Victorian Detective Fiction and the Nature of Evidence

Palgrave Studies in Nineteenth-Century Writing and Culture

General Editor: **Joseph Bristow**, Professor of English, UCLA

Palgrave Studies in Nineteenth-Century Writing and Culture is a new monograph series that aims to represent the most innovative research on literary works that were produced in the English-speaking world from the time of the Napoleonic Wars to the *fin de siécle*. Attentive to the historical continuities between "Romantic" and "Victorian," the series will feature studies that help scholarship to reassess the meaning of these terms during a century marked by diverse cultural, literary, and political movements. The main aim of the series is to look at the increasing influence of types of historicism on our understanding of literary forms and genres. It reflects the shift from critical theory to cultural history that has affected not only the period 1800–1900 but also every field within the discipline of English literature. All titles in the series seek to offer fresh critical perspectives and challenging readings of both canonical and non-canonical writings of this era.

Titles include:

Lawrence Frank
VICTORIAN DETECTIVE FICTION AND THE NATURE OF EVIDENCE
The Scientific Investigations of Poe, Dickens, and Doyle

Forthcoming title:

Laura Franey
VICTORIAN TRAVEL WRITING AND IMPERIAL VIOLENCE

Victorian Detective Fiction and the Nature of Evidence

The Scientific Investigations of Poe, Dickens, and Doyle

Lawrence Frank

First published 2003 by
PALGRAVE MACMILLAN
Houndmills, Basingstoke, Hampshire RG21 6XS and 175 Fifth Avenue, New York, N.Y. 10010
Companies and representatives throughout the world

PALGRAVE MACMILLAN is the global academic imprint of the Palgrave Macmillan division of St. Martin's Press, LLC and of Palgrave Macmillan Ltd. Macmillan® is a registered trademark in the United States, United Kingdom and other countries. Palgrave is a registered trademark in the European Union and other countries.

ISBN 1–4039–1139–8 hardback

This book is printed on paper suitable for recycling and made from fully managed and sustained forest sources.

A catalogue record for this book is available from the British Library.

Library of Congress Cataloging-in-Publication Data
Frank, Lawrence, 1933–
    Victorian detective fiction and the nature of evidence : the scientific investigations of Poe, Dickens, and Doyle / Lawrence Frank.
      p. cm.—(Palgrave studies in nineteenth-century writing and culture)
    Includes bibliographical references and index.
    ISBN 1–4039–1139–8
    1. Detective and mystery stories, English—History and criticism.
2. Doyle, Arthur Conan, Sir, 1859–1930—Characters—Sherlock Holmes.
3. Literature and science—Great Britain—History—19th century.
4. Detective and mystery stories, American—History and criticism.
5. Forensic sciences—Great Britain—History—19th century.
6. Dickens, Charles, 1812–1870. Mystery of Edwin Drood. 7. English fiction—19th century—History and criticism. 8. Poe, Edgar Allan, 1809–1849—Fictional works. 9. Dickens, Charles, 1812–1870. Bleak House. 10. Holmes, Sherlock (Fictitious character). 11. Evidence, Criminal, in literature. 12. Science in literature. I. Title. II. Series.
PR878.D4F73 2003
823'.08720908—dc21

                                       2002044800

10 9 8 7 6 5 4 3
12 11 10 09 08 07 06

Printed and bound in Great Britain by
Antony Rowe Ltd, Chippenham and Eastbourne

For my wife, Augusta

A bad earthquake at once destroys the oldest associations: the world, the very emblem of all that is solid, has moved beneath our feet like a crust over a fluid, – one second of time has conveyed to the mind a strange idea of insecurity, which hours of reflection would never have created.

Charles Darwin, *Journal* of the voyage of the *Beagle* (1839)

Contents

List of Illustrations

Acknowledgments

This book had its beginnings in an undergraduate course at the University of Oklahoma that originally concentrated upon nineteenth-century detective fiction and the psychoanalytic case history. Over the years, in response to questions posed by various students in the course, the emphasis changed to an examination of the relationship between the new genre of detective fiction and certain nineteenth-century historical disciplines, including cosmology, geology, paleontology, archaeology, and evolutionary biology.

Such an examination of the interrelationships between detective fiction and nineteenth-century scientific texts was made possible through the resources of the History of Science Collections at the University of Oklahoma and through the thoughtful support of members of the History of Science department. Duane H. D. Roller, formerly the Curator of the Collections, and Marcia Goodman, formerly the Collections librarian, welcomed me and guided me to those nineteenth-century texts that constitute but a part of the holdings of the Collections. Duane Roller was succeeded by Marilyn Ogilvie as Curator, Marcia Goodman by Kerry Magruder as librarian, each of whom generously followed their predecessors in being receptive to someone entirely new to the discipline of the history of science.

It was Kenneth Taylor of the History of Science department who first invited me to present a paper at one of the weekly department colloquia. Other invitations – from Peter Barker, Steven Livesey, and Gregg Mitman – followed, each providing another opportunity to explore the topic of the historical disciplines and their relationship to detective fiction.

Such opportunities to speak before friends led to other papers delivered over the years at the annual meetings of the Society for Literature and Science; at the Dickens Universe held each summer at the University of California, Santa Cruz, under the auspices of the Dickens Project directed by John Jordan; and at a conference in 1995 on "Sherlock Holmes: The Detective and the Collector," convened at the University of Minnesota.

From such occasions, there emerged early versions of Chapters 1, 6, and 7 that appeared in *Nineteenth-Century Literature*, and a version of Chapter 4 published in the *Dickens Studies Annual: Essays on Victorian*

Fiction. The revised chapters appear in the book with the permission of the University of California Press and the AMS Press.

Throughout the time that I worked on the manuscript, colleagues in the Department of English at the University of Oklahoma were kind enough to read drafts of various chapters. I wish to mention specifically Robert M. Davis, Vinay Dharwadker, George Economou, and Henry McDonald. Those at other universities read and commented upon the manuscript in its different forms, particularly Robert Hudspeth of Redlands University, James Kincaid of the University of Southern California, and J. Hillis Miller of the University of California, Irvine.

The book as it now stands has been vastly improved (and shortened) as the result of the astute comments of Joseph Bristow of the University of California, Los Angeles, editor of the Palgrave series, Studies in Nineteenth-Century Writing and Culture. In my experience Joseph Bristow has acted as the ideal editor, demanding, yet always thoughtful and encouraging.

Carol Roberts has patiently dealt with different drafts of the manuscript in completing the typescript.

However, fortunate as I have been to experience the generosity of spirit of so many, one person has sustained me through the visions and revisions of a project that must, at times, have seemed interminable: my wife, Augusta.

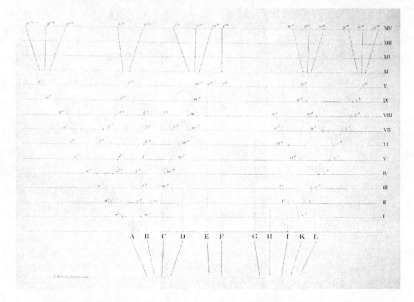

Charles Darwin's Tree of Life, from *The Origin of Species* (1859). Image reproduced courtesy of the History of Science Collections, University of Oklahoma.

Introduction: Contexts

It is easy to say that the truth of certain propositions is obvious to *common sense*. It may be so: but how am I assured that the conclusions of common sense are confirmed by accurate knowledge? Judging by common sense is merely another phrase for judging by first appearances; and every one who has mixed among mankind with any capacity for observing them, knows that the men who place implicit faith in their own common sense are, without any exception, the most wrong-headed and impracticable persons with whom he has ever had to deal.

John Stuart Mill, "The Spirit of the Age, II,"
Examiner, 23 January 1831

And thus, when a word entirely refuses to give up the secret of its origin, it can be regarded in no other light but as a riddle which no one has succeeded in solving, a lock of which no one has found the key – but still a riddle which has a solution, a lock for which there is a key, though now, it may be, irrecoverably lost.

Richard Chenevix Trench, *On the Study of Words* (1851)

I

Writing in the *Examiner* in the winter and spring of 1831, John Stuart Mill referred to the "SPIRIT OF THE AGE" as a "novel expression": "I do not believe that it is to be met with in any work exceeding fifty years in antiquity."[1] In invoking a new sense of history in which ages differ from each other, Mill wrote of his own time as "an age of transition"

1

(*Collected Works*, XXII, 230), characterized by his claim that "the modes of thinking of our ancestors" (XXII, 231) had become irrelevant given changed circumstances and an increase in the knowledge of certain empirically determined facts, particularly in the realm of the sciences. The old order of the landed gentry and aristocracy, supported by the doctrines of the Anglican Church, were no longer adequate. However, so Mill wrote, no new source of political, religious, or moral authority had appeared to command the assent of the ordinary man and woman: "The progress of inquiry has brought to light the insufficiency of the ancient doctrines; but those who have made the investigation of social truths their occupation, have not yet sanctioned any new body of doctrine with their unanimous, or nearly unanimous, consent" ("Spirit, II," *Collected Works*, XXII, 245).

Mill wrote, assuming the absence of a concensus, a new form of common sense, that could replace that sanctioned by the old hierarchical, semi-feudal deference society whose leaders were still clinging to power.[2] He hoped to call into existence a lay clerisy to displace the natural theologians of the old order, imagining in 1831 the ascendancy of men like Thomas Henry Huxley (1825–1895) who would, perhaps, forge a new concensus by which men and women were to live. But, at the moment, there was no social, political, or moral authority to encourage such a concensus: "society has either entered or is on the point of entering into a state in which there are no established doctrines; in which the world of opinions is a mere chaos" ("Spirit, III," *Collected Works*, XXII, 252). In his essay Mill later observed, "society is at one of those turns or vicissitudes in its history, at which it becomes necessary that it should change its opinions and its feelings" ("Spirit, IV," *Collected Works*, XXII, 294). However, Mill's own age was marked by a new, unprecedented circumstance, the reality of a widespread literacy: "In an age of literature, there is no longer, of necessity, the same wide interval between the knowledge of the old, and that which is attainable by the young. The experience of all former ages, recorded in books, is open to the young man as to the old" (XXII, 294). While, by implication, the writings of the day – like Mill's own essays in the *Examiner* and elsewhere – made available to readers a worldview in opposition to those opinions and feelings that had prevailed without challenge for centuries.

As Mill observed, "There are things which books cannot teach" ("Spirit, IV," *Collected Works*, XXII, 294), but in a period of transition and a new literacy, publications of all sorts become necessary to effect the changes – political, moral, and scientific – that he envisioned. Of course, the concept of an age of transition can be seen at best as a useful fiction, not only for Mill's program of reform, but for someone like myself setting out to provide a dissenting interpretation of nineteenth-century detective fiction from that which has been set forth by various literary critics over the last twenty years.[3]

Invoking Mill's age of transition, I represent the detective fictions of Edgar Allan Poe (1809–1849), Charles Dickens (1812–1870), and Arthur Conan Doyle (1859–1930) as participating in the critique of those traditional doctrines and a prevailing common sense that Mill challenged in "The Spirit of the Age." Poe, Dickens, and Doyle promoted a *new*, emerging worldview that was secular and naturalistic in opposition to nineteenth-century scriptural literalism, Natural Theology, and the vestiges of an Enlightenment deism that were often conservative in their political perspectives. As a new genre, nineteenth-century detective fiction in the hands of Poe, Dickens, and Doyle responded explicitly and implicitly to the scientific controversies of the day, particularly those surrounding the nebular hypothesis of Pierre Simon Laplace (1749–1827), a naturalistic explanation of the origin of galaxies from a diffused cloud of heated gases that, in cooling and condensing, formed stars and various solar systems, including our own. Laplace's hypothesis was appropriated and developed by various British and American writers, both natural historians and laymen, including John Pringle Nichol (1804–1859), Regius professor of astronomy at Glasgow University; Robert Chambers (1802–1871), the Edinburgh literary figure who, with his brother, published the *Chambers's Edinburgh Journal*; John Tyndall (1820–1893), the Irish-born physicist and polemicist who eagerly promoted Darwinian evolution; and Winwood Reade (1838–1875), the African adventurer and religious skeptic, no less a follower of Darwin than Tyndall. In their discussions of the nebular hypothesis (a precursor to the "Big Bang" theory), these writers set forth a naturalistic, potentially materialist vision of the universe, while offering an evolutionary perspective as a justification for political reforms resisted by defenders of a traditional hierarchical society, particularly natural theologians like Thomas Chalmers (1780–1847), Adam Sedgwick (1785–1873), and William Whewell (1794–1866) who, as the author of a history and a philosophy of empirical science and as Master of Trinity College, Cambridge, provided some of the more serious traditional responses to hypotheses concerning the transmutation of species. (Throughout the Introduction, the chapters to follow, and the Epilogue, I shall provide the dates of important figures and key texts in order to establish an historical context.)

Moreover, in alluding to the nebular hypothesis, with its speculations on the origins of galaxies and solar systems, Poe, Dickens, and Doyle were inevitably preoccupied with epistemological and narratological issues. The nebular hypothesis of Laplace was to become associated with those other historical disciplines that sought to reconstruct the past from fragmentary evidence surviving into the present in the form of fossils or archaeological remains.[4] Throughout the detective fictions of Poe, Dickens, and Doyle (unlike those of Wilkie Collins), there appear terms, figures of speech, and methodological practices indebted to nineteenth-century philology, geology and paleontology, archaeology, and evolutionary biology, disciplines that by mid-century were to share common preoccupations about the nature of evidence and narratological reconstructions of a past unavailable to the observer. A characteristic terminology and methodology established a continuum between the historical disciplines and were made available to the fictional detective who acted and spoke in a manner based on the models provided by such disciplines. In turning to these disciplines, and those who wrote about them, Poe, Dickens, and Doyle were to reject the prevailing common sense of the eighteenth and early nineteenth centuries and were to promote a new version of common sense that seemed to defy the everyday experiences of their readers. In this way the detective fictions of Poe, Dickens, and Doyle possess, to this day, a complex intellectual dimension: they promoted a worldview that many modern readers, particularly in the United States, still reject as they introduced a middle-class readership to a universe governed by chance *and* necessity.[5]

In the chapters that follow I resist the claims of various critics represented by Stephen Knight in *Form and Ideology in Crime Fiction* (1980) and by Dennis Porter in *The Pursuit of Crime: Art and Ideology in Detective Fiction* (1981). In his book Knight argues that detective fiction as a genre promotes "the ideology of the bourgeois professional intelligentsia" who constitute its "central audience," as it offers a consoling resolution of threats to a prevailing social and economic system.[6] Porter claims that "the popular literature of a consumer society in an age of mass literacy" can be regarded "as a reflector and valuable barometer of the society's ideological norms."[7] Both Knight and Porter can be seen to anticipate the thoroughgoing Foucauldian interpretations of nineteenth-century detective fiction offered by D. A. Miller in *The Novel and the Police* (1988) and, more recently, by Ronald R. Thomas in *Detective Fiction and the Rise of Forensic Science* (1999). In a tour de force Miller argues that detective fiction serves the aim of a bourgeois, panoptical society not only by promoting an existing ideology, but by creating in its readers certain anxieties that are then controlled as the reader polices his or her own consciousness to avoid deviant behavior. Ronald R. Thomas joins a new-historicist approach to a Foucauldian perspective by exploring various nineteenth-century and early twentieth-century forensic texts that, in concert with detective fiction, particularly in Great Britain, colluded to transform Romantic conceptions of consciousness, in the process "*conspiring* . . . to produce a complex set of discourses on subjectivity" that sought to "enforc[e] the limits of individual autonomy."[8] Such collusion transforms individuals into figurative machines denied the complex mental life that Romantic literature offered as a model of human consciousness.

Not only do I question the hegemonic coherence of any society, including the contemporary bourgeois, bureaucratic one that Thomas discusses, I question his claims that nineteenth-century detective fiction was not concerned with issues involving epistemology and narrative and that it introduced a "paradigmatic shift in the realm of subjectivity: the replacement of the entire ideologically laden notion of Victorian moral character . . . with the more physiologically based but socially-defined conception of Victorian identity" (*Detective Fiction*, p. 63). Rather than turn to the biological determinism that was to emerge in the late nineteenth century, the detectives of Poe, Dickens, and Doyle were to reaffirm Romantic conceptions of consciousness within the context of a thoroughgoing philosophical materialism. It is appropriate to speak of a Romantic materialism to which Poe, Dickens, and Doyle turned, retaining for human consciousness the aura of mystery and awe that was to be found in the writings of William Wordsworth (1770–1850), Thomas De Quincey (1785–1859), and Thomas Carlyle (1795–1881).

In my book I discuss in chronological order the detective fictions of Edgar Allan Poe, Charles Dickens, and Arthur Conan Doyle. Part One concentrates on Poe: Chapter 1 explores Poe's "The Murders in the Rue Morgue" (1841), Chapter 2 "The Gold-Bug" (1843), establishing a pattern followed throughout in succeeding chapters. I explore in Part One the significance of the nebular hypothesis for the worldview enacted in the stories and novels under consideration and then the problematic nature of historical knowledge, involving a consideration of epistemology and narratology, in a universe characterized by pure contingency. In "The Murders in the Rue Morgue" C. Auguste Dupin refers in passing to "the late nebular cosmogony" promoted by John Pringle Nichol in his *Views of the Architecture of the Heavens* (1837), suggesting a context involving current scientific disputes over the origins of the universe in which to consider the significance of the deaths of

Madame and Mademoiselle L'Espanaye at the hands of an Ourang-Outang.[9] In "The Gold-Bug" William Legrand, entomologist and natural historian, reconstructs the past from dubious evidence, leading him to pirate treasure, perhaps by chance alone.

In turning to the novels of Charles Dickens in Part Two, I trace in Chapter 3 implicit allusions in *Bleak House* (1852–53) to Nichol's *Architecture of the Heavens* and to the anonymous *Vestiges of the Natural History of Creation* (1844) as Dickens exploited the famous and problematic double narrative through which to dramatize competing worldviews – one secular and naturalistic, the other Christian – at a moment when it could not be predicted which might triumph among people of science and the men and women who were reading the novel. In Chapter 4 I concentrate on Dickens's last, uncompleted novel, *The Mystery of Edwin Drood* (1870), as the significance of Charles Darwin's *Origin of Species* (1859) and Charles Lyell's *Geological Evidences of the Antiquity of Man* (1863) for the novel becomes clear: through a complex geological and archaeological perspective, *Edwin Drood* investigates the difficult process of reconstructing past events from fragmentary and inadequate evidence.

Part Three considers Arthur Conan Doyle's Sherlock Holmes stories and novels. In Chapter 5 I discuss the significance of Winwood Reade's *The Martyrdom of Man* (1872) – recommended by Holmes to Dr. Watson in *The Sign of Four* (1890) – for an understanding of the evolutionary worldview informing Holmes's investigations. In his book Reade returned to "the nebula of the sublime Laplace," proceeded to offer an evolutionary investigation of the origins of life and consciousness, and engaged in a hyperbolic attack upon "Supernatural Christianity."[10] In concluding with a discussion of *The Hound of the Baskervilles* (1901–02) in Chapter 6, I investigate the way in which historical disciplines, both the geology of Lyell and the evolutionary biology of Darwin, inform Holmes's methodology, raising again the epistemological and narratological issues addressed in Poe's "The Gold-Bug" and in Dickens's *Edwin Drood*. In the concluding Chapter 7 I reconstruct implicit allusions to various expositions of the nebular hypothesis, leading to John Tyndall's promotion of a Romantic materialism that sought to retain the mystery of human consciousness as depicted by Wordsworth, De Quincey, and Carlyle, thus preserving the complexities of individual motivation denied by the biological determinism of Sir Francis Galton (1822–1911) and Cesare Lombroso (1835–1909).

II

Throughout I will be engaged both in close readings of various kinds of texts – literary and scientific – and in the reconstruction of an intellectual tradition sharing common figures of speech and methods of proceeding that informed the naturalistic worldview they were in the process of constructing. In the stories and novels under consideration there occur allusions and a characteristic language revealing shared assumptions that point to controversies about the origins of the universe, the age of the earth, the transmutation of species, and the very existence of prehistoric peoples. I conduct what might be termed an act of literary and intellectual paleontology in which the past is haphazardly preserved in literary and scientific texts that, in defiance of conventional generic classifications, interact with each other to point to a coherent intellectual tradition reaching into a past without a definable origin.

Such an investigation need not rely upon, although it must acknowledge, theoretical speculations of recent decades, particularly those of Hayden White in *Metahistory: The Historical Imagination in Nineteenth-Century Europe* (1973); of Dominick LaCapra in *Rethinking Intellectual History: Texts, Contexts, Language* (1983); and, more recently, those of James Chandler in *England in 1819: The Politics of Literary Culture and the Case of Romantic Historicism* (1998) and of Catherine Gallagher and Stephen Greenblatt in their *Practicing New Historicism* (2000). In *Metahistory* White emphasizes "the fictive character of historical reconstructions" as he argues that so-called historical events are depicted through "modes of emplotment" that correspond to the categories of Romance, Tragedy, Comedy, and Irony set forth in Northrop Frye's *The Anatomy of Criticism* (1957).[11] White states that his "method, in short, is formalist" (p. 3), an orientation that LaCapra modifies by invoking both Mikhail Bakhtin (1895–1975) and Kenneth Burke (1897–1993). In his version of intellectual history there are no longer reliable documents, but texts that claim to correspond to reality and that demand, as literary texts do, the kind of close reading engaged in by literary critics. In examining a text of any sort, LaCapra argues, the intellectual historian cannot isolate it from various other texts with which it is engaged in a Bakhtinian dialogue that may constitute a particular moment in time. In this way LaCapra dismisses the conventional distinction between a text and its so-called intellectual and historical background: there is, implicitly, only intertextuality, part of that "unending conversation" that constitutes Kenneth Burke's drama of history.[12]

In *England in 1819* James Chandler relies more fully on the writings of Burke to investigate the idea of the "historical situation" as a construct, the creation of Romantic writers, Sir Walter Scott (1771–1832) and John Stuart Mill (1806–1873) among them, who perceived their own age as different from other preceding ages.[13] Romantic historiography presented a model for the identification of periods organized around certain individuals of genius, Percy Bysshe Shelley's poets as legislators of the world, or around a representative form of thought revealed in a pervasive figure of speech as Thomas Carlyle suggested in the *Edinburgh Review* in "Signs of the Times" (1829). Periods were to be identified chronologically by dates, clustered around a synecdochic event, idea, or individual identified, if not arbitrarily, then at least through an act of interpretation. Catherine Gallagher and Stephen Greenblatt finally assert that an "entire culture is [to be] regarded as a text."[14] There is no verifiable reality; there are only "representations" that claim to point to the real, representations that, in a Foucauldian sense, always contend with other representations for authority. All of these writers reject appeals to empirically verifiable facts to settle disputes among historians. There is no end to the scope of interpretation in an activity that must resist, so Gallagher and Greenblatt argue, the seductive notions of the period, the stability of genre, and any recourse to the quasi-miraculous activity of the transhistorical genius.

No one currently engaged in the practice of literary and intellectual history should ignore the contributions of those critics who have responded in various ways to post-structuralist and post-modernist thought. But, in considering the relationship between the historical disciplines of nineteenth-century science – including cosmology, paleontology, archaeology and, later, evolutionary biology – and nineteenth-century detective fiction, I have sought out a text central to the century, one that anticipated and sanctioned the kind of paleontological reconstructions in which I intend to engage. Such a text is to be found in Charles Darwin's *Origin of Species* (1859), read not as the classic investigation into the transmutation of species, but as a form of historiography that anticipated late twentieth-century speculations about the practice of any historical discipline.

As Ernst Mayr has noted in *The Growth of Biological Thought* (1982), "It was Darwin more than anyone else who showed how greatly theory formation in biology differs in many respects from that of classical physics."[15] Darwin was engaged in the construction of "historical narratives" that "can only rarely (if at all) be tested by experiment" (p. 521). In the *Origin* Darwin's long argument became an historical enterprise based upon the study of living organisms and on the examination of fossil remains constituting the geological record that Darwin, in part following Charles Lyell's three-volume *Principles of Geology* (1830–33), treated as a fragmentary archive in which fossil remains were to be seen, figuratively, as the relics of extinct dialects and languages. To illustrate his practice and to defend his hypothesis from those who emphasized the inadequacy of his evidence, Darwin concluded the chapter "On the Imperfection of the Geological Record" with an elaborate metaphor: "I look at the natural geological record, as a history of the world imperfectly kept, and written in a changing dialect; of this history we possess the last volume alone, relating only to two or three countries. . . . Each word of the slowly-changing language, in which the history is *supposed to be written*, being more or less different in the interrupted succession of chapters, may represent the apparently abruptly changed forms of life, entombed in our consecutive, but widely separated formations."[16]

The figure of speech, with its emphasis on the geological record "as a history of the world imperfectly kept, and written in a changing dialect," provides a context in which to consider Darwin's diagrammatic Tree of Life in the chapter on "Natural Selection" as a Tree of Language indebted not only to Lyell's comparison of "the first [geological] theorists" to "novices, who attempt to read a history written in a foreign language, doubting about the meaning of the most ordinary terms," but also to the discipline of historical philology that was to lead to Richard Chenevix Trench's two papers presented to the Philological Society of London in November 1857.[17]

Trench's proposal for a New English Dictionary grounded on historical principles was to become the *Oxford English Dictionary* (1884–1928) under the general editorship of James A. H. Murray (1837–1915). However, the worldview and the characteristic vocabulary that was to inform Trench's call for a New English Dictionary had already been suggested by the Orientalist, Sir William Jones (1746–1794), who was to serve as a judge in the Supreme Court at Fort William in Calcutta and who helped to found the Asiatic Society of Bengal in 1784 and then became its first president. In his annual addresses to the Society – his Anniversary Discourses – Jones set forth the principles that were, in part, to inspire Trench and others who wished to establish a dictionary designed to record the history of the English language.[18] The goal of Jones's inquiries was to study the written records of the Asian past in order to establish the "true centre of population, of knowledge, of languages, and of arts" that "expanded in all directions to all the regions of the world."[19] In calling for the study of "the *languages* and *letters, reli-*

gion and *philosophy*, and . . . the *arts* and *sciences*, of the ancient *Persians*"
(*Works*, III, 111), as well as of the Indians, the Arabs, and the Tartars,
Jones revealed his Eurocentric and racist determination to trace the
origins of civilization, after the Fall, to Iran and to a written language
no longer available for study. He wrote assuming the historical accuracy
of Genesis and accepting the Christian chronology set forth by
Archbishop Ussher (1581–1656) that began with the creation of the
universe in 4004 B.C.

As he traced the origins of the peoples of India, Arabia, and Tartary,
Jones turned unselfconsciously to the vocabularies of horticulture,
animal husbandry, and genealogy. He wrote of "the three stocks"
(*Works*, III, 111) to which Hindus, Arabs, and Tartars belonged, while
he repeatedly invoked the family tree of genealogy. In his fourth
Anniversary Discourse of 15 February 1787, Jones set forth his plan
"to discourse . . . on the *five* principal nations, who have peopled the
continent and islands of *Asia*; so as to trace, by an historical and philological analysis, the number of ancient stems, from which those five
branches have severally sprung, and the central region, from which they
appear to have proceeded" (III, 47). Such an investigation should
demonstrate that just "as the *Indian* and *Arabian* tongues are severally
descended from a common parent, so those of *Tartary* might be traced
to one ancient stem essentially differing from the two others" (III, 85).
The "common source" (III, 34) of all existing languages may no longer
exist, but they do point to some common origin. With such observations Jones was to prepare for Darwin in the *Origin of Species* as he wrote
throughout of the common parents of species and genera, particularly
in his explication of the Tree of Life.

Anyone turning to Darwin's 35-manuscript-page "Sketch" (1842) and
to his 231-manuscript-page *Essay* (1844) will find, particularly in the
Essay, a thoroughgoing exposition of the long argument of the *Origin
of Species*.[20] In the "Sketch" and the *Essay* Darwin was preoccupied
with the response to an hypothesis that he hoped would not seem "*so
monstrous as it at first appears*" and with "*the difficulty of imagining*" the
gradual process by which the transmutation of species occurs.[21] In the
Essay he observed:

> The mind cannot grasp the full meaning of the term of a *million or
> hundred million years*, and cannot consequently add up and perceive
> the full effects of small successive variations accumulated during
> *almost infinitely many generations*. The difficulty is the same with that
> which, *with most geologists*, it has taken long years to remove, as when

Lyell propounded that great valleys were hollowed out ... by the slow action of the waves of the sea.

(p. 249, emphasis added)

The allusion to Lyell returns us to the earlier "Sketch" in which Darwin appropriated a figure of speech for the geological record from Lyell: "If geology presents us with mere pages in chapters, towards [the] end of a history, formed by tearing out *bundles of leaves*, and each page illustrating merely a small portion of the organisms of that time, the facts accord perfectly with my theory" (p. 63, emphasis added). The word "leaves" suggests a possible pun, the transformation of the leaves of the philological tree into the pages of an incomplete volume, a transformation that was developed in the *Essay* by a passage that was to recur, almost verbatim, in the *Origin*: "In the same manner as during changes of pronunciation certain letters in a word may become useless in pronouncing it, but *yet may aid us in searching for its derivation*, so we can see that rudimentary organs, no longer useful to the individual may be of high importance in ascertaining its descent" (p. 237, emphasis added).

Darwin's recourse to the analogy involving spelling and pronunciation in the 1844 *Essay* anticipated Richard Chenevix Trench's discussion of orthography and pronunciation in his *English Past and Present* (1855). Hans Aarsleff has observed in *The Study of Language in England, 1780–1860* (1967) that "language study was beginning [in Victorian England] to form an alliance with geology" (p. 208). But his words suggest something more: the ways in which historical philology was not merely illustrative for Lyellian geology and Darwinian evolutionism, but rather constitutive in providing a vocabulary, a methodology, and a worldview. In fact, Trench's various publications of the 1850s – *On the Study of Words* (1851), *English Past and Present*, and *On Some Deficiencies in Our English Dictionaries (1857)* – not only served to popularize his version of historical philology, but to mediate between Darwin's "Sketch" and *Essay* and the *Origin of Species*.

Trench wrote as an Anglican clergyman who succeeded William Buckland (once Oxford University's first professor of geology) as Dean of Westminster in 1856 and who was to become Archbishop of Dublin in 1863.[22] As a graduate of Cambridge University, Trench participated in the tradition of Natural Theology promoted by the *Bridgewater Treatises* of the 1830s, whose eight volumes were underwritten by the Earl of Bridgewater in the attempt to reconcile nineteenth-century science and revealed Christianity.[23] Even before joining the Philological Society in 1857, Trench had sought to promote historical philology within the context established by Sir William Jones in his Anniversary Discourses. Trench's Anglican perspective was explicit. In *On the Study of Words* he argued "that God gave man language, just as He gave him reason. . . . he could not be man, that is, a social being, without it. . . . [Man] did not thus begin the world *with names*, but *with the power of naming*."[24] Here, Trench seemed to acknowledge the claims of Jean-Jacques Rousseau (1712–1778) and Johann Gottfried Herder (1744–1803) without relinquishing his neoplatonic orientation in which language originally revealed the mind of God and the structure of the universe. Since the Fall language had become debased, particularly among those designated as savages. But the English language, so Trench claimed in *English Past and Present*, participated in certain "historic evolutions" with which the philologist must be acquainted "because the present is only intelligible in the light of the past, often of a very remote past indeed": "There are those who may seek *to trace* our language to the forests of Germany, to investigate its relation to all the *kindred tongues* that were there spoken; again, to follow it up, till it and they are seen *descending from an elder stock*; nor once to pause, till they have assigned to it its place . . . in respect of all the tongues and languages of the earth."[25] Trench was to make larger claims: the English language was determined to "have a great part in the Providence of God to play for the reconciling of a divided Christendom." He quoted Jacob Grimm: "In truth the English language, which by no mere accident has produced and upborne the greatest and most predominant poet of modern times [Shakespeare] . . . may with all right be called a world-language; and like the English people appears destined hereafter to prevail with a sway more extensive even than its present over all the portions of the globe" (*English*, pp. 38–39).

With such observations, Trench embraced a philological version of the doctrine of special creation by celebrating the mysteries of genius even as he offered a providential sanction for British imperialism. Yet, he also set forth a program for the study of language that would appear thoroughly historical and empirical.[26] Borrowing from Ralph Waldo Emerson's vision of language as "fossil poetry," he wrote of words as "fossil history" (*Study*, pp. 12–13): each word becomes representative of an age, offering "a deeper insight into [a people's] real condition, their habits of thought and feeling, than whole volumes written expressly with the intention of imparting this insight" (p. 84). Following Carlyle's "Signs of the Times," he suggested that words were to be seen as "epoch-making" (p. 131), a "record of passages in . . . history" (p. 157).

He wrote: "It is a signal evidence of the conservative powers of language, that we may oftentimes trace in speech the records of customs and states of society which have now past so entirely away as to survive nowhere else but in these words alone" (p. 122).

None of this occurs by accident: "there is a [secondary] law here at work, however hidden it may be from us" (*English*, p. 108). And it is in changes of spelling of the written word that the past, if not the law, is revealed: "And then what light . . . does the older spelling of a word often cast upon its etymology; how often does it clear up the mystery, which would otherwise hang about it" (p. 200). But such changes in the spoken or the written dialect challenge the imagination. In *English Past and Present*, Trench observed: "Indeed it is hard to imagine anything more gradual, more subtle and imperceptible than [this] process of change" (p. 158). Significantly, Trench invoked the Tree of Language of Herder and, of course, of Sir William Jones:

> It is not for nothing that we speak of some languages as living, of others as dead. . . . Our own language is of course a living language still; it is therefore gaining and losing; it is a tree in which the vital sap is yet working, *ascending from its roots into its branches*; and as this works, *new leaves* are being put forth by it, old are dropping away and dying.
>
> (*English*, pp. 40–41, emphasis added)

The figurative tree of language whose leaves become associated with the pages of ancient volumes where words are preserved was to inform Trench's proposal for a New English Dictionary in November of 1857. Throughout the two papers that constituted *On Some Deficiencies in Our English Dictionaries*, Trench was to mute his theological convictions as he called for "an inventory of the [English] language" that was not to promote a preferred usage, but "to collect and arrange all the words, whether good or bad." The maker of such an inventory "is an historian . . . not a critic."[27] Rather, such "a Dictionary is an historical monument, the history of a nation contemplated from one point of view, and the wrong ways into which a language has wandered, or attempted to wander, may be nearly as instructive as the right ones in which it has travelled" (p. 6). The passage reveals the persisting teleological assumptions central to Trench's understanding of languages, particularly the English language. With his emphasis on the citation of written documents and the reliance upon literary figures as authorities for the histories of words, he could not shake those metaphysical assumptions that were to compromise the creation of a natural history of the language by the compilers of the *Oxford English Dictionary*. Yet, there was on his part the attempt to be historical *and* empirical, particularly with his emphasis on the chronological ordering of the changes in meaning that a word had undergone: "Our Dictionaries do not always take sufficient care to mark the period of the rise of words, and where they have set, of their setting. . . . It is in every case desirable that the *first* authority for a word's use in the language [which occurs] should be adduced; . . . Of course no Dictionary can accomplish this completely" (*Deficiencies*, pp. 22–23). Nevertheless, the entry for a word is like a biography:

> A word's birth may not be as important as a man's birth; but a biography which should omit to tell us when [a man] was born whose life it professes to record, would not . . . be a whit more incomplete . . . than is the article in a lexicon which makes no attempt to fix, *where there are any means for doing so*, the date of a word's first appearance in the language. And as with birth, so also with death. Where a word is *extinct*, not to note, *where this is possible*, the time of its extinction, seems . . . as serious an omission as in the life of a man not to tell us the time, . . . when that life was ended.
>
> (*Deficiencies*, pp. 33–34, emphasis added)

Trench's popularization of the study of language throughout the 1850s had its parallel in the *Origin of Species*, perhaps nowhere more explicitly than in Darwin's discussion of classification in chapter XIII as he turned to "the case of languages":

> If we possessed a perfect pedigree of mankind, a genealogical arrangement of the races of man would afford the best classification of the various languages now spoken throughout the world; . . . [and] it might be that some very ancient language had altered little, and had given rise to few new languages, whilst others (owing to the spreading and subsequent isolation . . . of the several races, *descended from a common race*) had altered much, and had given rise to many *new languages and dialects*.
>
> (p. 406, emphasis added)

Further on in the same chapter Darwin returned to his discussion of orthography in the 1844 *Essay*, repeating the earlier observation that "rudimentary organs may be compared with the letters in a word, still retained in the spelling, but become useless in the pronunciation, but which serve as a *clue* in seeking for its derivation" (p. 432, emphasis added).

The *Origin of Species* was to become an enterprise not unlike that proposed by Trench to the Philological Society. Without a science of genetics, Darwin was to consult a geological record perceived as a fragmentary document in order to reconstruct a Tree of Life akin to Trench's tree of language in *English Past and Present*. In his explication of the diagram of the Tree of Life, Darwin explained that the common parents of successive generations of organisms were indicated by upper-case characters in the Roman alphabet, while those varieties that over millenia were to become extinct or to produce new species were designated by lower-case, italicized characters accompanied by superscribed numbers. Horizontal lines in the diagrammatic tree suggested the different formations that constituted geological epochs, identified by characteristic fossil remains that were preserved by chance haphazardly in the earth's crust. In the Tree of Life Darwin announced his evolutionary hypothesis:

> The affinities of all the beings of the same class have sometimes been represented by a great tree. I believe this *simile* largely speaks the truth. The green and budding twigs may represent existing species; and those produced during each former year may represent the long succession of extinct species. . . . Of the many twigs which flourished when the tree was a mere bush, only two or three, now grown into great branches, yet survive. . . . As buds give rise by growth to fresh buds, and these, if vigorous, branch out and overtop on all sides many a feebler branch, so by generation I believe it has been with the great *Tree of Life*.
>
> (*Origin*, pp. 171–72, emphasis added)

The Tree of Life becomes Darwin's elegant solution to the problem of representing a difficult hypothesis that challenges the human imagination.[28] Yet, "this simile" suggests the language tree of nineteenth-century philology. The upper-case and the italicized letters that represent varieties and species through the millennia of geological time invoke both the arbitrary characters upon which the domestic breeder seizes, and the equally arbitrary characters that constitute the written languages of Richard Chenevix Trench. Such characters, like the writing in the figurative volume of the earth's crust, reveal those foreign languages (literal and figurative) that the literary and intellectual historian consults in the attempt to reconstruct the spirit of ages past. The Tree of Life, understood as a Tree of Language, offers a model for such practices.

But, in Darwin's hands, the Tree of Language was shorn of Trench's central philosophical and religious assumptions. Concepts central to philology, evolutionary biology, and *any* historical discipline seeking to reconstruct the past become, at best, necessary fictions. In rejecting the doctrine of special creation, Darwin offered a natural history of the origin of species, precluding a neoplatonic tradition that sanctioned divine interventions in acts of special creation, essentialism, and the immutability of species. By analogy – since Trench's philological tree points to a world of written texts – the literary historian may dispense with appeals either to the agency of genius or to the reality of stable genres. Species, and genres, are human constructs only. As Darwin observed: "we shall have to treat species in the same manner as [some] naturalists treat genera, . . . [as] merely artificial combinations made for convenience. . . . we shall . . . be freed from the vain search for *the undiscovered and undiscoverable essence* of the term species" (*Origin*, p. 456, emphasis added). For the literary and intellectual historian there cease to exist generic boundaries separating literary texts or, for that matter, any text from others. The old-fashioned recourse to intellectual and historical "background" becomes suspect. There exist only innumerable texts that, like fragmentary fossil remains in the earth's crust, point to a complex set of associations. Illusory generic boundaries become porous, permeated by a characteristic vocabulary, an alphabet and a grammar that constitute the spirit of an age.

Moreover, as both Ernst Mayr and Stephen Jay Gould insist, in different ways, Darwin believed only in the individual: he was a nominalist.[29] Yet, as a nominalist seeking to reconstruct the past, Darwin was compelled to treat individual fossil remains as parts of groups, to classify them as members of fictional categories. Darwin rejected the reality of species and emphasized the incompleteness of the geological record only in part to refute those critics who would claim, as they did (and still do), that he lacked the paleontological evidence to support his hypothesis. But, he also had to posit gaps in the geological record that permitted him to order individuals into groups: "for if every form which has ever lived on this earth were suddenly to reappear, . . . it would be quite impossible to give definitions by which each group could be distinguished from other groups, as all would blend together" (*Origin*, p. 413), rendering a history impossible.

Like Darwin consulting the geological record depicted "as a history of the world imperfectly kept, and written in a changing dialect," the intellectual historian encounters an overwhelming array of primarily printed texts that would seem to elude classification and understanding, forming a continuum that would defy any reconstruction of past epochs. Such a situation demands the practice of canon formation as certain texts become representative, indices to a posited historical period. But as texts, like fossils, are only individuals defying generic classification, such a process of selection is rendered problematic: the formal, linguistic, and evaluative criteria for identifying canonical texts become arbitrary, excluding other texts that, through a complex intertextual association, might be considered as equally or more truly representative of an era. Finally, if there are only individual texts participating in an unbroken temporal continuum, the act of periodization is itself rendered suspect. Like the "imaginary" breaks in Darwin's diagrammatic Tree of Life (*Origin*, p. 163), literary periods become necessary fictions in a chronological reconstruction of the past. The figurative alphabet and grammar that constitute an historical period become "epoch-making" in a sense quite different from Trench's claim that words, as "fossil history," are "epoch-making" (*Study*, p. 131).

The recourse to chronology in philology, geology, and evolutionary biology (as in intellectual history) becomes no less a convention. Darwin's version of a genealogy of species relying on a chronological organization was itself conventional, not unlike Trench's proposal for a New English Dictionary organized not on the preferred usage of a word, but on the chronological history of a word as documented in certain prescribed texts. But such a convention reveals that speculations about causal relationships in the philological or paleontological past become pure metonymies, like those examined by David Hume in his discussion "Of the idea of necessary connexion" in *A Treatise of Human Nature* (1739–40). In the practice of intellectual history, the study of causal relationships and of influence becomes problematic, grounded in fictions and figures of speech. And, within the context of the *Origin of Species* read as a form of historiography, teleology is precluded: "Looking to the future, we can predict that the groups of organic beings which are now large and triumphant . . . will for a long period continue to increase. But which groups will ultimately prevail, no man can predict" (*Origin*, pp. 168–69). Ultimately, the struggle between worldviews – to appropriate a metaphor from Darwin – is to be reconstructed from fragmentary evidence provided by selected texts upon which the literary and intellectual historian ponders without recourse to causal relationships or teleological necessity.[30]

As a piece of historiography, the *Origin of Species* codified Romantic conceptions of history with the reliance upon the representative author or text, the belief in identifiable epochs manifesting the spirit of an age, and the transition (gradual or abrupt) from one worldview, perhaps never fully coherent, to another that over the course of time supplanted it, even as the older, now obsolete worldview was to persist as a living fossil. However, Darwin's Tree of Life – understood as a Tree of Language – subtly subverted assumptions central to Romantic historiography, anticipating later, skeptical investigations of the methods, practices, and assumptions of a positivistic history of ideas that served to illustrate the seemingly inevitable triumph of the modern over the course of centuries.[31]

III

If contributors to the proposed New English Dictionary were directed to certain volumes in their search for prescribed words, if the nineteenth-century paleontologist was encouraged by T. H. Huxley to seek out the fossil remains of the requisite ancestor of the modern horse, Gillian Beer's *Darwin's Plots: Evolutionary Narrative in Darwin, George Eliot and Nineteenth-Century Fiction* (1983) and George Levine's *Darwin and the Novelists: Patterns of Science in Victorian Fiction* (1988) have opened a field of study in which nineteenth-century scientific and literary texts inter-act, responding to each other across arbitrary generic boundaries.[32] Both Lyell and Darwin, in keeping with the conventions of the day, wrote as men of letters as well as men of science, resorting to allusions to classical literature and to British literature, past and present. They self-consciously turned to figurative language, not only to render the diffi-cult intelligible, but to constitute the fields of study that they, along with others, were in the process of creating. It becomes possible, even neces-sary, to read scientific writings as literary texts, engaged in the represen-tation of phenomena that may, finally, defy the structures of language.

With *Darwin's Plots* and *Darwin and the Novelists* as models, it becomes possible to find in Arthur Conan Doyle's *Memories and Adventures* (1924) clues to the complexity of his Sherlock Holmes stories and novels. In offering an account of his religious crisis as a medical student at Edinburgh University in the 1870s Doyle mentioned familiar names – Darwin, Huxley, John Stuart Mill, Herbert Spencer (1820–1903) – even as he introduced someone less familiar to us, like John Tyndall, physi-cist, religious skeptic, ardent polemicist. In mentioning Tyndall in his memoir, Doyle leads us to *Fragments of Science* and Tyndall's essay, "Scientific Use of the Imagination," first published in 1870. In this essay Tyndall speculated upon Laplace's cosmology, the "Evolution hypoth-esis," and the nature of human consciousness in a universe constituted only of matter.[33] Throughout the essay Tyndall was to allude both to the anonymous *Vestiges of the Natural History of Creation* and to Nichol's earlier *Views of the Architecture of the Heavens*. As the Dr. Nichol of whom C. Auguste Dupin speaks in "The Murders in the Rue Morgue," he was one of the foremost proponents in the 1830s and 1840s of "the late nebular cosmogony" ("Murders," p. 404).[34] Significantly, the title of Tyndall's essay recurs without attribution in *The Hound of the Baskervilles*, as Sherlock Holmes speaks of "the scientific use of the imagination."[35] In this way a fleeting allusion suggests a complex genealogy of which Doyle himself need not have been fully aware. This example illustrates the relevance of Mikhail Bakhtin's observation in "The Problem of the Text in Linguistics, Philology, and the Human Sciences: An Experiment in Philosophical Analysis": "Each large and creative verbal whole is a very complex and multifaceted system of relations. . . . there are no voiceless words that belong to no one. Each word contains voices that are sometimes infinitely distant, unnamed, *almost impersonal* . . . , *almost undetectable*, and voices resounding nearby and simultaneously."[36]

Unfortunately, no practitioner of an historical discipline – the philologist, the paleontologist, the intellectual historian – comes upon evidence in the chronological order of its production. In piecing together the "complex and multifaceted system of relations" that characterizes a literary or intellectual tradition, someone like myself inevitably resorts to a chronological narrative in which texts, come upon quite randomly, offer only fleeting allusions, recurring figures of speech, and a shared vocabulary that may be epoch-making, that may embody a worldview, perhaps one in the process of constituting itself even in the face of opposition.

A chain of allusions, perceived as paleontological clues, may be reconstructed, if only by chance. The chain may lead to the promoters of a potentially naturalistic worldview, men like Darwin, Huxley, Tyndall and Winwood Reade, but also to their opponents, defenders of the old order. This is the case of Hugh Miller (1802–1856), the Scottish stonemason and popularizer of geology whose language Tyndall parodied in "Scientific Use of the Imagination," as he mocked defenders of Natural Theology who invoked the "fiat" of God in successive acts of special creation over the eons.

It was in 1857 – the year of Trench's papers on the deficiencies of English dictionaries – that Miller's *Testimony of the Rocks* appeared posthumously after his suicide in 1856.[37] Like other proponents of Natural Theology, Miller accepted the uniform operation of natural laws to explain geological phenomena. Genesis was to be read figuratively as the historical Moses's account of a visionary experience akin to Adam's introduction to the creation by Raphael in Book VII of *Paradise Lost* (1667, 1674). In this way Miller could depict the "Noachian deluge" as a local event, accept the extinction of species, and argue for an age of the earth far greater than that proposed by Archbishop Ussher in the seventeenth century. He skirted scriptural literalism, defended Genesis – properly understood – yet retained the doctrine of special creation, the immutability of species, and a belief in teleology.

In spite of a certain brand of protestant orthodoxy, Miller was to challenge an existing common sense that denied that the earth had once been radically different in climate or topography, inhabited by monstrous, extinct dinosaurs. In *Testimony of the Rocks* he observed: "It has been well remarked, that when two opposing explanations of extraordinary natural phenomena are given, – one of a simple and seemingly *common sense* character, the other complex and apparently absurd, – it is almost always safer to adopt the apparently absurd than the seemingly *common sense* one." Those who invoked miracles to explain certain geological events were sure to err: the "'plain man,' yielding to the dictates of what he would deem *common sense*, – which, of course, in questions of *natural science* is tantamount to *common nonsense*, – would be sure to go wrong."[38]

In *Testimony of the Rocks* Miller was writing as if in anticipation of the *Origin of Species*, aware that traditional appeals to the common sense of everyday life or to that of nineteenth-century Natural Theology were imperiled. For Miller, writing in 1856, the Book of Nature of the New Science and of Natural Religion no longer attested to "the authorship of the heavens and earth, which the science of La Place [*sic*] failed of itself to discover." Geology had now become "as thoroughly a physical science as either geography or astronomy"; but, "while the Scriptures do not reveal the form of the earth or the motions of the planets, they *do* reveal the fact that the miracle of creation was effected, not by a single act, but in several successive acts" (*Testimony*, pp. 381, 382–83, emphasis added) in the form of divine fiats. In the face of a naturalistic cosmology and the new geology, Miller had retreated from an earlier reaffirmation of the Book of Nature made less than a decade before in *Foot-Prints of the Creator* (1849), a polemic directed against the naturalistic thrust of *Vestiges of the Natural History of Creation*.

In *Foot-Prints of the Creator* Miller had harkened back to *Robinson Crusoe* (1719), using allusions to Daniel Defoe's novel to illustrate the Natural Theology of Chalmers, Sedgwick, and Whewell. As Anglicans *and* men of science, the three accepted the Argument from Design of the eighteenth century in which a universe governed by immutable natural laws provided evidence of the existence of an omnipotent, omniscient, and benevolent God. As promoters of science, they endorsed Newtonian physics, astronomy, and the new geology as empirical, rejecting appeals to the supernatural to explain physical phenomena, except in explaining the origins of the universe and the appearance of immutable species over the eons. But, characteristically, Chalmers, Sedgwick, and Whewell were not to follow Enlightenment Deists in their skepticisim about the divinity of Christ and a miraculous resurrection. Although Genesis was no longer to be read literally, the New Testament – the revealed Word – demonstrated Christ's divinity and as a true history attested to the miracles that He performed and to the reality of the resurrection.[39]

In mentioning Robinson Crusoe, Miller assumed that even in 1849 men and women still resorted to the supernatural rather than to a material chain of events to explain certain phenomena, as he invoked the sudden appearance of stalks of English barley on Crusoe's island: "Had Robinson Crusoe failed to remember that he had shaken the old corn-bag where he found the wheat and barley ears springing up on his island," he might have treated the event as miraculous: "And the process analogous to the shaking of the bag is frequently a process *not* to be remembered."[40] Throughout Defoe's novel Crusoe resorts to a version of the Natural Theology that Miller was then promoting. In the barley episode, Crusoe first assumes "that God had miraculously caus'd this Grain to grow without any Help of Seed sown, and that it was directed purely for [his] Sustenance."[41] But he will reject a superstitious belief in miracle: "at last it occur'd to my Thoughts, that I had shook a Bag of Chickens Meat out in that Place, and then the Wonder began to cease" (*Crusoe*, p. 58). Crusoe's rejection of the appearance of the barley as "a Prodigy of Nature" (p. 58) enacts a version of common sense that was to sustain men and women of various religious persuasions well into the nineteenth century. Later in the novel, in his attempt to convert Friday, Crusoe observes:

I began to instruct him in the Knowledge of the true God: I told him that the great Maker of all Things liv'd up there, pointing up towards Heaven: That he governs the World by the same Power and Providence by which he had made it: That he was omnipotent, could do every Thing for us, give every Thing to us, take every Thing from us; and thus by Degrees I open'd his Eyes.

(p. 156)

Crusoe resorts to a version of the Argument from Design to demonstrate the existence of God and to infer His attributes. But such an appeal takes Crusoe only so far; finally, he understands the limits of "the meer Notions of Nature":

> nothing but divine Revelation can form the Knowledge of *Jesus Christ*, and of a Redemption purchas'd for us, of a Mediator of the new Covenant, and of an Intercessor, at the Foot-stool of God's Throne; I say, nothing but a Revelation from Heaven, can form these in the Soul, and that therefore the Gospel of our Lord and Saviour, *Jesus Christ*; I mean, the Word of God, and the Spirit of God . . . are the absolutely necessary Instructors of the Souls of Men, in the saving Knowledge of God, and the Means of Salvation.
>
> (p. 158)

By 1856, Miller sensed that the fragile concensus that was Natural Theology was challenged both by a lingering scriptural literalism *and* by the emerging naturalism of John Stuart Mill (and Darwin). In the *Testimony of the Rocks*, he was seeking to forge a new concensus that might reconcile science and revealed religion without recourse to the Book of Nature of *Robinson Crusoe*.

In directing his readers to Defoe's novel in his *Foot-Prints of the Creator* in 1849, Miller had invoked a fictional character with whom his readers were apparently familiar. In doing so, he revealed his understanding of the role of popular literature in the construction of common sense. He saw the serious function of a literature that in the nineteenth century now included the new genre of detective fiction. Writing in January, 1856, for the *Witness* – the evangelical periodical that he edited – Miller discussed "Our Novel Literature." He argued that "the most influential writings of the present time, – the writings that tell with most effect on public opinion," were newspaper articles and novels. Such classics of the eighteenth century as Hume's "Essay on the Human Understanding," Montesquieu's "Spirit of Laws," and Smith's "Wealth of Nations" had been displaced by periodical publications (where Poe's stories and Doyle's Sherlock Holmes adventures were to appear) and by serialized novels, especially those of Dickens. Although, he observed, some "grave and serious people [continue] to speak of novels as mere frivolities," the novel was in fact "a tremendously potent instrument for the *origination* or *the revolutionizing of opinion*." Miller went on to argue that it would be unwise to ignore the political and religious significance of *Bleak House* or *Little Dorrit* (1855–57):

Some of our great lawyers could make sharp speeches, about two years ago, against what they termed the misrepresentations of "Bleak House," evidently regarding it, as they well might, as the most formidable series of pamphlets against the abuses of Chancery, and the less justifiable practices of the legal profession, that ever appeared. We are by no means sure, however, that the Church is as thoroughly awake to the tendencies of his present work [*Little Dorrit*], as members of the legal faculty . . . were to the design of his last.

Here Miller sensed something heterodox both in *Bleak House* and in *Little Dorrit*. As examples of detective fiction in their excavations of a buried past, the novels suggested to Miller a power "for the origination or the revolutionizing of opinion" that would subvert not only the Natural Theology that he defended, but that Enlightenment common sense that the historical disciplines and detective fictions were in the process of challenging.[42]

Miller's observations in the *Witness* suggest that those literary historians who trace the genealogy of detective fiction back to Voltaire's *Zadig* (1748) are, in fact, mistaken.[43] In the English translation of his *Discours préliminaire* (1812), Georges Cuvier invoked *Zadig* only to dismiss it as representative of a worldview in the process of being rendered obsolete. As he discussed his reconstructions of extinct animals from incomplete fossil remains, he set out to

lay down empirical rules on the subject, which are almost as certain as those deduced from rational principles, especially if established upon careful and repeated observation. Hence, any one who observes merely the print of a cloven hoof, may conclude that it has been left by a ruminant animal, and regard the conclusion as equally certain with any other in physics or in morals. . . . It is much surer than all the marks of Zadig.[44]

Cuvier placed himself within the empirical tradition that Voltaire promoted in *Zadig* and, later, in *Candide* (1759). He was to continue Voltaire's crusade against superstition and those chimeras like the griffin and the basilisk that Zadig dismisses in his travels through an Orient of the Western imagination, travels that are to demonstrate universal human folly and cruelty. In *Zadig* there is no genuine interest in history. Rather, Voltaire wrote of exemplary figures to be found in all times and all places.[45] Even Zadig's ability to infer the existence of the queen of Bablyon's bitch or to describe with exactitude the runaway stud of the king, neither of which he has laid eyes upon, involves the use of a common sense altogether different than that which Cuvier invoked. Zadig uses his experience of dogs and horses to read the signs they leave. From fossil remains Cuvier reconstructed animals that no longer existed and that he, unlike a Zadig, had never seen. He imaginatively moved back into a past extending far beyond the chronology of Archbishop Ussher to reconstruct geological and zoological epochs at least tens of thousands of years prior to the existence of human beings.[46]

There is an ironic dimension to Cuvier's allusion to *Zadig*. As "an antiquary of a new order" (*Essay*, p. 1), he sought to discover "the ancient history of the globe": "enlightened men . . . if they take any interest in examining, in the infancy of our species, the almost obliterated traces of so many nations that have become extinct, . . . will doubtless take a similar interest in collecting, amidst the darkness which covers the infancy of the globe, the traces of those revolutions which took place anterior to the existence of all nations" (p. 3). The world of Voltaire's *Zadig* was to lose its reassuring familiarity. The common sense of the Enlightenment was being transformed as Victorian men and women were compelled to contemplate natural processes and alien terrains from a geological past no longer immediately available to sense experience. They were encouraged by Cuvier, Lyell, William Buckland, and others to imagine a time when the now temperate and cultivated British Isles were inhabited by extinct mammals whose descendants were currently to be found only in the tropics of Africa or Asia.

In the famous chapter 5 of volume I of the *Principles of Geology*, Lyell was to turn to the difficulties to be met by the geologist or the layperson in the attempt to grasp the geological processes uniformly at work in the natural world. He observed: "The first and greatest difficulty, then, consists *in our habitual unconsciousness* that our position as observers is essentially unfavourable, when we endeavour to estimate the magnitude of the changes now in progress. . . . it requires an effort *both of the reason and the imagination* to appreciate duly their importance" (*Principles*, I, 81, emphasis added).

Even more difficult was the effort required to understand and, as Lyell suggested, to imagine the earth and its inhabitants in geological ages of the deep past. Thus, Cuvier's "antiquary of a new order" must be possessed of the power "to penetrate *the mystery that veils* the earliest condition of the earth," in the words of Gideon Mantell, physician turned popularizer of Lyell's geology.[47] In his *Wonders of Geology* (1838) Mantell celebrated the almost preternatural power of the geologist who "learns that most important of all lessons – to doubt the evidence of his senses, until confirmed by cautious and patient observation" (I, 9) as he "proceed[s] from the consideration of what is known, to that which is unknown" (I, 123). In the process he must accept "the sublime discoveries of modern astronomers [that] have shown that every part of the realms of space abounds in large expansions of attenuated matter, termed *nebulæ*" from which "suns and planets like our own" (I, 22) are formed, as well as "a period in which the earth . . . teemed with enormous mammalia" (I, 123). So it is that "the palæontologist, in his inquiries into . . . fossil remains . . . is enabled to call forth from their rocky sepulchres, the beings of past ages, and like the fabled sorcerer, give form and animation to the inhabitants of the tomb" (I, 181).

The geologist becomes shrouded in the aura of the Romantic poet, a figure associated with Lord Byron whose *Childe Harold's Pilgrimage* (1812) Lyell and Mantell were to quote in emphasizing the mutability of things in a universe of endless change.[48] It is this aura, indebted at once to the Romantic poet and to those practitioners who proceed "from the consideration of what is known, to that which is unknown" that was to be bestowed upon the fictional detective, yet another "antiquary of a new order." For Poe, Dickens, and Doyle the fictional detective was to be as concerned with epistemological and narratological issues as any practitioner of an historical discipline who set out to reconstruct the history of the universe, the changes in the earth's surface over time, or those species that had become extinct. In the act of solving a mystery, Dupin, Legrand, and Sherlock Holmes were to reject the orthodoxies of a Natural Theology that embraced empiricism – up to a point – and was to prove vulnerable to the speculations of cosmology, geology, and paleontology in the decades before the publication of the *Origin of Species* in 1859.

As in the *Principles of Geology* and, later, the *Origin of Species*, detective fiction in its inception explored a variety of practices and narrative structures by which to make sense of things in a new way. It appropriated the procedures and the language of the "palætiological sciences" as defined by William Whewell in 1837, "those researches in which the object is, to ascend from the present state of things to a more ancient condition, from which the present is derived by intelligible causes."[49] Detective fiction did not, then, simply reinforce a prevailing orthodoxy or ideology; nor did it reductively police consciousness. Through this new genre, men and women of the nineteenth century were to be introduced to a way of imagining themselves in a universe radically altered by the historical disciplines, each of them characterized by their narrative practices. Ross Macdonald (the American author of the Lew Archer mysteries) once observed, "Popular fiction, popular art in general, is the very air a civilization breathes. . . . Popular art is the form in which a culture comes to be known by most of its members. It is the carrier and guardian of the spoken language. A book which can be read by everyone, a convention which is widely used and understood in all its variations, holds a civilization together as nothing else can."[50] But such a civilization is never without its contradictions, its competing, often irreconcilable, worldviews. Nor is any worldview itself thoroughly coherent, free of contradictions.[51] In introducing readers to a new way of construing reality, nineteenth-century detective fiction may have sought, perhaps without success, to initiate a transition from one version of common sense to another. But, such fiction in the hands of Poe, Dickens, and Doyle also pointed to the inadequacies of the various disciplines – philology, geology, paleontology, and evolutionary biology – that informed it, subverting its own claims to the truth.

There was no necessary transition effected by nineteenth-century detective fiction from one worldview to another. Then, as now, controversies abounded both in the scientific and lay communities about the nature of evidence; about the origins and age of the earth, the solar system, and the universe; and about competing evolutionary hypotheses. Although in the chapters that follow I shall move chronologically from "The Murders in the Rue Morgue" to *The Hound of the Baskervilles*, I do not intend to suggest that I follow a necessary teleological trajectory, ending with the triumph of modernity. Rather, *The Hound of the Baskervilles* may not, after all, suggest the final consolidation of a Darwinian worldview in late-Victorian Britain. If detective fiction in the nineteenth century responded to various historical disciplines, it revealed that in excavating the past, the detective encounters an infinite regress without a point of origin: there is no firm grounding for any hypothesis. The requisite "retrospection" of the detective story never provides an end to speculation. In the same way there is no end to the scientific and religious controversies of the nineteenth century that continue to this moment at the beginning of the twenty-first century.[52]

Part One
Edgar Allan Poe

Nebula in Orion, from John Pringle Nichol's *Views of the Architecture of the Heavens*, 3rd edn (1839). Image reproduced courtesy of the History of Science Collections, University of Oklahoma.

1

"The Murders in the Rue Morgue": Edgar Allan Poe's Evolutionary Reverie

> Origin of man now proved. – Metaphysic must flourish. – He who understands baboon ⟨will⟩ would do more towards metaphysics than Locke
>
> Charles Darwin, Notebook M, 16 August 1838

In *The Dialogic Imagination* Mikhail Bakhtin uses evolutionary metaphors to argue that as historical circumstances change, certain literary genres become extinct or endure at best as living fossils, while new genres appear in response to new and perplexing situations. Of the novel, Bakhtin observes:

> Among genres long since completed and in part already dead, the novel is the only developing genre. It is the only genre that was born and nourished in a new era of world history and therefore it is deeply akin to that era, whereas the other major genres entered that era as already fixed forms, as an inheritance, and only now are they adapting themselves – some better, some worse – to the new conditions of their existence.[1]

Such new eras of history appear perhaps after a period of transition, even of crisis, that precedes the fragile consolidation of what may only seem to be a newly-triumphant and prevailing worldview. From such a perspective, Michael McKeon has suggested that changes in genre and in the generic categories of the literary historian register "an epistemological crisis, a major cultural transition in attitudes toward how to tell the truth in narrative."[2] Bakhtin and McKeon imply that both generic classes and truth become relative, products of a particular historical situation. New genres not only posit new truths; they provide narrative models for arriving at the truth of the moment. It is possible, then, to argue that the detective story, not unlike the novel, appeared at a moment of social and intellectual crisis that it both recognized and defined, even as it promoted the transition from one worldview, generally Christian and ahistorical, to another, profoundly historical worldview that remains to this day unsettling.[3]

A case in point is Edgar Allan Poe's "The Murders in the Rue Morgue" (1841), arguably the first detective story, the first indication of a new genre "born and nourished in a new era of world history." The story introduces the eccentric detective in the character of C. Auguste Dupin as he solves the grotesque murders of Madame and Mademoiselle L'Espanaye (mother and daughter) who were brutally killed and mutilated in their locked apartment in the Rue Morgue by an unknown intruder that will prove to be an Ourang-Outang transported to Paris from the Malay archipelago. Through allusions to the nebular hypothesis of Pierre Simon Laplace (1749–1827) "The Murders in the Rue Morgue" hinted at the existence of a contingent universe denied the trappings of divinity in which the detective finds himself as he sets out to render the apparently unintelligible intelligible without recourse to supernatural explanations. The story appeared in 1841 at a time in which both a resurgent evangelicalism and a conservative Natural Theology were confronted by a positivist science that was to have its nineteenth-century culmination in Charles Darwin's *Origin of Species*.[4] Of course, transitions in worldview do not occur within a few decades; no worldview ever sweeps the field. The mysterious universe of *The Pilgrim's Progress* (1678), in which divine intervention and the supernatural abound, was never to be displaced completely by that version of what was to become Natural Theology that Robinson Crusoe enacts in Daniel Defoe's 1719 novel. The transition from the Natural Theology of William Paley (1743–1805) or of the authors of the Bridgewater Treatises, with their attempts to reconcile science and revealed religion, to a Darwinian universe of natural law and chance has never been consolidated within Western consciousness – as the rise of scientific creationism and, more recently, of the argument for intelligent design reveals.[5]

As a representative of detective fiction, "The Murders in the Rue Morgue" participates in an endless conversation, perhaps a cacophony of dispute, that has never ended.[6] The story itself depicts a culture in which disagreement and discord are everywhere. Men and women of different nationalities and languages are gathered in Paris, a world-city that becomes a nineteenth-century Babel. The witnesses to the carnage in the house in the Rue Morgue are unable to agree about the language spoken in the shrill – or was it a harsh? – voice that they had heard, about the gender of the speaker, or perhaps about anything else. They speak, literally and figuratively, in foreign languages to each other. The situation points to the debates of the 1830s and 1840s about the origins and meaning of the universe. When C. Auguste Dupin dismisses the acumen of the Paris police as mere cunning, he observes that "there is no method in their proceedings, beyond the method of the moment."[7] With these words Dupin is not simply endorsing a generalized scientific and empiricist method to be demonstrated through his solution to the murders that occurred within the locked apartment of the L'Espanayes. Rather, he alludes to a specific worldview and to the controversies surrounding Pierre Simon Laplace's nebular hypothesis and to one version of it set forth by John Pringle Nichol (1804–1859), Regius professor of astronomy at the University of Glasgow. In his scorn for the method, the common sense, of the moment, Dupin will ally himself with a vision of the universe that, as its critics understood, could lead to religious skepticism.[8]

All of this is clarified in the episode in which Dupin engages in what will prove to be his first tour de force of detection for our benefit. Dupin and the narrator have been walking at night through the streets of Paris without having spoken for some fifteen minutes. Suddenly, Dupin remarks to his companion: "He is a very little fellow, that's true, and would do better for the *Théâtre des Variétés*" ("Murders," p. 402). The astounded narrator feels that Dupin has fathomed his soul; he demands to know the method – "if method there is" – that according to Dupin has led to the links in a chain that run "Chantilly [the cobbler turned tragedian], Orion, Dr. Nichol, Epicurus, Stereotomy, the street stones, the fruiterer" (p. 403). In his explanation of his inferences Dupin will demonstrate a method and, in discussing the topics the narrator dwells upon, allude to an embryonic worldview. Poe's narrator may emphasize the almost preternatural nature of Dupin's gifts; but Dupin himself scorns recourse to the supernatural: he pursues explanations always grounded in empiricist assumptions about causation and human consciousness. In retracing his companion's thoughts, Dupin uses the reconstructive models of nineteenth-century historical disciplines associated with geology and archaeology and later with evolutionary biology. He returns to a posited "starting-point" – the narrator's encounter with a fruiterer that had "thrust [him] upon a pile of paving-stones collected at a spot where the causeway is undergoing repair" (p. 403). From this accidental event Dupin creates a chronological, an associative, and, implicitly, a causal sequence of ideas based on the assumption that law governs not only all natural phenomena, but also the workings of the human mind.[9]

From the start, the episode touches upon debates central to a time when nineteenth-century geology, particularly that of Charles Lyell and his *Principles of Geology* (1830–33), challenged the literal status of Genesis and a chronology claiming that the universe had been created in 4004 B.C. The narrator's meditations have begun after the brush with the fruiterer. Dupin observes: "You stepped upon one of the loose fragments [of paving-stone], slipped, slightly strained your ankle, appeared vexed or sulky, muttered a few words, turned to look at the pile, and then proceeded in silence" ("Murders," p. 403). The loss of his footing initiates the narrator's musings upon origins. With challenges to Genesis and to traditional conceptions of time, the ground beneath his feet has shifted; he undergoes a version of what Darwin experienced on the voyage of the *Beagle* during the Chilean earthquake of 1835: "A bad earthquake at once destroys the oldest associations: the world, the very emblem of all that is solid, has moved beneath our feet like a crust over a fluid; – one second of time has conveyed to the mind a strange idea of insecurity, which hours of reflection would never have created."[10] When he comes upon what seems to be firmer footing in the interlocked paving-stones, the narrator only finds that the term "Stereotomy" reminds him of the chaos of atoms from which the universe had arisen, by chance, according to the Epicurean cosmogony of Lucretius's *De rerum natura*.

It is at this point that the narrator thinks of Dr. Nichol, the author of *Views of the Architecture of the Heavens* (1837). Except for a reference to the "late nebular cosmogony," Dupin neglects to explain how thoughts of Nichol might lead the narrator to look up to Orion. But anyone turning to Nichol's book would find that it offered an exposition of the nebular hypothesis that Laplace first sketched out in 1796 in his *Exposition du système du monde*.[11] In place of Isaac Newton's world-machine, created and periodically regulated by God, Laplace posited the existence of an original matter existing in a heated, gaseous form that, through the laws of physics, cooled over vast periods of time. As the matter cooled, it began to rotate around emerging centers due to the force of gravity; in this way stars and solar systems would be formed. One such center of cooling gas was to become our sun, orbited by planets that were the condensed remnants of rings of vapor thrown off by centrifugal force from the cooling, rotating sun. Laplace's hypothesis had been influenced by the astronomer, William Herschel (1738–1822), who had claimed to have found within the constellation Orion a luminous nebula of heated gases. Those gases were the precursors of yet other stars and solar systems, a revelation from the depths of space and time of their origins. It was Herschel who wrote in 1789 of the histories of different celestial systems as akin to "the germination, blooming, foliage, fecundity, fading, withering, and corruption of a plant."[12] Both Herschel and Laplace were to contribute to a worldview that, if Herschel's account is to be trusted, would lead Laplace in his confident theism to observe to Napoleon that he had no need to turn, as Newton had, to a First Cause to explain the origins of the universe.[13]

With its materialist implications, the nebular hypothesis could be associated, as indeed it was, with a Lucretian atheism, a sweeping away of the foundations of everyday life. Early in the nineteenth century William Paley attacked the nebular hypothesis, citing it as one among several hypotheses about the origins of the universe offered by "those who reject an intelligent Creator."[14] Later in the century, in the first of the Bridgewater Treatises written to promote Natural Theology, Thomas Chalmers (1780–1847) specifically mentioned Laplace, holding him responsible for "the tendency of atheistical writers . . . to reason exclusively on the laws of matter, and to overlook its dispositions": "Could all the beauties and benefits of the astronomical system be referred to the single law of gravitation, it would greatly reduce the strength of the argument for a designing cause. . . . as if to fortify still more the atheism of such a speculation[,] . . . La Place [*sic*] would have accredited the law, *the unconscious and unintelligent law, that thing according to him of blind necessity,* with the whole of this noble and beautiful result," that is, the solar system and the universe.[15] Writing in 1833, Chalmers sensed to what speculations the nebular hypothesis might lead: "Insomuch, that though we conceded to the atheist, the eternity of matter, and the essentially inherent character of all its laws – we could still point out to him, in the manifold adjustments of matter . . . the most impressive signatures of a Deity" (pp. 19–20): "That *blind and unconscious matter* cannot, by any of *her* combinations, evolve the phenomena of mind, is a proposition seen in its own immediate light, and felt to be true with all the speed and certainty of an axiom" (p. 27, emphasis added). Of course, not all proponents of the nebular hypothesis perceived themselves either as skeptics or as potential transmutationists. In other Bridgewater Treatises, religious men of science like William Whewell (1794–1866) of Cambridge and William Buckland (1784–1856) of Oxford could provide thorough expositions of Laplace's ideas: it was, in fact, Whewell who coined the term, nebular hypothesis.[16] Gideon Mantell, the popularizer of Charles Lyell's dynamic geology, could endorse the nebular hypothesis in his *Wonders of Geology* in 1838 and remain thoroughly conventional in his religious beliefs.[17]

There are, then, good reasons for not explaining why the narrator's thoughts have moved from Epicurus to Dr. Nichol, rather than to Whewell, Buckland, or Mantell. Dupin's companion is preoccupied with one version of the nebular hypothesis that can be seen as a challenge to orthodoxies of all sorts – religious, scientific, and social. Nichol was an advocate of political economy and, in its name, social change, one of a group of self-styled reformers including John Stuart Mill (1806–1873) and George Combe (1788–1858), the phrenologist. They invoked the rule of natural law and the notion of a changing universe to attack entrenched social and religious institutions. Inevitably, they found themselves in conflict with defenders of the existing social order – with those like Whewell and Adam Sedgwick (1785–1873), first professor of geology at Cambridge and a patron of Charles Darwin, who tried to dominate the emerging sciences in the name of Anglicanism. In their defense of society as it existed, the dons of Cambridge and Oxford could be expected to respond to Nichol and to others with charges of political radicalism and religious impiety.[18]

In his *Views of the Architecture of the Heavens*, Nichol wrote with a keen awareness of potential critics. Throughout his book Nichol celebrated "that BEING, who amid change alone is unchangeable – whose glance reaches from the beginning to the end – and whose presence occupies all things" to quell "uneasy feelings" aroused by "the idea of a process which may appear to substitute *progress* for *creation*, and place *law* in the room of *providence*."[19] He proceeded to expatiate upon "Laplace's bold and brilliant *induction*" (p. 185) that had revealed a "System of Evolution of which Creation as it exists is only one phase," by which "to develope all possible variety, to exhibit how, without infraction of stedfast law, Being may be infinitely diversified, and room found for unfolding the whole riches of the Almighty" (pp. 45–46): "Who can ascend so far up that vast chain which unites the eternal past with the fleeting present; who – to go no higher – can dwell on the idea of our Sun being born from one of those dim nebulæ, order growing within him by effect of law, and the worlds he illumines and sustains, springing gradually into being, – without engrossing emotions!" (pp. 187–88). Yet such emotions must encompass the possibility that matter itself "may bear within it, laid up in its dark bosom – the germs, the producing powers of that LIFE, which in coming ages will bud and blossom, and effloresce, into manifold and growing forms" (p. 138). Within a universe so conceived "the existence of the human race is an invisible speck, [that] will have resulted during a stage of condensation in a secondary nebula": "In relation to the nebulæ, Man is only an Ephemeron" (pp. 151–52). Nichol's vision of Man as a "transient organization, with whose progress the education of a Spiritual Being has been for a moment connected" (p. 188) might arouse anxiety, as Nichol substituted for a single act of creation an evolving process governed only by natural law. Yet he argued that such anxiety arises from a misunderstanding, for law cannot be separated from Mind:

> Law is a mere name for a long order – an order unoriginated, unupheld, unsubstantial, whose floor sounds hollow beneath the tread, and whose spaces are all void; an order hanging tremblingly over nothingness, and of which every constituent – every thing and creature fails not to beseech incessantly for a substance and substratum in the idea of ONE – WHO LIVETH FOR EVER!
>
> (pp. 189–90)

Nichol captured the agony of those who feel that they tread upon nothing, only to console his readers with, in the eyes of his critics, a convenient abstraction. He could only further stir uneasiness as he observed that "absolute permanence is visible nowhere around us, and the fact of change merely intimates, that in the exhaustless womb of the future, unevolved wonders are in store." But such wonders require "the close of one mighty cycle in the history of the solar orb – the passing away of arrangements which have fulfilled their objects that they might be transformed into new. Thus is the periodic death of a plant perhaps the essential to its prolonged life, and when the individual dies and disappears, fresh and vigorous forms spring from the elements which composed it" (*Architecture*, pp. 194–95).

It is not surprising that Poe's narrator may not find solace in Nichol's claim that "a time may come, when the veil can be drawn aside – when spirit shall converse *directly* with spirit, and the creature gaze without hinderance on the effulgent face of its Creator" (*Architecture*, p. 196). Only as he finds surer footing in the pavement of the alley, Lamartine, does he regain what Nichol called "the solid ground of fact and observation" (p. 122): at that moment he casts his "eyes upward to the great *nebula* in Orion" ("Murders," p. 404). It was, after all, William Herschel's speculations on the luminous clouds he claimed to have discovered in the constellation of Orion that had influenced Laplace's formulation of the nebular hypothesis.[20] The narrator gazes upward to glimpse the birth of other stars, perhaps of other solar systems, that could eventually give rise to life itself. Yet, in contemplating Orion, the narrator inevitably is reminded of a recent attack upon the would-be tragedian, Chantilly, in which the critic in the *Musée* mocked the actor's change of name by citing a Latin line about which he and Dupin have often talked: "Perdidit antiquum litera prima sonum" (p. 404). The line is from the *Fasti*, Ovid's uncompleted calendar that included an account of the birth of Orion. In the *Fasti* Ovid told the story of Jupiter, Neptune, and Mercury, who urinate upon a bull's hide from which, after being covered by earth, a boy is born some ten months later. The child is originally called Urion, from the Greek "ouron," for urine; the name is altered to obscure his true origins and the curious fact that he is not born of woman.[21] The "pungencies connected with this explanation," so Dupin claims, has led the narrator "to combine the two ideas of Orion and Chantilly" (p. 404). In thinking of the cobbler who has changed his name, the narrator thinks of an act of self-transformation from some ignominious condition. Yet the creation of Orion out of urine, earth, and the bull's hide – out of matter in its least pleasant forms – suggests not only the diminutive, perhaps comic Chantilly; it stands as a curious parody of any evolutionary account of human origins that might suggest, as the *Architecture of the Heavens* had, that matter itself bears within it germs that may produce life without an act of special creation. In drawing himself to his full height, Dupin's companion not only thinks of the cobbler's stature; he asserts his own dignity and humanity within the context of certain accounts of human origins. In his erect posture the narrator, who to that point has "been stooping in [his] gait" (p. 404), would seem to shrug off any hypothesis that would suggest that he is related to creatures of some lower order.

Although Dupin's reconstruction of his friend's thoughts would seem to bring to an end the preoccupations that bother him, "The Murders in the Rue Morgue" becomes an extension of the narrator's reverie, even a confirmation of his fears. Dupin's revelation that an Ourang-Outang had been the killer of Madame and Mademoiselle L'Espanaye only further develops the possibilities that have proven to be so disconcerting to the narrator. In his efforts to persuade his friend that the marks on the throat of Mademoiselle L'Espanaye have not been left by a human hand, Dupin turns to a passage from Georges Cuvier: "It was a minute anatomical and generally descriptive account of the large fulvous Ourang-Outang of the East Indian Islands. The gigantic stature, the prodigious strength and activity, the wild ferocity, and the imitative propensities of these mammalia are sufficiently well known to all. I understood the full horrors of the murder at once" ("Murders," p. 424). Burton R. Pollin has already recognized that Dupin has referred his friend to Cuvier's *Animal Kingdom* (1817), and Pollin has further noted that the entry on the Ourang-Outang does not, in fact, mention the ferocity of the animal.[22] More suggestive is the fact that Cuvier is careful to qualify the claims of those who would argue that the Ourang-Outang approaches "most nearly to Man in the form of his head, height of forehead, and volume of brain." Yet, in a passage omitted from "The Murders in the Rue Morgue" – paralleling the omission of the significance of Dr. Nichol – Cuvier went on to discuss the Ourang-Outang's imitative talents and then turned to deal with the Pongo, which resembles the Ourang-Outang and "in size is nearly equal to Man." The full implications of the entry are revealed in a footnote explaining the etymology of the animal's name: "*Orang* is a Malay word, signifying *reasonable being*, which is applied to man, the ourang-outang, and the elephant. *Outang* means *wild*, or *of the woods*; hence, Wild Man of the Woods."[23] Cuvier's etymology may well be a pure fiction, a repetition in the story of Ovid's account of the derivation of the name, Orion, from Urion. But just as the *Fasti* suggests Orion's humble origins, Cuvier's discussion of the name, Ourang-Outang, connects the animal with the human species, perhaps as its ancestor.

Given the scientific debates of the time and an anxiety about the implications of the nebular hypothesis, someone reading the *Animal Kingdom*, with Cuvier's account of the successive appearance of living organisms over time, might well think of James Burnett, Lord Monboddo (1714–1799), the eighteenth-century Scottish polymath who had become notorious for his account of the origin of language.[24] In *Of the Origin and Progress of Language* (1773–92) and in *Antient Metaphysics* (1779–99), Monboddo, like Cuvier after him, translated Ourang-Outang as "Wild Man of the Woods." For Monboddo, the Ourang-Outang was a necessary stage in the progression of the human species; indeed, he *is* a man as suggested by the name, "*Man of the Woods*, . . . by which he is called by the people of Africa, where he is to be seen, and who do not appear to have the least doubt that he is a man; which, as they live in the country with him, they should know better than we do."[25] Accounts of the Ourang-Outang provide a description of "man, in his first state":

for man is said first to creep, that is, to go upon all four. . . . After that, he is erected, and gets the use of an artificial weapon, such as the

Ourang Outang uses. Next, he invents rude and barbarous cries . . . by which men communicated their sensations, appetites, and desires to one another. And, last of all, they formed ideas, and invented words to express them. . . . But this is a step in the progress towards the civilized life, which the Ourang Outang has not yet made.

(IV, 31–32)

In fact, Monboddo argued that the Ourang-Outang has a fully developed larynx – "the upper part of the larynx, which is called in English *the knot of the throat*, and in French *la glotte*" (IV, 110) – exactly like that of man. As the self-proclaimed promoter of the theism of Plato and Aristotle, Monboddo claimed, however improbably, that

it was of absolute necessity that, in the progress of the human species, man should at some time or another be such an animal: For, if he was originally a quadruped, as I think I have proved by facts incontestible, with only a natural aptitude, more than any other animal, to walk on two, as Aristotle has said, the first step in his progression was to become a biped.

(IV, 26)

As further proof of his claims Monboddo stated that the Ourang-Outang can copulate with human females and produce offspring. Out of a hodge-podge of philosophy, anecdotal reporting, and flights of fancy, Monboddo depicted the Ourang-Outang as man in his natural state before the invention of the art of language that was necessary for his progression towards full humanity.

It is perhaps with such discussions of the Ourang-Outang in mind that Dupin seizes upon the confusing testimony about the language and even the gender of one of the voices heard behind the locked door to the L'Espanaye apartment. He comments: "Now, how strangely unusual must that voice have really been . . . in whose *tones*, even, denizens of the five great divisions of Europe could recognise nothing familiar!" ("Murders," p. 416). With a characteristic racism, Dupin and his friend descend a hierarchy from the apex constituted by speakers of Indo-European languages to Asiatics and Africans, with their "barbarous tongues," to those excluded from the human community through the unintelligibility of the sounds that they produce. In response to Dupin's observation that the voice was "devoid of all distinct or intelligible syllabification," the narrator at last exclaims that "a madman . . . has done this deed – some raving maniac, escaped from a neighboring *Maison de*

Santé" (p. 423). Asians, Africans, lunatics – and perhaps, by implication, women – become associated with the Ourang-Outang. Without language, whatever creature had uttered such sounds and brutally killed the two women is exiled from the human species and ceases, in its apparent motivelessness, to be a responsible agent.[26]

In emphasizing that "madmen are of some nation" and in dismissing "the blundering idea of *motive"* ("Murders," pp. 423, 421), Dupin introduces the Ourang-Outang as the culprit, reducing the murders to purely contingent events without purpose and meaning. He denies that any significance is to be found in the accidental intrusion of the Ourang-Outang into the L'Espanaye apartment or in its frenzied attack upon the mother and the daughter. Yet the fate of the two women demands some response: they had been so violated that the daughter's tongue had been bitten through, the mother's throat cut – I would suggest at the larynx, Monboddo's knot of the throat – so that her head had been severed from her body.[27] A psychological reading of the story would emphasize the misogyny of the murders: the imitative behavior of the Ourang-Outang and the name "Wild Man of the Woods" – suppressed in the story itself – would transform the creature into the Double of its master, the sailor, acting out his fantasies upon the two women. In destroying the women's organs of speech, the Ourang-Outang blindly denies their status as human beings, confirming the darkest implications of male attitudes toward women.[28]

But such a reading complements the one I am suggesting. In the figure of the Ourang-Outang and its attack upon the organs of speech, "The Murders in the Rue Morgue" points to Lord Monboddo's speculations on the progress of the human species in its development from lower animals. As it thrusts the corpse of Mademoiselle L'Espanaye up the chimney, feet first, the Ourang-Outang enacts male terror of the female body and captures, in another sense, the terror and confusion of those who suddenly find themselves in a contingent universe. In his Bridgewater Treatise Thomas Chalmers had said that "blind and unconscious matter cannot, by any of her combinations, evolve the phenomena of mind." In his discussion of the nebular hypothesis John Pringle Nichol had written of the "womb of the future." Both, as men are wont to do, associate matter and nature with the female, implicitly denying women consciousness and the power of speech. But, in association with a rage directed toward women, the murders reveal an act of retribution directed against a universe that is itself the result of an accidental birth out of matter in a gaseous state; that has produced life in ways not fully understood; and that is, even now, moving toward its inevitable death.

In the midst of debates about the implications of the nebular hypothesis, "The Murders in the Rue Morgue" offered all that the critics of Laplace most feared: a harrowing vision of a Lucretian universe. It was a vision recorded by Charles Darwin in his personal notebooks in the spring and summer of 1838. In terms curiously like those we have seen in Poe's detective story, Darwin wrote,

> —look abroad, study gradation. Study unity of type—Study geographical distribution
>
> study relation of fossil with recent. the fabric falls! But Man——wonderful Man. "divino ore versus cœlum attentus" is an exception.— He is Mammalian. . . . he is not a deity, his end ⟪under present form⟫ will come, (or how dredfully we are deceived) then he is no exception. . . .
>
> Let man visit Ourang-outang in domestication, hear expressive whine, see its intelligence when spoken; as if it understood every word said . . . ⟪let [man] look at savage, roasting his parent, naked, artless, not improving yet improvable⟫ & then let him dare to boast of his proud preeminence.— ⟪not understanding language of Fuegian, puts on par with Monkeys⟫[29]

The fabric that falls for Darwin must be that of Natural Theology, with its emphasis on the doctrine of special creation and the uniqueness of humanity. For Darwin, as for Poe, Man is mammalian, not a deity, perhaps separated from other animals only by a face turned toward the heavens and by the power of speech.

In the decade after Darwin's notebook entry it is understandable, then, that opponents of the nebular hypothesis were not to be reassured by the purportedly theistic vision of the 1844 *Vestiges of the Natural History of Creation* or Poe's 1848 lecture on the Universe and its published version, "Eureka."[30] The anonymous author of *Vestiges* – Mr. Vestiges as he came to be called – was Robert Chambers, coeditor of the *Chambers's Edinburgh Journal*, in which, appropriately, an abridged version of "The Purloined Letter" appeared in 1844. John Pringle Nichol would accuse Mr. Vestiges of plagiarism in his uniting of the nebular hypothesis with Lamarckean premises to argue that a "First Cause" – "a primitive almighty will" – has produced the two laws that govern the universe: "The inorganic has one final comprehensive law, GRAVITATION. The organic, the other great department of mundane things, rests in like manner on one law, and that is, – DEVELOPMENT."[31] In the nebula of

Orion we have glimpsed "the process through which a sun goes between its original condition, as a mass of diffused nebulous matter, and its full-formed state as a compact body" (*Vestiges*, p. 8). With the laws of gravitation and development, there is no need to invoke miracle or the doctrine of special creation. Over the course of time the solar system has been formed; even "the first step in the creation of life upon this planet was *a chemico-electric operation, by which simple germinal vesicles were produced*" (pp. 204–5), initiating a process that led from simple organisms to complex ones that include human beings. God willed into existence a process that permitted Mr. Vestiges to deny the dualism of Mind and Matter and to suggest that "the difference between mind in the lower animals and in man is a difference in degree only" (pp. 335–36). There are even echoes of Lord Monboddo as Mr. Vestiges discussed the larynx, the trachea, and the mouth to argue that language is not a new gift of the Creator but that "man" has possessed a physiological organization that was ready for the production of intelligible sound. For those who might be taken aback by his attacks on divine intervention in human affairs or visions of an anthropomorphic God, Mr. Vestiges offered a vista of unending progress in civilization and the further development of human reason in an unimaginable future.

Those who heard Poe's lecture on the Universe and read his "Eureka: A Prose Poem" in 1848 recognized the unacknowledged influence of *Vestiges*.[32] With explicit references to Epicurus, William Herschel, and Nichol's *Architecture of the Heavens* – and a footnote referring to "The Murders in the Rue Morgue" – Poe proceeded to offer his own interpretation of "*the Material and Spiritual Universe: – of its Essence, its Origin, its Creation, its Present Condition and its Destiny*" ("Eureka," p. 1261). Like Mr. Vestiges, Poe wrote of a divine Unity that, through an act of pure volition, "*now* exists solely in the diffused Matter and Spirit of the Universe; and — [of] the regathering of this diffused Matter and Spirit [that] will be but the re-constitution of the *purely Spiritual* and Individual God" (p. 1357). In place of Mr. Vestiges' laws of Gravitation and Development, Poe introduced the rule of Repulsion and Attraction that governs the inanimate and the animate realms. He offered an idiosyncratic pantheism that some associated with Spinoza to explain the origins of the universe and consciousness and to reveal, through the power of Attraction, an inevitable return to the primal unity from which all has come. Unlike Mr. Vestiges, Poe rejected the possibility that "the Universe has no conceivable end": without an end "Creation would have affected us as an imperfect *plot* in a romance, where the *dénoûment* is awkwardly brought about by interposed incidents external and foreign to the main subject;

instead of springing out of the bosom of the thesis" (p. 1352). Human beings demand plots with teleological implications: "The plots of God are perfect. The Universe is a plot of God" (p. 1342). God's plot demands that the universe of matter and spirit through which divinity has diffused itself will finally, and satisfyingly, be rejoined with the unity from which they have proceeded.

But those who were skeptical of the unorthodox implications of the nebular hypothesis would have nothing to do with "the sublime chronology" (*Vestiges*, p. 22) of a Mr. Vestiges or with Poe's version of the universe as a "plot of God." In his anonymous review of *Vestiges* in the *Edinburgh Review*, Adam Sedgwick could write of the book as "the raving madness of hypothetical extravagance," mention Lucretius and his *De rerum natura*, and yoke Mr. Vestiges with Lord Monboddo, each of whom "brooded over the fantasies of his mind till his dreams became to him as substantial realities."[33] The responses to Poe's lecture and "Eureka" were mixed, but the unsigned review of "Eureka" in the *Literary World* attacked Poe's speculations as "extraordinary nonsense, if not blasphemy; and it may very possibly be *both*" (*Poe Log*, p. 746). The unorthodox speculations in *Vestiges* and "Eureka" were properly seen as threats to traditional Christianity and to an existing social order in Great Britain and the United States. Those who would have known of the feverish dreams of Mr. Vestiges or Poe feared that the act of divine volition that created an evolving universe, with or without an end, might well be but a step away from a purely contingent originating event from which the solar system and life itself were to arise. In the place of a divine chronology or a plot of God we may be left perhaps with a romance, a plot in the mind of C. Auguste Dupin, reconstructed only after a series of coincidences that led, with a seeming inevitability, to the murders in the Rue Morgue.

In 1841 "The Murders in the Rue Morgue" explored the implications of the nebular hypothesis at a moment when the contest between differing worldviews had not been decided and when the future could not be predicted. Poe's story did not simply reinforce a prevailing orthodoxy: at the time, Natural Theology and evangelicalism remained powerful voices in the ongoing, and unending, conversation about the origin and nature of the universe. The story may, in fact, have been in the service of an emerging perspective whose full implications were to be clarified in 1859 with the publication of the *Origin of Species*. Poe himself, as "Eureka" suggests, remained undecided, perhaps divided, about the speculations of John Pringle Nichol or Mr. Vestiges. Instead, "The Murders in the Rue Morgue" suggests the situation of the individual within a Parisian Babel of controversy, anticipating in its own outré way the possible ascendancy of one evolutionary vision of the universe. In the figure of C. Auguste Dupin, Poe depicted the individual as a creature of history who must reconstruct the past even as he comes upon the fact of the contingency of certain events, without any reassuring knowledge of the future. It becomes a harrowing vision, centered upon the presence of the Ourang-Outang – the ominous "it" – that in a seemingly motiveless frenzy introduces the terror of a history secularized and devoid of design. In such a world there is no longer the solace provided by claims that "the plots of God are perfect. The Universe is a plot of God." Rather, we are left with the reconstructions of a Dupin and, later, of a William Legrand in "The Gold-Bug" (1843), for whom *"perfection* of plot is really, or practically, unattainable . . . because it is a finite intelligence that constructs" ("Eureka," p. 1342). Such plots, like "an imperfect *plot* in a romance" (p. 1352), become a mark of the detective story as it responds to a new era of world history. Through the creation of plot, both Dupin and Legrand struggle against that "temporary paralysis" that coincidence induces: each establishes "a connexion – a sequence of cause and effect" ("Gold-Bug," p. 511) – in the face of what may prove to be mere chance.[34] Through an almost preternatural will to power, Dupin and Legrand create contexts for the literal and figurative texts before them. In this way they regain their footing and walk again in a world that has once been, but may never again be, the "very emblem of all that is solid."

2
"The Gold-Bug," Hieroglyphics, and the Historical Imagination

> I could not, therefore, but conclude, that a most extraordinary
> chance had brought into my possession a document which was
> not very likely, in the first place, ever to have existed, still less
> to have been preserved, uninjured, for my information, through
> a period of near two thousand years.
>
> Thomas Young, *An Account of Some Recent Discoveries in*
> *Hieroglyphical Literature, and Egyptian Antiquities* (1823)

I

In the universe of pure contingency depicted in "The Murders in the Rue Morgue" (1841) there is only – history. Once the universe is denied design and purpose through the skeptical implications of the nebular hypothesis, the human situation and the mysteries that constitute it are to be understood only through the reconstruction of those contingent events that have led to the present moment, for example, to the murders of Madame and Mademoiselle L'Espanaye. The fictional detective becomes a practitioner of those historical disciplines – philology, geology, and archaeology – that were in the process of consolidation in the middle of the nineteenth century both in Britain and in the United States, often under the figurative aegis of Jean-François Champollion's decipherment of the Rosetta Stone, a feat announced to the world in his famous 50-page letter to M. Dacier that was read before the Académie Française on 27 September 1822.[1]

"The Murders in the Rue Morgue" alludes to the significance of Champollion's achievements for detective fiction as the anonymous narrator of the story meditates upon "the mental features discoursed of as the analytical [that] are, in themselves, but little susceptible of analysis."[2] The individual possessed of, or possessed by, such analytical powers "glories . . . in that moral activity which *disentangles*": "He is fond of enigmas, of conundrums, of hieroglyphics; exhibiting in his solutions of each a degree of *acumen* which appears to the ordinary apprehension præternatural. His results, brought about by the very soul and essence of method, have, in truth, the whole air of intuition" (p. 397). But neither C. Auguste Dupin, nor his equally idiosyncratic counterpart, William Legrand of "The Gold-Bug" (1843), exercises unnatural powers as each disentangles a snarled thread of events to create the story line that is meant to explain them through a sequence of natural causes and effects.[3]

In introducing William Legrand in "The Gold-Bug," Poe returned to a detective figure confronted by a conundrum. Coming upon a new species of beetle on the South Carolina coast, Legrand and his black man-servant, Jupiter, also find by chance a parchment with which to handle the pesky *scarabæus* that has already bitten Legrand. Through a series of fortuitous events Legrand discovers a coded message on the apparently blank parchment that, deciphered, leads him to a buried pirate treasure with which to restore the fortunes of his Huguenot family. A story that seems to celebrate the powers of the human intellect, nevertheless, suggests the limits of reason as it points to Legrand's non-rational *will* to meaning that produces pirate treasure while, in a larger context, his feverish desire to see the universe as intelligible is rendered suspect.

As Dupin and Legrand seek out solutions to the mysteries that confront them, the "essence of [their] method" remains obscured: the mysteriousness of their solutions is not to be ignored, remaining finally at the very center of the situations in which they are involved. Poe's detective fictions become extended meditations upon what his Pundita of "Mellonta Tauta" (1849) calls the "*two possible roads*" to truth, the deductive road of Aristotle or the inductive road that she attributes to a nineteenth-century empiricism with its purportedly "Baconian" foundation (pp. 874–75). In "Mellonta Tauta" Pundita proceeds by considering how "the truth of Gravitation" was attained: "Newton owed it to Kepler. Kepler admitted that his three laws were *guessed at* – these three laws of all laws which led the great Inglitch mathematician to his principle, the basis of all physical principle – to go behind which we must enter the Kingdom of Metaphysics. Kepler guessed – that is to say, *imagined*" (p. 877). Such comments ironically subvert any claim to a systematic method upon which Newtonian physics is founded. Pundita continues: "Would it not have puzzled these old moles, too, to have explained by which of the two 'roads' a cryptographist unriddles a cryptograph of more than usual secrecy, or by which of the two roads Champollion directed mankind to those enduring and almost innumerable truths which resulted from his deciphering the Hieroglyphics?" (p. 877). The implication is clear. Champollion's achievement was no less a feat of the imagination than Kepler's; and it is no less mysterious. The foundations of human knowledge have been questioned both in the realm of physics and in the realm of those historical disciplines that work with literal and figurative documents surviving from the past by which that past is to be reconstructed. Written in the year 2848, Pundita's letter to her beloved Pundit ends as she tries to understand *"an inscription – a legible inscription"* (p. 883), found on a marble slab, apparently erected by the tribe called Knickerbocker in 1847, to commemorate George Washington's defeat of Lord Cornwallis at Yorktown in A.D. 1781. The intact inscription leads Pundita to comic misinterpretations as she speculates that "Lord Cornwallis was surrendered (for sausage)" to those "savages [who] were undoubtedly cannibals . . . 'under the auspices of the Washington Monument Association'" (p. 884).

Pundita's observations may occasion a moment of hilarity, yet they nevertheless point to the challenge that the fictional detective faces as he tries to interpret a murder scene, often relying on various newspaper accounts as C. Auguste Dupin does both in "The Murders in the Rue Morgue" and in "The Mystery of Marie Rogêt" (1842–43), a story in which he never visits the scene of the crime. In "The Gold-Bug" Poe will examine the methods of William Legrand, yet another detective figure, to suggest that beneath "the very soul and essence of method," with its "air of intuition" ("Murders," p. 397), there lies a will to meaning that defies rational understanding even as it becomes the foundation of that historical knowledge that is the special domain of the detective. Legrand's discovery of a new species of *scarabæus* is accompanied by the equally fortuitous discovery of a piece of parchment in which to wrap the beetle that has already bitten him once. The coincidental discovery of a beetle and a blank parchment on the coast of the South Carolina mainland abutting Sullivan's Island initiates a series of events that culminate in the excavation of treasure buried, it would seem, in the late seventeenth century by the notorious William Kidd.[4]

Both Pundita and William Legrand become figurative archaeologists and cryptographers who set out to decipher writings from the past. Pundita discusses an inscription in English from a thousand years earlier, an inscription that nevertheless defies her understanding.

Legrand comes upon a perfectly blank parchment that, through a series of complex operations, will yield first a death's-head and then a curious figure that he will treat as "a kind of punning or hieroglyphical signature" ("Gold-Bug," p. 585) to a non-existent message. In explaining to his physician friend how he has found a coded message upon the parchment, Legrand dwells upon the coincidence – in fact, the series of coincidences – that has led to his discovery of a skull drawn "immediately beneath [the] figure of the *scarabæus*" that Legrand himself has drawn on the parchment: "I say the singularity of this coincidence absolutely stupified me for a time. This is the usual effect of such coincidences. The mind struggles to establish a connexion – a sequence of cause and effect – and, being unable to do so, suffers a species of temporary paralysis" (p. 581). Throughout the story Legrand will dramatize the human need to avoid such paralysis, a need that may appear as a form of madness to someone like the narrator, at ease with his common-sense understanding of things. The narrative follows the methods by which Legrand proceeds to establish, even to create, a "sequence of cause and effect" that may satisfy his will to order and meaning.

It is significant that Legrand, who shares with Dupin a loss of patrimony that haunts him, is both a solitary *and* a natural historian. The narrator of the story introduces him as a conchologist and entomologist of note, with a "collection of [insects that] might have been envied by a Swammerdamm" ("Gold-Bug," p. 561). Jan Swammerdam (1637–1680) was a Dutch entomologist, most famous for his three-volume *Biblia naturae* (1737), a pioneering study of insects based upon his use of microscopic investigations of various specimens. Swammerdam participated in the seventeenth-century creation of that common sense that was to inform both Deism, with its skeptical tendencies, and nineteenth-century Natural Theology. In his *Biblia naturae* Swammerdam challenged prevailing misconceptions about insects, arguing that like larger organisms they were deserving of scientific study. In his book he set out to disprove traditional claims about the spontaneous generation of insects and to explain in empirical terms the metamorphosis from larva to chrysalis to imago. With his celebration of nature as God's creation, Swammerdam promoted the natural religion of the seventeenth and eighteenth centuries, a tradition in which Legrand would seem to participate as a classifier of shells and insects.[5]

However, as a nineteenth-century natural historian, Legrand need not be compared to the legendary Swammerdam. Rather, the narrator of "The Gold-Bug" could find models closer to hand, including that of the famous French comparative anatomist, Georges Cuvier (1769–1832) to whose *Animal Kingdom* C. Auguste Dupin has turned in solving the murders in the Rue Morgue. Cuvier participated in the Enlightenment tradition that Swammerdam and others helped to shape, retaining his Christian belief in the doctrine of special creation and the immutability of species. Yet, he accepted the extinction of species and rejected supernatural causes for those geological catastrophes that produced the phenomenon of extinction. In Great Britain Cuvier was the authority to whom proponents of Natural Theology turned. Men like Oxford's William Buckland (1784–1856) and Cambridge's William Whewell (1794–1866) often cited Cuvier in their efforts to refute any hypothesis about the transmutation of species.[6] In his three-volume *History of the Inductive Sciences* (1837) Whewell celebrated Cuvier's skills in the reconstruction of extinct mammals from their fragmentary remains. As he provided a history of physiology, Whewell turned to Cuvier's methods of reconstruction with a suggestive analogy: "He proceeded in his investigations like the decipherer of a manuscript, who makes out his alphabet from one part of the context, and then applies it to read the rest."[7]

Here, Whewell implicitly invoked Jean-François Champollion's decipherment of the Egyptian hieroglyphs on the Rosetta Stone, even as he responded to Cuvier's *Discours préliminaire*, translated into English as an *Essay on the Theory of the Earth* (1813). In his own way Cuvier had anticipated Whewell's association of the comparative anatomist and the philologist by observing, "As an antiquary of a new order, I have been obliged to learn the art of deciphering and restoring these remains [of extinct animals], of discovering and bringing together, in their primitive arrangement, the scattered and mutilated fragments of which they are composed, of reproducing, in all their original proportions and characters, the animals to which these fragments formerly belonged."[8] Practicing "an art which is almost unknown" (*Essay*, p. 2), Cuvier proceeded to reconstruct "the ancient history of the globe" (p. 3), turning to an archaeological metaphor to illustrate it: "Every part of the globe bears the impress of those great and terrible [catastrophic] events . . . [that] must be visible to all who are qualified to read their history in the remains which they have left behind" (p. 17). Such remains, in the form of fossil bones, are to be treated as "historical documents" providing evidence of the "successive epochs in the formation of [the] earth" (p. 54).

In "The Gold-Bug" William Legrand will proceed under the aegis both of Cuvier and Champollion: as a natural historian, he will become "an antiquary of a new order," a practitioner of one of those "palætiological sciences" that endeavor, in the words of William Whewell, "to

ascend to a past state of things, by the aid of the evidence of the present"
(*History*, III, 482). In recovering from the mental paralysis induced by
the inexplicable appearance of a death's-head on a blank parchment,
Legrand has already invoked Champollion by speaking of the punning
or the hieroglyphical signature that he has found diagonally opposite
to the death's-head. As he explains all of this to his physician friend,
Legrand's language echoes Whewell's *History*: the parchment remains
blank; he is "sorely put out by the absence . . . of the *body* to [his]
imagined instrument – of *the text for [his] context*" ("Gold-Bug," p. 585,
emphasis added).

In fact, Legrand's determination to find "the body to [his] imagined
instrument" has already been fired by his desire to regain a lost patrimony and to reestablish the wealth and the repute of "an ancient
Huguenot family" ("Gold-Bug," p. 560). The discovery of the beetle
on the mainland offers the opportunity for which he has long been
waiting. He has, indeed, been bitten by Jupiter's "goole bug" (p. 562)
long ago; he has been "dancing mad," to quote the epigraph to the
story, prepared to seize upon the occasion that finally presents itself.[9]
He is alert to the talismanic significance of the *scarabæus* in Egyptian
mythology: for the scarab was recognized as an emblem to be found on
Egyptian monuments and in hieroglyphic writings often bearing upon
it a royal name, suggestive of a regal paternity. The *scarabæus* is immediately suggestive to Legrand, as any reader acquainted with the
controversy involving claims to priority over the decipherment of the
Rosetta Stone might recognize. Such a reader need not have read
Thomas Young's *Account of Some Recent Discoveries in Hieroglyphical
Literature, and Egyptian Antiquities* (1823) or Champollion's *Précis du
système hiéroglyphique des anciens Égyptiens* (1824) in which he set forth
fully the system of the hieroglyphics. A passing acquaintance with
essays and reviews in various British and American periodicals might
serve to acquaint someone with the story of Champollion's claim to priority as well as with the rudiments of the hieroglyphic inscriptions
found on the Rosetta Stone.

In 1831 there appeared in *The North American Review* a review of Isaac
Stuart's translation of J. G. H. Greppo's *Essay on the Hieroglyphic System
of M. Champollion, Jun.* (1830), a work first appearing in French in
1829.[10] The anonymous reviewer noted that Champollion's writings
were "not translated into English, nor of common occurrence in this
country." The reviewer went on to touch upon the Thomas Young–
Champollion controversy, to explain the hieroglyphic system and,
perhaps most significantly, to reject the neoplatonic, hermetic tradition

that had seen in Egyptian hieroglyphs arcane symbols of a higher truth intelligible only to the initiate. Near the conclusion of the essay the reviewer proceeded to emphasize that in his decipherment of Egyptian hieroglyphs "M. Champollion pursued the inductive method, and ascertained the alphabetical value of these hieroglyphical characters, by examining the different words where they occur."[11] Just as occult meanings were to be ignored, Champollion's methods were not to suggest preternatural powers unavailable to the average person.

In turning to Greppo's *Essay on the Hieroglyphic System*, a reader of *The North American Review* would find a defense of Champollion's claims to priority in the decipherment of the demotic and hieroglyphic inscriptions on the Rosetta Stone; a discussion of the hieroglyphic system itself; and the use of Egyptian texts and inscriptions both to establish an absolute chronology of scriptural events within the time scheme of Archbishop Ussher (1581–1656) and to locate the sites mentioned in scriptural accounts. It is, particularly, Greppo's discussion of the various functions of the hieroglyphic characters that offers an insight into William Legrand's responses to the gold-bug, the parchment, and the message that appears on its blank surface after he exposes it to the fire in his hut on Sullivan's Island. In his essay Greppo stressed as the key to Champollion's achievement his recognition of the phonetic significance of the hieroglyphic characters. But he also discussed their other functions as well. Greppo explained that the hieroglyphic characters were originally ideographic, imitations of the objects represented (figurative in Greppo's terminology). Over time they became less representational and finally acquired a phonetic significance: the representational hieroglyph could indicate the first sound of the word in the spoken language. Casting aside the hermetic tradition, Greppo proceeded to demonstrate that hieroglyphic characters could also indicate abstract ideas, either as figures of speech or as symbols, totally arbitrary signs for abstract ideas. As figures of speech, hieroglyphs might be understood as metonymies or synecdoches, literal objects connected by association with the ideas represented. But symbols, the true enigmas of the hieroglyphic system according to Saint Clement, were purely arbitrary in their meanings: to understand *them*, it was necessary to understand the conventions of Egyptian culture. To illustrate the nature of the symbol, Greppo turned to the *"scarabee,* [as] a symbol of *the world,* of the *male nature* or *paternity,"* meanings unintelligible outside of the context of the Egyptian system of belief.[12] All of this becomes relevant to Poe's "The Gold-Bug," especially since Greppo emphasized Champollion's *"analytic* method which discloses the facts, and then the *synthetic* method, which arranges the materials and puts them together in a systematic manner" (*Essay*, p. 4). In rejecting hermetic doctrines concerning the hieroglyphs, Greppo argued that Champollion offered a "positive, methodical, and lucid system" (p. 19), one within the tradition of eighteenth- and nineteenth-century empiricism. But Greppo's language returns us to "The Murders in the Rue Morgue" that opens as the narrator observes that "the mental features discoursed of as the analytical are, in themselves, but little susceptible of analysis" (p. 397); and to Pundita in "Mellonta Tauta" as she rejects the deductive and inductive "roads of Truth" by suggesting that Champollion turned to the imagination in "direct[ing] mankind to those enduring and almost innumerable truths which resulted from his deciphering the Hieroglyphics" (p. 877).

In "The Gold-Bug," Legrand (Jupiter's Massa Will) acts upon a yearning both for treasure and for meaning. Such a desire has only been intensified by the discovery of the *scarabæus* that becomes for Jupiter a literal bug of gold since its "brilliant metallic lustre," as Legrand observes, "is really almost enough to warrant Jupiter's idea" (p. 562). Behind his racist condescension, Legrand comments upon a naiveté that is pervasive among those who cannot recognize the purely conventional nature of all language, oral and written, and the ambiguity inherent in any system of meaning.[13] Jupiter's apparent error points to the ambiguous status of a beetle that Legrand has transformed into a sign. He may well recognize that in ancient Egypt the scarab, in Greppo's words, represents "the *male nature* or *paternity.*"

But Legrand never shares with the narrator the symbolic meanings of the *scarabæus* for the ancient Egyptians. Yet, such meanings induce him to carry the beetle with him on the expedition to the mainland. He wields it as a talisman, purportedly to produce "a little bit of sober mystification" ("Gold-Bug," p. 595). However, Legrand may have himself succumbed to his own act of mystification. He carries the gold-bug to reassure himself that the cipher he has found on the parchment and has decoded will, in fact, lead him to the treasure for which he has been on the lookout. For the significance that he has attributed to the parchment, once the narrator discovers the death's-head on it, rests upon a series of suspect conjectures, based always upon "a *desire* [more] than an actual belief" (p. 585, emphasis added). It is the desire for treasure that impels Legrand to "[establish] a kind of *connexion,*" to forge "two lengths of a great chain" between the parchment and the long boat "lying on [the] sea-coast . . . not far from . . . a parchment – *not a paper* – with a skull depicted on it" (p. 583).

It is, above all, desire that leads Legrand to observe that "parchment is durable – almost imperishable. Matters of little moment are rarely consigned to parchment" ("Gold-Bug," p. 583). And it is desire that permits him to associate what seems to be the beached carcass of a long boat with the parchment. The discovery of the death's-head on the vellum has posed "a mystery which [he feels] it impossible to explain; but, even at that early moment, there seem[s] to glimmer, faintly, within the most remote and secret chambers of [his] intellect, a glow-worm-like conception of [the] truth" (p. 582). So moved, he reconstructs "the hull of what *appeared* to have been a ship's long boat . . . for the resemblance to boat timbers could scarcely be traced" (p. 582, emphasis added). Legrand transforms the shore into an archaeological site, creating rather than perceiving connections between the wreck and the parchment, all the while conjuring up an historical context for, as yet, a non-existent text.

Legrand has encountered a series of seeming coincidences that he proceeds to transform into a causal chain through an act of will. Throughout his paleontological and archaeological reconstruction of the past, he relies upon assumptions that are increasingly suspect. In his investigation he assumes, from the start, that the blank parchment must bear a message that is not esoteric. He posits that the skull on the parchment is "the well-known emblem of the pirate. The flag of the death's-head is hoisted in all engagements" ("Gold-Bug," p. 583). But, if the parchment is to yield an intelligible message, Legrand must perpetrate an anachronism to fulfill his desire. William Kidd was, in fact, executed in 1701 when he may well have been a licensed privateer, authorized to raid the ships of hostile nations by a group of prominent Whig politicians. When the historical Kidd sailed the seas, he operated most notoriously in the Indian Ocean; and, in the 1690s, the emblem of the pirates was not the skull and crossbones, but the red flag.[14]

However, Legrand's error is a necessary one as he prepares for his interpretation of the curious figure that he will find "diagonally opposite to the spot in which the death's-head was delineated" ("Gold-Bug," p. 584). In order to coerce the figure into existence, Legrand kindles a fire, subjecting the parchment to its heat as well as to the heat of his ardent desire. He will conjure up a sign to satisfy his need for treasure and for meaning. So it is that the parchment, exposed to the fire's "glowing heat," yields up "the figure of what [Legrand] at first supposed to be a goat," but which upon "closer scrutiny" proves to be "intended for a kid" (pp. 584–85). But Legrand's interpretation of the figure that he will treat as a punning signature depends on other assumptions. He relies on negative evidence, arguing that persisting rumors of pirate treasure "must have had some foundation in fact . . . [and] that the rumors have existed so long and so continuously . . . only from the circumstance of the buried treasure still *remaining* entombed" (p. 586). Legrand's conviction of the existence of a buried treasure informs his claim that all human signs "convey a meaning": "it may well be doubted whether human ingenuity can construct an enigma of the kind which human ingenuity may not, by *proper application*, resolve" (p. 587, emphasis added). Such an article of faith smacks more of desire than method. For Legrand, as for others, it involves the creation of an historical context by which to render any text intelligible.

Every one of William Whewell's "palætiological sciences" – philology, paleontology, geology, and archaeology – proceed in this way, transforming everything into a figurative document by which to read the past. In his further investigation of the parchment, Legrand will perform other acts of interpretation that suggest that the "proper application" of method involves a willing of evidence and of meaning into existence. Coming upon a shape diagonally opposite to the death's-head, perhaps a blot of ink left accidentally upon the parchment, Legrand will not perceive it as fortuitous and, thus, meaningless. He must see it first as a goat, then as a kid, as if it were indeed possible to perceive in a thing so small a recognizable design.[15]

Throughout "The Gold-Bug" the narrator's account suggests that through the heat of his desire Legrand has willed the appearance of the ink figure: it will not be his last feverish operation upon the vellum. Before proceeding further, he has already begun to treat the figure of the kid as the key to any memorandum that has been inscribed on the parchment in "secret writing" ("Gold-Bug," p. 587): for a buried treasure demands a coded message to obscure its location. It is only later, after the appearance of the requisite cipher, that Legrand notes that "in all cases of secret writing – the first question regards the *language* of the cipher; for the principles of solution . . . depend upon, and are varied by, the genius of the particular idiom" (p. 587). His words suggest that in identifying the ink figure as a kid, he has already determined that if a cipher were to appear, it will be based on English.

In acting as a morphologist, Legrand follows Cuvier and Champollion who in their acts of decipherment had to ascertain the nature of the literal and figurative characters before them. But in seeing the ink figure as a hieroglyphic signature with both an ideographic and phonetic meaning, Legrand has already engaged in yet another act of historical mystification. As others have noted, William Kidd was not commonly associated with the southeastern coast of North America. It was Edward Teach, Blackbeard, who had at one time blockaded Charleston Harbor in 1718 and who might have been expected at that later date to have flown the skull and crossbones from the mast of his ship. Neither the name, Teach, nor the pseudonym, Blackbeard, would serve so nicely as the basis of a punning signature to be read both ideographically and phonetically. In Legrand's conflation of Edward Teach with William Kidd, "The Gold-Bug" continues its ironic commentary on the historical imagination and on the reconstructive disciplines that work with ambiguous evidence from the past to satisfy the desires of an interpreter in the present.[16]

II

"The Gold-Bug" continues its subversion of the historical imagination as it follows William Legrand in his quest for "a lost record of the place of deposit" (p. 586) of a rumored pirate treasure. There is as yet no "text for [Legrand's] context" (p. 585), only a blank surface with a death's-head and a purported signature diagonally juxtaposed to each other. Legrand's activities suggest that there is never a text without a pre-existing context that is itself a construct based upon seemingly empirical observations. Akin to Cuvier and Champollion, Legrand is "like the decipherer of a manuscript, who makes out his alphabet from one part of the context, and then applies it to read the rest" (*History*, III, 474). Throughout the story, Legrand's surmises about the parchment continue to be implicitly subjected to a skeptical scrutiny. For he already knows what he will find, "to [his] inexpressible joy," as he holds "the vellum again to the fire," rinses it in warm water, and "place[s] it in a tin pan . . . upon a furnace of lighted charcoal" (p. 586). He acts in ways that the narrator takes for lunacy until even *he* succumbs to the contagion of Legrand's convictions.

Legrand compels the vellum to yield to the heat of his expectations as it produces the secret writing that will confirm his hopes. The language that Legrand has used to describe his discovery echoes that of Cuvier and Whewell, implicating all of the historical disciplines that were consolidating themselves in the nineteenth century, including not only philology and archaeology, but the uniformitarian geology of Charles Lyell and, later, the evolutionary hypotheses of Darwin. "The Gold-Bug" implies that acts of reconstruction, including those of the fictional detective, involve the production of the evidence that they require in the study of monuments inscribed with foreign, perhaps dead, languages, the ruins of ancient edifices, and errant manuscripts, all preserved haphazardly if only in a fragmentary, mutilated form. In this way the story alludes to the *Principles of Geology* (1830–33) in which Lyell, self-consciously following Cuvier and Champollion, transformed the strata of the earth into figurative documents bearing hieroglyphic inscriptions in the form of embedded fossil remains. In volume one of the *Principles*, Lyell sought to dismiss those who still relied on literal readings of the Old Testament, with its supernatural events, by turning to an archaeological analogy. He invoked Jean-François Champollion who, in first visiting Egypt, might have assumed "that the banks of the Nile were never peopled by the human race before the beginning of the nineteenth century," only to come upon "the sight of pyramids, obelisks, colossal statues, and ruined temples, [that] would fill [Champollion and his companions] with such astonishment, that for a time they would be as men spell-bound – wholly incapacitated to reason with sobriety." In Legrand's words, they would "[suffer] a species of temporary paralysis" ("Gold-Bug," p. 581), after which they "might incline at first to refer the construction of such stupendous works to some superhuman powers of a primeval world."[17] Eventually, Champollion and his fellow antiquarians would reject such supernatural explanations, according to Lyell, and would achieve a truly historical understanding of the Egyptian past.

In volume three of the *Principles* Lyell returned to the analogy: "All naturalists, who have carefully examined the arrangement of the mineral masses composing the earth's crust, and who have studied their internal structure and fossil contents, have recognized therein the signs of a great succession of former changes; and the causes of these changes have been the object of anxious inquiry" (III, 1). In the past, Lyell claimed, "the student [of geology], instead of being encouraged with the hope of interpreting the enigmas presented to him . . . was taught to despond from the first": "Even the mystery which invested the subject was said to constitute one of its principal charms, affording, as it did, full scope to the fancy to indulge in a boundless field of speculation" (III, 3).

William Legrand's philological and archaeological investigation of the parchment, seemingly so shrouded in the aura of mystery, nevertheless proceeds within the naturalistic context of Cuvier, Champollion, and Lyell.[18] In applying the vellum to the heat of the fire, he restores a secret writing that proves not to be esoteric, intelligible only to the initiate. He has already determined that any cryptograph to be discovered will be based upon the English language since "the pun on the word 'Kidd' is appreciable in no other language" ("Gold-Bug," p. 588). He identifies the letters for which the coded characters stand by establishing the frequency of their repetition and the probability that they reflect the frequency of the appearance of certain letters in written English. He has grasped the alphabet of the cipher and proceeds to establish its grammar. However, "the characters upon the parchment, as unriddled," offer only another enigmatic text whose English letters must be divided "into *the natural division intended* by the cryptographist" (p. 591, emphasis added).[19]

Like the Rosetta Stone with its Greek, demotic, and hieroglyphic scripts, the parchment will present three figurative languages, one a cipher, another that, decoded, remains equally enigmatic, and a third to be understood through another act of interpretation. Legrand proceeds in a manner akin to that of C. Auguste Dupin in his investigations into the murders in the Rue Morgue and the affair of the purloined letter, by comprehending the mind of another, in this case the Captain Kidd possessed of but "the crude intellect of the sailor" ("Gold-Bug," p. 587). With such an assumption about Kidd, Legrand constructs potentially coherent sentences by detecting pauses in the hand-written cipher or places where the characters of the cipher run together. But the deciphered message offers yet another puzzle, written in what Legrand assumes to be a figurative language that, through further interpretation, will provide the requisite directions to the location of the rumored treasure.

Legrand now sees in the curious language of the deciphered cryptograph references to identifiable geological formations on the mainland in the vicinity of Sullivan's Island. To determine their locations, he plays the philologist as he traces the meanings of phrases like *"the bishop's hostel," "the devil's seat,"* and the *"main branch seventh limb east side"* ("Gold-Bug," p. 591). In reconstructing the history of *"bishop's hostel,"* he finds that it refers to *"Bessop's Castle,"* the colloquial name for "an irregular assemblage of cliffs and rocks" (pp. 592–93). Here, the figurative devil's seat proves to be a narrow ledge in the face of the rocks providing a unique vantage point from which to locate with a telescope a majestic tulip tree with a human skull on one of its limbs. So construed, the message provides a map and a set of coordinates leading to a specific site at which Legrand, with the narrator and the hapless Jupiter, will find not only a buried treasure, but "a mass of human bones, forming two complete skeletons" (p. 577). As archaeologists and paleontologists, Legrand and his companions have come upon a site offering up ambiguous evidence in the form of gold coins "of antique date and of great variety" – some "so worn that [they] could make nothing of their inscriptions" (pp. 579–80) – and those human bones that, once reconstructed, lead Legrand to infer a past event of which they have previously had no knowledge.

In his discovery of the pirate treasure Legrand would seem to have followed the practice of J. G. H. Greppo in his *Essay on the Hieroglyphic System of M. Champollion, Jun*. As part of his enterprise Greppo sought to use the historical evidence provided by the decipherment of inscribed monuments and hieroglyphic manuscripts to establish the geographical location of Old Testament place names and to construct an absolute chronology of scriptural events within the time scheme of Archbishop Ussher. He traced the etymology of names in the Vulgate, the Greek, and the Hebrew back to their Egyptian originals in an attempt to identify existing sites in the Middle East of the nineteenth century. Such sites could be subjected to archaeological investigations to provide evidence in support of Old Testament accounts and the miracles recorded in them (*Essay*, pp. 150–61). Such place names would "afford [the] occasion for [those] very interesting geographical researches as connected with Scripture" (pp. 160–61) that would lead to the archaeological expeditions of Austen Henry Layard (1817–1894) who was to use both scriptural and classical texts to guide him to a grassy mound near the town of Mosul in present-day Iraq. In November 1845 he began the excavations that uncovered a buried and long-forgotten city that he identified as the Biblical Nimrud, part of the Assyrian empire whose capital was Nineveh. A similar spirit was to inform Heinrich Schliemann's quest for the Troy of the *Odyssey* and the *Iliad*: these and other classical texts led him to Hissarlik on the Anatolian peninsula of Asia Minor where he began the excavations in the 1870s that led him to the site of a settlement that he proclaimed was the historical Troy.[20]

Legrand's feat uncannily anticipates the way in which nineteenth-century archaeologists were moved by a "preconceived idea" ("Gold-Bug," p. 593), a desire for a buried treasure of sorts that would lead Layard or Schliemann to the recovery of a scriptural or a classical patrimony. As an antiquarian of a new order, Legrand sees in the deciphered message a map, a template, that he imposes upon "a tract of country excessively wild and desolate, where no trace of a human footstep [is] to be seen." The mainland proves to be as blank as the parchment has once been until Legrand establishes "certain landmarks of his own contrivance" (p. 570) by which to negotiate his return to the tulip tree that towers above all else. As he approaches it, the narrator observes that the tulip tree "surpasse[s] . . . all other trees which [he] had then ever seen, in the beauty of its foliage and form, in the wide spread of its branches, and in the general majesty of its appearance" (p. 570).

In a story preoccupied with ciphers, hieroglyphs, and enigmas that "human ingenuity may . . . by proper application, resolve" ("Gold-Bug," p. 587) the tulip tree itself becomes an ambiguous sign. It is not to be understood only ideographically (in Greppo's terminology) as a representation of a tree: it may also function phonetically, figuratively (as a synecdoche) and, finally, symbolically in accordance with the complex status of the Egyptian hieroglyphs. Read phonetically, the tulip tree becomes a homonym, introducing once more the theme of the woman and the woman's body that figures so prominently in "The Murders in the Rue Morgue," "The Mystery of Marie Rogêt," and "The Purloined Letter" (1844). With the discovery of the human skeletons beneath the tree whose cylindrical trunk and limbs are so emphasized by the narrator, the story again poses the mystery of the female body. With the skull attached to a dead limb, the tulip tree alludes, however indirectly, to the fate of Madame and Mademoiselle L'Espanaye, Marie Rogêt, and the royal personage, perhaps the queen, who becomes associated with the purloined letter that Minister D— soils, crumples, and tears nearly in two. The "oblong chest of wood" (p. 578) found in association with human bones announces the fact of human mortality, the fate of all those born of woman.[21]

But the tulip tree becomes suggestive of other meanings. In practicing an historical discipline in his decoding of the cipher, Legrand emulates Champollion who had successfully traced the relationship between the Greek, the demotic, and hieroglyphic inscriptions on the Rosetta Stone, accidentally discovered in August 1899 while French troops were "digging the foundations of the fort St. Julien, [when] they found a large mutilated block of black basalt, which was covered with a considerable portion of *three inscriptions in different characters*" (Greppo, *Essay*, p. 16). Later, Champollion was to follow the lead of England's Thomas Young who had established the phonetic function of some hieroglyphic characters by rejecting a prevailing esoteric tradition. Champollion then engaged in a genealogical study of the three inscriptions. In the words of the reviewer of Greppo's *Essay* in *The North American Review*, philologists studied the history of language, "going back in its origin to a period alike beyond history and tradition." Continental philologists, the reviewer observed, had found "a similarity between the languages of the Teutonic stock and the sacred dialect of Hindostan, which must have had its origin in a consanguinity of nations, dating from a period anterior to all our historical traditions. So permanently does a language take root!"[22]

The clearing over which the tulip tree presides in "The Gold-Bug" has become a site of ambiguous origins: associated with the Tree of Life in Genesis and with the philological tree of the Indo-European family of languages, as a synecdoche it points backward in time to the figurative ground of a European and an American tradition that may well be purely imaginary.[23] Yet, it will fulfill another hieroglyphic function, that of the symbol, "the *enigmatic method*," in Greppo's words, designed "to conceal the mysteries of the sacerdotal caste and of the initiated" (*Essay*, pp. 33–34). In his use of the gold-bug as the weight for his plumb-line, Legrand announces his own status as one of the initiate. As the beetle hangs from the tulip tree, it becomes "visible at the end of the string, and glisten[s], like a globe of burnished gold, in the last rays of the setting sun" ("Gold-Bug," p. 574). It has become "the index of [Legrand's] fortune" (p. 575), a bearer of meanings accessible only to someone steeped in Egyptian mythology. One meaning that would appeal to the ardent Legrand could be found in the Supplement to the fourth and subsequent editions of the *Encyclopædia Britannica* (1824). In the fourth volume of the Supplement there appeared an article on Egypt written, appropriately, by Thomas Young who was to argue his claim to priority for the decipherment of the Egyptian hieroglyphs in his *Account of Some Recent Discoveries in Hieroglyphical Literature, and Egyptian Antiquities* (1823). Young's article on Egypt dealt, in part, with the "Rudiments of a Hieroglyphical Vocabulary" and with the purely conventional meaning of certain Egyptian characters and objects. Of the beetle, Young observed that

> [it] is frequently used for the name of a deity whose head either bears a beetle, or is itself in the form of a beetle; and in other instances the beetle has clearly a reference to generation or reproduction, which is a sense attributed to this symbol by all antiquity; so that it may possibly sometimes have been used as a synonym for Phthah, as the father of the gods.[24]

From the start William Legrand has sought to restore more than his family fortune: he has desired to reestablish a more significant patrimony, faith in a universe governed by a Fortune or by a Fate ("Gold-Bug," p. 568) that suggests divine design. "The Gold-Bug" would seem to celebrate his achievement: the triumph of the historical imagination

in the service of Greppo's desire "to render still more firm the belief of
Christians in the truth and faithfulness of [those] sacred writers" of the
Old Testament (*Essay*, p. v). But from the beginning of the anonymous
narrator's account, the contingent nature of the events recorded have
been suggested. It is important to remember that both the narrator and
Legrand emphasize, to different ends, the series of accidents that have
led Legrand not only to the gold-bug and the parchment, but to the discovery of the cipher and to its decipherment. The narrator has first met
Legrand "by mere accident" ("Gold-Bug," p. 560) sometime before the
events of which he writes. The fall day in the middle of October upon
which the narrator unexpectedly visits Legrand's hut is unusual for "a
rare event," a "remarkable chilliness" that necessitates the "novelty" of
a fire (p. 561). He awaits the return of Legrand and Jupiter who inform
him that they have chanced upon a rare *scarabæus* that has bitten the
naturalist. At this precise moment, Jupiter happens upon the scrap of
parchment – conveniently in the vicinity of what is taken for the
remains of a wrecked long boat – in which to wrap the beetle. Then,
Lieutenant G— fortuitously appears, asking to take the beetle back to
Fort Moultrie: "without being conscious of it" Legrand places the parchment in his pocket (p. 582). Later, in his hut, he looks for paper to draw
a sketch of the gold-bug, finds there is "no paper where it [is] *usually
kept*" (p. 583, emphasis added), reaches into his pocket, "hoping to find
an old letter," and comes upon the parchment. He hands the parchment with his drawing of the beetle to his friend when Wolf, the
Newfoundland, "rushe[s] in, leap[s] upon [the narrator's] shoulders"
(p. 562), and initiates a new sequence of purely fortuitious events.[25]

Yet, such purely contingent events can be reconstructed as Legrand
has proceeded to do:

> "With your left hand you [the narrator] caressed [Wolf] . . . while
> your right, holding the parchment, was permitted to fall listlessly
> between your knees, and in close proximity to the fire. At one
> moment I thought the blaze had caught it. . . . When I considered all
> these particulars, I doubted not for a moment that *heat* had been the
> agent in bringing to light, on the parchment, the skull which I saw
> designed on it."
>
> ("Gold-Bug," p. 584)

Legrand has reconstructed what he calls a chain of events, not one of
them necessary, that could have led to the destruction of the precious
parchment. He even comments on "the series of accidents and coinci-

dences" that are "so *very* extraordinary" (p. 585), as if each one is part
of a larger design that has governed the events of the day.

Legrand's words reveal how his own desire has led him to the discovery of the cipher upon the parchment. In reconstructing the events
of that October day, he remarks upon the "fire [that] was blazing on the
hearth" and upon the fact that he "was heated with exercise" ("Gold-
Bug," p. 584), a condition that persists and one that the narrator treats
as a symptom of fever. But the fever with which Legrand burns is the
desire for meaning in a universe of purely contingent events, events
that Legrand reads as "the index of his fortune" (p. 575). The nebular
hypothesis of Pierre Simon Laplace (1749–1827) and John Pringle
Nichol (1804–1859) remains relevant to Legrand's determination to find
meanings through a chain of cause and effect that suggests that there
is, indeed, a design that governs his life. "The Gold-Bug" suggests that
no one practicing an historical discipline proceeds according to conventional notions of empiricism. It dwells upon the element of chance
that leads to the survival of even fragmentary evidence from the past
and to its fortuitous discovery. From the start a desire for meaning
informs a trajectory, a telos, that produces a sequence of cause and effect
constructed out of the innumerable coincidences of everyday life.
Legrand *must* live in a teleological universe, tending to a preordained
end governed by what he calls Fortune or Fate. The great chain of
history *must* lead to an origin beyond chance.[26]

It is the narrator of "The Gold-Bug" who suggests the larger context
in which to place his account. Responding to Legrand's explanation of
the discovery and the deciphering of the secret writing, he asks, "How
then do you trace any connexion between the boat and the skull – since
this latter . . . must have been designed (God only knows how or by
whom) at some period subsequent to your sketching the *scarabœus*?"
("Gold-Bug," p. 583). The narrator's recourse to the banal parenthetical
observation, almost emptied of meaning, reveals the enduring need to
believe that divine and human designs coincide. The story has moved
from a critique of historical knowledge to an exploration of nineteenth-
century theism with its reliance upon the traditional Book of Nature
and the Argument from Design.[27] Such a context has been suggested
early on when the narrator compares Legrand to Jan Swammerdam
whose *Biblica naturae* was translated into English in 1758 as *The Book of
Nature; or, the History of Insects*. From his study of insects, the least of
animals, Swammerdam argued that "all [animals] are under the direction and controul of a supreme and singular intelligence; which, as in
the largest, it extends beyond the limits of our comprehension, escapes

our researches in the smallest." There is within the smallest or largest organism a structure, a design, attesting to the existence of "the Great Creator." However mysterious the metamorphoses of insects may seem, they are susceptible to a purely naturalistic explanation that proves, in spite of "the great obscurity of the human understanding ... [that] all we have, we receive from the gracious hands of the Supreme Being."[28]

In treating the parchment as he does, Legrand has followed those who have turned the natural world into a text, one more reliable than scripture itself. The purely conventional nature of the cipher on the parchment – with its Arabic numerals, punctuation marks, asterisks, and other signs – can return us to the Copernican revolution and to Galileo's claims in *The Assayer* (1623):

> Philosophy is written in this grand book – I mean the universe – which stands continually open to our gaze, but it cannot be understood unless one first learns to comprehend the language and interpret the characters in which it is written. It is written in the language of mathematics, and its characters are triangles, circles, and other geometrical figures, without which it is humanly impossible to understand a single word of it; without these, one is wandering about in a dark labyrinth.[29]

The tradition in which Galileo wrote had its most enduring English affirmation in Francis Bacon's *Advancement of Learning* (1605), that touchstone both of empiricism and theism to which defenders of Natural Theology were to return in the nineteenth century in their attempts to refute speculations on the transmutation of species. Bacon's words were used to perpetuate the distinction between Scripture and the Book of Nature:

> when a man passeth on farther [from the study of second causes to the first cause], and seeth the dependence of causes and the works of Providence; then, according to the allegory of the poets, he will easily believe that the highest link of nature's chain must needs be tied to the foot of Jupiter's chair. To conclude therefore, let no man, upon a weak conceit of sobriety or an ill-applied moderation, think or maintain that a man can search too far or be too well studied in the book of God's word or in the book of God's works; divinity or philosophy; but rather let men endeavour an endless progress or proficience in both.[30]

With its reference to Jupiter, Bacon's circumlocution for God, the *Advancement* may, in part, explain the presence of the manumitted Jupiter in "The Gold-Bug" as a comic deity, reduced to confusion over the most fundamental distinctions between left and right. The "link[s] of nature's chain" as reconstructed by Legrand may lead to the foot of the tulip tree and to buried treasure, but not to evidence of God's design for the universe. In alluding to the Book of Nature – Bacon's "book of God's works" – the story subverts the argument of the *Advancement of Learning*, even as it implicitly invokes Sir Thomas Browne's "Hydriotaphia: Urne-Burial" (1658), the essay that provided the epigraph for "The Murders in the Rue Morgue": "What song the Syrens sang, or what name Achilles assumed when he hid himself among women, although puzzling questions, are not beyond *all* conjecture" ("Murders," p. 397). In "Urne-Burial" Browne wrote about the recent discovery of ancient burial urns and of the coins and other artifacts found in their vicinity. He sought to establish "a sure account" of the urns of whose "precise Antiquity . . . nothing [is] of more uncertainty."[31] For the seventeenth-century antiquarian such relics "arose as they lay, almost in silence among us" (I, 132), posing another version of those "enigmas, . . . conundrums, . . . [and] hieroglyphics" ("Murders," p. 397) that C. Auguste Dupin and William Legrand encounter.

In "Urne-Burial" Browne not only dealt with ambiguous "Urnes, Coynes, and Monuments" (I, 135) from a time some 1300 years in the past. He also dwelled upon the Christian rejection of human cremation as he considered the significance of the practice for those who seemed not to believe in the resurrection of the body. He referred both to Epicurus and to Lucretius, those materialist philosophers for whom there was no Elysium, no life after the death of the body: "It is the heaviest stone that melancholy can throw at a man, to tell him he is at the end of his nature; or that there is no further state to come," for "we are more than our present selves" (I, 163–64).

In "The Garden of Cyrus" (1658), a companion piece to "Urne-Burial," Sir Thomas Browne claimed that evidence that "we are more than our present selves," was to be found everywhere in "the great Volume of nature" (I, 217). Writing within a neoplatonic, hermetic tradition, Browne set out to demonstrate that "the verdant state of things is the Symbole of the Resurrection" (I, 177). After a passing reference to Tulipists and tulipomania in the essay's dedicatory epistle, he argued that "in the orderly book of nature" can be discerned "the Elegancy of her hand in other correspondencies" (I, 206), particularly in the recurring figure of the quincunx, the geometrical shape manifesting the mystical number five: the quincunx – to be found, however mysteriously, in the triangle, the circle, the cross – becomes a fundamental emblem of a higher reality. The number five is anounced hieroglyphically in many biological forms of growth. The "higher Geometry of nature" (I, 201), Browne argued, was to be seen in "trees [that are] ordained not only to protect and shadow others, but by their shades and shadowing parts, to preserve and cherish themselves": "And therefore providence hath arched and paved the great house of the world" (I, 217).

The "Cylindrical figure of Trees" ("Garden," I, 215) becomes at once an emblem of a higher order, and a model for a human architecture that expresses the mysteries revealed by natural forms, whether in the Cretan labyrinth or the architectural feats of ancient Egypt: "And if Ægyptian Philosophy may obtain, the scale of influences was thus disposed, and the geniall spirits of both worlds do trace their way in ascending and descending Pyramids, mystically apprehended in the Letter X, and the open Bill and straddling Legges of a Stork, which was imitated by that Character" (I, 220). Through the "magicall Characters" of the "Hieroglyphicks," so Browne maintained, "the Ægyptians thereby expressed the processe and motion of the spirit of the world, and the diffusion thereof upon the Celestiall and Elementall nature" (I, 182).

But, in "The Gold-Bug," William Legrand no longer works within a hermetic tradition like that espoused by Sir Thomas Browne. He departs from that tradition to embrace the naturalistic program of Francis Bacon's *Advancement of Learning* and the post-Enlightenment perspectives of Georges Cuvier, Thomas Young, and Jean-François Champollion. The tulip tree, that "most magnificent of American foresters," whose "trunk peculiarly smooth" the narrator compares to a "huge cylinder" ("Gold-Bug," p. 571), loses its hermetic significance to become an arbitrary human sign denoting the site of buried treasure. Legrand lives within the shadow of an Enlightenment skepticism that J. G. H. Greppo was to excoriate in his *Essay* on the hieroglyphic system: in the last century, Greppo wrote, "there arose a sect of unbelievers, who with an avowed aim to overturn Christianity, unceasingly attacked the holy books, and attempted in every way to prove them to be error, or an imposture, or a contradiction and absurdity." With Voltaire in mind – "the philosopher of Ferney" – Greppo proceeded to denounce further "the sophists of this new school [who] sought . . . for arms to use against Christianity. Geology, astronomy, geography, chronology, history, the knowledge of ancient languages, and *all branches of science* were put in requisition, in a perfidious attempt to decry the august claims of our faith" (p. 163, emphasis added). Various historical disciplines seem to be marshaled against orthodox faith, including an astronomy that had led to the nebular hypothesis of Pierre Simon Laplace.[32] However, as Greppo argued, Champollion appeared as "a new Alexander . . . to cut the Gordian knot [of the hieroglyphics] which men had vainly sought to untie" (*Essay*, p. 184). In his feat he redeemed the historical disciplines that, now, were to verify the historical accuracy of the Old Testament. Bacon's "book of God's word" and his "book of God's works" remain to explain the human situation: "Providence, whose operations are so sensibly exhibited in the whole physical constitution of the world, has not abandoned to chance the government of the moral or intellectual world" (*Essay*, p. 187).[33]

But chance, as "The Gold-Bug" suggests, may in fact reign in the physical world as well as in the moral and the intellectual world. The account of William Legrand's discovery of the pirate treasure has moved beyond a rejection of Sir Thomas Browne's hermetic musings in "The Garden of Cyrus" to a critique of Baconian empiricism and of those "palætiological sciences" that, in William Whewell's words, "endeavour to ascend to a past state of things, by the aid of the evidence of the present" (*History*, III, 482). The parchment that Legrand happens upon has survived by accident. His sketch of the rare *scarabæus* leads fortuitously to the narrator's discovery of the death's-head on the parchment. Only through the exercise of his willful desire for treasure, and for meaning, does Legrand find the secret writing that he deciphers, providing a map to the site beneath the tulip tree.

But in sketching the gold-bug on the parchment that he has unthinkingly placed in his pocket, Legrand raises the question of the significance of signs in the largest sense. As he and his physician friend quarrel about the accuracy of his drawing of the beetle, the narrator observes, "this *is* a strange *scarabæus*, I must confess: new to me: never saw anything like it before – unless it was a skull, or a death's-head" ("Gold-Bug," p. 563). Of course, the narrator is not looking at Legrand's sketch, but at a figure on the opposite side of the vellum that has mysteriously appeared on it. His words point to the ambiguity of any conventional sign. But, in observing to Legrand, "I fear you are no artist," he inevitably raises other issues: "I presume you will call the bug *scarabæus caput hominis*, or something of that kind – there are many similar titles in the Natural Histories. But where are the *antennæ* you spoke of?" (p. 563).

Rather than suggesting human immortality and a providential design, the *scarabæus* speaks only of universal mortality. Unlike the lavish illustrations of insects in Jan Swammerdam's *Biblia naturae*, the drawing does not attest to the existence of a Creator. Legrand's response to the narrator clarifies the issue: "I am sure you must see the *antennæ*. I made them as distinct as they are in the original insect" ("Gold-Bug," p. 563). Their exchange has become a parody of neoplatonism, either in interpretations of Plato's *Timæus* or of the Gospel according to John, in which ideas in the mind of God are transformed into the objects of the phenomenal world. The formerly blank parchment suggests that the Book of Nature of Francis Bacon, Galileo, or Sir Thomas Browne is radically imperfect, or, that it is a perfect and absolute blank, the inscriptions found upon it only the production of the human desire for meaning, rather than the revelation of a divine order. At this moment, "The Gold-Bug" anticipates *Beyond Good and Evil* (1886) and Friedrich Nietzsche's claim that even physics "is only an interpretation and exegesis of the world (to suit us, if I may say so!) and *not* a world-explanation":

> The strange family resemblance of all Indian, Greek, and German philosophizing is explained easily enough. Where there is affinity of languages, it cannot fail, owing to the common philosophy of grammar – I mean, owing to the unconscious domination and guidance by similar grammatical functions – that everything is prepared at the outset for a similar development and sequence of philosophical systems; just as the way seems barred against certain other possibilities of world-interpretation.

Nietzsche's conclusion becomes inevitable: "So much by way of rejecting Locke's superficiality regarding the origin of ideas."[34] Locke's "white paper" of the human mind, "void of all characters, without any ideas," has been transformed into the white paper of the universe upon which human beings write.[35]

At best, William Legrand's parchment is the fragment of a human document yielding a coded message that, deciphered, leads to pirate treasure – and to buried human corpses. The parchment has become a figurative palimpsest; it produces another enigmatic text that must be properly construed if it is to lead to those arbitrary landmarks that Captain Kidd has imposed upon the barren landscape of the mainland. However, the buried treasure itself will offer yet another set of mysteries, both in the form of the human skeletons next to the wooden chest and in the coins that the chest contains: "All was gold of antique date and of great variety – French, Spanish, and German money, with a few

English guineas, and some counters, of which we had never seen specimens before. There were several very large and heavy coins, so worn
that we could make nothing of their inscriptions. There was no
American money" ("Gold-Bug," pp. 579–80). The treasure seekers have
been returned to their original plight, contemplating coins without
intelligible inscriptions whose country of origin is not to be determined.
Like those practitioners of other historical disciplines – Greppo's geologist, astronomer, historian, philologist – they are engaged in an unending quest for historical meaning that leads only to an infinite regress.[36]

In this way "The Gold-Bug" suggests that there are occasions, perhaps
only fortuitous, when the human desire for meaning may be tem-
porarily satisfied, and there occur correspondences between a text, perceived as divine or human, and the universe. Ultimately, the story
mocks the act of interpretation that it seems to celebrate. For as William
Legrand observes, "it may well be doubted whether human [or divine?]
ingenuity can construct an enigma of the kind which human ingenuity may not . . . resolve" ("Gold-Bug," p. 587). But if the contriver of the
enigma is not what the interpreter imagines the contriver to be, if he
becomes not the Jupiter of Francis Bacon's *Advancement of Learning*, or
not even Captain Kidd, Legrand's simple-minded pirate, but the befud-
dled Jupiter of the story, the pursuit of meaning, even purely historical
meaning, will prove fruitless.

And, should the Divine Artist fail in the act of creation to reproduce
his original design, the Book of Nature will not offer hieroglyphical evidence to the existence of its Creator. The "highest link of nature's chain"
may not "be tied to the foot of Jupiter's chair" (*Advancement*, p. 126),
but to an unending chain of natural events that are transformed by a
desire rather than a belief into "a sequence of cause and effect" created
to stay "a species of temporary paralysis" ("Gold-Bug," p. 581) aroused
by the possibility that coincidence rather than design reigns in human
and natural affairs. For rumors of God that "have existed so long and
so continuously" (p. 586) may not attest to the fact of His existence.

Part Two
Charles Dickens

Temple of Jupiter Serapis, frontispiece to volume one of Charles Lyell's *Principles of Geology* (1830). Image reproduced courtesy of the History of Science Collections, University of Oklahoma.

3

Bleak House, the Nebular Hypothesis, and a Crisis in Narrative

"It is a coincidence," said Mr. Kenge, with a tinge of melancholy in his smile, "one of those coincidences which may or may not require an explanation beyond our present limited faculties, that I have a cousin in the medical profession."

Bleak House

I

It may not be immediately apparent that Charles Dickens's *Bleak House* (1852–53), like Edgar Allan Poe's "The Murders in the Rue Morgue" (1841), should be read within the context of ongoing controversies over the nebular hypothesis. On the face of it, *Bleak House* is distinguished by a double narrative constituting an experiment in detective fiction that leaves at least one mystery unresolved, the identity of the author of the present-tense narrative that exists in a curious relationship to the illegitimate Esther Summerson's retrospective account characterized as "A Progress."[1] As readers, we follow both narratives as each pursues a central mystery that will lead to their convergence: through the anonymous present-tense narrative we are present at the arrest of Mademoiselle Hortense for the murder of Mr. Tulkinghorn, attorney to Sir Leicester Dedlock and his wife, Lady Dedlock; while Esther discovers, reluctantly, the identities of her mother, who proves to be Lady Dedlock, and her father, a Captain Hawdon who, as Nemo the lawwriter, dies early on in the novel. However, at the end of *Bleak House* the writer of the present-tense narrative – so often considered by critics as omniscient – remains unidentified, someone with whom Esther has inexplicably been in correspondence.[2] In bringing her own story to its ambiguous close, Esther observes: "Full seven happy years I have been the mistress of Bleak House. The few words that I have to add to what I have written, are soon penned; then I, and the *unknown friend* to whom I write, will part for ever. Not without much dear remembrance on my side. Not without some, I hope, on *his or hers*" (p. 877, emphasis added). Esther's habitual, self-deprecating stance reveals her correspondent as someone not unlike herself, a character living in the midst of a figurative "London particular" (p. 28), challenged by bewildering events that may defy understanding. Like Esther, her unknown friend must ponder the significance of the seemingly coincidental meetings and occurrences that he – or she – records. Inevitably, characters in *Bleak House* must determine whether they find themselves in a teleological universe governed by divine providence or one, in the words of Jacques Monod, of *chance and necessity*.[3]

Bleak House opens as Esther's unidentified correspondent engages in a narrative tour de force, announcing that something out of the ordinary is afoot:

> London. Michaelmas term lately over, and the Lord Chancellor sitting in Lincoln's Inn Hall. Implacable November weather. As much mud in the streets, as if the waters had but newly retired from the face of the earth, and it would not be wonderful to meet a Megalosaurus, forty feet long or so, waddling like an elephantine lizard up Holborn Hill. Smoke lowering down from chimney-pots, making a soft black drizzle, with flakes of soot in it as big as full-grown snow-flakes – gone into mourning, one might imagine, for the death of the sun.
>
> (*Bleak House*, p. 1)

The passage introduces Victorian London not through an allusion to Genesis, but to nineteenth-century cosmology, geology, and paleontology. The "death of the sun" is not merely hyperbolic, but suggests *Views of the Architecture of the Heavens* (1837) and John Pringle Nichol's Laplacean argument that our sun and solar system had been condensed out of a diffused cloud of "Nebulous matter" to which, in a departure from Newton and Pierre Simon Laplace (1749–1827), it must some day return.[4] The description of London further acknowledges the extinction of enormous, terrestrial reptiles, the "dinosaurs" of William Buckland (1784–1856) and of Richard Owen (1804–1892) whose existence in the geological past had rendered a literal reading of Genesis difficult, if not impossible, to maintain.[5] Recent cosmological and paleontological speculations had led, in the words of Nichol, to "the land of clouds and doubts – the solid ground of fact and observation is rapidly retiring from below us" (*Architecture*, p. 122).

From the start Laplace's *Exposition du système du monde* (1796) – translated into English as *The System of the World* (1809) – had been seen to encourage religious doubt, if not downright atheism. In an account directed to his sister, Caroline, the astronomer William Herschel (1738–1822), whose papers had influenced both Laplace and Nichol, described an 1802 interview involving himself, Laplace, and Napoleon: "The first Consul . . . asked a few questions relating to Astronomy and the construction of the heavens. . . . He also addressed himself to Mr Laplace on the same subject, and held a considerable argument with him. . . . [A] difference was occasioned by an exclamation of the first Consul, who asked . . . 'And who is the author of all this!' Mons. De la Place [*sic*] wished to shew that *a chain of natural causes would account for the construction and preservation of the wonderful system.*"[6]

Herschel's anecdote points to the naturalistic implications of Laplace's hypothesis, implications suggested but not fully developed by Nichol in *Architecture of the Heavens* and, later, in his *System of the World* (1846).[7] In offering a potentially evolutionary perspective, Nichol invoked the Deity and prudently refrained from applying his vision of a "System of Evolution" (*Architecture*, p. 45) to a full-scale discussion of living organisms on our planet. It was left to the anonymous author of *Vestiges of the Natural History of Creation* (1844) to take the step that defenders of religious orthodoxies expected and feared. Mr. Vestiges followed Laplace and Nichol by describing "a universal Fire Mist" out of which various galaxies and solar systems, including our sun and its orbiting planets, had condensed.[8] After the earth had cooled, developed a hardened crust and an atmosphere that could sustain life, Mr. Vestiges argued – as we have seen – that "the first step in the creation of life upon this planet was *a chemico-electric operation, by which simple germinal vesicles were produced*" (*Vestiges*, pp. 204–5). For Mr. Vestiges, God had no need to intervene directly to initiate the formation of galaxies and solar systems or to introduce living organisms on the earth. The Deity operates solely through the law of Gravitation in the realm of inert matter and the law of Development in the realm of the organic (p. 360). Once biological organisms appeared, the law of Development led chronologically from Georges Cuvier's radiata through the mollusca and articulata, to the vertebrate class (*Vestiges*, pp. 226–27). The geological record, "the *Stone Book*" (p. 57), reliably documents a progression among the vertebrates from fish, to reptiles, birds and, finally, to mammals, culminating in the appearance of the human species. Even human consciousness ceases to be different in kind from that of animals: "The difference between mind in the lower animals and in man is a difference in degree only; it is not a specific difference" (pp. 335–36).

Fifteen years before the publication of the *Origin of Species* (1859), Mr. Vestiges had abandoned the doctrine of special creation, the immutability of species, and the mind–body dualism so central to Western philosophy and to Christianity. Nonetheless, Mr. Vestiges presented himself as a theist with a profound respect for "the authority of the Mosaic record. . . . may not the sacred text, on a liberal interpretation, or with the benefit of new light reflected from nature, or derived from learning, be shewn to be as much in harmony with the novelties of this volume [*Vestiges*] as it has been with geology and natural philosophy?" (*Vestiges*, p. 389). In spite of such a claim, Mr. Vestiges had offered a thoroughgoing naturalistic account of the origins and the development of life, inevitably anathema both to scriptural literalists and to proponents of Natural Theology.[9]

Dickens may well have known the identity of Mr. Vestiges, the Robert Chambers who, with his brother William, published *Chambers's Edinburgh Journal*. William Henry Wills, subeditor to Dickens's *Household Words*, had served as assistant editor of *Chambers's Journal* and was married to Janet Chambers, sister of the Chambers brothers. He may have been privy to the identity of the author of *Vestiges* and shared his knowledge with his employer.[10] Whether Dickens knew the identity of Mr. Vestiges or not, he did know *Vestiges* itself and seemed undisturbed by its heterodox tendencies. In the 9 December 1848 *Examiner* review of Robert Hunt's *The Poetry of Science* (1848), Dickens defended *Vestiges* from Hunt's more-or-less conventional criticism of it. He praised the book and its author for "rendering the general subject [of science] popular, and awakening an interest and spirit of inquiry in many minds, where these had previously lain dormant, [creating] a reading public – not exclusively scientific or philosophical – to whom such offerings can be hopefully addressed." Dickens wrote of *Vestiges* as "that remarkable and well-abused book," even as he proceeded to praise the *Poetry of Science*.[11]

Disavowing any tendency to materialism, Hunt was to return in the *Poetry of Science* to the nebular hypothesis, appropriating language from Nichol's *Architecture of the Heavens* as he wrote of "Magellanic clouds [of matter], and other singular patches of light [in the heavens], exhibiting changes, which can only be explained on the theory of their slow condensation."[12] He followed the changes in the earth's surface over eons and the appearance of living creatures in a universe constituted of matter in perpetual motion. The atom of inorganic matter was transformed into the living cell that became the basis of animate nature. This phenomenon remains "one of the mysteries of creation," hidden from human eyes "until this 'mortal coil' is shaken off" (*Poetry*, p. 339). Although he defended the doctrine of special creation, Hunt nevertheless celebrated the achievements of the physical sciences: "Remembering that the revelations of natural science cannot in any way injure the revelation of eternal truth, . . . we need never fear that we are proceeding too far with any inquiry so long as we are cautious to examine the conditions of our own minds" (p. 386). Ultimately, the revelations of science were to be viewed as "a grand epic," a "great didactic poem" of Miltonic scale (p. 397).

The opening paragraphs of *Bleak House* constitute Hunt's scientific epic in small. Beginning *in medias res*, the present-tense narrative returns to a time when, in Hunt's words, "a monstrous race of reptiles [lived] . . . [of which] we have the megalosaurian remains" (*Poetry*, p. 318). In the paragraphs that follow the moment when "the waters had but newly retired from the face of the earth" (*Bleak House*, p. 1), the anonymous writer chronicles the history of the vertebrate class as the elephantine megalosaurus initiates the evolutionary process that will lead, in time, to dogs, horses, and those human "foot passengers . . . losing their foothold at street-corners, where tens of thousands of other foot passengers have been slipping and sliding since the day broke (if this day ever broke), adding new deposits to the crust upon crust of mud." The crusts, "accumulating at compound interest," allude to the economic activities and to the accounting ledgers central to London life, but also to geological time and to the crust of the earth, composed of those strata in which had been discovered the fossil remains that, decomposed, fuel the gas lamps burning in place of a sun that only looms through the fog and the smoke. The pervasive November fog suggests those Magellanic clouds of vapor from which the solar system has emerged and to which it may one day return. Through the fog it is possible to glimpse "chance people on the bridges peeping over the parapets into a nether sky of fog, with fog all round them, as if they were up in a balloon, and hanging in the misty clouds" (p. 1).

Such people may suffer a vertigo induced by speculations on the nebular hypothesis that raise the specter of materialism and a contingent universe. It was such a specter that critics of *Vestiges* – that "remarkable and well-abused book" – feared in their various responses to it. Particularly, defenders of a prevailing, but endangered, Natural Theology, rose to the occasion. One of the most famous attacks upon *Vestiges* appeared in the *Edinburgh Review* of July 1845. The anonymous review was, in fact, written by Adam Sedgwick (1785–1873), first professor of geology at Cambridge University. His vitriolic review began with a curious speculation upon the identity of the anonymous author: "We thought, when we began . . . 'The Vestiges,' that we could trace therein the markings of a woman's foot."[13] However, the reviewer relented, for he had seen in *Vestiges* "a scheme of nature against common sense, reason, and experience" (82:12) that threatened the social and the moral order. No woman whose education would limit her "to the science gleaned at a lady's boarding-school" would descend to such "rank materialism" (82:27). Rather, Mr. Vestiges was to be associated with Lucretius, Lord Monboddo, and their ilk, potential monomaniacs all, suffering from diseased imaginations. The review was to continue with its hyperbolic assault on Mr. Vestiges by attacking his understanding of the geological record, "the *Stone Book*," upon which, according to Sedgwick, he had mistakenly based his hypothesis of the transmutation of species. In his review Sedgwick observed:

> Had he told us that our geological documents were mutilated and obscure – that, like the worm-eaten parchments of an old record-office, they were so far gone that no mortal could make a connected history out of them – and that he would work up an historical tale from his imagination – using the old documents now and then to eke out an hypothesis . . . a fictitious narrative: . . . we could have understood him.
>
> (82:44)[14]

In a more temperate response, William Whewell (1794–1866), Sedgwick's colleague as Master of Trinity College, Cambridge, gathered together extracts from his earlier writings on the history and the philosophy of the inductive sciences to produce his *Indications of the Creator* (1845). He wrote as a proponent of natural science and a defender of the revelations of the New Testament, promoting the synthesis that constituted Natural Theology in nineteenth-century Britain. Although Genesis was no longer to be read literally, Whewell was determined to argue for the doctrine of special creation and the immutability of species. In doing so, he returned to Pierre Simon Laplace's speculations on the origins of the universe that Whewell himself had named the nebular hypothesis in his 1833 Bridgewater Treatise, *Astronomy and General Physics*. He was writing with an awareness of William Herschel's anecdote about Laplace's indifference to teleological assumptions and the

Argument from Design. In response Whewell argued that, even if one were to accept the nebular hypothesis, it did not prove "that the solar system was formed without the intervention of intelligence and design."[15]

Like Adam Sedgwick in his review of *Vestiges*, Whewell considered the status of the geological record, invoking Georges Cuvier as the model reader of that figurative document. Cuvier was able to reconstruct extinct animals from fragmentary remains because he assumed "not only that animal forms have *some* plan, *some* purpose, but that they have an intelligible plan, a discoverable purpose." Whewell returned to his *History of the Inductive Sciences*, citing Cuvier who "proceeded in his investigations like the decipherer of a manuscript, who makes out his alphabet from one part of the context, and then applies it to read the rest" (*Indications*, p. 48). Writing as a Kantian, Whewell argued that any interpretation of the geological record must rest upon teleological assumptions: "the assumption of an end or purpose in the structure of organized beings, appears to be an intellectual habit which no efforts can cast off" (p. 37). But such a cast of mind is not simply habitual: it is necessary if someone is to read correctly the geological record that is yet another version of Galileo's "grand book – I mean the universe – which stands continually open to our gaze, but [which] cannot be understood unless one first learns to comprehend the language and interpret the characters in which it is written."[16]

However, the bête noire opposed to Cuvier was not for Whewell, Laplace; it was the French naturalist Étienne Geoffroy Saint-Hilaire (1772–1844) whose words he cited: "I ascribe no intention to God, for I mistrust the feeble powers of my reason. I observe facts merely, and go no further. I only pretend to the character of the historian of *what is*" (*Indications*, pp. 42–43). Whewell dismissed Geoffroy's position, reasserting his conviction that teleological assumptions, involving a belief in design and purpose, were fundamental conditions for knowledge:

> If any one were to suggest [as Mr. Vestiges has] that the nebular hypothesis countenances the Scripture history of the formation of [the solar] system, by showing how the luminous matter of the sun might exist previous to the sun itself, we should act wisely in rejecting such an attempt to weave together these two heterogeneous threads; – the one a part of a providential scheme, the other a fragment of physical speculation.
>
> (p. 134)

Writing within a context suggested by the controversies surrounding *Vestiges*, Esther Summerson and her anonymous correspondent will offer two rather different accounts, distinguished by Whewell's "two heterogeneous threads," one a retrospective, at once providential and teleological, after the fact; the other naturalistic, eschewing a concern with divine intention. Esther conceives her figurative progress as necessarily part of "a providential scheme"; the anonymous man or woman with whom she corresponds offers in the present tense a history "of *what is*," Whewell's "fragment of physical speculation" uninformed by teleological assumptions.[17]

As a character in *Bleak House*, Esther writes with an awareness of the pervasive misogyny of Victorian society, revealed so starkly in Adam Sedgwick's initial identification of the author of *Vestiges* as a woman, someone who will prove to be a man suspected of the heresy of philosophical materialism, and of madness. Tainted by her illegitimacy, educated at Greenleaf – a version of Sedgwick's "lady's boarding-school" – Esther has learned to be circumspect and guarded. She avoids controversy, in part by invoking that mysterious providence that seems to inform her life. In a pilgrim's progress written in the past tense, Esther will apparently reaffirm religious orthodoxy.

Esther's account contrasts with the flamboyant, speculative narrative written by her unknown friend. As if emulating a Mr. Vestiges, the writer of the present-tense narrative remains anonymous, conscious of the scientific controversies upon which he or she will touch. In that narrative Esther's correspondent acknowledges the newly-created awareness of geological time, transforming a London day into an ephemeral moment in the measureless history of the universe.[18] The narrative knowingly alludes to the extinction of species and to the debates over the fossil evidence used to promote evolutionary hypotheses. However, any reconstruction of the geological past is rendered difficult, if not impossible, in the reference to the crusts of mud "accumulating at compound interest" (*Bleak House*, p. 1) as the pedestrians slip and slide at the London street-corners. Beyond the suggestion of the account books so central to the economic activities of the city, "the crust upon crust of mud" (p. 1) points to the earth's crust, the figurative geological record that is Mr. Vestiges' "*Stone Book*" upon which, according to Adam Sedgwick, he had mistakenly based his hypothesis of the transmutation of species.

All of this suggests the potentially radical status of a present-tense narrative that will enact the excavation of the world of Victorian London, proceeding without teleological assumptions or claims to omniscience. As a geological account, it will engage in a morphological investigation of resemblances between institutions, characters, and events. The nar-

rative announces its experimental nature in its use of a series of fragmentary and participial constructions without the subject and predicate
of standard English. Conventional notions of agency are subverted: the
narrative reveals neither the identity of its author, nor posits the presence of a divine Author presiding over a creation that is no longer static.
Its meaning is rendered ambiguous, suggesting the exchange between
Napoleon and Pierre Simon Laplace who – so we are told – answered
Napoleon's query, "And who is the author of all this!" by invoking only
"a chain of natural causes [to] account for the construction and preservation of the wonderful system" that is the solar system and the
universe.

Inexorably, both Esther Summerson's narrative and that of her anonymous correspondent move toward Krook's Rag and Bottle Warehouse.
As a parody of the Court of Chancery, Krook's establishment houses
discarded objects, "heaps of old crackled parchment scrolls, and discoloured and dog's-eared law-papers" (*Bleak House*, p. 50), as well the
crazed Miss Flite and the law-writer known only as Nemo. The warehouse becomes the novel's version of Sedgwick's "old record-office" with
its "worm-eaten parchments" ("*Vestiges*," 82:44) that seem to defy interpretation. These remnants of the past, figurative fossils all, become
the basis upon which various characters in the novel, including Mr.
Tulkinghorn and Mr. Guppy the law clerk, are drawn to Krook's, as they
try to reconstruct the past, perhaps a fictitious one, that will lead to
Lady Dedlock and Captain Hawdon, reduced to his shadowy existence
as Nemo.[19]

Esther Summerson will find herself at Krook's, conducted there by "a
curious little old woman" (*Bleak House*, p. 32) whom she, Ada Clare, and
Richard Carstone have met after their interview with the Lord High
Chancellor in Lincoln's Inn Hall. In the window of Krook's establishment she will notice, if only in passing, a card "written in law-hand,
like . . . the letters [she] had so long received" from Kenge and Carboy's.
The card "announc[es] that a respectable man aged forty-five wanted
engrossing or copying to execute with neatness and dispatch: Address
to Nemo, care of Mr. Krook within" (p. 50). Chance – some would call
it providence – has led Esther to the residence of the man who will prove
to be her father, someone who writes under an assumed name and in
an altered hand, nevertheless leaving traces of a past that he has sought,
in his despair, to obliterate.

In her only meeting with Krook, Esther will look on as the illiterate
old man laboriously spells out the name, Jarndyce, each letter a separate and unintelligible character until joined into a coherent whole.

Quite without knowing it, he is a comic version of the paleontological and geological novices in Charles Lyell's *Principles of Geology* (1830–33), confounded by the fossil remains with which they were confronted: in examining "the earth's crust . . . and [the] fossil contents" that are "the signs of a great succession of former changes" in the earth's surface, they could only "attempt to read a history written in a foreign language, doubting about the meaning of the most ordinary terms; disputing, for example, whether a shell was really a shell, . . . and a thousand other elementary questions which now appear to us so easy and simple."[20] Esther is no less a novice than Krook as she becomes the unwilling excavator of her own past, compelled to acknowledge that the signs and tokens that she encounters are figurative hieroglyphs to be deciphered into an alphabet and a grammar providing a key to her own history.

II

Writing in the past tense, Esther Summerson can be aware only after the fact of the significance of events that she might otherwise have neglected to mention. Her retrospective narrative will, inevitably, suggest the workings of a design in human affairs. Others, however, must negotiate the labyrinth of the present-tense narrative without the benefit of hindsight. Esther's nameless correspondent will set out to establish "a chain of natural causes," in Laplace's words, by excavating the London scene at a moment in time so fleeting, so geologically insignificant, that the past tense – with its implications of omniscience – is to be avoided. The narrative is written with a wry awareness of the deceased Professor Dingo, that "eminent scientific man" (*Bleak House*, p. 228), who succeeded Captain Swosser as the second husband of Mrs. Bayham Badger, now married to the gentleman to whom Richard Carstone has been apprenticed in his pursuit of a medical career. Expatiating on that celebrated figure "of European reputation," Mrs. Badger remembers her honeymoon "in the North of Devon" when Professor Dingo disconcerted Devonians by "disfigur[ing] some of the houses and other buildings, by chipping off fragments of those edifices with his little geological hammer" (p. 230). Mrs. Badger appears only in Esther's account: neither she nor Esther may be aware of any allusion to the great Devonian controversy involving Sir Roderick Murchison and Adam Sedgwick. But the anonymous person with whom Esther corresponds may well know of it and of the issues concerning geological evidence and the speculations built upon contested facts.[21]

Professor Dingo and his geological hammer appear in the novel shortly after the often quoted meditation on the nature of connections in which Esther Summerson's unknown correspondent engages:

> What connexion can there be, between the place in Lincolnshire, the house in town, the Mercury in powder, and the whereabout of Jo the outlaw with the broom, who had that distant ray of light upon him when he swept the churchyard-step? What connexion can there have been between many people in the innumerable histories of this world, who, from opposite sides of great gulfs, have, nevertheless, been very curiously brought together!
>
> *(Bleak House*, p. 219)

The reference to "that distant ray of light" would seem to affirm a providential design that connects all the characters in the novel. But in its recognition of the "opposite sides of great gulfs" from which characters are "curiously brought together," the meditation hints at Laplace's nebular hypothesis and the gradual concentration of matter into galaxies and solar systems through the operation of natural law alone. There are connections that exist and that can be explained naturalistically even in a universe of chance and necessity teeming with those coincidences which, in the words of Conversation Kenge, "may or may not require an explanation beyond our present limited faculties" (p. 171). There may, in fact, be only the imperative to imagine a causal chain to connect those seemingly random events that lead a Mr. George to ponder whether he lives in a universe of "chance people" (p. 342) like those who visit his shooting gallery or in a universe governed by a "Providence" (p. 347) that has led him to a meeting with Esther Summerson whose face reminds him of Captain Hawdon's paramour.[22]

In its excavation of the figurative site of Victorian London, the present-tense narrative will examine a variety of social strata, constituting meaning out of apparent chaos. With the help of Mrs. Badger's Professor Dingo, we are returned to Adam Sedgwick who in response to successive editions of *Vestiges* was to renew his attack upon its anonymous author. In the fifth edition of his *Discourse on the Studies of the University of Cambridge* (1850), Sedgwick devoted only 90 of some 600 pages to the nominal topic of curricular reform: in the rest of the *Discourse* he once again defended the traditional social order and Natural Theology against the "mischievous, immoral, and antisocial" arguments of "the Author of the *Vestiges*."[23] In his renewed attack Sedgwick was to point to the dangers of a naturalistic account of a universe in which "we behold . . . only a chain of second[ary] causes of which we know neither the beginning nor the end" (*Discourse*, p. xvi). Here, Sedgwick implied that the refusal to deal with final causes must lead to an infinite regress, inducing the vertigo of those chance people who peep over the parapets of London bridges into a nether sky. Throughout the *Discourse* Sedgwick sought to foreclose a purely naturalistic examination of the universe with its disavowal of teleology. In identifying Mr. Vestiges as someone who had irresponsibly offered suspect hypotheses, he turned to demonstrate the proper "manner [in which] geologists try to clear their way among the broken fragments of a former world":

> They examine these fragments one by one, and learn to arrange them, in the exact order of their history: and taking the analogies of living nature as *their clew through the dark labyrinths of the earth*, they do their best to interpret the past by help of the present – what is dark by what is light – what is unknown by what is known. They are not anxious to form any theory: . . . and at every moment of their progress they are ready either to modify it, or to abandon it altogether, as new phenomena rise up before them.
>
> (*Discourse*, pp. lxxvii–lxxviii, emphasis added)

Read not as a warning against wrong-headed interpretations of the geological record, but as an unintended credo for any narrative that seeks out only naturalistic explanations, the passage describes the activities of the fictional detective from Edgar Allan Poe's C. Auguste Dupin to Arthur Conan Doyle's Sherlock Holmes. It anticipates the attempts of Mr. Tulkinghorn and Mr. Guppy to negotiate a figurative labyrinth as each comes upon apparent clues to the past.

Ironically, Adam Sedgwick's words point to the labyrinthine nature of the account that the present-tense narrative both constructs and negotiates.[24] Esther Summerson's past-tense account offers one way to make sense of things as a retrospective that discerns a providential design. However, the thread of the present-tense narrative begins arbitrarily with the contingent events that have brought Ada Clare, Richard Carstone, and an unnamed Esther Summerson into the presence of the Lord High Chancellor. It proceeds with a naturalistic account, uninformed by a commitment to teleology. The narrative moves from the Court of Chancery to "the world of fashion," both "things of precedent and usage" (*Bleak House*, p. 8). The two institutions are morphologically related in structure and function, living fossils that have survived into the present. The fashionable world is but "a very little speck" in "this world of ours," utterly oblivious both to "the larger worlds . . . [that] circle round the sun" and to "the void beyond" (p. 8). The language self-consciously alludes to Laplace's *Exposition du système du monde*, anticipating the "haut monde" depicted in Tony Jobling's Galaxy Gallery of British Beauty. In the introduction of Sir Leicester and Lady Dedlock, the narrative insists that it is by chance, on this particular November day in the Dedlock London town-house, that Mr. Tulkinghorn comes upon the clue for which he may long have been looking: "It *happens* that the fire is hot, where my Lady sits; . . . My Lady, changing her position, sees the [legal] papers on the table – looks at them nearer – looks at them nearer still – asks impulsively: 'Who copied that?'" (p. 14, emphasis added). When in the next moment Lady Dedlock faints, Tulkinghorn performs an act of interpretation, causally connecting her swoon to the law-hand that she has just glimpsed. Tulkinghorn has been astute enough to see that the "legal character" of the writing "was acquired after the original hand was formed" (p. 14). He has begun his own paleontological investigation of the document before him, but only within a context that *he* has created as he puzzles over the copied text.

Of course, Mr. Tulkinghorn may begin his inquiry into the identity of the person who has copied the legal document with a design or, perhaps, a wish of his own. But he is not concerned with the providential nature of the events that precipitate his investigation: teleological speculations would seem to be the last thing on his mind. In fact, the writer of the present-tense narrative refrains from direct revelations into the minds of various characters: "while Mr. Tulkinghorn may not know what is passing in the Dedlock mind . . . it is very possible that he may" (*Bleak House*, p. 13). Nevertheless, Lady Dedlock's fainting spell has suggested a history waiting to be excavated, a history about which Tulkinghorn may have already fantasized. So motivated, Tulkinghorn will find his way to Krook's warehouse, to the dead law-writer Nemo, and to the letters that will point to the liaison between Captain Hawdon and the woman who is the present Lady Dedlock.[25]

In scrupulously avoiding omniscience, the writer of the present-tense narrative will remain true to the paleontological enterprise that has been undertaken. It is a fact that, at one point, Esther's unidentified correspondent observes, "While Esther sleeps, and while Esther wakes, it is still wet weather down at the [Dedlock] place in Lincolnshire" (*Bleak House*, p. 81). The observation acknowledges Esther's account, written some seven years after the events recorded in the novel, perhaps her response to the present-tense narrative that offers what Hugh Miller, the Scottish stonemason turned popularizer of geology, might call "a congeries of biographies." In his *Foot-Prints of the Creator* (1849) – yet another attack upon *Vestiges* – Miller observed: "all Natural History, when restricted to the passing *now* of the world's annals, is simply a congeries of biographies. It is when we extend our view into the geological field that it passes from *biography* into *history proper*." But, according to Miller, "the *biography* . . . of an individual animal" can be understood only through a concern with "*final causes*."[26] Concentrating on "the passing *now* of the world's annals," the anonymous author of the present-tense narrative traces various personal histories on the principle of metonymy alone, foregoing the conventions of realism with its reliance on the past tense, causality, and omniscience.[27] The method informing the narrative would seem to reflect Richard Chenevix Trench's claim in *On the Study of Words* (1851) that language is "fossil history." In fact, so Trench argued, the spoken language is superior to "all written records," for it "stretches back and offers itself for our investigation . . . [as] a far more ancient monument and document than any writing which employs it. These written records, moreover, may have been falsified by carelessness, by vanity, by fraud, by a multitude of causes: but *it* [the spoken language] is never false, never deceives us, if we know how to question it aright."[28]

True to Trench's observations on the spoken language, the present-tense narrative offers a history of Sir Leicester and Lady Dedlock that can be picked up from the fashionable intelligence that it deftly parodies: "A whisper still goes about, that [Lady Dedlock] had not even family; howbeit, Sir Leicester had so much family that perhaps he had enough, and could dispense with any more." Anyone might learn from the "Honourable Bob Stables" that Lady Dedlock is "the best-groomed woman in the whole stud" (*Bleak House*, p. 10). Surely, everyone living in the neighborhood of Chesney Wold would know the story of Mrs. Rouncewell, the Dedlock housekeeper, and her troubles: "She has had two sons, of whom the younger ran wild, and went for a soldier, and never came back" (p. 84). The narrative proceeds by following various characters who are introduced only by themselves or by other characters. In this way each character's name becomes a form of fossil history, a synecdochal biography that "stretches back and offers itself for our investigation." For example, the narrative follows a "young gentleman" – addressed by "the *name* of Guppy" (p. 35, emphasis added) by Mr. Kenge in Esther's presence – as he reappears at Chesney Wold. Guppy is introduced to Mrs. Rouncewell and to us by the card he presents to her, to be read aloud by her grandson, Watt. It need not be providence but only a chain of circumstances that causes Guppy to visit Chesney Wold, an estate connected with the eminent Mr. Tulkinghorn. For "Tulkinghorn is, in a manner, part and parcel of the place" and, although "he is not in Mr. Tulkinghorn's office," Guppy "is sure that he may make use of Mr. Tulkinghorn's name" (p. 86). There is nothing unusual in a vulgar clerk's desire to look in upon the world that Tulkinghorn serves. At Chesney Wold, Guppy will be struck by the portrait of Lady Dedlock that reminds him of Esther Summerson. Now *he*, like Tulkinghorn, will begin a morphological and genealogical investigation into the past, trying to connect Esther to Lady Dedlock.

Through Guppy, the narrative comes upon Bartholomew Smallweed: it follows him as he saunters home after a dinner with Guppy and Tony Jobling, soon to be known by the name of Weevle. Smallweed is likened to "a kind of fossil Imp," yet one with no traceable genealogy: "to account for [his] terrestrial existence it is reported at the public offices that his father was John Doe, and his mother the only female member of the Roe family" (*Bleak House*, p. 275). However, where records do not provide a reliable genealogy, one will be created. The Smallweed family, presided over by Bart's nominal grandfather, has its own curious "family tree" that "has had no child born to it," but only "complete little men and women" who "bear a likeness to old monkeys" (p. 288). The narrative offers a paleontological account of the Smallweeds as living fossils who defy the principle of change, each a reversion to an earlier, more primitive time. The charming family group includes Bart's sister Judy, who "appears to attain a perfectly geological age, and to date from the remotest periods" (p. 293). At this point, the Smallweed servant girl to whom Judy refers as Charley appears. Charley, of course, is the orphaned daughter of Mr. Neckett who has first been known only as Coavinses through his relationship to the firm for which he works. As Charley sits down to her tea and "a Druidical ruin of bread-and-butter" (p. 293), there is a knock at the Smallweed door and Mr. George announces himself:

> He is a swarthy brown man of fifty; well-made, and good-looking;
> . . . he sits forward on his chair as if he were, from long habit, allow-
> ing space for some dress or accoutrements that he has altogether laid
> aside. . . . He is close-shaved now, but his mouth is set as if his upper
> lip had been for years familiar with a great moustache; . . . Altogether,
> one might guess Mr. George to have been a trooper once upon a time.
>   (p. 295)

It is all too tempting to dismiss the speculation and the ensuing aside – "if trooper he be or have been" (*Bleak House*, p. 297) – as Dickensian coyness, rather than to acknowledge the experiment in narrative that is suggested. The anonymous author has joined the amateur detectives of *Bleak House*, most notably Mr. Tulkinghorn and Mr. Guppy, to engage in speculations upon the histories of the chance people who present themselves in the present-tense narrative. Mr. George's appearance at the Smallweeds' to pay the interest on the loan that he inevitably renews provides an opportunity to perform a feat of analysis that repeats those of C. Auguste Dupin in "The Murders in the Rue Morgue" (1841) and antici-pates those of Sherlock Holmes in *A Study in Scarlet* (1887). It is Holmes who claims, interestingly, in an anonymous magazine article, that it is possible "on meeting a fellow-mortal . . . to distinguish the history of the man, and the trade or profession to which he belongs."[29] Just as Holmes is to claim the ability to read the histories of strangers from their appear-ances and their garb, the anonymous author of the present-tense narra-tive reads the histories of those chance people who appear in the account either by coincidence or through Laplace's "chain of natural causes."

Mr. George – who will prove to be the long-lost son of Mrs. Rouncewell, the housekeeper at Chesney Wold – first appears in the present-tense narrative. It is by chance that he has come upon Grand-father Smallweed's advertisement seeking the whereabouts of a Captain Hawdon. Grandfather Smallweed observes, "If you could have traced out the Captain, Mr. George, it would have been the making of you" (*Bleak House*, p. 300). Instead, George has borrowed money from Smallweed and has become his pawn, a circumstance that will lead him to the chambers of Mr. Tulkinghorn who wants for his own reasons "to see some fragment in Captain Hawdon's writing" (p. 374). Grandfather Smallweed explains: "*Happening* to remember the advertisement con-cerning Captain Hawdon, . . . [Tulkinghorn] looked it up and came to me – just as *you* did, my dear friend" (p. 374, emphasis added). Equally by happenstance, Mr. George will become a murder suspect as a clerk hears Tulkinghorn speak of the dead Mr. Gridley as "a threatening, murderous, dangerous fellow." As the clerk passes Mr. George on the stairs to Tulkinghorn's chambers, he "evidently applies [the words]" to the man descending the stairs (p. 388).

III

As a form of fossil history, each name in *Bleak House* offers itself as a trace of the past by which to reconstruct a literal or a figurative genealogy. The illiterate Jo, of course, continually reminds us of those whose pasts may never be reconstructed, belying Trench's claim about the superiority of the living language to written texts. But for the other characters in the novel it is the death of the law-writer known only as Nemo that poses the problem: "And, all that night, the coffin stands ready . . . and the lonely figure on the bed, whose path in life has lain through five-and-forty years, lies there, with *no more track behind him, that any one can trace, than a deserted infant*" (*Bleak House*, p. 145, emphasis added). The words connect the dead Nemo both to Esther Summerson and to Jo. Yet, in spite of his obscured origins, it may become possible to trace out the history even of someone like Nemo who has tried to obliterate any track that he has left by changing his name and his hand. Those seeking, for whatever motives, to trace the pasts of various characters may well be able to do so if those literal and figurative documents that do survive are not so "mutilated and obscure" (Sedgwick, "*Vestiges,*" 82:44) that they defy interpretation.[30]

Mr. Tulkinghorn and Mr. Guppy are able to proceed in their investigations because various attempts to obliterate the past are frustrated. The law-writer, Nemo, has acquired a Latin name that denies his identity and a new law-hand. But, in the card at Krook's that advertises his services, he has left evidence that can connect him to Lady Dedlock and, quite by chance, to Esther Summerson who has been reminded of "the letters [she] had so long received from the firm" (*Bleak House*, p. 50) of Kenge and Carboy's. Nemo cannot fully obliterate his past: his acquired law-hand reveals an earlier one; and he has kept the letters written to him by his former lover. Even the woman whom Esther has known only as her godmother leaves clues to be sorted out. In naming the infant girl, Esther, she reveals her real relationship to the child, transforming her estranged sister into the Biblical Vashti. She adopts the name Barbary – one of the names Krook mentions to Esther as a party to the great suit – and betrays her stated desire to "[blot] out all trace of [Esther's] existence" (p. 237). Through the assumed name she asserts her connection to Jarndyce and Jarndyce, the suit to which her sister Lady Dedlock, in another name, remains a party. By writing to John Jarndyce on Esther's behalf, so that the child might not be left "entirely friendless, nameless, and unknown" (p. 237), Miss Barbary offers yet another clue that may lead someone, even Esther herself, through the labyrinth of the past.

Names alone, of course, are not the only clues by which to trace the tracks of various characters: a handkerchief once in the possession of Esther Summerson will do. But with her resemblance to Lady Dedlock,

Esther becomes a living clue to the past. Having survived childbirth, she poses a threat to her mother through the features to which Mr. Guppy, Mademoiselle Hortense, and Mr. George respond. In her illness she embraces her disfigurement so that she "never could disgrace her [mother] by any trace of likeness" (*Bleak House*, p. 509). Hers is a morphological transformation, perhaps more desired than real, the result of the fever of smallpox. Esther even burns the letter that Lady Dedlock has written to her after her illness, making sure that the fire "consume[s] even its ashes" (p. 513).[31]

Always, the two narratives – Esther Summerson's and that of her anonymous correspondent – return to the language of geology, paleontology, and nebular cosmology. Esther affirms that her life reveals "the providence of God" (*Bleak House*, p. 509). Her survival in infancy and her illness become part of a larger design: "For I saw very well that I could not have been intended to die, or I should never have lived; . . . I saw very well how many things had worked together, for my welfare" (pp. 515–16). Yet the language of the nebular hypothesis has insinuated itself into her account of her illness, ironically mocking her own avowed faith in providence:

> Dare I hint at that worse time when, strung together somewhere in great black space, there was a flaming necklace, or ring, or starry circle of some kind, of which *I* was one of the beads! And when my only prayer was to be taken off from the rest, and when it was such inexplicable agony and misery to be a part of the dreadful thing?
>
> (p. 489)

In her words there are echoes of Robert Hunt's *Poetry of Science* and Adam Sedgwick's 1850 *Discourse* as the nebular hypothesis offers a metaphor for her "strange afflictio[n]" (p. 489) that has become physical, psychological, and spiritual. In writing of "the mysterious processes of world-formation," Hunt referred to "those gems of light, which flicker at midnight in the dark distance of the starry vault" (*Poetry*, pp. 18, 21); they suggest the existence of "a mass of nebulous matter, only known by its dim and filmy light," from which the "Central Sun" emerged that "by some mighty convulsion" produced "the earth and the other members of the Solar System" (p. 19). In the Appendix to his discourse on curricular reform, Sedgwick wrote of the "*nebulæ*, or masses of cloudy light," that William Herschel and John Herschel had discovered as "a multitude of luminous points, which have been well compared to 'spangles of diamond-dust'" (*Discourse*, pp. 121–22).

Esther's narrative is not immune to the influence of the controversies over the nebular hypothesis: the potential skepticism of Laplace's speculations is suggested in her narrative in spite of herself. Her survival, the survival in various forms of evidence from the past, the continued survival of the universe itself, may finally be purely contingent. In its investigation of the evidence discovered in *Bleak House*, the present-tense narrative hints at the accidental nature of various events in a language that will implicitly challenge Esther's affirmations. Perhaps it is only by accident that the letters once written to Captain Hawdon survive the curious convulsion of Krook's spontaneous combustion or that they are later discovered by Grandfather Smallweed upon his coming into possession of the Rag and Bottle Warehouse. In the words of Inspector Bucket, the police detective, Smallweed has "rummage[d] among the papers as [he has] come into; . . . and so . . . chance[s] to find, you know, a paper, with the signature of Jarndyce to it" (*Bleak House*, p. 839) that may be the last will of the suicide, Tom Jarndyce.

The episode in which Grandfather Smallweed produces the will has been prepared for earlier as Bucket confronts Smallweed, accompanied by Mr. and Mrs. Chadband and Mrs. Snagsby, in the library of Sir Leicester's town-house. Smallweed has come upon incriminating letters to Captain Hawdon, signed by Honoria, a name "that's not a common name," a name used by a "lady in this house that signs [letters] Honoria, . . . in the same hand" (*Bleak House*, p. 731). But Smallweed had sold the letters to Mr. Tulkinghorn before his murder: they are now in Bucket's possession. There is now no evidence available to confirm the speculations of Mrs. Chadband, the former Mrs. Rachael who once served Miss Barbary, about Lady Dedlock's affair and Esther Summerson's origins. So Bucket negotiates with Smallweed and sends him and his companions packing. Once he has dispatched them, Bucket prepares for the arrest of Mademoiselle Hortense for the murder of Tulkinghorn. In spite of the letters in Hortense's hand that denounce Lady Dedlock as a murderess – or because of them – Bucket has convinced himself that his female lodger, Mademoiselle Hortense, is the true culprit. The man whom "time and place cannot bind" (p. 712) will reject circumstantial evidence that would point either to Lady Dedlock or to Mr. George. He revisits Tulkinghorn's rooms in Lincoln's Inn Fields, finding what he is looking for, "the wadding of the pistol with which the deceased Mr. Tulkinghorn was shot": "It was a bit of the printed description [for visitors] of [the Dedlock] house at Chesney Wold" (p. 741). Not particularly significant, Bucket observes, except that Mrs. Bucket – "a lady of a natural detective genius" (p. 712) – finds "the rest of that leaf" that

Hortense has torn up and "puts the pieces together and finds the wadding wanting" (p. 741).

Bucket and his wife produce a context for the otherwise meaningless paper wadding, a fragmentary text that has survived yet another form of combustion, the firing of the pistol with which Mademoiselle Hortense shoots Tulkinghorn. They follow in the footsteps of Edgar Allan Poe's William Legrand as he deals with the scrap of vellum that Jupiter has found on the shore of the mainland near Sullivan's Island. Like Legrand, Mr. Bucket – moved more perhaps by "a desire than an actual belief" – finds a text to confirm the context he has already constructed. He defies the stupefying effects of certain coincidences "to establish a connexion – a sequence of cause and effect" – that leads him to Mademoiselle Hortense.[32]

Every character in *Bleak House*, including the anonymous author of the present-tense narrative, has become a natural historian creating contexts for literal and figurative texts, establishing sequences of cause and effect pointing always to the past. The will that Grandfather Smallweed has accidentally come upon among "old pieces of furniter, and books, and papers, and what not" (*Bleak House*, p. 840) so avidly collected by the illiterate Krook assumes, then, a larger significance. The document itself is "a stained discoloured paper, which [is] much singed upon the outside, and a little burnt at the edges, as if it had long ago been thrown upon a fire, and hastily snatched off again" (p. 841). It is left to Conversation Kenge to say, "it is a Will of later date than any in the suit. It appears to be all in the Testator's handwriting. It is duly executed and attested. And even if intended to be cancelled, as might possibly be supposed to be denoted by these marks of fire, it is *not* cancelled. Here it is, a perfect instrument!" (p. 843).

Mr. Kenge's words are reported by Esther who, with her usual reticence, remains silent about their larger implications. Within the context of Adam Sedgwick's attacks upon *Vestiges*, the will is to be associated not only with the geological record, but also with the Book of Nature of Natural Theology. Sedgwick observed of "the documents of nature" ("*Vestiges*," 82:32) that the characters in which they are written are never "legible and clear." He quoted from the *Geology of the Lake District* (1843): "just where we begin to enter on the history of the physical changes going on before our eyes, and in which we ourselves bear a part, our chronicle seems to fail us – a leaf has been torn out from nature's book, and the succession of events is almost hidden from our eyes" ("*Vestiges*," 82:49). Written upon discolored paper, burnt at the edges, the Jarndyce Will hints darkly of God the great Testator whose purposes and intents are not to be read in such a document; for the true intent of the Author of the universe may remain unknowable. Perhaps, like Tom Jarndyce the suicide, the Author has had second thoughts about that "perfect instrument" and almost consigned it to the origi-nating "universal Fire Mist" (*Vestiges*, p. 30) from which, according to the nebular hypothesis, it has emerged. Perhaps "this world of ours," with its "larger worlds [that] . . . circle round the sun" has survived only by chance, fated to end in the future in the "great funeral pyre" (*Bleak House*, pp. 8, 7) that consumes the Jarndyce suit in legal fees.

With an awareness of a Book of Nature that may itself be anonymous – as Hugh Miller was later to argue in his *Testimony of the Rocks* (1857) – the author of the present-tense narrative never resorts to the New Testament as the basis of a revealed religion, the final recourse of natural theologians like Adam Sedgwick and William Whewell. Rather, the anonymous author suggests that the characters in *Bleak House*, Esther Summerson among them, may no longer find solace in "the great Cross on the summit of St. Paul's Cathedral, glittering above a red and violet-tinted cloud of smoke." To the illiterate Jo, the "sacred emblem" becomes "the crowning confusion of the great, confused city; so golden, so high up, so far out of his reach" (*Bleak House*, p. 271). The great Cross and the scriptures for which it stands no longer provide the final stay against the chaos of the great city. The present-tense narrative suggests a new perspective on that "Terewth" of which Mr. Chadband discourses before the dozing Jo and the captive Snagsbys: "it may be, Jo, that there is a history so interesting and affecting even to minds as near the brutes as thine, recording deeds done on this earth for common men, that . . . it might hold thee awake, and thou might learn from it" (p. 361). The words seem written from the perspective of the Higher Criticism with its vision of the Bible as a human product, created over time by many hands. They harken back to Dickens's *Life of Our Lord* (1849), the book written for his children that depicts Jesus as a good man, a model for all to emulate. Implicitly, the Gospels cease to be the revealed word of God: they offer a human history, a special one, that contributes to Hugh Miller's "congeries of biographies" constituting the potential history of the world.[33]

Even as Jo returns to Tom-all-Alone's to die, it will be Allan Woodcourt who will introduce him, at last, to the Lord's Prayer. The present-tense narrative follows "a brown sunburnt gentleman" (*Bleak House*, p. 628) into Tom-all-Alone's, finally identifying him as the Woodcourt now familiar from Esther Summerson's narrative. True to its experimental nature, the narrative again avoids any claim to omniscience as Woodcourt comes upon a woman whom he delicately addresses as a brickmaker's wife "from the colour of the clay upon [her] bag and on [her] dress" (p. 629). We, of course, recognize her as Jenny, whose child has died in a hovel near St. Albans. It is she who leads Woodcourt to a dying boy, the boy from the "Inkwhich," whom he has forgotten. The woman, whose name Woodcourt never learns, "unravel[s] the riddle" (p. 632) of the boy whom she calls Jo, revealing to Woodcourt that he is the one of whom Richard Carstone has spoken.

Woodcourt resists the revulsion that he feels for the boy who has infected Esther with smallpox. He performs his Christian duty as he sees it, finding a refuge for Jo at Mr. George's shooting gallery. As Jo finally succumbs, Woodcourt asks, "Jo! Did you ever know a prayer?", to which the boy responds, "Never knowd nothink, sir" (*Bleak House*, p. 648). Woodcourt proceeds with the words, "OUR FATHER," that Jo repeats. But the boy dies before he can fully repeat Woodcourt's "HALLOWED BE THY NAME!" Jo manages to say, "Hallowed be – thy –" (p. 649): the rest is silence. The words themselves, however powerful for Woodcourt, have been emptied of meaning. Yet, as it so often does, the present-tense narrative resorts to a character's speech, incorporating his words and cadences into the account it offers. So the anonymous author can be seen to speak for Woodcourt in addressing your Majesty, the lords and gentlemen, the Reverends of every denomination, the men and women in general who have forgotten "a history so interesting and affecting" (p. 361) that it suggests the "Heavenly compassion" (p. 649) that they ought to feel. In its rebuke of an entire society, the narrative does not quite endorse the tenets of a revealed religion.[34]

IV

The present-tense narrative has moved ever closer to the unorthodox implications of the nebular hypothesis, the implications so feared by the defenders of Natural Theology and a traditional social order. The skepticism that Adam Sedgwick had attacked as a Lucretian heresy, both in his *Edinburgh Review* essay on *Vestiges* and in his later *Discourse*, is hinted at in the episode in which Mr. George rides to visit his brother, Mr. Rouncewell, the ironmaster. Mr. George moves from Chesney Wold, where he now serves Sir Leicester, to the iron country: from a traditional, hierarchical society, sanctioned by the arguments of Natural Theology, to the world of the emerging factory system. He traverses a landscape of "coalpits and ashes, high chimneys and red bricks, blighted verdure, scorching fires, and a heavy never-lightening cloud of smoke"

(*Bleak House*, p. 845). He has come upon the beginning of a new world informed by a principle of directionless change.[35] He arrives, at last, at "a gateway in the brick wall" of his brother's ironworks and "sees a great perplexity of iron lying about, in every stage, and in a vast variety of shapes":

> in bars, in wedges, in sheets; in tanks, in boilers, in axles, in wheels, in cogs, in cranks, in rails; twisted and wrenched into eccentric and perverse forms, as separate parts of machinery; *mountains* of it broken up, and rusty in its *age*; distant *furnaces* of it glowing and bubbling in its *youth*; bright fireworks of it showering about, under the blows of the steam hammer; red-hot iron, white-hot iron, cold-black iron; an iron taste, an iron smell, and a *Babel* of iron sounds.
>
> (p. 846, emphasis added)

With its fragmentary constructions suggesting the absence of agency and design, the passage returns to the opening paragraphs of the novel. If *Bleak House* begins *in medias res*, here it offers the epic of the universe, the solar system, and the planet from its molten beginnings to its probable end. Although Mr. George gazes upon the future of an industrializing England, within a larger context the scene suggests the history of a cooling earth as it moves from the molten furnaces of its youth to the mountains of the Alps and the Andes, rusty in their age, as the earth cools over vast periods of time, forming a crust to sustain life, producing eccentric forms presided over only by a chaos of sounds that point to a purely materialist worldview almost Lucretian in its lack of meaning.

The characters in *Bleak House* no longer live unambiguously under the aegis of the Cross of St. Paul's, "so golden, so high up, so far out of [their] reach." Theirs may be a universe represented by Mr. Rouncewell's ironworks, a universe forever changing, "twisted and wrenched into eccentric and perverse forms," always in a condition of becoming. There may be neither the hope of progress, nor the traditional solace of a design beyond human comprehension. Yet, in such a universe it remains possible to make conditional sense of the human situation through reconstructions of the past, should evidence from the past fortuitously survive. But such a possibility need not endorse a belief in teleology, design, and providence. Neither Mr. Tulkinghorn nor Mr. Guppy is given to providential musings: each becomes "the historian of *what is*" (Whewell, *Indications*, p. 43) even as each is guided by his own desires. Perhaps a revised teleology begins to emerge in the novel, one informed by a naturalistic belief in the significance of any human action. There need be no metaphysical implications in Tulkinghorn's response to the fact that Lady Dedlock has fainted after glimpsing the hand in the legal document that she chances to see. We are returned to the passage on connections found in the present-tense narrative written by a man or a woman who chooses, like a Mr. Vestiges, to remain anonymous: "What connexion can there have been between many people in the innumerable histories of this world, who, from opposite sides of great gulfs, have, nevertheless, been very curiously brought together!" (*Bleak House*, p. 219). The passage only apparently endorses the tenets of Natural Theology with its commitment to teleology. There are, indeed, connections between "the innumerable histories of this world," Hugh Miller's "congeries of biographies" (*Foot-Prints*, p. 280), and such connections may be reconstructed to produce a coherent history. However, the evidence to establish the past survives in various forms only by accident. The connections that emerge are gleaned by chance happenings that are neither necessary nor inevitable.[36]

As *Bleak House* comes to its ambiguous close with the conditional last words of Esther Summerson "– even supposing –" (*Bleak House*, p. 880), the events recorded in the two narratives may only in retrospect appear providential.[37] Instead, it is possible to argue that the novel has stepped to the side of Natural Theology and other forms of Christian affirmation. A search for connections sanctioned by the various Bridgewater Treatises of the 1830s may lead to an affirmation of design in the universe, or to a profound skepticism about the status of those connections established through an act of the historical imagination. The novel can be seen particularly to challenge the orthodoxy of William Paley (1743–1805), William Buckland, Adam Sedgwick, and William Whewell, each of whom argued in various ways for a vision of the universe in which every organism and every human being has been created already adapted to its niche in nature or in society. Such views are parodied in the empty words of Mr. Chadband, the Dissenter: "I say, my friends, . . . why can we not fly? Is it because we are calculated to walk? It is. Could we walk, my friends, without strength? We could not. . . . Then from whence, my friends, in a human point of view, do we derive the strength that is necessary to our limbs? Is it . . . from bread in various forms, from butter which is churned from the milk which is yielded untoe us by the cow, from the eggs which are laid by the fowl, . . . and from such like? It is. Then let us partake of the good things which are set before us!" (pp. 263–64). Even Sir Leicester Dedlock may no longer be comforted by a Natural Theology that is reduced in Chadband's speech to Panglossian platitudes that, time out of mind, have sanctioned a static, hierarchical society whose "framework," so Sir Leicester believes, "[is] receiving tremendous cracks in consequence of people (ironmasters, lead-mistresses, and what not) not minding their catechism, and getting out of the station unto which they are called – necessarily and for ever" (p. 397).

It is enough, as Mr. George observes of his brother's ironworks, "to make a man's head ache" (*Bleak House*, p. 846), precisely the effect that the Roman figure of Allegory painted on the ceiling of Mr. Tulkinghorn's chambers has upon those who look up at it: "Allegory, in Roman helmet and celestial linen, sprawls among balustrades and pillars, flowers, clouds, and big-legged boys, and makes the head ache – as would seem to be Allegory's object always, more or less" (p. 130). The figure of Allegory displaces the great Cross of St. Paul's: it becomes the appropriate emblem for a newly envisioned universe. Allegory always "looks pretty cool in Lincoln's Inn Fields" (p. 305), possessed of the capacity to disconcert as it looks down, if it does, forever silent, "pointing, with no particular meaning, from that ceiling," until its outstretched hand will, apparently, point at the corpse of Tulkinghorn: "All eyes look up at the Roman, and all voices murmur, 'If he could only tell what he saw!'" (p. 664). For anyone now entering Tulkinghorn's chambers,

an excited imagination might suppose that there [is] something . . . so terrific, as to drive . . . not only the attendant big-legged boys, but the clouds and flowers and pillars too – in short, the very body and soul of Allegory, and all the brains it has – stark mad. It happens surely, that every one who comes into the darkened room . . . looks up at the Roman, and that he is invested in all eyes with mystery and awe, as if he were a paralysed dumb witness.

(p. 665)

As indeed, Allegory is: he answers the questions addressed to him – with silence.

The figure of Allegory recurs in *Bleak House* to challenge the claims of Natural Theology and to rebuke those, like William Whewell, who would invoke the finger and the tongue of God in their response to *Vestiges*. In his *Indications of the Creator* Whewell stated that the man of science and the man of religion "have both alike a need for understanding the Scripture in some way in which it shall be consistent with their understanding of nature. It is for their common advantage to conciliate, as Kepler says, the finger and the tongue of God, his works and his word" (p. 144). Whewell offered a defense of Natural Theology in terms that return to Francis Bacon's *Advancement of Learning* (1605) and his reference to the Book of Nature as the work of the finger of God. Through an examination of the Book of Nature, Whewell continued, "we cannot refuse to recognize Him as not only the Maker, but the Governor of the World; as not only a Creative, but a Providential Power; as not only a Universal Father, but an Ultimate Judge" (p. 168). He invoked Galen, Harvey, Cuvier and quoted Newton "[to] declare, still with Newton, that 'this beautiful system could have its origin no other way than by the purpose and command of an intelligent and powerful Being, who governs all things, . . . who is not only God, but Lord and Governor'" (pp. 169–70).

But if all else fails – if an application of Laplace's theory of the system of the world should lead to *Vestiges* and, later, to Darwin's *Origin of Species* – there remains the final stay against the abyss of skepticism. Whewell concluded:

> And when we recollect how utterly inadequate all human language has been shown to be, to express the nature of that Supreme Cause of the Natural, and Rational, and Moral, and Spiritual world, to which our Philosophy points with trembling finger and shaded eyes, we may receive . . . the declaration which has been vouchsafed to us:
> IN THE BEGINNING WAS THE WORD, AND THE WORD WAS WITH GOD, AND THE WORD WAS GOD.
>
> (*Indications*, pp. 170–71)

When the finger of God has failed, the tongue of God that speaks in the New Testament must prevail. However, in the Babel world of *Bleak House* characters can no longer resort either to the finger or to the tongue of God. Rather, they are left to contemplate the figure painted on the ceiling of Tulkinghorn's chambers, as Allegory makes the head ache "– as would seem to be Allegory's object always, more or less."

In *Bleak House* the present-tense narrative – in which the figure of Allegory appears – depicts a universe of pure contingency, governed not by design but by Laplace's "chain of natural causes," forged in the iron-works of time. A universe of chance and necessity is presented as a very real alternative to Whewell's providential universe – presided over by "a Universal Father" – in which Esther Summerson wills herself to believe. Of course, a universe characterized by chance and necessity "makes rather an indifferent parent" (*Bleak House*, p. 72), in John Jarndyce's words, emanating as it might from Mr. Vestiges' "universal Fire Mist."[38]

Under such conditions there remains only the recourse to historical knowledge, to the reconstruction of the past through literal and figurative documents that survive by chance and that, like Tom Jarndyce's Will, defy an understanding of their intent. Inevitably, the genealogical reconstructions in which various characters engage become suspect, as Mrs. Woodcourt's insistence upon her Welsh pedigree reveals: "She came from Wales; and had had, a long time ago, an eminent person for an ancestor, of the name of Morgan ap-Kerrig – of some place that sounded like Gimlet – who was the most illustrious person that ever was known, and all of whose relations were a sort of Royal Family. . . . a Bard whose name sounded like Crumlinwallinwer had sung his praises, in a piece which was called . . . Mewlinnwillinwodd" (pp. 238–39). Even Esther Summerson can be seen to mock, however gently, Mrs. Woodcourt's pretensions and her fabrication of a spurious pedigree. In the novel the determination of any pedigree remains at best a chancy business as Mr. Guppy finds in careening from name to name, from biography to biography, moving from the Snagsbys to the man called Nemo, to the Chadbands and the former Miss Rachael and, finally, to the illegitimate Miss Hawdon, whom he knows as Esther Summerson.

It is, indeed, enough to make the head ache, enough to drive Mrs. Snagsby to the abyss of madness. She willfully misreads various contingent events – particularly Mr. Chadband's fixing of his eye on the hapless Jo out of habit alone as he harangues this "Gentile and [this] Heathen . . . [d]evoid of parents, devoid of relations" (*Bleak House*, p. 358). She weaves these empty signs and tokens into a narrative in which Jo *must be* Mr. Snagsby's bastard child: "Jo was Mr. Snagsby's son," she knows, " 'as well as if a trumpet had spoken it' " (p. 734). She has, of course, gotten it all wrong through "a general putting of this and that together by the wrong end" (p. 355). Inspector Bucket must finally rebuke her. He suggests that she "go and see Othello acted," for her jealousy has led her to misconstrue the roles of all those who have quite by accident been "mixed up in the same business," including Jo, the dead law-writer Nemo, and her own hapless husband, "with no more knowledge of it than your great-grandfather" (p. 806). Bucket's words suggest that Mrs. Snagsby's jealousy, like Mrs. Woodcourt's vanity, can produce suspect genealogies with tragic consequences.

In the fictive world of *Bleak House* all of the characters have become chance people "peeping over the parapets into a nether sky of fog, with fog all round them, as if they were up in a balloon, and hanging in the misty clouds." No longer grounded by scriptural literalism, by the common sense of the Enlightenment, or by the fragile synthesis of science and revelation fashioned by Natural Theology, they may well become lost in a nebulous realm of smoke and fog. It is not surprising that "the unknown friend" from whom Esther Summerson "will part for ever" (*Bleak House*, p. 877) at the novel's apparent end has chosen, like the author of *Vestiges*, to remain anonymous. For Esther may well have been compromised by engaging in a correspondence that may be seen as illicit in its nature. Such a communication may finally induce "strange afflictions" (p. 489) that lead to doubt and despair. In spite of her avowal of her faith in Providence, Esther may finally speak for every character in the novel:

> Dare I hint at that worse time when, strung together somewhere in great black space, there was a flaming necklace, or ring, or starry circle of some kind, of which *I* was one of the beads! And when my only prayer was to be taken off from the rest, and when it was such inexplicable agony and misery to be a part of the dreadful thing?
>
> (p. 489)

4
News from the Dead:
Archaeology, Detection, and
The Mystery of Edwin Drood

> The pictures of the Dedlocks past and gone have seemed to
> vanish into the damp walls in mere lowness of spirits, as
> the housekeeper has passed along the old rooms, shutting up
> the shutters. And when they will next come forth again, the
> fashionable intelligence – which, like the fiend, is omniscient
> of the past and present, but not the future – cannot yet under-
> take to say.
>
> *Bleak House*

I

Charles Dickens's *Bleak House* (1852–53) was, to the end, to resist a
resolution between the two, opposing worldviews embodied in Esther
Summerson's self-styled Progress and in the present-tense narrative of
the "unknown friend" of undetermined sex with whom she has been
in correspondence.[1] The novel was to suspend its readers in a state of
doubt, transforming them into versions of those "chance people on
[London] bridges peeping over the parapets into a nether sky of fog,
with fog all round them, as if they were up in a balloon, and hanging
in the misty clouds" (*Bleak House*, p. 1). By the time that Dickens turned
to *The Mystery of Edwin Drood* (1870) some sixteen years later, Charles
Darwin's *Origin of Species* (1859) and Charles Lyell's *Antiquity of Man*
(1863) had been published, the nearly final consolidation of a paradigm
shift to a uniformitarian worldview of a universe governed solely by
natural law. Darwin had dispensed with the doctrine of special creation
and the immutability of species. Lyell had argued for the existence
of prehistoric peoples, living long before events recounted in the Old
Testament, therefore dismissing scripture as a true history of the human
race from its beginnings. Although Lyell was not publicly to accept

Darwin's evolutionary hypothesis until the tenth edition of his *Principles of Geology* in 1868, the die was cast for those ready to embrace a thoroughgoing naturalistic worldview.[2] Together, Darwin and a reluctant Lyell had effectively subverted the synthesis of science and revelation that had constituted the Natural Theology of Hugh Miller (1802–1856), Adam Sedgwick (1785–1873), and William Whewell (1794–1866).

Both the *Origin of Species* and the *Antiquity of Man* were reviewed in *All the Year Round*, the weekly periodical that had succeeded Dickens's *Household Words*.[3] Darwin was himself dismissive of "Species," the first of the two-part review of the *Origin* that appeared on 2 June 1860. However, the unidentified reviewer had a sure sense of Darwin's "one long argument."[4] In introducing readers to the transmutation of species in the first review article, the reviewer made the by now obligatory acknowledgment of Pierre Simon Laplace (1749–1827) in familiar language: a universe forever in the process of change had been anticipated by "Laplace's celebrated comparison of the nebulæ, in what are supposed progressive stages of forwardness, to the trees of different ages growing in a forest.... Certain stars called nebulæ ... have an ill-defined and cloudy look; others are less and less so, till we arrive at the perfect, point-like, glittering star, or cluster of stars, shining like diamonds in the sky."[5] In such a universe "God is Continuous and Unyielding Law, and Incessant Energy, and All-pervading Life" ("Species," 176). With such a vision, according to the reviewer, Laplace and Darwin had forever dismissed the transcendent Deity of "[William] Paley's Natural Theology" (175).

In the second of the two-part review, the reviewer suggested that Darwin was to be seen as a nineteenth-century heretic, "opposed to the belief of philosophers who hold that the various species of plants and animals have been independently created, and have been purposely fitted and adapted to the place in creation which they were intended to occupy" ("Natural Selection," 296). In the concluding paragraphs of "Natural Selection," the reviewer suggested a sure understanding of Darwin's heresy by paraphrasing, almost verbatim, a central passage from the "Recapitulation and Conclusion" of the *Origin*:

> [Darwin's] theory ... entails the vastest consequences. We are no longer to look at an organic being as a savage looks at a ship – as at something wholly beyond his comprehension; we are to regard every production of nature as *one which has had a history*; we are to contemplate every complex structure and instinct as the summing up

of many contrivances, each useful to the possessor, nearly in the same way as when we look at any great mechanical invention as the summing up of the labour, the experience, the reason, and even the blunders, of numerous workmen.

("Natural Selection," 299, emphasis added)[6]

No less revealing is the hyperbolic, almost Dickensian review of the *Antiquity of Man*. "How Old Are We?" (7 March 1863) opened with a flourish: "Dealers in ancient dates have broken down."[7] The chronology of Archbishop Ussher, based upon scripture understood as the history of the human race, was no longer viable, for "the antiquity and ancestry of man" had been demonstrated by "SIR CHARLES LYELL, one of the soundest and most reasonable of geologists that have been or that are" ("How Old Are We?", 32). Through his discussion of "Danish bog[s]" (33), "Swiss lake-villages" (34) of the Stone Age, and British and Continental bone caves in which human artifacts had been found in association with the fossilized bones of extinct mammals, Lyell had proved the existence of those pre-Adamites so abhorrent to Christian orthodoxy: "The issue of all these researches is, in the opinion now held by geologists, that although man, whose traces are found only in the post-tertiary deposits, is geologically a new comer upon earth, his antiquity is, nevertheless, much greater than chronologists have hitherto supposed" (37).[8]

The appearance of such reviews in *All the Year Round*, a periodical directed to the men and women who read Dickens's novels, introduced them to the controversies stirred by the *Origin of Species* and the *Antiquity of Man*. Dickens could, perhaps, expect them to recognize in *The Mystery of Edwin Drood* a Darwinian narrative offering an evolutionary vision of "natural history" (*Origin*, p. 456) modelled upon Lyell's enactment of the reconstruction of the human past as he helped to establish the discipline of prehistoric archaeology.[9] As a piece of detective fiction, the novel narrates the complex relationship involving a callow Edwin Drood, his fiancée Rosa Bud, and his youthful uncle, John Jasper, driven to the use of opium as a release from "the cramped monotony of [his] existence" as a cathedral choirmaster and from his frustrated desire for Rosa – and for Drood.[10] The disappearance of Drood upon a stormy Christmas morning was never to be explained, a riddle that endures to this day, sealed by Dickens's death in the early evening of 9 June 1870, leaving only six parts of the proposed twelve monthly parts that were to constitute the novel. Victorian readers were never to know if Drood is alive or dead, the victim of an accident or of foul play

The personal effects – an engraved watch, a chain, and a shirt-pin – that are retrieved from Cloisterham Weir would seem to be his. But, they remain mute, unresponsive to the inquiries of the various characters who, like amateur archaeologists, seek to interpret them.[11]

Appropriately, the events narrated in *Edwin Drood* occur primarily in Cloisterham, an "old Cathedral town" (*Drood*, p. 14), that is presented at first as an antiquarian curiosity. However, the novel proceeds to initiate a transition from one form of historical knowledge to another as it rejects the traditional antiquarianism of those who, like the defenders of Natural Theology, sought to perpetuate a social and intellectual status quo. Like Lyell's *Antiquity of Man*, the narrative of *Edwin Drood* explores the problematic nature of evidence, the art of reconstructing in narrative form the inaccessible past, and the challenges posed by the phenomenon of negative evidence. As a prolonged meditation upon historical knowledge, the novel recapitulates a shift from an established antiquarian perspective to a truly archaeological one, a transition from a prevailing concensus among men of science and gentlemen amateurs to a new concensus that would, for some, sweep away a traditional Biblical chronology to open up an abyss of time obscuring human origins altogether.[12]

II

In *The Mystery of Edwin Drood* the congenial optimism of the nineteenth-century antiquarian, with his confidence in Baconian empiricism and a providential history, is suggested, only to be parodied, in the opening description of Cloisterham. The history of the town apparently honors a philological and antiquarian model, following the successive peoples, with their differing languages, who once inhabited the spot. Cloisterham, "a fictitious name," has been "once possibly known to the Druids by another name, and certainly to the Romans by another, and to the Saxons by another, and to the Normans by another; and a name more or less in the course of many centuries can be of little moment to its dusty chronicles" (*Drood*, p. 14). The history of Cloisterham is founded upon surviving edifices and on documents that point backward in time as far as the Celts, who were believed to have inhabited England in the period immediately preceding the Roman occupation. The novel captures the cadences and the spirit of Richard Chenevix Trench's *On the Study of Words* (1851). For Trench the philologist becomes a figurative geologist engaged in the study of "moral and historical researches":

You know how the geologist is able from the different strata and deposits, primary, secondary, or tertiary, succeeding one another, . . . to arrive at the successive physical changes through which a region has passed, . . . to measure the forces which were at work to produce them, and almost to indicate their date. Now with such a composite language as the English before us, . . . [h]ere too are strata and deposits, not of gravel and chalk, sandstone and limestone, but of Celtic, Latin, Saxon, Danish, Norman, and then again Latin and French words . . . any one with [the] skill to analyze the language might re-create for himself the history of the people speaking that language.[13]

Trench's geological analogy remains illustrative and unproblematic.[14] His attitude, so representative of the Anglican establishment, seems to inform the history of Cloisterham, that "ancient city . . . so abounding in vestiges of monastic graves, that the Cloisterham children grow small salad in the dust of abbots and abbesses . . . ; while every ploughman in its outlying fields renders to once puissant Lord Treasurers, Archbishops, Bishops, and such-like, the attention which the Ogre in the story-book desired to render to his unbidden visitor, and grinds their bones to make his bread" (*Drood*, p. 14). But such passages in *Edwin Drood* will, finally, parody in a nuanced way not only someone like Trench, but those antiquarians who incorporated a philological model into their histories of Britain. The history of Cloisterham echoes other accounts of the past from the time of the Celts to the conversion of the Anglo-Saxons that was seen to mark the founding of the modern British nation. In *The Celt, the Roman, and the Saxon*, first published in 1852, Thomas Wright provided a characteristic British history. In his preface to the second edition of 1861, Wright observed: "There is hardly a corner in our island in which the spade or the plough does not, from time to time, turn up relics of its earlier inhabitants, to astonish and to excite the curiosity of the observer, who, when he looks to an ordinary history of England, finds that the period to which such remains belong is passed over with so little notice."[15] Wright then proposed to

give a sketch of that part of our history which is not generally treated of, the period before Britain became Christian England – the period, indeed which, in the absence of much documentary evidence, it is the peculiar province of the antiquary to illustrate. Every article which . . . is turned up by the spade or the plough, is a record of that history, and it is by comparing them together, and subjecting them to the assay of science, that we make them tell their story.

(pp. v–vi)

Although he acknowledged the fact of those "centuries which present little more than a blank in our ordinary annals" (p. vi), Wright was sure that he could, indeed, offer a reliable account of the past. He began with the Celts and the Druids, with a primeval period that antiquarians claimed immediately preceded the Roman presence in Britain: his was a strategy shared with others who, in their Christian orthodoxy and social conservatism, sought to truncate time and to deny a prehistoric age that would challenge the scriptural account of human history.[16]

Throughout *The Celt, the Roman, and the Saxon*, Wright touched upon topics relevant to the narrative of *Edwin Drood*. He dealt with the history of the names of contemporary British towns and cities, following the lead of Trench with his concern for words as "fossil history" (*Study of Words*, p. 13). He mentioned the various names of Rochester – Bremenium, Durobrivæ, Hrofes-ceaster – anticipating the history of the town fictionalized as Cloisterham.[17] Wright devoted page upon page to Roman funeral monuments and to their Latin inscriptions, foreshadowing the preposterous Mr. Sapsea, the mayor of Cloisterham, and the self-serving epitaph to be inscribed upon the monument to his dead wife. He discussed Roman and Saxon burial customs, including both cremation and the later, more common, interment of bodies in sepulchral chests and stone sarcophagi along with the personal effects of the dead.

These are tantalizing facts. But the significance of *The Celt, the Roman, and the Saxon* for *Edwin Drood* involves, more significantly, the antiquarian ethos that the novel will reject in its promotion of the archaeological perspective that was to inform a new scientific consensus in the 1860s and to provide a model for the act of detection.[18] The novel implicitly challenges Wright's confidence that he can subject various forms of evidence "to the assay of science" and make them tell "their story" (*Celt*, p. vi). It will raise questions about the developmental, progressive model of British history promoted in the decades prior to Darwin's *Origin* and Lyell's *Antiquity of Man*. The novel will subvert Wright's belief in a providential history that reveals God's plan for the British people and a British empire that was to rival, and to outlast, that of Rome. Even the belief in the continuity between Saxon Britain, with the "municipal constitutions" (p. 443) of its purportedly independent towns, and Victorian Britain will be parodied, particularly Wright's claim that such towns "hold a very important place in the history of social development . . . to which we owe that due mixture of Saxon and Roman that forms the basis of modern civilisation" (p. 455).[19] Such claims underlie Wright's hostility to theorizing and his dismissal of the Danish three-age model of human history. Two years after Lyell had endorsed the fact of human prehistory before the British Association for the Advancement of Science in 1859, Wright could still attack "the system of archæological periods which has been adopted by the antiquaries of the north. . . . It is true that there may have been a period when society was in so barbarous a state, that sticks or stones were the only implements with which men knew how to furnish themselves; but I doubt if the antiquary has yet found any evidence of such a period" (p. vii). Wright later concluded: "the most probable view of the case seems to be, that the mass of our British antiquities belong to the age immediately preceding the arrival of the Romans, and to the period which followed" (p. 82).

Wright promoted a dogmatic antiquarianism to preclude the union of natural history and human history that Lyell would seek to forge two years later in the *Antiquity of Man*.[20] But in its final paragraphs *The Celt, the Roman, and the Saxon* introduced an element of uncertainty that belied the claims that Wright had insistently made. He turned to a discussion of inscribed stones found in Wales and Cornwall, apparently belonging to "the period following immediately after that of the departure of the Roman legions." The inscriptions "are in Latin, but the names are apparently Celtic" (*Celt*, p. 461). The inscription on one such stone in Wales "was evidently written by one who spoke Latin corruptly; but its greatest singularity is the circumstance that the inscription is cut on the back of an older inscribed stone, dedicated to the emperor Maximinus; and although the pure Roman inscription is written in lines across the stone, the later inscription is written, like those found in Cornwall, lengthways." Apparently, several stones had "a cross at the top, so that there can be no doubt of the people to whom these belonged being Christians" (p. 462). With the interpretation the book ends, asserting the continuity between Celtic, Roman, and Christian Britain and offering a history that is documented and intelligible. But with its multiple inscriptions, the fragmentary stone becomes a figurative palimpsest: it reveals the existence of trace upon trace leading forever backward in time and inducing historical vertigo.

With its unintended implications, Thomas Wright's discussion of the stone suggests how the narrative of *Edwin Drood* can resist Victorian antiquarianism, with its faith in providence and progress, and mock those like the Reverend Septimus Crisparkle whose world may well be circumscribed by the Alternate Musical Wednesdays that he attends. The novel insistently chides those who would argue that a providential design governs British history and leads to the glories of the Victorian era: "A drowsy city, Cloisterham, whose inhabitants seem to suppose, with an inconsistency more strange than rare, that all its changes lie behind it, and that there are no more to come. A queer moral to derive from antiquity, yet older than any traceable antiquity" (*Drood*, p. 14). The reference to those traces that antiquarians like Thomas Wright pursue so assiduously mocks their project. Not only may history have no traceable beginning, there is no end to history, the design of which has only apparently led to the British empire and to those like Edwin Drood who complacently talks of those "triumphs of engineering skill" that are "to change the whole condition of an undeveloped country" (p. 21) like the Egypt that awaits him. His condescension reveals the condition of most of those associated with Cloisterham.

Edwin Drood dismisses any claim to progress, particularly if providential design has led to the insipid world of Minor Canon Corner where the reverend Mr. Crisparkle now resides with his quaint, elderly mother:

> Swaggering fighting men had had their centuries of ramping and raving about Minor Canon Corner, and beaten serfs had had their centuries of drudging and dying there, and powerful monks had had their centuries of being sometimes useful and sometimes harmful there. . . . Perhaps one of the highest uses of their ever having been there, was, that there might be left behind, that blessed air of tranquillity which pervaded Minor Canon Corner, and that serenely romantic state of the mind . . . which is engendered by a sorrowful story that is all told.
>
> (*Drood*, pp. 39–40)

The days, weeks, and months to pass will prove how illusory is the tranquillity of Minor Canon Corner and the belief that history is "a pathetic play that is played out" (p. 40). In the process, the novel explores the problematic nature of the evidence, documentary and otherwise, that Thomas Wright subjected to "the assay of science": for every artifact "turned up by the spade or the plough" does not tell its own story (*Celt*, p. vi), but is coerced into meaning by those who examine it.

As "the Cloisterham children grow small salad in the dust of abbots and abbesses, and make dirt-pies of nuns and friars" and as the "plough-man . . . grinds [the] bones" (*Drood*, p. 14) of the long-dead members of the clerical hierarchy, they blithely destroy relics of the past. Even those relics that do survive pose a challenge to the antiquarian: "In the midst of Cloisterham stands the Nuns' House; a venerable brick edifice whose present appellation is doubtless derived from the legend of its conventual uses" (p. 15). There may, in fact, be no proof that the building had once been a nunnery. Rather, its origins and the transformations it may have undergone through the centuries remain shrouded in myth and conjecture. It can only puzzle the historian, just as others in the future may be puzzled as they contemplate a "resplendent brass plate" from the nineteenth century, "flashing forth the legend: 'Seminary for Young Ladies. Miss Twinkleton'" (p. 15). Just as the inscribed stone in Wales defied Thomas Wright's interpretation, the Nuns' House resists attempts to reconstruct its history: the ironic legend proclaiming its current use can not tell its own story, either in the present or in the future.

Edwin Drood transforms monuments to the past into figurative texts that retain an irresolvable ambiguity. The novel begins to demonstrate a sophisticated archaeological awareness, first in the depiction of the Nuns' House, later in its introduction of "the mysterious inscription" over the portal to Mr. Grewgious's chambers in Staple Inn, located near "the most ancient part of Holborn," where the man who is Rosa Bud's guardian both works and lives. In its apparent simplicity the inscription reads, "J   P   T " (*Drood*, p. 88). The novel will return to the 1747 inscription with a curious insistence. Grewgious himself has never "troubled his head about [it], unless to bethink himself at odd times on glancing up at it, that haply it might mean Perhaps John Thomas, or Perhaps Joe Tyler" (pp. 88–89).[21] The narrative toys with the inscription, playing whimsically, it would seem, upon its possible meanings. In choosing his niche in life, Grewgious has settled down "under the dry vine and fig-tree of P. J. T., who planted in seventeen-forty-seven" (p. 89), an observation that invokes the family trees and genealogies of antiquarianism, but also the language tree of Victorian philology and, perhaps, the Tree of Life of Darwin's *Origin of Species*. As Grewgious entertains Edwin Drood on the night he entrusts the lad with the ring once belonging to Rosa Bud's mother, he emphasizes the solemnity of the moment with a special wine: "If P. J. T. in seventeen-forty-seven, or in any other year of his period, drank such wines – then, for a certainty, P. J. T. was Pretty Jolly Too" (p. 93). The evening ends as Grewgious addresses his image in a looking-glass: "there are such unexplored romantic nooks in the unlikeliest men, that even old tinderous and touch-woody P. J. T. Possibly Jabbered Thus, at some odd times, in or about seventeen-forty-seven" (p. 99).

Like the Nuns' House, the corner house in Staple Inn has become a
figurative document or manuscript from which a chronology and a
history, however whimsical, are to be constructed. But the narrative
insists that the inscription cannot be made to "tell [its] story," that it
refuses to become "a record of . . . history" (*Celt*, p. vi). All the verbal
playfulness with the inscription draws attention to the fact that an order
has been imposed upon the inscribed characters that is not sanctioned
by the triangular inscription in which no letter possesses an indis-
putable priority. The various renderings of the inscription arbitrarily
order the letters that could be arranged in other ways and suggest other
interpretations. The renderings seem to contextualize the letters by connecting the date with the erection of the building, with a purportedly
historical personage, and with an historical period. Inevitably, the
inscription remains mysterious, enigmatic, potentially without meaning, a reminder of the perils of creating accounts from ancient edifices,
in whatever condition, and from the inscriptions on them. For in the
"little nook" called Staple Inn there is "a little Hall, with a little lantern
in its roof: to what obstructive purposes devoted, and at whose expense,
this history knoweth not" (*Drood*, p. 88).

III

The Mystery of Edwin Drood has become a special kind of history, an
anonymous one that does not lay claim to omniscience. The status of
the narrative is more fully revealed later in the novel after Drood's
disappearance. Neville Landless, the orphaned twin from Ceylon, has
removed himself from Cloisterham to rooms in the vicinity of Staple
Inn. Mr. Grewgious, suspecting John Jasper of *something*, has been on
the lookout for the choirmaster who persecutes Landless for his interest in Rosa Bud by spying on him in his London retreat. In pondering
the significance of what he knows and what he suspects, Grewgious
finds himself, on one particular night, gazing at the stars "as if he would
have read in them something that was hidden from him": "Many of us
would if we could; but none of us so much as know our letters in the
stars yet – or seem likely to, in this state of existence – and few languages can be read until their alphabets are mastered" (*Drood*, p. 160).

The passage signals the transition from an antiquarian concern with
Latin, Saxon, and English inscriptions to other written languages –
Egyptian hieroglyphs and Assyrian cuneiform, whose alphabets and
grammars had only been deciphered in recent decades. Rosa Bud has
poutingly expressed her distaste for all things vaguely Middle Eastern

by dismissing "Arabs, and Turks, and Fellahs, and people." She professes to hate the pyramids and Miss Twinkleton's lectures on "tiresome old burying-grounds! Isises, and Ibises, and Cheopses, and Pharaohses; who cares about them? And then there was Belzoni or somebody, dragged out by the legs, half choked with bats and dust" (*Drood*, p. 21). Rosa's petulance serves to establish early on the preoccupation in *Edwin Drood* with British imperialism and with a provincialism that reveals itself as pure racism in Mr. Sapsea's and Mr. Honeythunder's denunciations of the dark-skinned Landless whom they suspect as the murderer of Drood.[22]

But other issues are suggested in Rosa's irreverent reference to Giovanni Battista Belzoni. In his popular *Narrative* (1820), Belzoni described several of his Egyptian exploits. One was his discovery in 1818 of the concealed passage in the second pyramid of Giza that led to the burial chamber of Rosa's tiresome Cheops. More important perhaps was Belzoni's rediscovery in 1817 of the buried temple of Abu-Simbel. In gaining access to the temple, Belzoni became perhaps the first European in a thousand years to see its interior. As a collector of Egyptian antiquities for the British Museum, Belzoni could be seen as an adventurer, perhaps even a grave-robber.[23] He lacked the kind of sophisticated archaeological awareness suggested by the moment in which Mr. Grewgious contemplates the stars as if they were some hieroglyphic or cuneiform script as yet undeciphered and untranslated. For many Victorians the moment would conjure up the dispute over priority in the decipherment of the Rosetta Stone involving Britain's Thomas Young (1773–1829) and Jean-François Champollion (1790–1832). More specifically, readers of *All the Year Round* might be reminded of "Latest News from the Dead" (11 July 1863). Its opening paragraph celebrates the archaeological feats of recent years, pointing particularly to the decipherment of Egyptian hieroglyphs and of Assyrian cuneiform: "Old Egypt is delivering up fresh secrets of her dead, at Thebes and elsewhere. . . . Nineveh and Babylon, having been in the hands of such resurrectionists as Mr. Layard, Sir Henry Rawlinson, and others, are left at peace for a short time."[24] By 1863 any news from Nineveh and Babylon might be seen as old news. The feats of Layard and Rawlinson belonged to the 1840s and 1850s when the two achieved fame, Layard for the excavation of sites near Mosul in present-day Iraq that he identified as the Biblical Nineveh and Nimrud, Rawlinson for the decipherment of the Assyrian cuneiform.[25]

In *Nineveh and its Remains*, an immediate sensation upon its publication in 1849, Layard provided an account of his excavations at Nimrud, evoking a sense of mystery and wonder surrounding his discovery of a high Assyrian civilization almost lost to human memory. In an introduction to the American edition of *Nineveh and its Remains*, Edward Robinson captured that wonder aroused by a figurative resurrectionist like Layard. Robinson distinguished "the classic lands of Greece and Rome" whose monuments and inscriptions had been known for centuries from the "hoary monuments of Egypt . . . [that] have presented to the eye of the beholder strange forms of sculpture and of language . . . mute for so many ages." Even more wonderful had been the recovery of Nimrud and Nineveh "whose greatness sank when that of Rome had just begun to rise": "Here we have to do, not with hoary ruins that have borne the brunt of centuries in the presence of the world, but with a resurrection of the monuments themselves." He concluded: "It is the disentombing of temple-palaces from the sepulchre of ages; the recovery of the metropolis of a powerful nation from the long night of oblivion."[26]

It is from Edward Robinson's "long night of oblivion" that Victorian Cloisterham whose monuments and inscriptions would seem to have "been known for centuries" will be resurrected as if by one of the fabled archaeologists of "Latest News from the Dead." The town will be transformed from a place of only antiquarian interest into an archaeological site as mysterious and foreign as Herculaneum, Pompeii, and Layard's Nineveh. It will become a figuratively buried city, disinterred to yield its secrets to an uncomprehending world. When, on the evening of John Jasper's midnight ramble through the Cathedral with the stonemason Stony Durdles, the ever-complacent Dean asks if the choirmaster plans "to write a book about us," he responds, "I really have no intention at all, sir, . . . of turning author, or archæologist. It is but a whim of mine" (*Drood*, p. 100). However, in Jasper's excursion with Durdles, Cloisterham and the Cathedral will be metamorphosed into a domestic version of the excavated Nimrud that Layard described in *Nineveh and its Remains*.

In the abridged account of the excavations at Nimrud that Dickens owned, Layard retained a De Quinceian set-piece from *Nineveh and its Remains* in which he evoked the dream-like splendor of the Assyrian city that he had discovered in a mound near the city of Mosul. It was a place totally foreign to the British imagination, unknown even to the Bedouins who "have lived on these lands for years."[27] In the words of one Sheikh Abd-ur-rahman, perhaps only apocryphal, his "father, and the father of [his] father, pitched their tents here . . . and none of them ever heard of a palace under ground" (*Discoveries*, p. 294). The sheikh can only proclaim, "Wonderful! Wonderful!", a response that Layard sought to evoke in his British readers by conducting them upon an imaginary tour of "the subterraneous labyrinth" where one encounters "colossal winged figures: some with the heads of eagles, others entirely human, and carrying mysterious symbols in their hands": "To the left is [a] portal, . . . formed by winged lions. . . . Beyond this portal is a winged figure, and two slabs with bas-reliefs; but they have been so much injured that we can scarcely trace the subject upon them" (p. 307). Farther on, "among these scattered monuments of ancient history and art, we reach another doorway, formed by colossal winged bulls in yellow limestone" (p. 308). In the revery Layard moves on to other galleries and chambers, "examining the marvelous sculptures, or the numerous inscriptions that surround [him]" (p. 310). He has created a phantasmagoric experience, suggesting that we may be "half inclined to believe that we have dreamed a dream" and that some, "who may hereafter tread on the spot when the grass again grows over the ruins of the Assyrian palaces, may indeed suspect that [he has] been relating a vision" (p. 311). An archaeological experience induces a new awareness of unimagined realms and an appreciation of the evanescent status of the evidence that attests to them.[28]

Ironically, it is an awareness that Dickens had already captured in his descriptions of Rome in *Pictures from Italy* (1846). In describing his visit to the Eternal City early in 1845, over six months before Layard began his dig near Mosul in November of that year, Dickens managed to transform Rome into yet another buried city quite as wonderful as the Nimrud of Layard, as it rises out of the "undulating flat" of the Roman Campagna. From afar he sees "innumerable towers, and steeples, and roofs of houses, . . . and high above them all, one Dome": "it was so like London, at that distance, that if you could have shown it me, in a glass, I should have taken it for nothing else."[29] In the transforming mirror of Dickens's imagination Rome becomes a figurative Herculaneum, Pompeii, Nineveh, or Babylon, one of the disinterred cities later to be celebrated in "Latest News from the Dead." It is a city of desolation, with the Colosseum, the Forum, and ancient temples offering a vision of ruin upon ruin. Beneath its streets lie the catacombs, "quarries in the old time, but afterwards the hiding-places of the Christians," whose "great subterranean vaulted roads" (p. 386) become a city beneath a city, suggesting the world of a barely imaginable past beneath contemporary Rome. In the streets of modern Rome "you pass by obelisks, or columns: ancient temples, theatres, houses, porticoes or forums: it is strange to see, how every fragment, whenever it is possible, has been blended into

some modern structure, and made to serve some modern purpose"
(p. 398).

Dickens's experience of the Eternal City culminates as he and his party
return at night from an excursion on the Campagna, an "unbroken
succession of mounds, and heaps, and hills, of ruin." The Campagna
becomes a figurative "Desert, where a mighty race have left their foot-
prints in the earth from which they have vanished" (*Pictures*, p. 396).
As early as 1845 Dickens engaged in his own revery that bespeaks a
complex archaeological awareness:

> To come again on Rome by moonlight, after such an expedition, is
> a fitting close to such a day. The narrow streets, devoid of footways,
> and choked, in every obscure corner, by heaps of dung-hill rubbish,
> contrast . . . with the broad square before some haughty church: in
> the centre of which, a hieroglyphic-covered obelisk, brought from
> Egypt in the days of the Emperors, looks strangely on the foreign
> scene about it.
>
> (p. 397)

The moon "gushes freely" through the "broken arches and rent walls"
of the Colosseum whose stones have been used to rear other "ponder-
ous buildings"; while an "ancient pillar, with its honoured statue over-
thrown, supports a Christian saint: Marcus Aurelius giving place to Paul,
and Trajan to St. Peter" (p. 397). Dickens responds to Rome with the
eye of the archaeologist, recognizing the existence of ancient Egypt,
the rise and fall of imperial Rome, the emergence of a Christian Rome
under Roman Catholic dominance; he even acknowledges the mundane
present in "the little town of miserable houses" where "the Jews are
locked up nightly, when the clock strikes eight" (p. 397). He has presented a multilayered past, a stratified archaeological site that, like
Layard's Nimrud, demands excavation and has at its center an obelisk
engraved with hieroglyphs to be deciphered and translated.

The perspective suggested in *Pictures from Italy* and in Layard's
abridged *Discoveries at Nineveh* provides a context in which to consider
John Jasper's moonlight excursion with Stony Durdles. The outing
should not be seen primarily as evidence that Jasper is plotting to kill
Edwin Drood and to conceal his corpse in the Cathedral crypt. Rather,
the Cloisterham through which they move has become an archaeological site: its various edifices contain vestiges of the past in "fragments
of old wall, saint's chapel, chapter-house, convent, and monastery"
(*Drood*, p. 14). Finally, Jasper and Durdles enter the Cathedral precincts

where "a certain awful hush pervades the ancient pile, the cloisters, and the churchyard" (p. 105). They descend into the Cathedral crypt where Durdles discourses of the "old-uns," those "buried magnate[s] of ancient time and high degree" (p. 29) whose corpses may have turned to dust. They leave the crypt, beginning their ascent to the great tower, stopping on "the Cathedral level" where "the moonlight is so very bright . . . that the colors of the nearest stained-glass window are thrown upon their faces." Durdles opens the door to the tower staircase, holding it for Jasper "as if [he is] from the grave" (p. 107). The two explorers toil up "the winding staircase," pausing at different stages, at places that include "low-arched galleries" from which they glimpse "the moonlit nave," while above them "the dim angels' heads upon the corbels of the roof, [seem] to watch their progress" (pp. 107–8).

Durdles and Jasper reenact the experience that Dickens has had of Rome by moonlight; they enter a realm like that of the excavated Nimrud, a realm of dream that reveals the enduring nature of the past. As the two attain the Cathedral tower itself, "they look down on Cloisterham, fair to see in the moonlight: Its ruined habitations and sanctuaries of the dead, at the tower's base: its moss-softened red-tiled roofs and red-brick houses of the living, clustered beyond: its river winding down from the mist on the horizon, as though that were its source, and already heaving with a restless knowledge of its approach towards the sea" (*Drood*, p. 108). A spatial journey has become a temporal one: there is a movement from the sepulchral depths of the Cathedral that suggest not only a medieval past, but the dust and soil prior to its erection, and the dust to which the Cathedral may return. Durdles and Jasper have moved through strata of human time, rising to the tower and to a prospect of present-day Cloisterham, so confident that all change lies behind it. As in Dickens's depiction of the broad square in Rome, with the obelisk and the statuary, a multilayered reality has been suggested, a rendering of human time indebted to philology, geology, and an archaeology that has opened new vistas of time through the excavation of "dead and buried cities that it is one of the labours of the living in our day to disentomb" ("News from the Dead," 473).

IV

But as Cloisterham's "river [winds] down from the mist on the horizon, as though that were its source," an even more profound sense of the past has been suggested, a past extending into epochs that far predate the time of Roman Britain, a time before the literate societies of Egypt,

Babylon, and Assyria. For Victorians living in the 1860s and 1870s, such mists were now associated with a preliterate world prior to that of the Celts: they were mists of time through which archaeologists were just beginning to peer. In 1875 William Gladstone would introduce Heinrich Schliemann to the London Society of Antiquaries in language that had become conventional and, to many, unexceptionable:

> When many of us who are among the elders in this room were growing up, the whole of the prehistoric times lay before our eyes like a silver cloud covering the whole of the lands that, at different periods of history, had become so illustrious and interesting; but as to their details we knew nothing. . . . Now we are beginning to see through this dense mist and the cloud is becoming transparent, and the figures of real places, real men, real facts are slowly beginning to reveal to us their outlines.[30]

Gladstone was referring to Schliemann's quest for Troy, but his words suggest that like-minded people, even the devoutly Christian, had accepted prehistory as a reality, an assumption that John Lubbock, now Lord Avebury, could question as he promoted the reality of human prehistory in the seventh edition, posthumously published in 1913, of his classic *Prehistoric Times* (1865).[31]

Perhaps for readers of *All the Year Round*, such mists had first been parted by the review of the *Antiquity of Man*, in which Charles Lyell argued that human "antiquity is . . . much greater than chronologists have hitherto supposed" ("How Old Are We?", 37). Those readers of *All the Year Round* who might have turned from "How Old Are We?" to the *Antiquity of Man* itself would have found in its pages not only an argument for the fact of human prehistory, but the demonstration of a methodology for reconstructing the past, a methodology to be replicated in detective fiction, particularly in *Edwin Drood*.

From the start Lyell understood the reluctance of those like Thomas Wright to accept human prehistory: "I can only plead that a discovery which seems to contradict the general tenor of previous investigations is naturally received with much hesitation."[32] Such hesitation was both religious and psychological in its basis. But it also reflected the nature of the evidence with which Lyell had to work. Earlier in the *Principles of Geology* (1830–33) and here again in the *Antiquity of Man*, Lyell stressed "the fragmentary nature of all geological annals" that he examined, producing gaps "in the regular sequence of geological monuments bearing on the past history of Man" (*Antiquity*, pp. 208, 207). Both the geological and archaeological records become an "interrupted series of consecutive documents" so that it is difficult to construct "any thing like a connected chain of history" (p. 208). As he pursued the evidence that he needed in "the dark recesses of underground vaults and tunnels, which may have served as places of refuge or sepulture to a succession of human beings and wild animals" (p. 94), Lyell became a self-conscious detective in a mystery novel: at one point, in discussing the effects of glacial action, he observed how difficult it was to read the geological and archaeological records "without having the ice-clue in his mind" (p. 139). In interpreting the incomplete annals that constitute such records, he dealt with fragmentary evidence, even with figurative pages erased by glacial action. He confronted the problem posed by the skepticism of Thomas Wright who saw worked flints as forgeries, or of those others who dismissed them as accidents of natural processes. Perhaps more daunting, Lyell acknowledged the challenge of the "negative fact" (p. 151): all too often, there were no fossilized human skeletons, whole or fragmentary, to be found in association with flint instruments and with fossilized remains of extinct mammals. Repeating observations in the *Principles*, he said: "Instead of its being part of the plan of nature to store up enduring records of a large number of the individual plants and animals which have lived on the [earth's] surface, it seems to be her chief care to provide the means of disencumbering the habitable areas . . . of those myriads of solid skeletons of animals" (p. 146).

Here Lyell struck a note to be heard throughout the *Antiquity of Man*: "in our retrospective survey, we have been obliged, for the sake of proceeding from the known to the less known, to reverse the natural order of history, and to treat of the newer before the older" (p. 108). With these words Lyell clarified the practices of the geologist, the paleontologist, and the archaeologist who move from fragmentary evidence in the present to a complex reconstruction of the past. He set forth the program of the *Antiquity of Man* as he discussed flint tools, fossilized animal bones, and geological formations to demonstrate to the skeptical the reality of human prehistory. He also alluded to the *Principles of Geology* in which he had sought to demonstrate the nature of geological changes over vast periods of time: "As examples of such [geological] changes . . . [which] have become accessible to human observation, I have adduced the strata near Naples in which the Temple of Serapis at Pozzuoli was entombed" (p. 45).

In referring to the Temple of Serapis, Lyell implied that his discussion of the temple in volume one of the *Principles of Geology* had become a model for the practice of the historical disciplines of geology and archaeology. He did so with confidence, relying upon the authority of William Whewell who had turned in his three-volume *History of the Inductive Sciences* (1837) to Lyell's discussion of the Temple of Serapis as exemplary of "those researches in which the object is, to ascend from the present state of things to a more ancient condition."[33] Whewell went on to clarify the nature of the "palætiological sciences." They involve

> inquiries concerning the monuments of the art and labour of distant ages; . . . examinations into the origin and early progress of states and cities, customs, and languages; as well as . . . researches concerning the causes and formations of mountains and rocks, the imbedding of fossils in strata, and their elevation from the bottom of the ocean. All these speculations are connected by this bond, – that they endeavour to ascend to a past state of things, by the aid of the evidence of the present.
>
> (*History*, III, 482)

Implicitly, philology and historical archaeology offered a methodology and a characteristic language for the geologist and paleontologist who became readers of literal and figurative documents. For Whewell, Georges Cuvier became the representative figure, " 'the geologist [as] an antiquary of a new order' ": "The organic fossils which occur in the rock, and the medals which we find in the ruins of ancient cities, are to be studied in a similar spirit and for a similar purpose. Indeed, it is not always easy to know where the task of the geologist ends, and that of the antiquary begins" (III, 482). The study of the history of the earth and that of the history of humankind merge into one coherent discipline governed by similar practices.

Whewell proceeded by observing, "It is more than a mere fanciful description, to say that in languages, customs, forms of society, political institutions, we see a number of formations superimposed upon one another, each of which is, for the most part, an assemblage of fragments . . . of the preceding condition" (*History*, III, 484). The "palætiological sciences" – those "sciences [which] might be properly called *historical*" (III, 486) – study a past embodied in the form of "the ruined temple [that] may exhibit the traces of time in its changed level, and sea-worn columns; and thus the antiquarian of the earth may be brought into the very middle of the domain belonging to the antiquarian of art" (III, 482–83). The temple to which Whewell alluded was Lyell's "temple of

Jupiter Serapis, near Puzzuoli" (III, 483). In invoking Lyell's discussion of this temple, he conferred upon it the status of a classic, the model for the reconstruction of the past. However, Lyell's account of the temple was to become the foundation for a subtle, yet potentially radical, historiography beyond the ken of the conventional antiquarian or even the sophisticated natural theologian. His discussion of the Temple of Serapis was to become an epistemological and narratological tour de force, an exemplum for the practice of the historical disciplines that, nevertheless, revealed the indeterminate nature of the reconstructions such disciplines offer.

Significantly, the frontispiece to volume one of the *Principles* was not an illustration of some geological wonder, as was the case in volumes two and three, but an engraving of the Temple of Jupiter Serapis, a Roman ruin on the Bay of Baiæ in the vicinity of Naples and the once-buried cities of Herculaneum and Pompeii. The frontispiece announced Lyell's strategy: throughout the three volumes of the *Principles* he would turn to philological and archaeological figures of speech, illustrating how to read the history of the inanimate and animate worlds. As a monument to a former age, the Temple of Serapis was to be approached as a figurative document inscribed by nature's own hand. Its periodic subsidence beneath and re-elevation above the waters of the Mediterranean demonstrated the unending cycle of subsidence and elevation that for Lyell prevails over the earth's surface, a cycle that refutes scriptural literalists and British catastrophists: his history of the temple was designed to document the processes of geological change that, within an appropriate time scheme, explained the submergence of continents and the elevation of the Alps and the Andes without recourse to catastrophic events or divine intervention.[34]

Before turning to his discussion of the Temple of Jupiter Serapis, Lyell observed: "Buildings and cities submerged for a time beneath seas or lakes, and covered with sedimentary deposits, must, in some places, have been re-elevated to considerable heights above the level of the ocean."[35] This, in part, had been the fate of the ruin whose history Lyell set out to reconstruct. All that was to be seen of it in 1828 were three erect, but broken columns, the pavement that supported them, and the remnants of toppled columns of African breccia and granite. From these remains Lyell reconstructed the original edifice: "The original plan of the building could be traced distinctly; it was of a quandrangular form, seventy feet in diameter, and the roof had been supported by forty-six noble columns" (*Principles*, I, 452–53). Yet Lyell acknowledged an unresolved issue: "Many antiquaries have entered into elaborate discussions

as to the deity to which this edifice was consecrated; but Signor Carelli
. . . endeavours to show that all the religious edifices of Greece were of
a form essentially different – that the building, therefore, could never
have been a temple – that it corresponded to the public bathing-rooms
at many of our watering-places" (I, 453). The plan of the original building may be reconstructed, but its real nature and use may, perhaps,
never be determined. All such remains become the subject of dispute;
interpretations must rely on other evidence that the antiquarian or the
archaeologist chooses to bring to bear upon the problem. For even if
the building were a temple, so Carelli claimed, "it could not have been
dedicated to Serapis, – the worship of the Egyptian god being strictly
prohibited at the time when this edifice was in use, by the senate of
Rome." Nonetheless, Lyell wryly deferred to the antiquarians, "desig-
nat[ing] this valuable relic of antiquity by its generally received name"
(I, 453).

The dispute over the name of the structure and its use alluded to
the heated debates over the status and meaning of fossils, whether they
were to be seen as sports of nature or the remains of dead, perhaps
extinct, organisms.[36] Yet Lyell's archaeological analogy pointed to the
elusive nature of all fragmentary evidence. He transformed the Temple
of Jupiter Serapis into an incomplete text to be deciphered and read as
he turned "to consider the memorials of physical changes, inscribed
on the three standing columns in most legible characters by the hand
of nature" (*Principles*, I, 453). He then proceeded to interpret the hieroglyphic cavities produced in the columns by marine mollusks when the
temple was partially submerged in the Mediterranean. From his reading of the various signs on the columns, Lyell constructed a relative
chronology of the subsidence and re-elevation of the coast on which
the temple stood: "as the temple could not have been built originally
at the bottom of the sea, it must have first sunk down below the waves,
and afterwards have been elevated" (I, 454). Just as marine fossils atop
mountains attest to the origin of the mountains beneath the sea in ages
long past, the history of the temple offers an index to the "alternate
elevation and depression of the bed of the sea and the adjoining coast
during the course of eighteen centuries" (I, 455).

But a relative chronology cannot be satisfying. Lyell had to establish
an absolute chronology for the subsidence and re-elevation of the
Temple of Serapis in order to illustrate further his own vision of cyclical geologic time and the incremental workings of geologic change. He
turned to a variety of texts, the first of which was the temple itself: "It
appears, that in the Atrium of the Temple of Serapis, inscriptions were

found in which Septimus Severus and Marcus Aurelius record their labours in adorning it with precious marbles" (*Principles*, I, 456). If the temple had originally reflected the influence of the Greek colonizers of Pompeii and Herculaneum, the Romans of "the third century of our era" had adapted it for their own uses, leaving their Latin inscriptions for later generations to read and puzzle over. Lyell now invoked literal documents, some to be seen as "the imperfect annals of the dark ages" (I, 456), before the emergence of a truly historical awareness. Written perhaps in medieval Latin, they recorded events in 1198 and 1488 which caused the subsidence beneath the Mediterranean of the tract upon which the temple was built. Lyell then turned to letters written, presumably in Italian, by Signor Falconi and Pietro Giacomo di Toledo that recorded the 1538 eruption of Monte Nuovo and the re-elevation of the sunken coast and the appearance, so Falconi wrote, of *"the newly discovered ruins"* (I, 457) of the temple.

As he proceeded, Lyell necessarily relied on documents recorded by other antiquarians, written in different centuries, presumably in two languages and perhaps in a variety of dialects; some of the documents – the letter by Pietro Giacomo di Toledo – did not even mention the temple itself. From these documents of varying reliability Lyell created a context for the figurative text of the Temple of Serapis. The history of the temple – if temple it had ever been – remains a narrative, chrono-logically and causally ordered, about an edifice whose nature and uses throughout the centuries remain undetermined and, finally, beyond determination. No one can more fully relish the nature of his interpre-tations than Lyell himself. In concluding his discussion of the temple, Lyell added:

> In 1828 excavations were made below the marble pavement of the Temple of Serapis, and another costly pavement of mosaic was found, at the depth of five feet or more below the other. The existence of these two pavements at different levels seems clearly to imply some subsidence previously to all the changes already alluded to. . . . But to these and other circumstances bearing on the history of the Temple antecedently to the revolutions already explained, we shall not refer at present, trusting that future investigations will set them in a clearer light.
>
> (*Principles*, I, 458)

Such investigations might reveal yet another pavement beneath the two already discovered. The study of the temple may well produce an infinite regress, revealing pavements beneath pavements, figurative texts beneath figurative texts, transforming the Temple of Jupiter Serapis, years before the *Suspiria de Profundis* (1845), into a De Quinceian palimpsest, awaiting future revelations.[37]

The *Antiquity of Man* was to become Lyell's discussion of the Temple of Jupiter Serapis writ large. In its pages Dickens – and perhaps those readers of the celebratory "How Old Are We?" who turned to it – would have found, not only a model for William Whewell's "palætiological sciences," but for the various acts of detection that occur in *The Mystery of Edwin Drood*. In Lyell's *Principles*, marine fossils and cavities in the columns of the Temple of Serapis became figurative signs. In the *Antiquity of Man* worked flints and other human artifacts also became a figurative writing found in "the pages of the peaty record" (*Antiquity*, p. 112) or in bone caves transformed into "sepulchral vault[s]" (p. 192). They offered fragmentary evidence by which to reconstruct a human past before written records. Once again Lyell encountered the inherent ambiguity of the evidence that he presented: for worked flints, "so irregular in form as to cause the unpractised eye to doubt whether they afford unmistakable evidence of design" (p. 379), might be dismissed by those like Thomas Wright who were opposed to the idea of human prehistory. Even if someone were to accept such flints as human artifacts, there remained the vexing fact that all too often Lyell found such relics only in association with the fossil remains of extinct elephants, rhinoceroses, and cave-bears. There were no human skeletal remains, intact or fragmentary, to demonstrate the coexistence of human beings with extinct mammals.

Inevitably, Lyell observed, "the thread of our inquiry into the history of the animate creation, as well as of man, is abruptly cut short" (*Antiquity*, p. 206). Geology and archaeology lead into a maze: there is no narrative thread by which such historical disciplines may penetrate to an ever-receding center.[38] This is the difficulty with which any practitioner of a palaetiological science is faced. William Whewell recognized that such disciplines that "travel back towards the origin, whether of inert things or of the works of man, . . . treat of events as connected by the thread of time and causation" (*History*, III, 488). But the figurative maze that Whewell and Lyell invoked may be transformed into the labyrinth of human motivation and consciousness. For Whewell the "palætiological sciences," dealing with "the past causes of events," lead to a "moral palætiology," the study of the human in a larger sense. Such disciplines offer "a ready passage from physiology to psychology, from physics to metaphysics. . . . we are, at a different point, carried from the world of matter to the world of thought and feeling, – from things to men" (III, 486–87).

The historical disciplines provide a ready passage into the maze that constitutes the heart of detective fiction, the labyrinth of human motivation and consciousness, to be negotiated by Whewell's "thread of time and causation." It is the maze into which the characters in *Edwin Drood* move when they attempt to reconstruct the events that have led up to the disappearance of Drood on the stormy Christmas morning when he has last been seen by Neville Landless. All of those concerned in the fate of Edwin Drood, John Jasper among them, become practitioners of a "moral palætiology," amateur detectives engaged in a geological and archaeological endeavor that will lead to those literal and figurative annals that Lyell consulted in the *Antiquity of Man*, writing with a full awareness of their inadequacy and of those, like Thomas Wright, who were reluctant to accept the fact of human prehistory.

The elaborate philological and archaeological figures of speech to which both Lyell and Darwin resorted in their various books suggest the problematic nature of any historical discipline working with fragmentary evidence from another time. They can return us to Mr. Grewgious contemplating the stars: for "none of us so much as know our letters in the stars yet – or seem likely to, in this state of existence – and few languages can be read until their alphabets are mastered" (*Drood*, p. 160). The future remains closed to the characters in the world of *Edwin Drood*; for them, the past exists in the form of mutilated texts written in languages whose alphabets are difficult if not impossible to master. Living in an unspecified decade after Lyell's *Principles of Geology*, but prior to the publication of the *Origin of Species* and the *Antiquity of Man*, they become engaged in attempts to reconstruct the past, to arrive at a history that has been forged "among the mighty store of wonderful chains that are for ever forging, day and night, in the vast iron-works of time and circumstance" (p. 118).[39]

Perhaps the one missing link in the chain exists in the form of the articles – the gold watch, the chain, and the shirt-pin – that Septimus Crisparkle has found in Cloisterham Weir. The articles, especially the watch engraved with the initials, E.D., become figurative monuments from the realms of geology and archaeology by which to reconstruct a temporal chain of events. Like the archaeologist, the would-be detectives of Cloisterham confront a fragmentary text, akin to the worked flints found in association with mammal bones, but unaccompanied by human remains: for Edwin Drood's personal effects do not lead to the recovery of his corpse. In spite of the efforts of John Jasper and others in dredging the river, nothing is to be found: "All the livelong day, the search went on; upon the river, . . . upon the muddy and rushy shore. . . . Even at night, the river was specked with lanterns, and lurid with fires." The searchers explore "far-off creeks, . . . remote shingly causeways near the sea, and lonely points off which there [is] a race of water . . . still no trace of Edwin Drood revisit[s] the light of the sun" (*Drood*, p. 136): he is lost in Edward Robinson's "long night of oblivion."

The people of Cloisterham are met with the fact of negative evidence, unable to prove that Edwin Drood is actually dead, the victim of an accident or of a violent attack. Yet with a parochialism that barely masks their racism, the townsfolk can be manipulated by John Jasper and led by Mr. Sapsea's distrust of Neville Landless's "Un-English complexion" (*Drood*, p. 135) to turn their suspicions upon the young man so recently arrived from Ceylon, an island associated in the British imagination with their own version of the Indian subcontinent.[40] With John Jasper's help Mr. Sapsea has created a context, one informed by the values of British imperialism, in which a collective attempt to reconstruct the past occurs. As detectives, the people of Cloisterham become unwitting practitioners of William Whewell's "moral palætiology." They first try to establish a relative chronology and, then, an absolute one with causal implications. To account for what *must* be Drood's jewelry, the townspeople create a narrative akin to that offered by Lyell in his discussion of the Temple of Jupiter Serapis. They organize the various meetings between Drood and Neville Landless, beginning with the night on which the two have almost come to blows, into a coherent chronology. Ignorant of John Jasper's obsession with Rosa Bud, they postulate a beginning that is necessarily arbitrary and suspect, as elusive as the mosaic pavements of the Temple of Serapis.

Into their account the characters weave Septimus Crisparkle's report of Landless's admiration for Rosa Bud, as well as the information about the mutual decision to break their engagement, with Drood's plan, according to Rosa, to await the arrival of Mr. Grewgious before leaving Cloisterham. These events preceded the Christmas Eve dinner attended by Jasper, Drood, and Landless that led, if Landless is to be believed, to the midnight walk along the river and the parting of the two young men at the Minor Canon's door, after which Drood was to return to the Gate House rooms of Jasper. When the town jeweler identifies the engraved watch as the "one he had wound and set for Edwin Drood, at twenty minutes past two" on Christmas Eve, any gaps in the narrative would seem to be filled:

it had run down, before being cast into the water; and it was the jeweller's positive opinion that it had never been re-wound. This would justify the hypothesis that the watch was taken from [Drood] not long after he left Mr. Jasper's house at midnight, in company with the last person seen with him, and that it had been thrown away after being retained some hours.

(Drood, p. 144)

The incomplete chronology would now seem to be complete, without any missing links in the chain of events. It would seem no longer to be a relative chronology, but an absolute one, crucial events associated with specific times. As detectives the people of Cloisterham have engaged in "researches in which the object is, to ascend from the present state of things to a more ancient condition, from which the present is derived by intelligible causes" (*History*, III, 481).

But the hypothesis, like one in any of William Whewell's palaetiological sciences, remains at best an interpretation of fragmentary evidence, including Drood's personal effects and the negative fact that there is no corpse. The account has been worked out within the context of a provincial fear of the foreign Neville Landless who becomes the object of the prejudices of British imperialism: "Before coming to England he had caused to be whipped to death sundry 'Natives' – nomadic persons, encamping now in Asia, now in Africa, now in the West Indies, and now at the North Pole – vaguely supposed in Cloisterham to be always black, always of great virtue, always calling themselves Me, and everybody else Massa or Missie" (*Drood*, p. 143). The passage may well satirize a belief in the noble savage that is condescending and misconceived in a time before the Great Mutiny of 1857–58 and the Jamaican uprising of 1865. Yet it suggests how such parochialism may become transformed so that the apparently submissive native, "supposed . . . to be always black," may be demonized into a savage brute who must be controlled by agents of the Crown for his own good.[41]

Such prejudices become pervasive, a "maze of nonsense" (*Drood*, p. 135), obstructing other possible interpretations of the evidence that the townspeople might consider. So, it is not clear how the good people of Cloisterham would respond to information that they might dismiss as untrue or unthinkable. They have produced an account satisfying to everyone but the laconic Mr. Grewgious and those remaining loyal to Neville Landless, including Mr. Crisparkle and Neville's twin sister, Helena. From the start Helena Landless has understood John Jasper's obsession with Rosa Bud and the extremes to which it might lead. But she is from Ceylon, possessed of an awareness quite foreign to the world of Cloisterham. Grewgious, alone, has watched as Jasper has collapsed into "a heap of torn and miry clothes" (p. 138) upon learning of the broken engagement after the futile search for Drood's body. Perhaps Grewgious connects that episode with the fact that the ring he has entrusted to Drood is not among the personal articles that Crisparkle has recovered from Cloisterham Weir. He may be able to use such a negative fact to create an alternative account of Drood's disappearance.

But in its fragmentary form *Edwin Drood* provides information that neither Helena Landless, Mr. Grewgious, nor anyone else currently in Cloisterham possesses, including that old codger, Mr. Datchery, who arrives in town to conduct yet another investigation into Drood's disappearance. No one knows of the chance meeting on Christmas Eve, before he joins Landless and Jasper, between Drood and the old woman who only later will be identified by the young urchin, Deputy as " 'Er Royal Highness the Princess Puffer" (*Drood*, p. 214). As he talks with the woman, Drood notes that "a curious film passes over her, . . . 'Like Jack that night!' " (p. 126) during the dinner at the Gate House when Jasper has confessed that he has been "taking opium for a pain – an agony – that sometimes overcomes [him]" (p. 10). Drood learns that the old woman smokes opium too and that Ned is "a threatened name. A dangerous name." Yet he resolves to say nothing of the meeting to Jack, "who alone calls him Ned" (p. 127), until the following day. Drood has the opportunity to play detective, to engage in an act of moral palaetiology. No one can know if he creates his own harrowing narrative out of the fragments of evidence that have been presented by coincidence to him: a narrative by which to glimpse Jasper's complex motives and his ambiguous passion for Rosa Bud. He may well be prepared for his return to the Gate House after his midnight ramble along the river with Neville Landless. If Jasper awaits Drood's return, under the influence of the opium to which he turns for relief, no one can reconstruct the bizarre midnight struggle, if any, that may have occurred in Jasper's rooms.[42]

For the knowledge to which acts of detection in *The Mystery of Edwin Drood* drive is never of the future, but only of the past: in the universe of Darwin's *Origin of Species* and of Lyell's *Antiquity of Man*, such knowledge involves the reconstruction of events not witnessed, always based upon fragmentary and ambiguous evidence. In the course of the novel, Edwin Drood has had the opportunity to engage in a form of moral palaetiology, to play detective. But so too has the reader who has been invited to scrutinize and to rewrite the generally accepted account arrived at by the people of Cloisterham. In this way *Edwin Drood* engages us in the act of constructing interpretations, internalizing the practices and the worldview of those historical disciplines that can be seen to culminate, to the dismay of Charles Lyell and defenders of Natural Theology, in the *Origin of Species*. Darwin demanded of his readers an understanding of the nature of the historical imagination, as the unsigned 1860 review of the *Origin* in *All the Year Round* recognized. The reviewer had knowingly alluded to a passage central to Darwin's long argument:

> When we no longer look at an organic being as a savage looks at a ship, as at something wholly beyond his comprehension; when we regard every production of nature as one which has had a history; when we contemplate every complex structure as the summing up of many contrivances, each useful to the possessor, nearly in the same way as when we look at any great mechanical invention as the summing up of the labour, the experience, the reason, and even the blunders of numerous workmen; ... how far more interesting ... will the study of natural history become!
>
> (*Origin*, p. 456)

With these words, as the reviewer of the *Origin* understood, Darwin had renounced the world of Paley's *Natural Theology* (1802): we are now all to be seen as creatures of history in a universe without design.

In this context *Edwin Drood* offers a performance of how to read the world. The methodology suggested in the novel and the worldview implicit in it can be grasped through the reader's participation in an act of interpretation demanded by the disappearance of Edwin Drood and by the fragmentary status of a novel that Dickens did not live to complete. The novel dramatizes a method of making sense out of apparently indecipherable events, of ordering into narrative form that which can disconcert, puzzle, even paralyze. In a universe no longer intelligible according to a literal reading of scripture or to William Paley's Natural Theology, the narratives of the historical disciplines initiate new paradigms in which many of us continue to find solace.[43]

V

But, as *The Mystery of Edwin Drood* suggests, such solace is illusory, always to be tempered by an awareness of the stubborn ambiguity of the fragmentary evidence with which any practitioner of an historical discipline must work. Like the geological and archaeological monuments for which it comes to stand, the Temple of Jupiter Serapis invites and resists interpretation, always pointing to elusive mysteries at the center of history. In his movement toward an uneasy acceptance of Charles Darwin's transmutation theory, Charles Lyell returned in the *Antiquity of Man* to the tenuous nature of the evidence with which the geologist and the paleontologist must work: "When we reflect, therefore, on the fractional state of the annals which are handed down to us, and how little even these have as yet been studied, we may wonder that so many geologists should attribute . . . every gap in the past history of the organic world, to catastrophes and convulsions . . . or to leaps made by the creational force from species to species" (*Antiquity*, p. 449). Here Lyell renewed his attack upon the catastrophists, even as he hinted at a rejection of the doctrine of special creation. He knew that the fact of negative evidence could not be used to refute Darwinism, even as it could not be used to deny the reality of human antiquity.[44]

Yet in the *Antiquity of Man* Lyell failed to follow the logic of his own argument and to heed his own warnings both about the misuse of the negative fact – the fossils to confirm the Darwinian hypothesis might well be found – and, more significantly, about the dangers of teleological speculations. He cited Darwin: "Progression . . . is not a necessary accompaniment of variation and natural selection. . . . One of the principal claims of Mr. Darwin's theory to acceptance is, that it enables us to dispense with a law of progression as a necessary accompaniment of variation" (*Antiquity*, p. 412). Nevertheless, Lyell concluded the *Antiquity of Man* by repeating Asa Gray's claim that the doctrine of Variation and Natural Selection could not weaken the foundations of Natural Theology, as he engaged in – a teleological speculation: "the supposed introduction into the earth at successive geological periods of life, – sensation, – instinct, – the intelligence of the higher mammalia bordering on reason, – and lastly the improvable reason of Man himself, presents us with a picture of the ever-increasing dominion of mind over matter" (p. 506).

Ironically, Lyell himself anticipated those who might yield to a "materialistic tendency" (*Antiquity*, p. 506) and who might see in such a progression, real or imagined, an inevitable development informed only by natural law. In 1863 he could foresee the evolutionary anthropology that, in the books of E. B. Tylor (1832–1917) and James Frazer (1854–1941), was to promote a purely naturalistic account based upon a Comtean, rather than a Darwinian, vision of human development.[45]

In *Primitive Culture* (1871) and in *The Golden Bough* (1890), Tylor and Frazer were to remain oblivious to warnings about the inadequacy of the annals – geological, archaeological, or anthropological – upon which any historical discipline must rely. In their confident rationalism Tylor and, later, Frazer ignored the possibility that progression is not a "necessary accompaniment" of historical change. In the opening chapter of *Primitive Culture* Tylor established the assumptions that form the foundation of his classical evolutionism:

> The condition of culture among the various societies of mankind, in so far as it is capable of being investigated on general principles, is a subject apt for the study of laws of human thought and action. On the one hand, the uniformity which so largely pervades civilization may be ascribed . . . to the uniform action of uniform causes: while on the other hand its various grades may be regarded as stages of development or evolution, each the outcome of previous history, and about to do its proper part in shaping the history of the future.[46]

With his Eurocentric parochialism Tylor – and Frazer after him – created a hierarchy of societies, each representing a stage in the evolutionary progress toward the reign of the positive. It was with remarkable self-confidence that Tylor concluded *Primitive Culture*:

> To impress men's minds with a doctrine of development, will lead them in all honour to their ancestors to continue the progressive work of past ages, to continue it the more vigorously because light has increased in the world, and where barbaric hordes groped blindly, cultured men can often move onward with clear view. It is a harsher, and at times even painful, office of ethnography to expose the remains of crude old culture which have passed into harmful super-stition, and to mark these out for destruction. Yet this work . . . is not less urgently needful for the good of mankind. Thus, active at once in aiding progress and in removing hindrance, the science of culture is essentially a reformer's science.
>
> (II, 453)

E. B. Tylor, the Comtean positivist with a "materialistic tendency," returned to the teleology of an antiquarian like Thomas Wright who offered in *The Celt, the Roman, and the Saxon* a providential history of Britain. As the practitioner of yet another historical discipline, Tylor reconstructed the barbaric past, even as it supposedly persisted into the present in the form of those savages and peasant folk whom he treated as living fossils. In doing so, Tylor relied on documentary evidence, often provided by the agents of the British empire, that he failed to treat with appropriate skepticism.

Appearing in 1870, in the year before the publication of *Primitive Culture*, Dickens's *The Mystery of Edwin Drood* repeated the warnings of Lyell's *Antiquity of Man*, hinting always at the unreliability of fragmentary evidence found in literal and figurative documents; it anticipated the dangers of a naive teleology, whether that of the fictitious Mr. Sapsea or the real-life E. B. Tylor, ever in the grips of an unexamined provincialism and an undisguised racism. The fragmentary novel reveals that it is impossible to know the ends of history: it points to the conditional nature of all historical knowledge through an awareness of "the fractional state of the annals which are handed down to us" (*Antiquity*, p. 449) and of the perils of self-serving teleologies. In the novel the Nuns' House has become a Dickensian version of the Temple of Jupiter Serapis. With its legendary and elusive origins, it endures in and through time, accruing new uses and new meanings that never quite pass away, but that elude understanding. The novel *will* call attention to the limits of historical knowledge, to the "little Hall [in Staple Inn], with a little lantern in its roof: to what obstructive purposes devoted, and at whose expense, *this history knoweth not*" (*Drood*, p. 88, emphasis added). The novel *will* remind us of the reality of chance and necessity, the unpredictable nature of the future, as Edwin Drood and Rosa Bud suddenly decide to end their engagement, to "change to brother and sister from this day forth" (p. 114). At that moment Drood has in his possession the ring of Rosa's dead mother, entrusted to him by Mr. Grewgious. He decides not to tell Rosa of the ring and to return it to Grewgious upon his next visit to Cloisterham. Decisions that could not have been anticipated will produce consequences that are never to be known: for "among the mighty store of wonderful chains that are for ever forging, day and night, in the vast iron-works of time and circumstance, there was one chain forged in the moment of that small conclusion, riveted to the foundations of heaven and earth, and gifted with invincible force to hold and drag" (p. 118).

Charles Dickens was himself to become caught up in an unpredictable chain of events, "for ever forging, day and night, in the vast iron-works of time and circumstance." On the evening of 8 June 1870, having "put a flourish to the end of the last chapter of the sixth number of *The Mystery of Edwin Drood*, exactly the halfway point of the novel," he was stricken at dinner and collapsed, unconscious.[47] With his death the following evening, he bequeathed to us the fragmentary *Edwin Drood*, a testament to the "fractured state of the annals which are handed down to us." Akin to fossil remains, to worked flints, and to ruined edifices inscribed in foreign characters that may defy translation, the novel dramatizes the difficulties – epistemological and narratological – upon which it meditates. Whatever has happened to Edwin Drood in the early hours of that Christmas morning – whether he has been murdered, suffered some fatal or deeply injurious accident, or spirited himself away – remains beyond our capacity to know. His disappearance poses an archaeological mystery as puzzling as that posed by the Temple of Jupiter Serapis or by Cloisterham itself, that ancient city "so abounding in vestiges of monastic graves," a city in which "fragments of old wall, saint's chapel, chapter-house, convent, and monastery, have got incongruously or obstructively built into many of its houses and gardens" (*Drood*, p. 14).

Each of us who reads *The Mystery of Edwin Drood* becomes a hypothetical visitor to a figurative Cloisterham, now an archaeological curiosity like the "dead and buried cities that it is one of the labours of the living in our day to disentomb": it can only offer us – "News from the Dead." Like Belzoni's Abu-Simbel, Layard's Nimrud, and Dickens's Rome, with the "hieroglyphic-covered obelisk" in the square fronting a "haughty church" (*Pictures*, p. 397), Cloisterham will challenge any would-be excavator. The buildings of Edwin Drood's time may no longer stand in their entirety. Perhaps the monument erected by the honorable Mr. Sapsea to the memory of a wife wise and humble enough to have married him is no longer intact; it may be in fragments, its inscription defaced by time, barely discernible, and written in an alphabet and a grammar of a dead language. Such inscriptions become enigmatic signs for a traveler to contemplate, someone not unlike the inquisitive Mr. Davis of *Pictures from Italy*. Dickens's fellow Englishman

> had a slow curiosity constantly devouring him, which prompted him to do extraordinary things, such as taking the covers off urns in tombs, and looking in at the ashes as if they were pickles – and tracing out inscriptions with the ferrule of his umbrella, and saying, with intense thoughtfulness, "Here's a B you see, and there's a R, and this is the way we goes on in; is it?"
>
> (p. 378)

Poking at inscriptions he can barely decipher, disappearing into sepulchers, Mr. Davis serves as an apt warning to anyone who would definitively resolve the mysteries posed by *The Mystery of Edwin Drood* and by those fractured annals, literal and figurative, left to us by the hand of time. We should never forget the comic anxiety of Mrs. Davis and her party that Mr. Davis might well become lost in the labyrinth of his antiquarian preoccupations: "This caused them to scream for him, in the strangest places, and at the most improper seasons. And when he came, slowly emerging out of some sepulchre or other, like a peaceful Ghoul, saying 'Here I am!' Mrs. Davis invariably replied, 'You'll be buried alive in a foreign country, Davis, and it's no use trying to prevent you!'" (p. 378). Fair warning to all practitioners of those historical disciplines to which a detective novel like the fragmentary *Edwin Drood* introduces us, for the past is, indeed, a foreign country where "they do things differently."[48]

Part Three
Arthur Conan Doyle

it possible that I am really in danger from so dark a cause? You don't believe it, do you, Watson?"

"No, no."

"And yet it was one thing to laugh about it in London, and it is another to stand out here in the darkness of the moor and to hear such a cry as that. And my uncle! There was the footprint of the hound beside him as he lay. It all fits together. I don't think that I am a coward, Watson, but that sound seemed to freeze my very blood. Feel my hand!"

It was as cold as a block of marble.

"You'll be all right to-morrow."

"I don't think I'll get that cry out of my head. What do you advise that we do now?"

"Shall we turn back?"

"No, by thunder; we have come out to get our man, and we will do it. We are after the convict, and a hell-hound, as likely as not, after us. Come on! We'll see it through if all the fiends of the pit were loose upon the moor."

We stumbled slowly along in the darkness, with the black loom of the craggy hills around us, and the yellow speck of light burning steadily in front. There is nothing so deceptive as the distance of a light upon a pitch-dark night, and sometimes the glimmer seemed to be far away upon the horizon and sometimes it might have been within a few yards of us. But at last we could see whence it came, and then we knew that we were indeed very close. A guttering candle was stuck in a crevice of the rocks which flanked it on each side so as to keep the wind from it, and also to prevent it from being visible, save in the direction of Baskerville Hall. A boulder of granite concealed our approach, and crouching behind it we gazed over it at

the signal light. It was strange to see this single candle burning there in the middle of the moor, with no sign of life near it—just the one straight yellow flame and the gleam of the rock on each side of it.

"What shall we do now?" whispered Sir Henry.

"Wait here. He must be near his light. Let us see if we can get a glimpse of him."

The words were hardly out of my mouth when we both saw him. Over the rocks, in the crevice of which the candle burned, there was thrust out an evil yellow face, a terrible animal face, all seamed and scored with vile

"I SAW THE FIGURE OF A MAN UPON THE TOR."

passions. Foul with mire, with a bristling beard, and hung with matted hair, it might well have belonged to one of those old savages who dwelt in the burrows on the hill-sides. The light beneath him was reflected in his small, cunning eyes, which peered fiercely to right and left through the darkness, like a crafty and savage animal who has heard the steps of the hunters.

Something had evidently aroused his sus-

"A Man upon the Tor," *The Hound of the Baskervilles, The Strand Magazine,* December 1901, drawn by Sidney Paget.

5
Sherlock Holmes and "The Book of Life"

> We are now in the dreary desert which separates two ages of Belief. A new era is at hand.
>
> Windwood Reade, *The Martyrdom of Man* (1872)

I

In the lives and in the fictions of Edgar Allan Poe (1809–1849), Charles Dickens (1812–1870), and Arthur Conan Doyle (1859–1930), it is possible to see the aptness of the claim of the biologist, Ernst Mayr that "the Darwinian revolution affected every thinking man [and woman]": "A world view developed by anyone after 1859 was by necessity quite different from any world view formed prior to 1859."[1] There are those, of course, who would dispute the notion of such a revolution. But we can see in the stories of Poe and in Dickens's *Bleak House* (1852–53) their attempts to come to terms imaginatively with various challenges to scriptural literalism and Natural Theology before 1859. Writing after the publication of the *Origin of Species*, Dickens could explore fully in *The Mystery of Edwin Drood* (1870) the implications of a universe denied divinity and design. But it was Doyle, born in 1859, who was to come of age in the aftermath of the publication of the *Origin* and the triumph, for some, of a uniformitarian science that had extended its reach from physics and geology into the realm of living organisms. Beyond would lie the ultimate domain, that of human consciousness.[2]

As an adolescent, Doyle was to experience during his years at Edinburgh University that figurative convulsion to which Darwin had alluded in his account of the Chilean earthquake of February 1835 when "the world, the very emblem of all that is solid, [had] moved beneath

[Darwin's] feet like a crust over a fluid."[3] Darwin's words can be seen to have their echo in Doyle's *Memories and Adventures* (1924) as he recalled his loss of faith during his years as a young medical student in the 1870s:

> both from my reading and from my studies, I found that the foun-
> dations not only of Roman Catholicism but of the whole Christian
> faith, as presented to me in nineteenth century theology, were so
> weak that my mind could not build upon them. It is to be remem-
> bered that these were the years when Huxley, [John] Tyndall, Darwin,
> Herbert Spencer and John Stuart Mill were our chief philosophers,
> and that even the man in the street felt the strong sweeping current
> of their thought, while to the young student, eager and impression-
> able, it was overwhelming.[4]

In response to the loss of his Christian faith, Doyle was to find a new foundation in various proponents and defenders of Darwinian evolu-tion and, later, to render that worldview imaginatively in the various adventures of Sherlock Holmes.

In his memoirs Doyle, however, did not mention Winwood Reade's *The Martyrdom of Man* (1872), a book that was committed to the erosion of Christian belief in any form. But, in *The Sign of Four* (1890), the second novella to deal with Sherlock Holmes, there is a passing refer-ence to Reade and to his *Martyrdom of Man*. Holmes and Dr. Watson wait with Inspector Athelney Jones for the steam launch *Aurora* that is to carry Jonathan Small and Tonga, the Andaman Islander, out of England to safety, a safety that they are never to enjoy. In a shipyard across the Thames they see workers "swarm[ing] ... in the gaslight." Holmes observes: "Dirty-looking rascals, but I suppose every one has some little immortal spark concealed about him. ... A strange enigma is man!"[5] Watson muses that "someone calls [man] a soul concealed in an animal." Holmes responds, "Winwood Reade is good upon the subject. ... He remarks that, while the individual man is an insoluble puzzle, in the aggregate he becomes a mathematical certainty" (I, 137). Here, Holmes paraphrases the *Martyrdom of Man* in which Reade observed that it is necessary to "look at men in the mass" if one is to understand "the life of an ordinary man."[6]

By recommending the *Martyrdom of Man* to Watson, Holmes has directed his friend to a book that Doyle might have read as a univer-sity student.[7] In its pages he would have found a recapitulation of themes and issues emanating from the nebular hypothesis, beginning with William Herschel's account of the exchange between Napoleon and Pierre Simon Laplace (1749–1827) in 1802 and culminating in a religious skepticism that natural theologians like Adam Sedgwick (1785–1873) and William Whewell (1794–1866) rightly feared. The *Martyrdom of Man* documented an intellectual and a psychological transformation that could lead Reade to claim that "Christianity is not in accordance with the cultivated mind; . . . It is . . . a superstition, and ought to be destroyed" (*Martyrdom*, p. 432).

Reade set out with zest to do just that. In the "Author's Preface" he identified his intellectual genealogy. He wrote of Darwin as "a Great Master" (*Martyrdom*, p. l) and then proceeded to acknowledge "that there is scarcely anything in this work which [he] can claim as [his] own": "I have taken not only facts and ideas, but phrases and even paragraphs, from other writers" (p. li). Reade's "chief guides" were certain nineteenth-century figures and titles that are, by now, familiar to us: for the "*Philosophy of History*, Herder, Buckle, Comte, Lecky, Mill, Draper; [for] *Science*, Darwin, Lyell, Herbert Spencer, Huxley, Tyndall, Vestiges of Creation, Tylor, and Lubbock" (p. li).

Reade's allusion to "Vestiges of Creation" identifies the complex generic status of the *Martyrdom of Man*, yet another compendium of scientific and philosophical opinion designed to promote a naturalistic worldview.[8] In various chapters Reade traced the stages of human development according to his own idiosyncratic perspective, suggesting the influence of Auguste Comte's three epochs of human thought, the Theological, the Metaphysical, and the Positive. In the *Martyrdom of Man* Adam Sedgwick (who was to die in 1873) might have come upon the realization of his worst fears. For in his Universal History of a universe governed only by natural law, Reade confirmed Segwick's warnings in the fifth edition of *A Discourse on the Studies of the University of Cambridge* (1850). Those who reject an appeal to a First Cause, Sedgwick had argued, will

behold in nature only a chain of second causes of which we know neither the beginning nor the end; [they claim] that we have no right to speak of a Creator or of a creative power; because the links of nature's chain may be infinite in number, and the order of nature may have been eternal. With such a view of nature we may end in downright atheism; or, if we accept the indications of intelligence in the natural world, we may . . . try to satisfy the longings of the mind in some cold scheme of pantheism.[9]

Sedgwick's words become premonitory. In writing of religion, Reade observed: "There was a time when the phrases of modern poetry were the facts of ordinary life. There was a time when man lived in fellowship with nature, believing that all things which moved or changed had minds and bodies kindred to his own" (*Martyrdom*, p. 134). A primitive animism was to give way over time to the monotheism of Judaism, Christianity, and Islam. But in the epoch of Intellect it is possible and necessary to provide a truly natural history of the physical universe, organic life, and consciousness. In the "splendid narrative" (p. 328) that was to constitute his Universal History, Reade returned not surprisingly to the nebular hypothesis:

> Even when science shall be so far advanced that all the faculties and feelings of men will be traced . . . to their latent condition in the fiery cloud of the beginning, the luminous haze, the nebula of the sublime Laplace: even then the origin and purpose of creation, the How and the Why, will remain unsolved. Give me the elementary atoms, the philosopher will exclaim; give me the primeval gas and the law of gravitation, and I will show you how man was evolved, body and soul, just as easily as I can explain the egg being hatched into a chick.
>
> (p. 364)

He then proceeded in a "sketch . . . taken from the writings of others" (p. 379) to follow Mr. Vestiges' account of the cooling earth, the formation of its crust, and "an interesting event," an "elaborate chemical operation" that was to produce first "embryonic plants," then "embryonic animals" (p. 327): "dots of animated jelly, without definite form or figure, swimming unconsciously in the primeval sea, were the ancestors of man. The history of our race begins with them, and continues without an interruption to the present day" (p. 328).

With a dollop of Darwinian evolutionism, Reade followed the appearance of "gelatinous plants and animals . . . at first simple in their forms" to arrive at the epoch when "enormous reptiles crawled upon the earth, frogs as large as elephants" (*Martyrdom*, pp. 379–80), versions of the megalosaurus of *Bleak House*, "waddling like an elephantine lizard up Holborn Hill."[10] Later, a "struggle for life" was to culminate in "a nation of apes, possessing peculiar intelligence and sociability": "exposed to peculiar dangers . . . they combined more closely; . . . their language was improved; . . . using their hands, they walked chiefly with their feet; the apes became *almost man*" (p. 380, emphasis added). Through a complicated process echoing Lord Monboddo (1714–1799) on the

Ourang-Outang as much as Darwin on the descent of man, Reade argued that "the lower animals . . . become Man" (p. 381).

Now Reade offered his Universal History of nations with its progression through the stages of War, Religion, Liberty, culminating in the current epoch, that of Intellect. Along the way he was to repeat some of the worst racial slurs that could be found in the writings of Sir William Jones (1746–1794), G. W. F. Hegel (1770–1831) and, of course, Darwin. For, "in the theatre of history," the "Old World" has not participated in the modern stages of the drama. Rather, it is "a huge body, with its head buried in eternal snows; . . . The lower extremities of this Old World are covered for the most part with thorny thickets and fiery plains" (*Martyrdom*, pp. 383–84), inhabited by natives beyond the reach of history. Africa and Asia constitute "the body in its ancient state," fixed in a condition of arrested development "entirely outside the stream of history" (p. 384). It is Europe, according to Reade, that has become "the centre of the human growth" with "mighty London, the metropolis of the earth" (p. 406), as its figurative heart. He then proceeded to sanction nineteenth-century colonialism, in an aside dismissing the "Indian Mutiny [as] a mutiny only, and not a rebellion." For, "the conquest of Asia by European Powers is . . . in reality Emancipation, and is the first step towards the establishment of Oriental nationality" (pp. 414–15). "Buried in the night" (p. 412), Africa and Asia must be rescued from an obsolete paternalism that denies those rights of private property upon which the development of the intellect rests.[11]

All of this serves as a prelude to the central goal of the chapter on "Intellect," the reformer's task of E. B. Tylor's *Primitive Culture* (1871) that is "to expose the remains of crude old culture which have passed into harmful superstition, and to mark these out for destruction."[12] For if Asia and Africa are in a condition of stasis, there are institutions closer to home that defy the law of development. In the concluding pages of the *Martyrdom of Man* Reade was to turn to the remaining vestiges of an obsolete theism, marking *them* out for destruction. With relish he offered critiques of the Higher Criticism, Deism, and that Natural Theology which remained the great stay against evolutionary hypotheses. He dealt with contempt of a surviving anthropomorphism, the "popular theory" that "the world was made by a Great Being [who] . . . is omnipotent and omnipresent. He loves men whom he has made, but sorrows over their transgressions. . . . those who have sinned and repent, . . . he will forgive. . . . Those who are wicked and stubborn, . . . he will punish" (*Martyrdom*, p. 424).

In turning to the traditional Book of Nature, Reade found a "book inscribed in blood and tears; it is when we study the laws regulating life, the laws of productive development, that we see plainly how illusive is this theory that God is Love" (*Martyrdom*, p. 427). Read through the prism of a Darwinian biology, the Book of Nature proclaims that "the law of Murder is the law of Growth. Life is one long tragedy; creation is one great crime" (p. 427). Reade moved beyond the theism of Mr. Vestiges to an emerging skepticism. For "the nature of the Deity is beyond the powers of the human intellect to solve. The universe is *anonymous*; it is *published* under secondary laws" (p. 428, emphasis added). With these words Reade made explicit what had remained implicit in Edgar Allan Poe's "The Gold-Bug" (1843) and in the present-tense narrative of Dickens's *Bleak House* as the novel opens with a series of fragmentary sentences that deny the existence of a creative mind that has authored the Book of Nature as a second revelation to humanity.

In the concluding pages of the *Martyrdom of Man* Reade turned to the necessary "destruction of [a] Christianity" (p. 430) that impeded human development. Ignoring those who read the Bible literally, he first considered the proponents of the Higher Criticism who hoped to rescue Christianity from a traditional dogmatism in the name of a humanism deeply influenced by Goethe and German *Naturphilosophie*. But, even these humanists are only "advocates for Christianity *versus* Truth" (p. 430). Reade went on to offer a parody of Ludwig Feuerbach (1804–1872) who, in George Eliot's translation of *The Essence of Christianity* (1854), argued that "all the attributes of the divine nature are, therefore, attributes of the human nature."[13] With the advocates of the Higher Criticism Reade granted that "Christianity . . . is human in its origin, erroneous in its theories, delusive in its threats and rewards." He continued: "Jesus Christ was a man with all the faults and imperfections of the prophetic character. . . . The miracles in the gospels are like the miracles in Plutarch's Lives: [however,] they do not lessen the value of the biography, and the value of the biography does not lessen the absurdity of the miracles" (*Martyrdom*, pp. 430–31). Reade's words summon up those of the anonymous author of the present-tense narrative of *Bleak House*, musing upon "a history so interesting and affecting . . . , recording deeds done on this earth for common men, . . . [that] it might hold [Jo] awake, and [he] might learn from it yet!" (*Bleak House*, p. 361).

So it is that, according to Reade, the Higher Criticism – and perhaps Dickens – would argue "that this religion with all its errors has rendered inestimable services to civilisation, . . . so inseparably associated in the minds of men with purity of life, and the precepts of morality, that it is impossible to attack Christianity without also attacking all that is good, all that is pure, all that is lovely in human nature" (*Martyrdom*, p. 431). Yet, Reade would have none of it. Ultimately, Christianity "is pernicious to the intellect" (p. 432). For Reade there is but one imperative: "To cultivate the intellect is . . . a religious duty" (p. 444). Even "the advocates of Deism . . . acknowledge that Christianity is unsuited to the mental condition of the [present] age." They acknowledge that "the fables of a god impregnating a woman, of a god living on the earth, are relics of pagan superstition." Yet Deists persist "that Christianity should not be destroyed but reformed; that its barbarous elements should be expelled, and then, as a pure God-worship, it should be offered to the world" (p. 433). But, Reade argued that to promote a belief "in a future state" in order to promote morality is only to live "under an illusion" (p. 434).

Now, with a feigned regret, Reade turned to "the existing generation" (*Martyrdom*, p. 444), to those who had followed in the footsteps of William Buckland (1784–1856), Adam Sedgwick, and William Whewell. In their attacks upon various evolutionary hypotheses, they are men "who endeavour to reconcile the fables of a barbarous people with the facts of science and the lofty conceptions of philosophy": "they are mostly serious and worthy men. Entering the Church in their youth, before their minds were formed, they discover too late what it is that they adore, and since they cannot tell the truth, and let their wives and children starve, they are forced to lead a life which is a lie" (pp. 444–45). With his closing words, he denounced the defenders of Anglican orthodoxy and those for whom "worship is a conventionality, churches are bonnet shows, places of assignation, shabby-genteel salons where the parochial At Home is given" (p. 445).

So it is that Reade could proclaim: "Supernatural Christianity is false. God-worship is idolatry. Prayer is useless. The soul is not immortal. There are no rewards and there are no punishments in a future state" (*Martyrdom*, p. 430). But, nonetheless, Reade was not to embrace atheism, but a version of "some cold scheme of pantheism" (*Discourse*, p. xvii) of which Adam Sedgwick had warned in 1850:

> We teach that there is a God, but not a God of the anthropoid variety . . . whose attributes can be catalogued by theologians. God is so great that he cannot be defined by us. . . . Those who desire to worship their Creator must worship him through mankind. Such it is plain is the scheme of Nature. We are placed under secondary laws, and

these we must obey. To develop to the utmost our genius and our
love, that is the only true religion.

(Martyrdom, p. 441)

The death of the individual leads to a reunion with "the glorious One
... of whom we are the elements, and who, though we perish, never
dies, but grows from period to period" (p. 442). There are parallels here
to Edgar Allan Poe's "Eureka" (1848) and his claim "that each soul is,
in part, its own God – its own Creator: – in a word, that God – the
material *and* spiritual God – *now* exists solely in the diffused Matter and
Spirit of the Universe; and that the regathering of this diffused Matter
and Spirit will be but the re-constitution of the *purely Spiritual* and
Individual God."[14]

Reade's "cold scheme of pantheism" was to become the basis of that
Unitarianism to which Arthur Conan Doyle turned after his religious
crisis: "It was, then, all Christianity, and not Roman Catholicism alone,
which had alienated my mind and driven me to an agnosticism, which
never for an instant degenerated into atheism" (*Memories*, p. 27). Doyle's
"non-conformity" was that of Reade's "glorious One ... of whom we
are the elements." And, like Reade, Doyle was to resist the pull of a
thorough-going philosophical materialism: "This negative position ...
seemed to me to be a terminus; whereas it proved only a junction on
the road of life where I was destined to change from the old well-worn
line on to a new one" (p. 27). Writing in the 1920s, some fifty years
after his time as a university student, Doyle was still to resort to the language and the idiosyncratic worldview of the *Martyrdom of Man*. Perhaps
he had skirted a vulgar materialism through Reade's reprisal of John
Tyndall's observation in his "Scientific Use of the Imagination" (1870)
that "the Evolution hypothesis" was not to be feared, because it did not
solve "the ultimate mystery of this universe," the mystery of human
consciousness.[15] For Reade followed Tyndall, arguing that "there can
be no mind without matter: there can be no matter without mind"
(*Martyrdom*, p. 336). Doyle avoided the abyss of skepticism, preparing
for his ambiguous statement, "I was a Unitarian," and his observation
that "every materialist ... is a case of arrested development" (*Memories*,
p. 27).

II

In *The Martyrdom of Man*, Arthur Conan Doyle found an epic in small,
a condensed reenactment of a loss of faith in the nineteenth century

that, for some, began with speculations on the nebular hypothesis and culminated with the publication of the *Origin of Species*. Traces of the *Martyrdom of Man* are to be found throughout Dr. Watson's accounts of the exploits of Sherlock Holmes. But the imprint of the book may be seen most clearly, perhaps, in the first two novellas that introduced Holmes to the British reading public. In them Watson offers a pastiche, "not only [of] facts and ideas, but [of] phrases and even paragraphs, from other writers" (*Martyrdom*, p. li) whom Winwood Reade had mentioned in his "Author's Preface," among them those whom Doyle was later to identify as "our chief philosophers" so well known "that even the man in the street felt the strong sweeping current of their thought" (*Memories*, p. 26). In the first of the Holmes stories, *A Study in Scarlet* (1887), Watson sees the man with whom he shares lodgings as a curiosity, someone ignorant not only "of contemporary literature, philosophy and politics," but "of the Copernican Theory and of the composition of the Solar System" (II, 21). However, the Holmes of *The Sign of Four* has become a Victorian polymath, someone not unlike Winwood Reade, versed in Thomas Carlyle, Jean-Paul Richter, and Goethe. Holmes now embodies a nineteenth-century worldview that had emerged out of the various challenges to the Higher Criticism, Deism, and Natural Theology summarized by Reade. Such challenges had, according to Doyle himself, offered a "negative position . . . so firm" that "it proved only a junction on the road of life where [Doyle] was destined to change from the old well-worn line to a new one" (*Memories*, p. 27), a figurative crust of certainty upon which Holmes was to tread in his investigations.

The Sign of Four opens as Holmes turns to his hypodermic needle and to a 7 percent solution of cocaine in an attempt to relieve the ennui induced by "the dull routine of existence" (*Sign*, I, 90). Watson sets out both to rouse Holmes and to rebuke him for "the somewhat dogmatic tone which he occasionally assume[s]" (I, 92). He is thinking of the magazine article, "The Book of Life," that Holmes had published anonymously, an article that Watson has once dismissed as "ineffable twaddle!" (*Study*, I, 23).[16] He alludes to the article by observing, "I have heard you say it is difficult for a man to have any object in daily use without leaving the impress of his individuality upon it in such a way that a trained observer might read it" (*Sign*, I, 92). He then offers Holmes "a watch which has recently come into [his] possession," daring him to provide "an opinion upon the character or habits of the late owner" (I, 92). From the initials engraved upon the watch, as well as from the dents and scratches that he detects, Holmes reconstructs the history of Watson's older brother who had experienced vicissitudes in his life and had died, leaving perhaps only this memento of his existence. The watch has become an archaeological or paleontological fragment from which Holmes infers the existence of someone of whom he has had no previous knowledge. Once he establishes that Watson has inherited the watch upon the death of an older brother, he offers the history of the man to whom it once belonged. By remarking upon "the numbers of the ticket[s]" scratched by pawnbrokers "upon the inside of the case" (I, 93), Holmes has once again transformed an object into a figurative manuscript, deciphering the hieroglyphic evidence on it. Even the scratches around the keyhole become "traces" left by the "unsteady hand" of a drunkard. In this way Holmes accurately recounts a life of dissipation and degradation that ends in an ignominious death.

The episode reveals, again, how the fictional detective practices an historical discipline, one of William Whewell's "palætiological sciences": "those researches in which the object is, to ascend from the present state of things to a more ancient condition, from which the present is derived by intelligible causes."[17] But the episode also implies that Holmes participates in what has come to be called the Darwinian revolution. For the watch of Watson's dead brother cunningly suggests Winwood Reade's attack upon "an anthropoid Deity, a Constructive Mind, a Deus Paleyensis, a God created in the image of a watchmaker" (*Martyrdom*, p. 428), and upon a worldview that Darwin, among others, had challenged.

Reade, of course, had alluded to William Paley's *Natural Theology* (1802) and to the famous analogy with which the book opened:

> In crossing a heath, suppose I pitched my foot against a *stone*, and were asked how the stone came to be there, I might possibly answer, that, for any thing I knew to the contrary, it had lain there for ever; . . . But suppose I had found a *watch* upon the ground, and it should be enquired how the watch happened to be in that place, I should hardly think of the answer which I had before given.[18]

In the passage Paley offered a classic version of the Argument from Design: he posited a Newtonian, mechanistic universe created by an omnipotent, omniscient, and benevolent God. The watch was, of course, the received metaphor for a universe so conceived. But, Paley went on: "the contrivances of nature surpass the contrivances of art, in the complexity, subtlety, and curiosity of the mechanism; and still more, if possible, do they go beyond them in number and variety; yet, in a multitude of cases, are not less evidently mechanical, not less evidently contrivances, not less evidently accommodated to their end" (p. 19).

The watch has now become a metaphor for a living organism, that, like William Buckland's exemplary Nautilus in his *Geology and Mineralogy* (1836), becomes a mechanism contrived by God, already adapted to its circumstances, immutable.[19]

Paley was writing before a consensus had emerged about fossils as the remains of living and extinct species. The British natural theologians who were to follow him – William Buckland, Adam Sedgwick, and William Whewell among them – would accept, even argue for the extinction of species, all the while defending the doctrine of special creation, the immutability of species, and the teleological claim that each species, like every man or woman, has been placed in an appropriate niche in an unchanging universe. However, the universe of Sherlock Holmes is a Darwinian one in which change prevails. It is appropriate that he would write an essay entitled "The Book of Life," implicitly rejecting the static universe both of Deism and Natural Theology. The title announces that Holmes's essay participates in a tradition associated with Robert Chambers's *Vestiges of the Natural History of Creation*, Robert Hunt's *The Poetry of Science* (1848), and Darwin's *Origin of Species*. The anonymous article offers a worldview: "From a drop of water . . . a logician could infer the possibility of an Atlantic or a Niagara without having seen or heard of one or the other. So all life is a great chain, the nature of which is known whenever we are shown a single link of it" (*Study*, I, 23). The article continues:

> Let [the inquirer], on meeting a fellow-mortal, learn at a glance to distinguish *the history of the man*, and the trade or profession to which he belongs. . . . By a man's finger-nails, by his coat-sleeves, by his boots, by his trouser-knees, by the callosities of his forefinger and thumb, by his *expression*, by his shirt-cuffs – by each of these things a man's calling is plainly revealed.
>
> (I, 23, emphasis added)

Implicit in such claims is a Darwinian worldview that rejects teleological speculations, even as it finds purpose and meaning everywhere in the great chain of life. All organisms, human beings among them, engage in activities that reveal a motive and a history. In rejecting traditional preoccupations with teleology, Holmes has accepted the Darwinian conviction that the structure and activity of every organism reveal a purpose that contributes to the preservation of life.

"The Book of Life" draws upon the *Origin of Species* with its rejection both of the doctrine of special creation and the resort to teleological explanations.[20] Yet, after the *Origin*, Darwin was to return again and again to his critique of special creation and of appeals to teleology, for the two foreclosed his own understanding of the structures and functions of various organisms. He felt the need always to elaborate upon the implications of his argument in the *Origin*, particularly in *The Various Contrivances by which Orchids are Fertilized by Insects* (1862). In the introduction to the orchid book Darwin observed: "This treatise affords me . . . an opportunity of attempting to show that the study of organic beings may be as interesting to an observer who is fully convinced that the structure of each is due to secondary laws, as to one who views every trifling detail of structure as the result of the direct interposition of the Creator."[21] Through his meticulous study of the relationships between various kinds of orchids and the insects that fertilize them, Darwin revisited illustrations that he had offered of "nectar-feeding insects" in the chapter on "Natural Selection" in the *Origin of Species* in order to repudiate again the claims of Natural Theology that the study of organic beings – their structures and their functions – demands a teleological perspective.[22]

In his discussion of orchids and the insects that fertilize them, Darwin saw purpose everywhere. But, where the natural theologian found evidence of design, Darwin reconstructed a complex historical process, governed by natural law alone, by which plants and insects become adapted to each other by chance: "It is in perfect accordance with the scheme of nature, as worked out by Natural Selection, that matter excreted to free the system [of a plant] from superfluous or injurious substances should be utilized for [other] highly useful *purposes*. . . . The regular course of events seems to be, that a part which originally served for one *purpose*, becomes adapted by slow changes for widely different *purposes*" (*Orchids*, pp. 187, 198, emphasis added). Such adaptations are the result of complex, purely contingent events occurring over vast periods of time. In concluding his discussion of the fertilization of orchids, Darwin returned to a version of the passage paraphrased by the reviewer of the *Origin* in *All the Year Round*:

> Although an organ may not have been originally formed for some special purpose, if it now serves for this end, we are justified in saying that it is specially adapted for it. On the same principle, if a man were to make a machine for some special purpose, but were to use old wheels, springs, and pulleys, only slightly altered, the whole machine, with all its parts, might be said to be specially contrived for its present purpose.

(p. 199)

Darwin continued, to write of "the living machinery of nature" (p. 199), appropriating the language of Paley's *Natural Theology* only to mock it. He suggested that the formerly static Book of Nature was now to be read as a Book of Life that records "the incessant changes to which the organic and inorganic world has been exposed" (p. 173).[23]

III

Such a perspective enables Sherlock Holmes to look everywhere for purpose and, ultimately, for meaning. As a consulting detective, Holmes will dwell upon the "moral and mental aspects" (*Study*, I, 23) of a case. He will practice a form of Whewell's "moral palætiology" as he moves from "the world of matter to the world of thought and feeling, – from things to men" (Whewell, *History*, III, 486–87). However, he will do so in a universe changed by Darwinian hypotheses. He will even be in possession of an embryonic psychology, directed to it perhaps by the *Martyrdom of Man* in which Winwood Reade observed that he had abandoned a projected study, "The Origin of Mind," with the publication in 1871 of Darwin's "Descent of Man" (*Martyrdom*, p. 1).

However, it would be in Darwin's *Expression of the Emotions in Man and Animals* (1872) that someone like Arthur Conan Doyle could find a natural history of human emotions setting forth a psychology and a semiotics that could become the model for the acts of detection in which the fictional Holmes engages. In his *Expression of the Emotions* Darwin followed the naturalistic tradition associated in nineteenth-century Britain with George Combe, the phrenologist, whose *Constitution of Man* (1828) argued that "we are physical, organic, and moral beings, acting under the sanction of general laws."[24] Such a tradition was further articulated by men like John Elliotson, who became notorious for mesmeric experiments, and, of course, by "Mr. Vestiges." In the first issue of Elliotson's *Zoist* (1843–44), the essay on "Cerebral Physiology" stated, "we consider that the thoughts, actions, and feelings of men, can be made a subject of scientific investigation, . . . we avow that there is a constant and unchanging series of effects, resulting from recognized and specific causes, . . . let us not cloak our ignorance by the assumption of an air of mystery and the parade of unintelligible theories."[25] Such a tradition claimed, in Combe's words, that "the key to the true theory of the divine government of the world [is], . . . namely, THE INDEPENDENT EXISTENCE AND OPERATION OF THE NATURAL LAWS OF CREATION" (*Constitution*, p. 19). Combe's words informed Mr. Vestiges' claim that "the difference between mind in the lower animals and in man is a difference in degree only; . . . We see animals capable of affection, jealousy, envy; we see them quarrel, and conduct quarrels, in the very manner pursued by the more impulsive of our own race."[26]

Darwin wrote within the context of such a tradition, proceeding in the *Expression of the Emotions* according to uniformitarian principles, dismissing those who argued for a difference in kind between the mental acts of animals and human beings.[27] Not surprisingly, Darwin opened his examination of the emotions with the requisite attack upon the doctrine of special creation that would foreclose the kind of study to which he was turning: "No doubt as long as *man and all other animals* are viewed as independent creations, an effectual stop is put to our natural desire to investigate as far as possible the causes of Expression." He continued: "He who admits on general grounds that the structure and habits of *all animals* have been gradually evolved, will look at the whole subject of expression in a new and interesting light."[28] Darwin returned to the argument of the *Descent of Man*, further developing his vision of "man [who] once existed in a much lower and animal-like condition" (*Expression*, p. 12), even as he implemented the program to which Winwood Reade referred as he wrote of those "new fields of knowledge" through which "the abyss deepens, the horizon recedes": "The proximate Why may be discovered: the ultimate Why is unrevealed" (*Martyrdom*, p. 364). Concentrating on Reade's "proximate Why," Darwin set out to demonstrate that certain gestures, sounds, and facial expressions reveal feelings and states of mind in animals and in human beings. He proceeded to offer a natural history of those signs that he saw as universal among all men and women by treating them as vestigial traces of an entire sequence of actions that, in the past, served a useful purpose in the struggle for survival. Over time, a simple gesture – the raising of the hand or the apparent thrusting away of something not actually present – has become the substitute for the former act of striking at an enemy or of pushing away food that for one reason or another was repugnant. Through the association of ideas and habit, a sequence of actions that once involved hand gestures, facial expressions, and sounds has been reduced to a sign that indicates a feeling or a state of mind.[29]

Darwin's discussion of weeping in *Expression of the Emotions* becomes indicative of the way in which he proceeded: "when complex actions or movements have long been performed in strict association together, and these are from any cause at first voluntarily and afterwards habitually checked, then if the proper exciting conditions occur, *any part of the action or movement which is least under the control of the will*, will often still be *involuntarily performed"* (p. 173, emphasis added). Darwin offered an example:

> if our infants, during many generations, and each of them during several years, had almost daily suffered from prolonged choking-fits, during which the vessels of the eye are distended and tears copiously secreted, then it is probable, such is the force of associated habit, that during after life *the mere thought of a choke*, without any distress of mind, would have sufficed to bring tears into our eyes.
>
> (p. 174, emphasis added)

Darwin first turned to a tentative neurological explanation involving vague references to nerve-force and nerve cells. He continued with a physiological explanation, describing the contraction of muscles, the condition of blood vessels in the eye, and the accretion of tears that protect the eye from injury. But he entered the realm of the psychological as he observed that "the mere thought of a choke" produces tears: "as the lachrymal glands are remarkably free from the control of the will, they would be eminently liable still to act, thus betraying, though there were no other outward signs, the pathetic thoughts which were passing through the person's mind" (p. 173).

In his discussion of weeping, laughter, and other human expressions, Darwin moved at once toward a coherent psychology and a theory of signs. In describing the contraction of the brow and the depression of the corners of the mouth as expressions of grief, he offered a model for the psychological understanding of the origin and the function of such facial expressions. Following the argument of the *Descent of Man*, Darwin resorted to the anthropological analogy between the development of civilization and the maturation and socialization of the child into the adult. In the process the European male – as opposed to the savage, the child, the woman, and the lunatic – learned to suppress a sequence of actions, of which a facial expression becomes a vestigial trace. He observed:

> In all cases of distress, whether great or small, our brains tend through long habit to send an order to certain muscles to contract, as if we were still infants on the point of screaming out; but this order we, by the wondrous power of the will, and through habit, are able *partially* to counteract; although this is effected *unconsciously*, as far as the means of counteraction are concerned.
>
> (p. 191, emphasis added)

Again, Darwin moved from a tentative neurological account to a physiological one, finally to turn to a psychological and a semiotic analysis: "It is remarkable how small a depression of the corners of the mouth gives to the countenance an expression of low spirits or dejection, so that an extremely slight contraction of these muscles would be sufficient to betray this state of mind" (p. 193).[30]

Darwin concluded his discussion of grief by restating the model he used throughout his natural history of the emotions:

> as soon as some melancholy thought passes through the brain, there occurs a just perceptible drawing down of the corners of the mouth, or a slight raising up of the inner ends of the eyebrows, or both movements combined, and immediately afterwards a slight suffusion of tears. A thrill of nerve-force is transmitted along several habitual channels, and produces an effect on any point where the will has not acquired through long habit much power of interference. The above actions may be considered as *rudimental vestiges of the scream-ing-fits*, which are so frequent and prolonged during infancy. In this case . . . the *links are indeed wonderful which connect cause and effect* in giving rise to various expressions on the human countenance; and they explain to us the *meaning of certain movements*, which *we involuntarily and unconsciously perform*, whenever certain transitory emotions pass through our minds.
>
> (*Expression*, p. 195, emphasis added)

In the passage there are traces of nineteenth-century psychology in Darwin's treatment of the nervous system as an electrical one, as well as an evolutionary anthropology with its preoccupation with the vestigial remains of prehistoric customs and practices. In his naturalistic account Darwin argued that a sequence of actions that once served the purpose of self-preservation is interrupted over time through the interposition of society and the individual will and reduced to a symptomatic act, perhaps only a facial expression, that releases anxiety and conveys a meaning that suggests a state of mind. Yet, neither the purpose of the expression, nor its meaning was originally intended.

Darwin had returned both to Romantic speculations on human consciousness and to naturalistic examinations of brain and mind. There are echoes of "Characteristics" (1831) in which Thomas Carlyle observed that a study of the "curious relations of the Voluntary and Conscious to the Involuntary and Unconscious . . . might lead us into deep questions of Psychology and Physiology."[31] In a more conventional, naturalistic tradition Darwin resorted to W. B. Carpenter's introduction of the concept of *"Unconscious Cerebration"* in the fourth edition of his *Human Physiology* (1854).[32] In expanding previous investigations into the relationship of brain and mind, Darwin edged closer to a naturalistic psychology that anticipated Sigmund Freud's psychoanalytic theories. He wrote of expressions of grief, anger, and defiance as "abortive action[s]" (*Expression*, p. 251), a phrase suggesting the psychoanalytic concept of parapraxes so important to Freud's discussion of slips, dreams, and symptoms that become the vestigial traces of psychological conflict.[33]

However, it is in his discussion of blushing that Darwin most unambiguously entered the realm of psychology. He introduced "blushing [as] the most peculiar and the most human of all expressions" (*Expression*, p. 309). Once again, he touched upon the neurological and the physiological dimensions of a phenomenon, only to move beyond them: "we cannot cause a blush . . . *by any physical means*, – that is by any action on the body. *It is the mind which must be affected*. Blushing is not only *involuntary*; but the wish to restrain it, by leading to self-attention actually increases the tendency" (pp. 309–10, emphasis added). Darwin, thus, dismissed the traditional distinction between body and mind as he entered into "questions of Psychology and Physiology," into the realm of the "Involuntary and Unconscious." He began by insisting that blushing is a universal phenomenon, common, "in almost all the races of man" (p. 315). But it is the phenomenon of blushing among European men and women that most concerned Darwin.

Through a neurological and physiological process upon which Darwin did not elaborate, the face becomes the site of a capillary action that produces blushing. As he had done in his discussion of grief, despair, and love, he proceeded to explain how it has come to pass that "self-attention [originally] directed to personal appearance, in relation to the opinion of others, . . . through the force of association" is now related "to moral conduct" (*Expression*, p. 325). For, "it is not the simple act of reflecting on our own appearance, but the thinking what others think of us, which excites a blush" (p. 325). In the distant past "primeval man before he had acquired much moral sensitiveness would have been highly sensitive about his personal appearance, at least in reference to the other sex, and he would consequently have felt distress at any depreciatory remarks about his appearance; and this is one form of shame" (p. 328). Darwin continued: "as the face is the part of the body which is most regarded, it is intelligible that any one ashamed of his personal appearance would desire to conceal this part of his body. The habit having been thus acquired, would naturally be carried on when shame from strictly moral causes was felt" (p. 328).

Rejecting theological or metaphysical accounts of the sense of guilt or shame, Darwin engaged in his own version of Whewell's "moral palætiology," moving into the "world of thought and feeling." He observed: "It is not the conscience which raises a blush, for a man may sincerely regret some slight fault committed in solitude, or he may suffer the deepest remorse for an *undetected crime*, but he will not blush. . . . It is not the sense of guilt, but the thought that others *think* or *know* us to be guilty which crimsons the face" (*Expression*, p. 332, emphasis added). He continued his natural history, claiming that "some persons flush up . . . at any sudden and disagreeable recollection. The commonest cause seems to be the sudden remembrance of not having done something for another person which had been promised. In this case it may be that *the thought passes half unconsciously through the mind*, 'What will he think of me?'" (p. 334, emphasis added).

Deep into the Carlylean realm of "the Involuntary and Unconscious," Darwin disdained appeals to teleology and to "the belief that blushing was *specially* designed by the Creator" (*Expression*, p. 336). Instead, he insisted that a man or a woman "will blush under the vivid recollection of a detected fault, or of one committed in the presence of others, the degree of blushing being closely related to the feeling of regard for those who have detected, witnessed, or suspected [the] fault. Breaches of conventional rules of conduct, if they are rigidly insisted on by our equals or superiors, often cause more intense blushes even than *a detected crime*" (p. 345, emphasis added). Such observations, with their insistence upon "the meaning of the gestures which accompany blushing throughout the world" (p. 345), lead to Darwin's concluding observation in the last chapter of the *Expression of the Emotions*: "throughout this volume, I have often felt much difficulty about the proper application of the terms will, consciousness, and intention. Actions, which were at first voluntary, soon became habitual, and at last hereditary, and may then be performed even in opposition to the will. Although they often reveal the state of the mind, this result was not at first either intended or expected" (p. 356). With his concern over the legitimacy of a traditional philosophical vocabulary, Darwin was but a step away from the kind of observation that Sigmund Freud was to make in his "Fragment of an Analysis of a Case of Hysteria" (1905) in which he offered his account of the adolescent girl whom he called Dora:

When I set myself the task of bringing to light what human beings keep hidden within them . . . by observing what they say and what they show, I thought the task was a harder one than it really is. He that has eyes to see and ears to hear may convince himself that no mortal can keep a secret. If his lips are silent, he chatters with his finger-tips; betrayal oozes out of him at every pore. And thus the task of making conscious the most hidden recesses of the mind is one which it is quite possible to accomplish.[34]

The Expression of the Emotions in Man and Animals, like Lyell's *Antiquity of Man*, had become a detective story in which Darwin was ever on the alert to those clues – facial expressions, gestures, tears – that betray states of mind to the adept. In his anecdote of a personal experience in a railway carriage, Darwin was to become a character engaged in the art of detection as he provided "a trifling observation, [that] . . . serve[d] to sum up our present subject" (*Expression*, p. 193), the expression of grief:

An old lady with a comfortable but absorbed expression sat nearly opposite to me. . . . Whilst I was looking at her, I saw that her *depressores anguli oris* became very slightly, yet decidedly, contracted; but as her countenance remained as placid as ever, I reflected how meaningless was this contraction, and how easily one might be deceived. The thought had hardly occurred to me when I saw that her eyes suddenly became suffused with tears almost to overflowing, and her whole countenance fell. There could now be no doubt that some painful recollection, perhaps that of a long-lost child, was passing through her mind.

(p. 194)

At this moment, Darwin might well be thinking of his beloved Annie, the daughter who had died in the spring of 1851, twenty-one years before. His own melancholia may inform his concluding remark: "In this case, as well as in many others, the links are indeed wonderful which connect cause and effect in giving rise to various expressions on the human countenance; and they explain to us the meaning of certain movements, which we involuntarily and unconsciously perform, whenever certain transitory emotions pass through our minds" (p. 195).[35]

Darwin's investigations into those expressions and movements that "we involuntarily and unconsciously perform" would lead him on one occasion, as he dealt with the response of an epileptic woman in an

asylum under a physician's examination, to his own study in scarlet:
"The moment that [the physician] approached, she blushed deeply over
her cheeks and temples; and the blush spread quickly to her ears. . . .
He unfastened the collar of her chemise in order to examine the state
of her lungs; and then a brilliant blush rushed over her chest, in an
arched line over the upper third of each breast" (*Expression*, p. 313).
Here, Darwin risked the charge of indelicacy, as any detective must, even
as he revealed his curious blindness to the woman's plight.[36] In his
Expression of the Emotions Darwin had anticipated Doyle's *A Study in
Scarlet* as Sherlock Holmes investigates a murder at Number 3, Lauriston Gardens on the south bank of the Thames. Both texts become
primers in how to read certain expressions, gestures, and actions as they
constitute "the words of a language" (*Expression*, p. 352) – "the language
of the emotions" (p. 366) – to which the "Science of Deduction" must
turn in considering the "moral and mental aspects" of a crime (*Study*,
I, 23). So, in "The Book of Life" the anonymous author has written of
"all life [as] a great chain, the nature of which is known whenever we
are shown a single link of it" (I, 23). In his dismissal of the claims in
the article as rubbish, Watson issues a challenge to its anonymous
author in words that recall Darwin's anecdote of the railway carriage: "I
should like to see him clapped down in a third-class carriage on the
Underground, asked to give the trades of all his fellow-travellers. I would
lay a thousand to one against him." Holmes merely responds, "You
would lose your money" (I, 23), identifying himself as the author of the
article.

In this exchange Watson is introduced not only to Holmes's "trade"
as "a consulting detective" (*Study*, I, 24), but to a still-contested worldview. It is Watson who dwells "in the dreary desert which separates two
ages of Belief" (Reade, *Martyrdom*, p. 445). A "new era is at hand," in
the words of Winwood Reade, but it was not fully consolidated within
the consciousness of late-Victorian men and women. In the cases that
follow, Watson – like the readers of Doyle's Sherlock Holmes stories and
novels – will experience a protracted initiation into a worldview crafted
by those acknowledged by Winwood Reade in the "Author's Preface" to
The Martyrdom of Man and, later, by Doyle in his *Memories and Adventures*. Charles Lyell, Mr. Vestiges, Herbert Spencer, T. H. Huxley, John
Tyndall, John Lubbock, and E. B. Tylor all participated in the destruction of a prevailing common sense. Each repeated in various ways the
experience of Darwin in 1838 as, in his Notebooks, he proclaimed,
"Once grant that . . . one genus may pass into each other.—grant that
one instinct to be acquired . . . if this be granted!! . . . [the] whole fabric

totters & falls."[37] The "fabric falls," but a new one is to be constructed by the men who destroyed the old. They set out to offer a new form of common sense announced in small in "The Book of Life." As he accompanies Holmes to Lauriston Gardens, and the study in scarlet begins, Watson enters upon an apprenticeship in which he will try to learn his friend's methods and apply them. It is appropriate that he will be introduced to them through Holmes's investigation into the murder of the American Mormon and polygamist, Enoch Drebber, whose corpse is discovered in a room in which, on one wall, "there [is] scrawled in blood-red letters a single word – RACHE" (*Study*, I, 31). The enigmatic word – "the German for 'revenge'" (I, 32) – will prove to have been written in the blood of the murderer, Jefferson Hope. In writing the word in the blood from a nose-bleed, first in the Lauriston Gardens house and later in the hotel room of the murdered Joseph Strangerson, Hope has left not only a bloody clue for Holmes to follow, but a crimson memorial to the dead Lucy Ferrier, his violated fiancée. The word acknowledges the sense of guilt that he feels over a vengeance too long delayed as he pursues Drebber and Strangerson from the United States through the capitals of Europe to London. In his confession Hope observes that, after killing Drebber, "the blood had been streaming from [his] nose, but [he] had taken no notice of it." He continues: "I don't know what it was that put it into my head to write upon the wall with it. Perhaps it was some mischievous idea of setting the police upon a wrong track" (I, 81–82). But, as Charles Darwin had observed in his conclusion to the *Expression of the Emotions in Man and Animals*, emotions may produce physiological phenomena that "reveal the thoughts and intentions of others more truly than do words, which may be falsified" (p. 364). In the cases to follow, Watson may begin to understand the full implications of such an observation, empowering him to make sense of the human situation in a new era, transformed for many by the likes of Mr. Vestiges, Darwin, John Tyndall, and Huxley, the "chief philosophers" of the day who sought to consolidate, at last, a new consensus, a new common sense.

6
Reading the Gravel Page: Lyell, Darwin, and Doyle

> If the earth told a true story, then Stapleton never reached that
> island of refuge towards which he struggled through the fog
> upon that last night. Somewhere in the heart of the great
> Grimpen Mire, down in the foul slime of the huge morass
> which had sucked him in, this cold and cruel-hearted man is
> forever buried.
>
> *The Hound of the Baskervilles*

I

The first installment of Arthur Conan Doyle's *The Hound of the
Baskervilles* appeared in the August 1901 issue of *The Strand Magazine*.
The serialized novel, which was to run through to April 1902, reintro-
duced Sherlock Holmes to the readers of *The Strand* some eight years
after "The Adventure of the Final Problem" was published in December
1893. In that story Holmes's struggle with Professor Moriarty had
apparently ended as the two men, "locked in each other's arms," fell to
their deaths "in that dreadful cauldron of swirling water and seething
foam" into which Dr. Watson peered in his search for his friend.[1]
Holmes was to return unambiguously from the dead in *The Strand* only
in October 1903, in "The Adventure of the Empty House." The events
that Watson records in the case of the spectral hound of Dartmoor occur
in 1889, several years before those related in "The Final Problem," a
fictional circumstance that need not have guaranteed further adventures of Sherlock Holmes. *The Hound of the Baskervilles* was perhaps
Doyle's reluctant response to the clamor of his reading public and to
his publishers' entreaties, in Britain and the United States, for more of
Holmes. In 1893 Doyle had reportedly said to his friend Silas Hocking,

"I shall kill [Holmes] off at the end of the year. . . . If I don't . . . he'll kill me."[2]

Yet, in turning again to Sherlock Holmes in 1901, Doyle may have responded not only to the lure of profit – *The Hound of the Baskervilles* proved to be a great success – or to men and women demanding a good read.[3] The popularity of the Holmes stories suggests the satisfaction of other desires that Doyle shared with his readers, including a need for the rendering in detective fiction of a coherent vision of the universe in a post-Darwinian moment. The novel opens as Holmes provides Dr. Watson with yet another opportunity to embarrass himself. The walking stick left by a Dr. Mortimer, with its engraved silver band and teeth marks, invites interpretation, offering Holmes an occasion to reassert his superiority to the good doctor: "Well, Watson, what do you make of it?" With these words, we are again on firm ground: Holmes will prove to be at his best. But more is at stake than the reintroduction of old friends, as Holmes adds, "Let me hear you reconstruct the man by an examination of [the stick]" (*Hound*, II, 669). For the British reader of *The Strand Magazine* in August 1901, Holmes's challenge to Watson indicated that the worldview in Doyle's new serial would again be thoroughly native, at once geological and evolutionary.

Through the various adventures of Holmes and Watson, Doyle had for over a decade been transmitting to a newly literate mass audience an emerging worldview. At first glance he would seem to be writing unequivocally in the service of the historical consciousness that Charles Lyell and Charles Darwin, amongst others, had promoted in the *Principles of Geology* (1830–33) and the *Origin of Species* (1859) and in ensuing works like Lyell's *Antiquity of Man* (1863) and Darwin's *Descent of Man* (1871) and his *Expression of the Emotions in Man and Animals* (1872). Through their Uniformitarianism Lyell and Darwin proposed that true knowledge is informed by a belief in fixed natural laws working in and through time that can lead to the reconstruction of the past even from fragmentary evidence.[4] As self-conscious proponents of a worldview, the two proceeded to offer in their writings implicit models for the narrative accounts appropriate to historical understanding. Like Charles Dickens in *The Mystery of Edwin Drood* (1870), Doyle was alert to the figures of speech that Lyell and Darwin used: he responded to their discussion of the geological record as a fragmentary text written in different languages demanding decipherment and interpretation. However, Doyle did not unreservedly endorse the historicizing perspective of nineteenth-century science. Rather, he provided a critique of the historical imagination quite as sobering as that emerging from the stories of Edgar Allan Poe (1809–1849) or, ironically, from the writings of Lyell and Darwin.

By the time of the serial publication of *The Hound of the Baskervilles*, the new historical consciousness had apparently triumphed in England. Doyle would seem to acknowledge this triumph by organizing his novel upon a model that would be immediately accessible to his readers. Dr. Mortimer's walking stick, that "accidental souvenir," is akin to the comparative anatomist's fossil bone or to the geologist's pebble. Like the watch in *The Sign of Four* (1890), the stick becomes a piece of fragmentary evidence by which Watson, following France's Georges Cuvier (1769–1832) or England's own Richard Owen (1804–1892), reconstructs not a geological epoch or an extinct animal but a living man. Once again, such a reconstruction takes the form of a narrative modeled on those offered by nineteenth-century philology, geology, and paleontology. Early on, Richard Kirwan had written in the preface to his *Geological Essays* (1799) of the mineralogist as a figurative philologist sorting out individual minerals into an alphabet that enables someone "to read the huge and mysterious volume of inanimate nature" and to follow "a clew" through the "mazes" of various geological formations.[5] In the English translation of the *Discours préliminaire* (1812) Cuvier wrote, as we have seen, of "the art of deciphering and restoring [animal] remains, of discovering and bringing together, in their primitive arrangement, the scattered and mutilated fragments of which they are composed, of reproducing . . . the animals to which these fragments formerly belonged."[6] Throughout his *Essay on the Theory of the Earth* (1813) Cuvier negotiated Kirwan's geological labyrinth, tracing and reconstructing the "living language" of nature to which Charles Lyell turned in the *Principles of Geology*.[7] It was perhaps second nature for Lyell, when referring to fossil mollusks in an 1829 letter to his sister Marianne, to write: "It is the ordinary, or, as Champollion says, the demotic character in which Nature has been pleased to write all her most curious documents."[8]

No less under the spell of a linguistic figure of speech, Holmes and Watson will treat Dr. Mortimer's walking stick as a fossil remain: in the engravings on it, they see a demotic script from "The Book of Life" to be deciphered and translated. In reconstructing the man from the stick, Watson creates a narrative account of Mortimer's life and character. Of course, as Holmes is all too ready to observe, Watson gets it wrong: "It may be that you are not yourself luminous, but you are a conductor of light. Some people without possessing genius have a remarkable power of stimulating it" (*Hound*, II, 669). Holmes then proceeds to reconstruct more or less correctly the man from the stick, a feat that Watson con-

firms by turning to the Medical Directory that has all along been ready
to hand. But in his attempt to rival Holmes, Watson has revealed the
detective's method. Like the geologist or the paleontologist, the detective explains a fact or an event by placing it within a chronological
series; he then imaginatively transforms it into a chain of natural causes
and effects, leading backward in time to some posited originating
moment. Such a moment is arbitrary and hypothetical: like the origin
of the legend of the hound of the Baskervilles, it stands as a character
or hieroglyph to be read and interpreted.[9]

When Dr. Mortimer, under the influence of the Baskerville legend,
describes the circumstances of Sir Charles Baskerville's death and his
own discovery of "the footprints of a gigantic hound," perhaps no late-
Victorian reader would have been surprised by Holmes's response: "If I
had only been there! . . . It is evidently a case of extraordinary interest,
and one which presented immense opportunities to the scientific
expert. That gravel page upon which I might have read so much has
been long ere this smudged by the rain and defaced by the clogs of
curious peasants" (*Hound*, II, 679–80). With these words Holmes does
not simply invoke the geological commonplace comparing the earth's
crust to a page in a book or a document; he returns to an issue central
to geology and paleontology, one just as important in detective fictions
influenced by those historical disciplines. The soft gravel path of the
Yew Alley becomes a page from which tell-tale traces, as signs or characters to be read, may disappear; it is akin to the geological record
written in the living, but ephemeral, language of nature upon which
natural historians and others build their accounts of geological and
human origins.

Within *The Hound of the Baskervilles* the recurring nineteenth-century
struggle between scriptural readings of nature's documents and those
promoted by the historical disciplines is reenacted. Dr. Mortimer, the
man of science who has written papers on comparative pathology
and psychology, has lost confidence in the naturalistic explanations of
Lyell and Darwin. He is half-persuaded to believe the eighteenth-
century manuscript that offers a providential, Christian account of the
Baskerville family history. In fact, the legend recorded in the manuscript
impels him to look for the evidence of the hound's existence that he
finds on the gravel path of the Yew Alley. Without that narrative framework to inform his perspective, Mortimer would never have looked for,
and seen, the footprints that seem to confirm it. For Holmes, echoing
Winwood Reade, the legend is of interest only to the "collector of fairy
tales" (*Hound*, II, 676). Later he observes to Mortimer, "I see that you
have quite gone over to the supernaturalists" (II, 681). The rhetorical

strategy of Doyle's novel is that of Lyell's *Principles of Geology* and his *Antiquity of Man*. It offers an event that seems to encourage a supernatural explanation, only to dismiss that explanation and to substitute for it an account that affirms "the ordinary laws of Nature" (II, 684).

Nonetheless, in Holmes's efforts to resolve the mystery surrounding the death of Sir Charles Baskerville and the curious events that envelop the new baronet, Sir Henry, there occurs a rigorous examination of the nature of evidence and the status of narrative accounts. Like those in geology and evolutionary biology, the accounts in detective stories are far closer to fiction than many Victorians with confidence in reason and scientific progress might acknowledge. Such accounts often obscure their shaky foundations which may prove to be as deceptive as the Grimpen Mire towards which the action in the novel moves with an inevitability shaped by disciplines that offer explanations through the discovery, or the creation, of origins. All of this is anticipated by the various clues with which Holmes works at the start of the case: "the footmark [of the hound] is material" (*Hound*, II, 681); a bearded figure, who identifies himself as Sherlock Holmes, shadows Dr. Mortimer and Sir Henry Baskerville through the London streets; Sir Henry loses his new boot, then an old one, and receives a letter composed mainly of words cut from a newspaper and pasted upon a sheet of paper faintly smelling of perfume. Such clues lead to Holmes's boast in "A Retrospection": "I had made certain of the hound, and had guessed at the criminal before ever we went to the west country" (II, 765). Armed with his belief in the existence of a real hound and the presence of a human agent, Holmes takes apparently random and trivial events, places them in a roughly chronological order – it is crucial that Sir Charles dies on the night *before* his departure for London – and creates a causal narrative designed to explain . . . everything.[10]

But Holmes's narrative remains a fabrication, much of it based upon the mysterious warning to Sir Henry that has been pieced out of the lead article in the London *Times*. Holmes recognizes the type characteristic to *The Times* and turns to an article in the paper of the previous day. Just as Dr. Mortimer can "tell the skull of a negro from that of an Esquimau" (*Hound*, II, 686), Holmes is adept in the identification of printed type, those hieroglyphic signs by which he creates a narrative framework to guide his further investigation. His assumptions enable him to establish the random event as relevant fact and to place that fact in some relationship to other seemingly unrelated events. In the episode of the printed warning Holmes is engaged – like William Legrand in "The Gold-Bug" (1843) – in the reading of a figurative palimpsest. The warning message leads him to the previous day's *Times* and the article from which the words of the message come, but never to "the [actual] remains of the mutilated *Times* leader" (II, 688). His interpretation, brilliant as it will prove to be, rests finally on negative evidence, on the absent proof that would confirm the truth of his inferences.

The whole of the Baskerville case is shadowed by absent evidence, by a hypothetical origin that is never fully available to the detective. Even Watson's final rendering of the events of the case remains at best a pastiche. The first seven chapters of the novel are a narrative reconstruction of his experiences, culminating with his introduction to the Stapletons and to the Grimpen Mire. In the next two chapters Watson transcribes, verbatim, the letters he has written to Holmes to keep his apparently absent friend abreast of the goings-on in Devon: "One page is missing, but otherwise they are exactly as written and show my feelings and suspicions of the moment more accurately than my memory, clear as it is upon these tragic events, can possibly do" (*Hound*, II, 712). Watson's words not only cast doubt upon the status of the preceding chapters, apparently written with the aid of memory alone, they also allude to a missing page, for all we know an important, perhaps suppressed, one. In transcribing the letters for us, Watson has had to fill in the missing page from memory. But memory itself, even of the most graphic events, may deceive in spite of the claims that Watson makes as he turns from the letters to his diary and, finally, to his recollections: "I have arrived at a point in my narrative where I am compelled . . . to trust once more to my recollections, aided by the diary which I kept at the time. A few extracts from the latter will carry me on to those scenes which are indelibly fixed in every detail upon my memory" (II, 726–27). Watson, perhaps unwittingly, reveals the fragility of the account he is offering, even as he insists that only such a narrative, modeled on those offered by Lyell or Darwin, constitutes truth in a modern, scientific culture.[11]

II

The Hound of the Baskervilles returns insistently to the problem posed by the gravel walk of the Yew Alley, to the defaced page that alludes to the unreliable geological and archaeological records that so preoccupied Lyell and Darwin. In the *Origin of Species* – appropriately published in the year of Doyle's birth – Darwin was compelled to rely on negative evidence to support his evolutionary hypotheses. The geological record, with its fossil and mineralogical characters, demonstrated that species had become extinct; it did not prove that existing species had, in fact, evolved from now-extinct ancestors. The geological record was, and remains, simply too incomplete to provide the conclusive evidence that Darwin sought. By 1859 Darwin might at last assume that his readers would accept fossil remains for what they were. They were no longer, in Lyell's words, things "created in the beginning . . . by the fiat of the Almighty" or by some mysterious "plastic power which resided in the earth in the early ages of the world" (*Principles*, I, 85). Fossils were acknowledged as organic remains, although their significance was subject to dispute. And with the gaps in the geological record due to the absence of fossil remains in strata lying below or above formations rich in fossil evidence, there could be no proof of the transmutation of species from the simple to the complex. Darwin acknowledged that he must posit the inadequacy of the geological record lest it be turned against him to refute his claims:

> That the geological record is imperfect all will admit; but that it is imperfect to the *degree which I require*, few will be inclined to admit. If we look to long enough intervals of time, *geology plainly declares* that all species have changed; and they have changed in the manner which my theory *requires*, for they have changed slowly and in a graduated manner.[12]

If the earth tells a true story, it renders up evidence, once not even seen as such, that will confirm a pre-existing theory that provides a genealogical – a narrative – definition of species.

In 1859 Darwin had to argue for the flawed geological record; he had to assume a geological time vast beyond the reach of reason. In the *Origin of Species* he called upon the reader, as Lyell had in the *Principles* and later in the *Antiquity of Man*, to follow him on an imaginative flight through the seeming chaos of time: for "the number of [fossil] specimens in all our museums is absolutely as nothing compared with the countless generations of countless species which certainly have existed" (*Origin*, p. 439). Darwin, and Thomas Huxley (1825–1895) after him, pursued the fossil remains that might establish "intermediate links" between seemingly unrelated species. The goal, through an act of the imagination, was to establish links between apparently random facts to render a narrative account in the form of a family tree – Darwin's Tree of Life – that transforms morphological similarity into a temporal and causal sequence.[13]

Darwin's scrutiny of a geological record that all too often failed to provide the evidence sought anticipated Sherlock Holmes's recurring interest in footprints, traces, and tell-tale signs. Holmes, too, must deal with the elusive nature of evidence, with the problem of signs that apparently point to nothing material and, most perplexing of all, with the dilemma posed by the non-existent trace. Stapleton's disappearance at the end of *The Hound of the Baskervilles* crystallizes once more epistemological and narratological issues inherent in evolutionary theory and in the detective fiction it influenced. Watson comments on the search for Stapleton that fails:

> no slightest sign of [Stapleton's footsteps] ever met our eyes. If the earth told a true story, then Stapleton never reached that island of refuge towards which he struggled through the fog upon that last night. Somewhere in the heart of the great Grimpen Mire, down in the foul slime of the huge morass which had sucked him in, this cold and cruel-hearted man is forever buried.
>
> (*Hound*, II, 760)

Watson returns unerringly to the *Origin of Species*, to Darwin who wrote of a geology that only seems to declare plainly the evolution of species: "I look at the natural geological record, as a *history of the world* imperfectly kept, and written in a *changing dialect*; of this history we possess the last *volume* alone, relating only to two or three countries. Of this volume, only here and there a *short chapter* has been preserved; and of *each page*, only here and there a *few lines*" (*Origin*, p. 316, emphasis added).

Darwin's carefully developed figure of speech informs Watson's descriptions of the moor and the Grimpen Mire. The undulating surface is covered with stone monuments that indicate the former presence of prehistoric man; the trench in the hillside to which Stapleton points is, in his words, the "mark," the signature, of "Neolithic man – no date" (*Hound*, II, 709). The detective, like the geologist and the paleontologist, emulates Cuvier's interpretation of fragmentary evidence or Jean-François Champollion's decipherment of the Rosetta Stone whose three scripts appear one on top of the other in a fashion reminiscent of the palimpsest or of the earth's fossil-laden strata.[14] The impact of Champollion's achievement can be seen not only in Lyell's *Principles*, but in the writings of Gideon Mantell (1790–1852) who, with Oxford's William Buckland (1784–1856), was one of the most important popularizers of geology in England in the 1830s and 1840s. Mantell, a physician and a geologist, was a precursor both of Arthur Conan Doyle and the fictional Sherlock Holmes: he once intervened on behalf of a woman convicted of poisoning her husband with arsenic, securing her release and saving her from execution. Mantell's interest in the case of Hannah Russell led to a Holmes-like paper published in 1827 entitled, "Observations on the Medical Evidence Necessary to Prove the Presence of Arsenic in the Human Body in Cases of Supposed Poisoning by that Mineral."[15]

In *The Wonders of Geology* (1838) Mantell resorted to a characteristic language. Following Lyell in the *Principles of Geology*, he wrote of fossil remains as those "precious historical monuments of Nature" that would be to the geological novice as "unintelligible as were the hieroglyphics of Egypt, before [Thomas] Young and Champollion explained their mysterious import":

> It is only by an acquaintance with the structure of the living forms around us, and by acquiring an intimate knowledge of their osseous frame-work or skeleton, that we can hope to decipher the hand-writing on the rock, obtain a clue to guide us through the labyrinth of fossil anatomy, and conduct to those interesting results, which the genius of the immortal Cuvier first taught us how to acquire.[16]

With this hyperbolic language Mantell dwelt upon natural hieroglyphs, ciphers, characters written in stone, to persuade his readers to see the earth's surface as a volume rich in meaning. Through the force of his own enthusiasm, Mantell would make a stone speak. The geologist and the detective – for Mantell can be seen as both – inhabit a world of signs that to the unseeing eyes of others do not exist. Each performs an act bordering on the magical to conjure up meanings out of objects and traces that seem to point to some historical process or succession of events.[17]

It is not surprising that Watson, returning from his club after Dr. Mortimer's visit, has an almost hallucinatory experience as, opening the door to 221-B Baker Street, he finds a room "so filled with smoke that the light of the lamp . . . [is] blurred by it": "Through the haze I had a vague vision of Holmes in his dressing-gown coiled up in an armchair with his black clay pipe between his lips. Several rolls of paper lay around him" (*Hound*, II, 683). The geologist and the detective are sorcerers, part philologists, part Poe-esque cryptographers, living after Babel, who consult literal and figurative documents no longer written in a single, unchanging language.

But the sorcerer's task remains problematic in spite of Mantell's enthusiasm. Throughout the three-volume *Principles of Geology* Lyell offered his vision of geological processes in his discussion of the natural and human monuments that, properly understood, speak of endless change. Nowhere is this clearer, as we have seen, than in his discussion of the Temple of Jupiter Serapis in volume one. He returned again and again to the cyclical, non-linear nature of geological time, emphasizing the imperfections of the geological record in his attempt to thwart the claims of those who might read the story of the earth as an evolutionary tale. The geological record that, through "the fossilizing process," commemorates "the particular state of the organic world, at any given time, . . . may be said to move about, visiting and revisiting different tracts in succession" (*Principles*, III, 31). In this illustration Lyell personified the commemorating process as a census taker who cannot visit every province in a kingdom simultaneously and who may fail to return to the provinces at regular intervals of time: the statistics of such a census are inherently suspect. Thus the apparently intact geological record defies the evolutionist's efforts to document progressive changes in organic life. Moreover, there often occurs a blank or a missing page: just as civil chaos may involve the partial or total destruction of precious documents, the geological processes that produce metamorphic rock erase the fossil hieroglyphs that the geologist or the paleontologist seeks. In reconstructing geological epochs and their relative temporal relationships to each other, the geologist is engaged in the creation of a fictional construct, a history that for Lyell writing in the 1830s can yield no persuasive evidence of evolution.

The figurative census register anticipates a culminating moment in the *Principles of Geology*: Lyell again was to pick up the thread of his archaeological discussion of the Temple of Jupiter Serapis from the penultimate chapter of volume one:

> Suppose we had discovered two buried cities at the foot of Vesuvius, immediately superimposed upon each other, with a great mass of tuff and lava intervening. . . . An antiquary might possibly be entitled to infer, from the inscriptions on public edifices, that the inhabitants of the inferior and older town were Greeks, and those of the modern, Italians. But he would reason very hastily, if he also concluded from these data, that there had been a sudden change from the Greek to the Italian language in Campania.
>
> (III, 33)

In this passage, with its archaeological and philological references, Lyell attacked the catastrophists who opposed his version of gradual change. He emphasized the slow passage from Greek to Italian, with "some terms growing obsolete, while others were introduced from time to time" (III, 34). Through his extended metaphor, Lyell also hoped to deny any connection between geological processes and progressive changes in organic life: the inscriptions on the edifices of buried cities are like fossil remains; the physical laws that lead to the burial of cities are not in concert with the cultural forces governing gradual changes in the dialects of a family of languages. In the same way, the laws governing geological change are separate from those informing the appearance and extinction of species. It would be dangerous and irresponsible to argue for a connection between geological phenomena and a linear, progressive development of organic life, for "*such is not the plan of Nature*" (III, 34).[18]

In his *Principles of Geology* Lyell promoted a vision of unending, cyclical change that leads to the disappearance, but not to the evolution of species or empires: in this way he defended the doctrine of special creation and Natural Theology. His conservative view warranted an elegiac tone that led him to *Childe Harold's Pilgrimage* (1812) and to Byron's sea as "The image of Eternity": "Our modern poet . . . has finely contrasted the fleeting existence of the successive empires which have flourished and fallen, on the borders of the ocean, with its own unchanged stability" (*Principles*, I, 459). Lyell continued by quoting from canto four of *Childe Harold*: the ocean is "Unchangeable, save to thy wild wave's play:/ Time writes no wrinkle on thine azure brow;/ Such as creation's dawn beheld, thou rollest now" (I, 459). However, there are other images of an eternity unmarked by time's hand to which Lyell turned in the *Principles*. One of them, curiously enough, was the Solway Moss, a peat bog "on the confines of England and Scotland" into which, as legend has it, a troop of horse plunged during the Battle of Solway in 1542. The surface of the Moss

> is covered with grass and rushes, presenting a dry crust and a fair appearance; but it shakes under the least pressure, the bottom being unsound and semifluid. The adventurous passenger, therefore, who sometimes in dry seasons traverses this perilous waste . . . picks his cautious way over the rushy tussocks as they appear before him. . . . If his foot slip, or if he venture to desert this mark of security, it is possible he may never more be heard of.
>
> (II, 217)

In *The Hound of the Baskervilles* the Grimpen Mire would seem to emerge as much from the pages of Lyell's *Principles* as from Doyle's visit to Dartmoor in 1901. The enormous wilderness of peat and granite, as Watson describes it, is characterized by "undulating downs, [like] long green rollers, with crests of jagged granite foaming up into fantastic surges" (*Hound*, II, 707). A figurative ocean out of the *Principles of Geology* and the *Origin of Species*, the Grimpen Mire gives birth to life and reclaims its own creatures as if to eradicate any sign of their existence. Exotic plants, nearly extinct birds, rare moths, and butterflies flourish there, while a moor pony, "rolling and tossing among the green sedges" in its death throes, can be sucked down into a bog-hole in the midst of the waste (II, 707–8). Only Stapleton can penetrate to the heart of the Mire and return alive. Once they expose him, Holmes and Watson pursue the fleeing Stapleton to the bog through which he has created a pathway marked by small wands. In a realm of rank weeds, lush, slimy waterplants, and "miasmatic vapour," they find only one trace of Stapleton, Sir Henry's missing boot, on the surface of the Mire's "obscene depths." There is, however, "no chance of finding footsteps in the mire" (II, 759–60). On the island at the Mire's center – the site of an abandoned tin mine – there are only fragmentary traces of Stapleton and his activities, including the skeleton of Dr. Mortimer's missing spaniel. Holmes and Watson abandon their search: for if the earth tells a true story, they will find neither a living Stapleton nor the corpse that will attest to his final end.

Like the Solway Moss, the Grimpen Mire frustrates any investigator, even the inimitable Holmes. It consumes the traces of human and animal existence upon which satisfying solutions to the issue of origins or to crimes must rest. From the start Holmes has set out "to frame some scheme" into which a series of "strange and apparently disconnected episodes could be fitted" (*Hound*, II, 696). Each incident becomes a clue to be woven by Holmes into a coherent whole, into a narrative from which nothing, not even the disappearance of Dr. Mortimer's spaniel, is to be omitted. There is always an aesthetic dimension to Holmes's activity, the purely aesthetic pleasure that coherence, conjured up by a Romantic virtuoso, yields. Beyond the aesthetic there is the problem of human knowledge itself. As he gathers disparate threads into his hands, Holmes weaves a web of meaning through the story that he creates. But the story is not enough: as he and Watson stand over the body of Selden the escaped convict, "black and clear against the silvered stones" (II, 745), Holmes says, "now we have to prove the connection between the man [Stapleton] and the beast. Save from what we heard [upon the moor], we cannot even swear to the existence of the latter. . . . Our case is not complete. . . . It is not what we know, but what we can prove" (II, 744). There will be proof only when the web of meaning ensnares Stapleton. Holmes's "single connected narrative" (II, 753) must culminate in a moment when the entomologist, the avid collector of rare species, will himself "be fluttering in [Holmes's] net as helpless as one of his own butterflies": "A pin, a cork, and a card, and we add him to the Baker Street collection!" (II, 750). But if the rare specimen were to elude Holmes, if the Grimpen Mire takes back that to which it has given life, Holmes's figurative net, woven from a series of narrative threads, will engulf only empty air: it will remain only an elaborate fiction uncorroborated by Stapleton's necessary confession.[19]

Holmes's words, "It is not what we know, but what we can prove," go to the heart of a recurring nineteenth-century dilemma. In an 1870 lecture entitled "Palæontology and the Doctrine of Evolution," Thomas Huxley worried aloud about the fact that the paleontological record shows "no evidence of [evolutionary] modification, or demonstrates [that] such modification as has occurred to have been very slight."[20] He acknowledged the inconclusive nature of the fossil remains that might establish connections between species or types. The genealogical tree of the evolutionists "must be regarded as provisional, except in those cases in which, by a fortunate accident, large series of remains are obtainable from a thick and widespread series of deposits" ("Palæontology," p. 354). Darwin's Tree of Life remains a fiction, a figure of speech that, without adequate proof, only suggests connections between species. In the *Origin of Species* Darwin's imagination had driven him beyond the evidence available to him and beyond those who could not grasp the sweep of his vision. But Huxley, sustained by a robust optimism, remained confident that the geological record would yield the evidence to support Darwin's all-encompassing metaphor. In *The Meaning of Fossils* Martin J. S. Rudwick recounts an episode in which Huxley predicted – on the basis of what he knew rather than on the basis of what he could prove – the existence of an as-yet-undiscovered precursor to the three-toed ancestor of the modern horse. In his 1870 lecture Huxley had already talked of the logical necessity of the existence of such a precursor if evolutionary hypotheses were true. In 1876 Huxley was on a lecture tour in the United States; on the basis of the recent speculations of the American paleontologist, O. C. Marsh, Huxley predicted, in Rudwick's words, "the probable form of an ancestral *Eohippus*, which was duly discovered only two months later."[21]

In *The Hound of the Baskervilles* Sherlock Holmes follows Huxley, as geologist and paleontologist, when he sees in the portrait of Sir Hugo Baskerville a resemblance to Stapleton. Holmes infers the genealogical connection between the two. He posits a missing link that fills in a gap in the Baskerville family tree, creating a genealogical narrative that suggests an ostensible motive for Stapleton who becomes a throwback to Sir Hugo whose violation of feudal principles was the originating cause of the Baskerville legend. In spite of the fact that he is never to have his account of the case confirmed by Stapleton, Holmes would seem to enjoy yet another triumph.

III

But, Arthur Conan Doyle, and writers of detective fiction in general, tend not to be as healthily optimistic as Thomas Huxley or as confident as the fictional Sherlock Holmes.[22] *The Hound of the Baskervilles* was neither the first, nor the last, examination of epistemological and narratological issues by Doyle in a post-Darwinian situation. From the start, in *A Study in Scarlet* (1887), Dr. Watson was to remark upon Holmes's seemingly eccentric behavior as he studies the pathway leading to the house at Number 3, Lauriston Gardens for tell-tale marks: "There were many marks of footsteps upon the wet clayey soil; but since the police had been coming and going over it, I was unable to see how my companion could hope to learn anything from it. Still . . . I had no doubt that he could see a great deal which was hidden from me" (*Study*, I, 28). Later, in the room in which the corpse of Enoch Drebber lies, Holmes "whip[s] a tape measure and a large round magnifying glass from his pocket": "With these two implements he trotted noiselessly about the room, sometimes stopping, occasionally kneeling, and once lying flat upon his face" (I, 31). In *The Sign of Four* (1890) Holmes scrutinizes the room in which the body of Bartholomew Sholto has been found, a "ghastly, inscrutable smile upon his face" (I, 109). He proceeds to read the floor like a printed page, finding "a circular muddy mark" first upon the window sill, "and here again upon the floor, and here again by the table" (I, 110). Through such evidence he confirms the existence of a "wooden-legged man" (I, 111), someone he has not yet laid eyes upon, but whose description he confidently reconstructs from the anecdotal evidence provided by Thaddeus Sholto and the examination of the murder scene.

In the thirteen stories that followed *The Hound of the Baskervilles*, constituting *The Return of Sherlock Holmes*, Doyle revisited such issues. In

"The Adventure of the Priory School" (February 1904), a case involving the kidnapping of a ten-year-old boy who is heir to a title and great wealth, Holmes reads the terrain for the marks of various bicycle tracks that will lead to the discovery of the victim's location. In "The Adventure of the Golden Pince-Nez" (July 1904), the case is introduced on "a wild, tempestuous night" as Holmes is "engaged with a powerful lens deciphering the remains of the original inscription upon a palimpsest" ("Pince-Nez," II, 607). He will solve the murder of Willoughby Smith, private secretary to a Professor Coram who will prove to be a Russian emigré, a former Nihilist who betrayed his companions and even his wife who has unearthed him in England, seeking her revenge. Again, Holmes will examine a garden path leading to the back door of the professor's house. He observes that, after an intervening rain, the path "will be harder to read . . . than that palimpsest" (II, 611). Even the cocoanut matting that covers the corridor connecting the study in which the corpse has been found and the bedroom of the invalided Professor Coram becomes yet another figurative palimpsest that has "taken no impression of any kind," thus "leaving no traces" (II, 611, 614). Yet, from a golden pince-nez found near the corpse of Smith, Holmes will reconstruct the woman who will prove to be the murderer, quite by accident, of the innocent secretary.

In *The Return of Sherlock Holmes* Doyle examined such issues perhaps most subtly in "The Adventure of the Abbey Grange" (September 1904). In a mystery story exploring the complex relationship between empirical evidence and what Jerome Bruner in *The Culture of Education* recently has called the "narrative construal of reality," "The Abbey Grange" demonstrates the way in which nineteenth and early twentieth-century detective fiction promoted a secular, naturalistic worldview, even as it ruthlessly examined the foundations of a naive empiricism.[23] "The Abbey Grange" offers a fascinating illustration of the methods of the fictional detective and of the way in which narrative is essential to the solution of a crime that, on the face of it, has already been solved. The story suggests that narrative, even a false one, may be necessary to the discovery of those facts that will provide the basis of a new, more viable account that leads to the true culprit. More radically, as in the case of Dr. Mortimer and his response to the legend of the hound of the Baskervilles, the story suggests that narrative is necessary to the act of perception, enabling the discovery of those "facts" whose existence would be otherwise undetectable. In "The Abbey Grange" Holmes and Dr. Watson are called into Kent to participate in the investigation into the death of Sir Eustace Brackenstall, apparently the victim of three notorious burglars. On the train carrying them to Marsham, Holmes complains of Watson's accounts of his various cases: "Your fatal habit of looking at everything from the point of view of a story instead of as a scientific exercise has ruined what might have been an instructive and even classical series of demonstrations" ("Abbey Grange," II, 636). With these words Holmes will become the target of the story's irony as he "propose[s] to devote [his] declining years to the composition of a textbook, which shall focus *the whole art of detection* into one volume" (II, 636, emphasis added). But Watson's account will demonstrate the art of detection as clearly as any textbook, even one by the Master: it will not prove to be empirical in the so-called Baconian tradition promoted by nineteenth-century antiquarians and the practitioners of the various historical disciplines. Rather, "The Abbey Grange" dramatizes the complex dynamic between the power of narration to constrain one's vision or to enable someone like Holmes to perceive anomalies, to conjure up a new narrative, and to come upon facts that have, in a sense, been created by narrative itself.

At the Abbey Grange, Inspector Stanley Hopkins greets Holmes and Watson with these words: "[Lady Brackenstall] has given so clear an account of the affair that there is not much left for us to do" ("Abbey Grange," II, 637). She then proceeds to repeat her account of the events of the previous night: she tells of three intruders, the "savage blow" that "felled [her] to the ground" (II, 638), her being bound to a chair by a piece of bell-rope, the murder of her husband, and the departure of the three with their loot. As she talks, "the keen interest . . . passe[s] out of Holmes's expressive face," as "with the mystery all the charm of the case [has] departed" (II, 639). The story, verified by Lady Brackenstall's maid, has its inconsistencies. But, after an examination of the dining room that for a moment "recall[s] his waning interest," Holmes observes, "The lady's story certainly seems to be corroborated, if it needed corroboration, by every detail which we see before us" (II, 639, 641). The story seems to account for all of the evidence before them, except for the puzzle posed by three wine glasses from which the murderers have apparently drunk: the cork of the wine bottle has been removed by a knife, not by a corkscrew; one of the glasses is full of beeswing, a detail that perplexes Holmes.

But Holmes does not, at first, know what to do with these details. He has not yet turned them into anomalies that will require a new, perhaps a radically new, narrative to account for them. He observes: "Perhaps, when a man has special knowledge and special powers like my own, it rather encourages him to seek out a complex explanation when a simpler one is at hand. Of course, it must be a *mere chance* about the glasses" ("Abbey Grange," II, 642, emphasis added). For a moment, Holmes doubts himself in his own egocentric way. But on the return journey to London, he impulsively leaves the train, explaining to Watson, "I simply *can't* leave that case in this condition. Every instinct that I possess cries out against it. It's wrong – it's all wrong – I'll swear that it's wrong. And yet the lady's story was complete, the maid's corroboration was sufficient, the detail was fairly exact" (II, 642). At this moment Holmes relives in a minor key the experiences of which Charles Lyell had written in his *Principles* and in his *Antiquity of Man*. Holmes struggles to resist an account that can become official dogma, a police-sanctioned version of events that precludes objection, even in the face of annoying discrepancies. The moment anticipates Thomas Kuhn's discussion of scientific revolutions:

> Anomaly appears only against the background provided by [a] paradigm. . . . If [an] awareness of anomaly plays a role in the emergence of new sorts of phenomena, it should surprise no one that a similar but more profound awareness is prerequisite to all acceptable changes of theory. . . . Let us then assume that crises are a necessary precondition for the emergence of novel theories.[24]

In "The Abbey Grange" Holmes clarifies the epistemological problem by observing to Watson, "if I had not taken things for granted, if I had examined everything with [the] care which I should have shown had we approached the case *de novo* and had no cut-and-dried story to warp my mind, should I not then have found something more definite to go upon? Of course I should" (II, 642). Here Holmes acknowledges the power of narrative to influence the very act of perception. He has become like Lyell's Champollion and his companions in volume one of the *Principles of Geology*, visiting Egypt with the "firm belief that the banks of the Nile were never peopled by the human race before the beginning of the nineteenth century," a "dogma . . . as difficult to shake as the opinion of our ancestors, that the earth was never the abode of living beings until the creation . . . of the species now existing," and now forced "to account for the monuments [they] discovered" (*Principles*, I, 76–77). Holmes, however, will not resort to what Lyell called "fanciful speculations" (I, 77). If he can resist the spell of Lady Brackenstall's story, he can reinterpret certain anomalies, turning them into those facts upon which he will proceed to construct a new narrative.[25]

Holmes must "dismiss from [his] mind the idea that anything which the maid or her mistress may have said must necessarily be true" ("Abbey Grange," II, 642). Neither social position nor force of personality should influence Holmes. He begins by re-examining Lady Brackenstall's story. But, he is not really approaching the case *de novo* as he claims. Lady Brackenstall's account, invented for reasons Holmes has yet to discern, serves its purpose: it offers the narrative frame by which he determines how adequately it might explain a broad range of facts. Holmes proceeds to revise the original story that he has been told, creating a new one covering all the facts and, perhaps, leading to the discovery of facts of which he has been unaware. Narrative is in the process of becoming, in the words of William C. Dowling, "like the Kantian concepts of space and time": "that is, narrative may be taken not as a feature of our experience but as one of the abstract or 'empty' coordinates within which we come to know the world, a contentless form that our perception imposes on the raw flux of reality." Narrative has become "an epistemological category." But, the form is never without content; it is an account conditioned always by historical circumstances. The "world comes to us in the shape of stories" that guide or coerce perception: they may blind us or make available perceptions that would otherwise never occur.[26]

In "The Abbey Grange" Holmes provides a case study in the art of detection as compelling as any that he might offer in his proposed textbook. As he extricates himself from the web of Lady Brackenstall's account, he identifies anomalies that reveal "a certain element of improbability" ("Abbey Grange," II, 643). Without having yet revisited the scene of the murder, he contemplates the three wine glasses "in [his] mind's eye," concluding that the beeswing in one glass suggests that only two people had, in fact, shared the wine: "But if I have hit upon the true explanation of this one small phenomenon, then . . . it can only mean that Lady Brackenstall and her maid have deliberately lied to us" (II, 643). The "case rises from the commonplace to the exceedingly remarkable" precisely because of the way in which it dramatizes the methodology of the fictional detective and of Lyell, Darwin, and Huxley who engaged in reconstructing the past in narrative form.

On their return to the Grange, Watson watches Holmes re-examine the dining room "like an interested student who observes the demonstration of his professor" ("Abbey Grange," II, 643). Holmes examines the cord with which Lady Brackenstall has been tied to a chair, the bell-rope from which it was cut by a knife, a wooden bracket on the wall where someone supported himself in reaching the rope. Finally, he can state, "We have got our case. . . . Now, I think that, with a few missing links, my chain is almost complete" (II, 644). Again, Holmes has resorted to the characteristic language of nineteenth-century geology, archaeology, and evolutionary biology, each a narrative science. He has reconstructed the events leading up to and following the murder of Sir Eustace Brackenstall, inferred the existence of a single culprit, and edged toward the conclusion that Sir Eustace had been killed by someone in defense of the abused Lady Brackenstall. Particularly telling has been the fact that the rope was not worn and frayed, but cut some three inches from the bell-wire to which it was attached. Such a "clue" has permitted Holmes to "reconstruct what occurred" (II, 644). He goes on to describe the actions of an unidentified man whose existence he has not even suspected until now: "a very formidable person. Strong as a lion. . . . Six foot three in height, active as a squirrel, dexterous with his fingers, finally, remarkably quick-witted, for this whole ingenious story is of his concoction" (II, 644). However, Holmes is once again in the situation that he has experienced in *The Hound of the Baskervilles*: "Our case is not complete. . . . It is not what we know, but what we can prove" (*Hound*, II, 744). He must produce the man himself if he is to confirm his own version of the murder, as he does by luring Jack Crocker to 221-B Baker Street (much as C. Auguste Dupin lures the Maltese sailor to his apartments in "The Murders in the Rue Morgue").

Perhaps more importantly, the account that he has reconstructed enables Holmes to see something previously ignored or dismissed. As he and Watson leave the Grange to return to London, Holmes leads his friend to "a pond in the park": "It was frozen over, but a single hole was left for the convenience of a solitary swan. Holmes gazed at it, and then passed on to the lodge gate [where] he scribbled a short note for Stanley Hopkins" ("Abbey Grange," II, 645). The hole becomes a version of Charles Lyell's "ice-clue" in his *Antiquity of Man*, the place where the few valuables removed from the Grange to deceive the police were deposited. The frozen pond, white on this wintry day, suggests the blank parchment of Poe's "The Gold-Bug" and the "single hole" in it the figure that William Legrand interprets as a kid rather than a goat. Without the new narrative that Holmes has woven, the hole remains insignificant, perhaps even unperceived, until it assumes a new reality, a new meaning, within the context provided by a new narrative.

Both *The Hound of the Baskervilles* and "The Adventure of the Abbey Grange" recall the radical implications of "The Gold-Bug" by which every student of a literal or a figurative text may well be moved more by "a desire [rather] than an actual belief," imposing a narrative upon the blank page of the natural world.[27] That the events recorded in "The Abbey Grange" occur on a day succeeding "a bitterly cold night and frosty morning, towards the end of the winter of '97" (II, 635) suggests even other texts: Poe's "The Narrative of Arthur Gordon Pym" (1837–38) that ends as Pym finds himself adrift in a canoe in the Antarctic Ocean, "white ashy material [falling] now continually," to confront "in [his] pathway a shrouded human figure, very far larger . . . than any dweller among men. And the hue of the skin of the figure [is] of the perfect whiteness of the snow" ("Pym," p. 1179); and, of course, Samuel Taylor Coleridge's "The Rime of the Ancient Mariner" (1798/1817) and the land of mist and snow into which the Mariner and his companions sail prior to the killing of the albatross.[28]

C. Auguste Dupin, William Legrand, and Sherlock Holmes become lineal descendants of Romantic poets as well as of those natural historians who, like Lyell and Mantell, quote Byron, associating themselves with those poets (Percy Bysshe Shelley among them) who dwell on mutability. But the Romantic poet, the geologist, and the paleontologist share another experience. Perhaps Lyell, Mantell, and even Hugh Miller in his attack upon "common nonsense," realized that they, like Coleridge or Poe, had made imaginative voyages and offered accounts of them that could prove unsettling to readers.[29] Even Darwin in his *Journal* (1839) of the voyage of H.M.S. *Beagle* must have thought of "The Rime of the Ancient Mariner" as he sailed southward to Tierra del Fuego, the southernmost point of South America, where he came upon a "landscape . . . widely different . . . from any thing [he] had ever beheld."[30] In his two visits to Tierra del Fuego – the first in December and January of 1832–33, the second in June, 1834 – he was to encounter the Fuegians who were to change forever his understanding of the human situation:

> Viewing such men, one can hardly make oneself believe they are fellow-creatures, and inhabitants of the same world. . . . Whilst beholding these savages, one asks, whence have they come? What could have tempted, or what change compelled a tribe of men to leave the fine regions of the north, to travel down the Cordillera or backbone of America; to invent and build canoes, and then to enter on one of the most inhospitable countries within the limits of the globe?
>
> (*Journal*, pp. 235, 236–37)

Finally, in June of 1834 Darwin and the crew of the *Beagle* were to work their way "into the open Pacific," leaving behind them Sarmiento, one of the highest peaks in Tierra del Fuego, "its base . . . clothed by dusky woods, and above this a field of snow extend[ing] to the summit":

> These vast piles of snow, which never melt, and seem destined to last as long as the world holds together, present a noble and even sublime spectacle. The outline of the mountain was admirably clear and defined. Owing to the abundance of light reflected from the white and glittering surface, no shadows are cast on any part; and those lines which intersect the sky can alone be distinguished: hence the mass stood out in the boldest relief.
>
> (p. 306)

Perhaps with thoughts of Shelley's "Mont Blanc" (1817) and of Mary Shelley's *Frankenstein* (1818/1831) in mind, Darwin was to navigate the Pacific Ocean that lay before him, holding the Galapagos Archipelago, Tahiti, New Zealand, and Australia with their various revelations. So it was that in crossing in December 1835 what would become the international dateline, Darwin observed: "The meridian of the Antipodes . . . has now been passed; and every league . . . which we travel onwards, is one league nearer to England. . . . Only the other day, I looked forward to this airy barrier, as a definite point in our voyage homewards; but now I find it, and all such *resting-places for the imagination,* are like shadows which a man moving onwards cannot catch" (*Journal,* p. 496, emphasis added).[31] With these words Darwin identified himself with Coleridge's Ancient Mariner who sails southward into an inhospitable and icy realm that forever changes his vision of the universe, and of himself. For the Romantic poet and for the natural historian – as for the fictional detectives who follow them – there are no resting places for the imagination: everything is reduced to the conventional depictions on a map "where dots, shading, and names are crowded together" (*Journal,* p. 496). Each has become a voyager, both in the natural world and in the realm of human consciousness. Like the Ancient Mariner, each returns with a tale that is profoundly disturbing and necessarily incomplete. In one way or another each encounters a figurative gravel page or a frozen waste bereft of reassuring landmarks. Instead, the Romantic poet, the natural historian, and the fictional detective encounter curious hieroglyphs, enigmatic signs (some white upon white), or blank pages that yield no final clue to the various mysteries before them. When he addresses the Wedding Guest, Coleridge's

Mariner – like Darwin in his *Journal* or the detective in the requisite retrospective – puts into words an experience that may defy language itself. The reassuring summation of the detective becomes inherently suspect. There are no "resting-places for the imagination": no narrative account can ever explain mysteries that originate from and disappear into the sea-like depths of a Grimpen Mire.[32]

7

The Hound of the Baskervilles, the Man on the Tor, and a Metaphor for the Mind

By the scientific use of the imagination we may penetrate this mystery also.

John Tyndall, "Scientific Use of the Imagination" (1870)

I

In his accounts of the investigations conducted by Sherlock Holmes, Dr. Watson has become Arthur Conan Doyle's fictionalized "man in the street," responding to "the strong sweeping current of . . . thought" of the "chief philosophers of the age."[1] Through such accounts Watson offers a brief for a worldview that, nevertheless, points to the problematic and contradictory nature of a Darwinian perspective that was not then, as it is not now, a single, coherent one. Rather, a variety of materialist perspectives existed in late-Victorian Britain, vying for the status of a prevailing common sense. In a novel like *The Hound of the Baskervilles* (1901–02) there is to be found evidence for Mikhail Bakhtin's claim that "each large and creative verbal whole is a very complex and multifaceted system of relations": in the novel "there are no voiceless words that belong to no one. Each word contains voices that are sometimes infinitely distant, unnamed, almost impersonal . . . , *almost undetectable*, and voices resounding nearby and simultaneously."[2] The "voices resounding nearby and simultaneously" may be those of Charles Darwin (1809–1882), Thomas Huxley (1825–1895), Francis Galton (1822–1911), and even Cesare Lombroso (1835–1909), while the other voices that are "unnamed, almost impersonal" may be those of John Tyndall (1820–1893), the Irish physicist and polemicist, and Robert Chambers (1802–1871), John Pringle Nichol (1804–1859), even John

Milton (1608–1674). Through a fleeting allusion to Tyndall's "Scientific Use of the Imagination" (1870) – an essay which promoted a materialist vision of the human mind with its origins in Pierre Simon Laplace's cloud of heated gases – *The Hound of the Baskervilles* suggests a genealogy that leads backward in time to *Vestiges of the Natural History of Creation* (1844), *Views of the Architecture of the Heavens* (1837) and, ultimately, but not finally to *Paradise Lost* (1667, 1674). The intellectual genealogy will then point forward in time from Milton's epic poem to Romantic speculations on the nature of mind by William Wordsworth (1770–1850) and Percy Bysshe Shelley (1792–1822). It will, for our purposes, lead to the moment when Watson glimpses a man on a tor, *brooding* over the Grimpen Mire before him. In the episode Watson offers an iconographic rendering of human consciousness that challenges a lingering Enlightenment rationalism and a current biological reductionism, to suggest the enduring mystery of the mind beyond the reach of nineteenth-century physiology.[3]

Such issues are introduced from the start.[4] The Dr. Mortimer who presents himself to Sherlock Holmes and Dr. Watson is a man of a Galtonesque, Lombrosian persuasion. The "Medical Directory" indicates that he has won a prize for an essay entitled, "Is Disease a Reversion?"; he has also published "Some Freaks of Atavism" and "Do We Progress?"[5] He is eager to obtain a cast of Holmes's skull for an anthropological museum and admires the work of Alphonse Bertillon (1853–1914), the chief of criminal identification for the Paris police and the creator of anthropomorphy, a dubious system of physiological measurement for the identification of criminals. Mortimer seems tempted to reduce disease and criminality to physiology and heredity by invoking the concept of atavism. Yet he is someone so shaken by the death of Sir Charles Baskerville and so influenced by the legend of a hell-hound that he has been willing to entertain a supernatural explanation for that mysterious event. Mortimer's contradictory inclinations point not only to the fact that a naturalistic perspective has not yet fully consolidated itself even within the scientific community, but also that there are various materialist and rationalist responses to the questions posed by criminal acts.[6]

Later in the novel Holmes himself associates the portrait of Sir Hugo Baskerville with the naturalist Stapleton, speaking of him as "an interesting instance of a throwback, which appears to be both physical and spiritual" (*Hound*, II, 750). Yet in his next statement – "A pin, a cork, and a card, and we add [Stapleton] to the Baker Street collection!" (II, 750) – Holmes associates himself with Stapleton, the naturalist and entomologist who collects rare moths and butterflies. From the moment that the disguised Stapleton, who has been shadowing Sir Henry Baskerville from a hansom cab, tells the cabbie that *he* is Sherlock Holmes, the motif of the double has been imported into the novel: Holmes and Stapleton are connected as two manifestations of a complex, mysterious human nature that may elude explanation. Through Watson's account the novel offers an alternative to Lombroso's atavism, an alternative that Havelock Ellis (1859–1939) had already touched upon in his popularizing work, *The Criminal* (1890).[7] Throughout his book Ellis engaged with the Lombrosian concept of the born criminal, finally to edge away from an emphasis on physiology and heredity. In his response to Lombroso's discussion of "the full biological and psychical significance" of the practice of tattooing among the lower orders and the so-called criminal classes, Ellis observed that "Lombroso attaches prime importance to atavism." He went on to disagree, suggesting that tattooing "is better described as a survival."[8] For British readers, including Doyle, the term "survival" would suggest the writings of John Lubbock and E. B. Tylor, for whom, in Lubbock's *The Origin of Civilisation* (1870) and Tylor's *Primitive Culture* (1871), certain practices and beliefs that lingered into the nineteenth century become vestiges of the mental life of primitive peoples living and dead.[9]

Ellis rejected a reductive emphasis on physiognomy and heredity, acknowledging the significance of environment and other contingent circumstances that include the biological and the social: "we cannot deal wisely with the social factor of crime . . . unless we know something of the biology of crime, of the criminal's anatomical, physiological, and *psychological nature*" (*The Criminal*, pp. 24–25, emphasis added). In qualifying Lombroso's reductive explanations, Ellis turned away from the terms "born criminal" or "congenital criminal" (p. 17 n. 2). He had opened up, perhaps without fully appreciating it, the possibility of a psychological understanding of criminal and other behavior. Indeed, he might share Watson's complex responses to the death of Sir Charles Baskerville and to the mysteries associated for Watson with the identity of a figure that he glimpses by chance, the figure of a man upon Black Tor.

Dr. Watson and Sir Henry Baskerville have just abandoned their pursuit of Selden, the notorious murderer who has escaped from Princetown prison, someone who would seem to be living proof of Lombrosian atavism. When he first sees Selden on the moor, Watson associates him at once with the prehistoric peoples who once lived there: "there was thrust out [Selden's] evil yellow face, a terrible animal face, all seamed and scored with vile passions. Foul with mire, with a bristling beard, and hung with matted hair, it might well have belonged to one of those old savages who dwelt in the burrows on the hillsides" (*Hound*, II, 725). Watson's words reveal the influence of Lombroso's *Crime: Its Causes and Remedies*, a work translated into French in 1899 and into English in 1911: "the atavism of the criminal, when he lacks absolutely every trace of shame and pity, may go back far beyond the savage, even to the brutes themselves. . . . [The] facts prove clearly that the most horrible crimes have their origin in those animal instincts of which childhood gives us a pale reflection." Such instincts break out in the born criminal as atavistic regressions that "are governed by silent laws, which never fall into desuetude and rule society much more surely than the laws inscribed in [its] codes." For Lombroso, with his debt to the *Origin of Species* (as Ellis argued in *The Criminal*), such laws are biological and hereditary. Lombroso quoted Wagner von Jauregg, who equated the atavism of criminals with "the reappearance of intermediate and indistinct fossil forms. We see very clearly, then, that influences capable of producing a disease can bring about atavistic morphological retrogressions."[10] Watson apparently sees in Selden proof that atavism occurs, that it is organic in its causes and can produce a freak like the Notting Hill murderer, a physiological and moral reversion to a past type.

"With the activity of a mountain goat" (*Hound*, II, 725), Selden eludes Watson and Sir Henry. They abandon their pursuit and turn homeward across the moor toward Baskerville Hall. "At this moment" Watson experiences "a most strange and unexpected thing" that will suggest in the course of his narrative a new way of imagining the nature of the criminal and of human consciousness in general:

> The moon was low upon the right, and the jagged pinnacle of a granite tor stood up against the lower curve of its silver disc. There, outlined as black as an ebony statue on that shining background, I saw the figure of a man upon the tor. . . . As far as I could judge, the figure was that of a tall, thin man. He stood with his legs a little separated, his arms folded, his head bowed, as if he were brooding over that enormous wilderness of peat and granite which lay before him.
>
> (II, 726)

In an instant, the "man [is] gone": "There was the sharp pinnacle of granite still cutting the lower edge of the moon, but its peak bore no trace of that silent and motionless figure" (II, 726).

The figure will prove to be Sherlock Holmes dwelling upon the implications of the Devon moor, the Grimpen Mire, and the stone relics
attesting to the presence, long ago, of "Neolithic man – no date" (*Hound*,
II, 709).[11] The moment crystallizes the questions posed by Watson's narrative, even as his description of the experience invites an archaeological excavation of the allusions that inform his response. Of course,
contemporary readers of *The Hound of the Baskervilles* did not have the
advantage, as we do, of knowing Doyle's *Memories and Adventures*, with
its discussion of the impact of Darwin and Huxley upon him. But as followers of nineteenth-century science and of the controversies generated
by geology, evolutionary biology, and anthropology, they could well
have recognized the figurative rendering of a generalized evolutionary
perspective in the description of the Man on the Tor. In this figure they
might glimpse allusions both to Darwin's *The Descent of Man* (1871) and
to Huxley's less recent (but no less controversial) *Man's Place in Nature*
(1863) that reveal, yet again, Holmes's association with the uniformitarian science of Darwin and Huxley. As "the very spirit of that terrible
place" (*Hound*, II, 726), Holmes ponders issues beyond those raised by
the case of the spectral hound: he broods upon the implications of
human origins and the possibility – perhaps the inevitability – of extinction. But as he considers the landscape before him, he will find that it
offers metaphors for the mind that will restore to human consciousness
the aura of mystery that a biological determinism would seem to deny.[12]
The granite tor upon which Holmes stands will literally and figuratively
connect him not only to the moor and to its now-extinct neolithic
inhabitants, but also to the origins of the solar system and of intelligent life in the fires of the sun. He will be associated with those obscure
realms of human consciousness suggested both by Romantic writers and
by nineteenth-century speculations upon the nebular hypothesis: he *is*
"the heart of the mystery" (II, 732) to which Watson's narrative moves.

However muted, Watson's allusions to *The Descent of Man* and *Man's
Place in Nature* can be detected. As the Man on the Tor, Holmes stands
bowed, silhouetted against the silver disc of the half-moon. His apparent sadness would suggest the conclusion to the *Descent of Man* in which
Darwin wrote of men and women as atop "the very summit of the
organic scale":

> we must acknowledge . . . that man with all his noble qualities, with
> sympathy which feels for the most debased, with benevolence which
> extends not only to other men but to the humblest living creature,
> with his god-like intellect which has penetrated into the movements

and constitution of the solar system – with all these exalted powers – Man still bears in his bodily frame the indelible stamp of his lowly origin.[13]

With the cautionary words, "though not through [their] own exertions" (*Descent*, II, 405), Darwin emphasized that human beings have achieved a precarious prominence not through choice but rather through the workings of laws of heredity (which were not yet understood) and chance. The "great principle of evolution" demonstrates that it is no longer possible to believe "that man is the work of a separate act of creation"; rather, all facts "point . . . to the conclusion that man is the co-descendant with other mammals of a common progenitor" (II, 386). Inevitably, "every one who admits the general principle of evolution, must see that the mental powers of the higher animals . . . are the same in kind with those of mankind, though so different in degree" (II, 390).

Darwin's reference to man at the summit of the organic scale recapitulates a figure of speech in *Man's Place in Nature*, as Huxley observed that

> our reverence for the nobility of manhood will not be lessened by the knowledge, that Man is, in substance and in structure, one with the brutes; for, he alone possesses the marvellous endowment of intelligible and rational speech, whereby . . . he stands raised . . . as on a mountain top, far above the level of his humble fellows, and transfigured from his grosser nature by reflecting, here and there, a ray from the infinite source of truth.[14]

Outlined against the shining background of the moon, as if "reflecting . . . a ray from [an] infinite source of truth," Holmes contemplates the wilderness of peat and granite before him. In standing upon the tor that both elevates him above the moor and connects him to it, he embodies the seeming paradox of the human situation: joined to the world of animals and savage prehistoric peoples, yet possessed of intellectual capacities that elevate him above his ancestors.

But there are other allusions in the episode of the Man on the Tor that become more fully clarified by an event early on in the case. Soon after meeting Sir Henry Baskerville, Holmes is presented with the warning that the baronet has received, a single sentence composed (except for the word "moor") of words cut out of a London *Times* article. The note provides the occasion for another virtuoso act of detection, one that leads Dr. Mortimer to cry out in exasperation, "We are coming now rather into the region of guesswork." Holmes replies: "Say, rather, into the region where we balance probabilities and choose the most likely. It is the *scientific use of the imagination*, but we have always some material basis on which to start our speculation" (*Hound*, II, 687, emphasis added). In his response to Mortimer, Holmes has appropriated the title of John Tyndall's 1870 essay, which was reprinted in the various editions of his *Fragments of Science*, a collection of scientific papers, talks, and occasional pieces by the Irish physicist and mathematician to whom Doyle referred in passing in his *Memories and Adventures*.[15] As a follower of Darwin, Tyndall was an original member of the X Club along with, among others, Huxley, Herbert Spencer, and John Lubbock, coiner of the terms "neolithic" and "paleolithic" in his *Pre-historic Times* (1865).[16] Tyndall was an inveterate critic of religious orthodoxies, perhaps most notorious for his "Belfast Address," delivered before the British Association for the Advancement of Science in 1874, in which he expressed his desire to "wrest from theology, the entire domain of cosmological theory" (*Fragments*, p. 530). In his subsequent "Apology for the Belfast Address" Tyndall went further, arguing that "the Book of Genesis has no voice in scientific questions. . . . It is a poem, not a scientific treatise" (*Fragments*, p. 548).

I would like to believe that a seventeen-year-old Doyle, entering upon his days as a medical student at Edinburgh University in 1876, might have come upon the fifth edition of the *Fragments of Science*, perhaps led to it by Winwood Reade's *The Martyrdom of Man* (1872), and sensed that Tyndall was addressing him directly as an "able Catholic student" encouraged to "sit under the immeasurable heavens, watch the stars in their courses, scan the mysterious nebulæ, and try to realise what it all is and means"; "he will see and feel what drivellers even men of strenuous intellects may become, through exclusively dwelling and dealing with theological chimeras" ("Introduction" to Part II, *Fragments*, p. 328).

Such an attitude could well inform Holmes's response to Dr. Mortimer's inclination to believe in a hell-hound. Besides the allusion to Winwood Reade in his dismissal of the demon hound as a fairy tale, Holmes's reference to Tyndall's "Scientific Use of the Imagination" suggests the extent to which his own experience upon Black Tor, and Watson's account of it, have been informed by the heterodox materialism of each man. Like Reade, Tyndall celebrated uniformitarian science, even as he emphasized the imaginative activity necessary to its conduct. In the closing paragraphs of his essay Tyndall recalled a moment in July 1868 as he stood upon the Matterhorn, contemplating the implications of Darwin's "Evolution hypothesis" (*Fragments*, p. 454). He found that his thoughts had run back to the remote "origin and sculpture" of the Alps:

> "Nor did thought halt there, but wandered on through molten worlds to that nebulous haze which philosophers have regarded, and with good reason, as the proximate source of all material things. I tried to look at this universal cloud, containing within itself the prediction of all that has since occurred. . . . Did that formless fog contain potentially the *sadness* with which I regarded the Matterhorn? Did the *thought* which now ran back to it [the nebulous haze] simply return to its primeval home?"
>
> (pp. 457–58)

In his reflections Tyndall invoked the nebular hypothesis as, through an act of the imagination, he returned to contemplate a moment "which no eye had previously seen, and which no mind had previously imagined" (p. 429) in order to consider once again the origins of the solar system, organized life, and even human consciousness, all through the operation of natural law alone.

Tyndall's essay was to become a paean to the wonders of the mind: "Nourished by knowledge patiently won; bounded and conditioned by co-operant Reason; imagination becomes the prime mover of the physical discoverer" (*Fragments*, p. 426). Even Darwin, Tyndall wrote, had used "observation, imagination, and reason combined, [to] run back with wonderful sagacity and success over a certain length of the line of biological succession" to place "at the root of life a primordial germ" (p. 450). Such an achievement, beyond the realm of the purely empirical, led Tyndall to acknowledge "in the human intellect a power of expansion – I might almost call it a power of creation – which is brought into play by the simple *brooding* upon facts. The legend of the Spirit *brooding* over chaos may have originated in a knowledge of this power" (p. 428, emphasis added).

Sherlock Holmes's scientific use of the imagination reveals the way in which the detective is never only the rationalist and the empiricist: after the initial interview with Dr. Mortimer, Holmes's "spirit has hovered . . . all day" (*Hound*, II, 683) over the Ordnance map of the Devon moor. He is possessed of a power that eludes explanation, that can be suggested only through the use of a figurative language that possesses its own history. It is a figurative language provided by earlier discussions of the nebular hypothesis that had influenced Tyndall's "Scientific Use of the Imagination" and – "infinitely distant, unnamed, . . . almost undetectable" – Watson's account of the Man on the Tor. In his essay Tyndall self-consciously responded to Robert Chambers and, before him, to John Pringle Nichol, Regius professor of astronomy at the University of Glasgow. In *Vestiges of the Natural History of Creation* (1844) the anonymous Chambers, "Mr. Vestiges," had written of the now familiar "universal Fire Mist" from which our solar system had emerged through a process governed at first by the law of Gravitation and, later, by the law of Development that governed the appearance of organized life and consciousness.[17]

Of course, the heterodox, materialist implications of *Vestiges*, which outraged both scriptural literalists and natural theologians, had been anticipated in 1837 by John Pringle Nichol in his *Views of the Architecture of the Heavens*.[18] In *his* account of the nebular hypothesis Nichol resorted to language to which John Tyndall returned in "Scientific Use of the Imagination." Nichol sought to describe the birth of the stars and our solar system from the cooling of heated gases "as if we had even attained the privilege of witnessing the arranging influence of that Dove Spirit which erst brooded over chaos."[19] At first glance Nichol (and Tyndall) would seem to allude to the King James Genesis where "the Spirit of God moved upon the face of the waters" (Genesis 1:2). But within the materialist tradition that the two shared, Nichol and Tyndall invoked another cosmological work, Milton's *Paradise Lost*, with its own heterodox and, for some, materialist implications.[20] In writing of the "legend of the Spirit brooding over chaos," Tyndall appropriated Nichol's words about the birth of the universe, of stars, and of the solar system, and used them to describe the mental activity in which he engaged while upon the Matterhorn – an activity in which Holmes as the Man on the Tor is later to engage, "brooding over that enormous wilderness of peat and granite which [lies] before him" (*Hound*, II, 726).

Nichol, Tyndall, and Doyle explicitly and implicitly invoked Romantic interpretations of Raphael's account of the Creation in *Paradise Lost*, as the Son rides "Far into *Chaos*, and the World unborn": "He took the golden Compasses, prepar'd / In God's Eternal store, to circumscribe / This Universe, and all created things." In this way "God the Heav'n created, thus the Earth, / Matter unform'd and void":

> on the wat'ry calm
> His brooding wings the Spirit of God outspread,
> And vital virtue infus'd, and vital warmth
> Throughout the fluid Mass.[21]

In his allusion to *Paradise Lost* Nichol sought perhaps to mute the more sombre implications of his version of the nebular hypothesis. Unlike the more sanguine Mr. Vestiges, for whom the process of development offered only hope, Nichol had observed that "in relation to the nebulæ, Man is only an Ephemeron" (*Architecture*, p. 152). He claimed that "absolute permanence is visible nowhere around us": "the history of the solar orb," and, inevitably, that of humankind may well have its close" (pp. 194–95).

In his own melancholic brooding upon evolution and the origins of human consciousness, Tyndall echoed Mr. Vestiges, Nichol, and Milton. But he also appropriated them for his own ends. At one point Tyndall observed, "I have no right to intrude upon you, unasked, the unformed notions which are floating like clouds, or gathering to more solid consistency, in the modern speculative scientific mind" (*Fragments*, p. 451). The process by which galaxies, suns, and planetary systems have appeared approximates the activity of human consciousness, the coalescing of amorphous intuitions into coherent ideas. With these words Tyndall placed himself within a Romantic tradition that responded in sharply diverging ways to Raphael's account of the Creation in *Paradise Lost*. In the nebular hypothesis Tyndall found a contemporary version of the Miltonic spirit brooding upon unformed matter; and he transformed this hypothesis, as William Hazlitt once transformed Milton's description of the Creation, into a Romantic metaphor for the mind. Writing of Wordsworth's *Excursion* in the *Examiner* in August and October of 1814, Hazlitt observed that Wordsworth "may be said to create his own materials. . . . His imagination *broods* over that which is 'without form and void,' and 'makes it pregnant.'"[22]

Hazlitt's *Examiner* review suggests the tradition in which Tyndall consciously participated. Throughout "Scientific Use of the Imagination" Tyndall discussed his solution to the phenomenon of the blueness of the sky, referring to experiences that he had had on Mont Blanc and Mount Snowdon. His celebration of the human imagination became implicitly associated with Percy Bysshe Shelley's "Mont Blanc" (1817) and with Wordsworth's *Prelude* (1850), two strikingly different meditations on the nature of consciousness, each with its own Miltonic allusion. Shelley's poem opens: "The everlasting universe of things / Flows through the mind, and rolls its rapid waves, / Now dark – now glittering – now reflecting gloom – / Now lending splendour, where from secret springs / The source of human thought its tribute brings / Of waters, – with a sound but half its own."[23] The poem ends by tracing the source of those springs to the summit of Mont Blanc:

> Its home
> The voiceless lightning in these solitudes
> Keeps innocently, and like vapour *broods*
> Over the snow. The secret Strength of things
> Which governs thought, and to the infinite dome
> Of Heaven is as a law, inhabits thee!

(ll. 136–41, emphasis added)

The borrowing from Milton's cosmological epic renders more ironic the ambiguity, bordering on skepticism, with which "Mont Blanc" concludes: "And what were thou, and earth, and stars, and sea, / If to the human mind's imaginings / Silence and solitude were vacancy?" (ll. 142–44). The potential skepticism of "Mont Blanc" is countered in Book XIV of Wordsworth's 1850 *Prelude* when, atop Mount Snowdon in the moonlight, the poet looks up: "The Moon hung naked in a firmament / Of azure without cloud, and at my feet / Rested a silent sea of hoary mist."[24] The "full-orbed Moon / . . . gaze[s] / Upon the billowy ocean" (XIV, ll. 53–55); from a rift in the mist "Mount[s] the roar of waters, torrents, streams / Innumerable, roaring with one voice!" (XIV, ll. 59–60). Finally, the Moon becomes "the emblem of a mind / That feeds upon infinity, that *broods* / Over the dark abyss . . . / . . . a mind sustained / By recognitions of transcendent power" (XIV, ll. 70–75, emphasis added).

In his musings upon the Matterhorn, Tyndall reenacted those of Shelley and Wordsworth, with their differing responses to Mont Blanc and Mount Snowdon. As a Darwinian, a materialist, and a skeptic, Tyndall was led back in time to "that nebulous haze which [natural] philosophers have regarded . . . as the proximate source of all material things," even "potentially [of] the *sadness*" with which he contemplated the Matterhorn (*Fragments*, p. 457). Like Nichol and Mr. Vestiges before him, Tyndall argued that there was no need for divine intervention in the formation of galaxies and our solar system or in the generation of life on earth. He imaginatively returned to a moment long past when "matter in a nebulous form preceded matter in its present form" (p. 450). Tyndall followed Mr. Vestiges, and Darwin, in endorsing the nebular hypothesis:

> There are the strongest grounds for believing that during a certain period of its history the earth was not, nor was it fit to be, the theatre of life. Whether this was ever a nebulous period, or merely a molten period, does not much matter. . . . Our question is this: Did creative energy pause until the nebulous matter had condensed, until the

earth had been detached, until the solar fire had so withdrawn . . .
as to permit a crust to gather round the planet? . . . Having waited
through those æons . . . did it send the fiat forth, "Let there be Life!"?
(pp. 452–53)

In his ironic play on Genesis and the Gospel of John, Tyndall rejected
theistic versions of origins, with their reliance on the doctrine of special
creation.[25]

Yet, throughout his broodings upon origins Tyndall responded to the
figurative implications of his own language in order to avert the melancholy he might feel, turning the nebular hypothesis into a metaphor
for the mind. As a friend of Thomas Carlyle and Ralph Waldo Emerson,
as a devotee of Goethe, Tyndall remained too much the Romantic in
spirit to give himself over to a version of materialism, a form of "arrested
development" (Doyle, *Memories*, p. 27), that could lead to Lombroso's
biological determinism. For Tyndall the mystery of human consciousness endures. Although he acknowledged that "there is but a step from
the atom to the organism" (*Fragments*, p. 447), he still asserted: "Spirit
and matter have ever been presented to us in the rudest contrast, the
one as all-noble, the other as all-vile. But is this correct? Upon the
answer to this question all depends" (p. 454). He wondered what would
follow had we "been taught to regard [spirit and matter] as equally
worthy, . . . as two opposite faces of the self-same mystery" (p. 454), as
Goethe had proposed. The mystery of human consciousness endures in
the union of matter and spirit. Thus Tyndall proclaimed: "not alone the
more ignoble forms of animalcular or animal life, not alone the nobler
forms of the horse and lion, not alone the exquisite and wonderful
mechanism of the human body, but . . . the human mind itself –
emotion, intellect, will, and all their phenomena – were once latent in
a fiery cloud" (p. 453). He was determined to retain the sense of mystery
at the heart of Romantic speculations upon consciousness and the
imagination: "Fear not the Evolution hypothesis. . . . It does not
solve – it does not profess to solve – the ultimate mystery of this
universe. It leaves, in fact, that mystery untouched" (p. 455).

Elsewhere in the 1876 edition of *Fragments of Science* Tyndall clarified
his choice among varieties of materialisms. In "Scientific Materialism"
(1868) he acknowledged "the association of two classes of phenomena,"
the material and the conscious, "of whose real bond of union [the
materialist] is in absolute ignorance" (*Fragments*, p. 421). Tyndall recognized that "for every fact of consciousness, whether in the domain
of sense, of thought, or of emotion, a definite molecular condition, of
motion or structure, is set up in the brain. . . . But the passage from the

physics of the brain to the corresponding facts of consciousness is unthinkable" (pp. 419–20). He concluded "Scientific Materialism" with an observation that returns us to *The Hound of the Baskervilles* and the Man on the Tor: "The problem of the connection of body and soul is as insoluble, in its modern form, as it was in the pre-scientific ages. . . . Let us *lower our heads*, and *acknowledge our ignorance, priest and philosopher, one and all*" (*Fragments*, p. 421, emphasis added).

II

What is both explicit and implicit in Tyndall's speculations upon mind – including distant, barely discernible allusions – informs Dr. Watson's vision of the Man on the Tor. Shelley contemplating Mont Blanc, Wordsworth atop Mount Snowdon, and Tyndall on the Matterhorn in July 1868 all prepare for an episode and a novel in which the nature of human consciousness is explored. An evolutionary perspective joins the nebular hypothesis and the confirmation in 1859 of the antiquity of man, the reality of the existence of prehistoric peoples – those extinct inhabitants, in Stapleton's words, of the stone wigwams that, with the trench in the hillside of the Devon moor, become the marks "of our worthy ancestors" (*Hound*, II, 709). With lowered head Holmes acknowledges the various mysteries posed by the scene before him; as he broods upon it, he seeks to engender order out of chaos. In the granite-strewn moor, the Grimpen Mire, and the prehistoric stone huts, Holmes gazes upon the evidence to which classical evolutionists turned to support their claims about the origins of life and consciousness.

Holmes engages in such speculations amid a setting reminiscent of "some fantastic landscape in a dream" (*Hound*, II, 700). The railway journey that has carried Dr. Watson, Dr. Mortimer, Sir Henry Baskerville, and, later, Holmes from London to Devon has become a journey both in space and in time. With its rare butterflies and moths, the nearly-extinct bittern, and the moor ponies that fall prey to the bog-holes of the Grimpen Mire, the landscape before Holmes suggests the world of the *Origin of Species*, governed by a struggle for survival and haunted by the threat of extinction. With its "undulating downs, long green rollers, with crests of jagged granite foaming up into fantastic surges" (II, 707), the moor becomes for Watson a primeval ocean out of which life has emerged and evolved. Stapleton speaks of "the wonderful secrets which it contains. It is so vast, and so barren, and so mysterious" (II, 707). He then directs Watson's attention to the Grimpen Mire, which seems to offer "a rare place for a gallop" but lures animals and human beings to their deaths. Later, in their pursuit of Stapleton, Holmes and Watson embark from a peninsula of peat into the bog: "a false step plunged us more than once thigh-deep into the dark, quivering mire, which shook for yards in soft undulations around our feet. Its tenacious grip plucked at our heels as we walked, and when we sank into it it was as if some malignant hand was tugging us down into those obscene depths" (II, 759–60).

The figurative ocean of the Devon moor and the Grimpen Mire becomes suggestive not only of Darwinian nature but of the depths of the Romantic mind that Hazlitt wrote of in his 1814 review of *The Excursion*. The poetic "imagination brood[ing] over that which is 'without form and void' and '[making] it pregnant'" becomes embodied in Sherlock Holmes, the Romantic spirit surviving after Darwin. For Holmes, who has been known to quote Goethe in the German and to recommend Carlyle and Jean-Paul Richter to Watson, the landscape may conjure up Carlyle's review-essay "Characteristics" (1831) and his investigations into the "curious relations of the Voluntary and Conscious to the Involuntary and Unconscious," investigations that "might lead us into deep questions of Psychology and Physiology." For

> Nature, it might seem, strives, like a kind mother, to hide from us even this, that she is a mystery: she will have us rest on her beautiful and awful bosom as if it were our secure home; on the bottomless boundless Deep, whereon all human things fearfully and wonderfully swim, she will have us walk and build, as if the film which supported us there ... were no film, but a solid rock-foundation.[26]

In his first written report to Holmes, Watson echoes Carlyle: "The longer one stays here the more does the spirit of the moor sink into one's soul. ... When you are once out upon its bosom you have left all traces of modern England behind you, ... you are conscious everywhere of the homes and the work ... of these forgotten folk" (*Hound*, II, 712).

The landscape suggests Carlylean depths of the mind that remain indefinable, perhaps unconstituted, until the emergence of an evolutionary perspective and, in the 1860s and 1870s, the rise of a prehistoric archaeology. In the form of the nebular hypothesis, nineteenth-century cosmology had posited the unimaginable age of a universe forever in the process of change; Lyellian geology had demonstrated the vast history of the earth and those subterranean phenomena that produce earthquakes and volcanic eruptions and, in concert with the forces of erosion, the elevation and subsidence of entire continents; paleontology had revealed the tenuous nature of the very ground upon which men and women walked, its immediate surface composed of the transformed remains of dead organisms. Now prehistoric archaeology had added yet another dimension to the human situation: those periods of time in which people lived millennia before events recorded in scripture or other ancient documents.

We have seen such vistas of time discussed in nineteenth-century Britain in a characteristic language that included Tyndall's "universal cloud" and "formless fog" that served as the "primeval home" of the universe and consciousness. Antiquarians and archaeologists, lay-people and professionals, invoked a similar vocabulary in discussing the antiquity of man. Thus, in introducing Heinrich Schliemann to the Society of Antiquaries in 1875, William Gladstone had observed that in the recent past "the whole of the prehistoric times lay before our eyes like a silver cloud covering the whole of the lands that, at different periods of history, had become so illustrious and interesting; but as to their details we knew nothing. . . . Now we are beginning to see through this dense mist and the cloud is becoming transparent."[27] A few years later a pioneer in the excavation of prehistoric sites in Great Britain, General Lane-Fox Pitt-Rivers, could bring the issue closer to home. In a meeting of the Archaeological Institute in 1887 he remarked: "No individual amongst those who assembled here in 1849 [when the Institute first met] had the least idea that beneath his very feet were to be found relics of man's workmanship at a time when he was contemporary with the elephant and other extinct animals."[28] So in the evening of a rainy day Watson dons his waterproof to venture out once more upon the Carlylean bosom of the moor, ready to respond to the landscape. He finds the Black Tor upon which he has seen "the unseen watcher, the man of darkness" (*Hound*, II, 730). From the summit of the tor he looks out across the downs to see, perhaps, what the Man on the Tor has already seen, "the fantastic hills" below him: "In the distant hollow on the left, half hidden by the mist, the two thin towers of Baskerville Hall rose above the trees. They were the only signs of human life which I could see, save only those prehistoric huts which lay thickly upon the slopes of the hills" (II, 730).

For Watson, as for Holmes, depths and elevated heights are joined; past and present coexist in the stone huts and the towers of the hall, glimpsed through Gladstone's transparent mist of time. Yet "nowhere [is] there any trace" (*Hound*, II, 730) of the lonely figure that Watson has seen on the tor two nights before. The rocky slopes below Black Tor, however, will finally yield traces that serve as clues to the larger mystery to which the Man on the Tor points. It is ironic that it will be the corpse of Selden, the escaped convict – driven to his death by the hound of the Baskervilles – that will clarify the issues that the novel explores. After their reunion on the moor, Holmes and Watson respond to a cry of agony. On a slope they find "spread-eagled some dark, irregular object," a "vague outline [that hardens] into a definite shape" (II, 744). Clad in the cast-off wardrobe of Sir Henry Baskerville and displayed against the slope, the body becomes an ambiguous sign that Holmes and Watson misread as they mistake the dead Selden for Sir Henry. Their error serves only further to blur the differences between the male figures involved in the case, a process that began when the bearded man in the London cab who was shadowing Sir Henry told the driver that he was Sherlock Holmes. The blurring continues when Watson realizes that there is not one man, but that there are two, living on the moor in the abandoned stone huts. The dead Selden – perceived by Watson as a prehistoric savage – becomes associated with the Man on the Tor through the language that Watson has used upon first seeing him: he was "outlined as black as an ebony statue" against the background of "the lower curve of [the moon's] silver disc" (II, 726). Now, as Watson, Holmes, and a frustrated Stapleton go their separate ways after realizing that the corpse is not that of Sir Henry but of Selden, Watson looks back to see "the figure [of Stapleton] moving slowly away over the broad moor, and behind him that one black smudge on the silvered slope which [shows] where the man [is] lying who had come so horribly to his end" (II, 747).

In his backward glance at Stapleton and the black smudge, Watson transforms the silvered slope into another figurative palimpsest that harkens back to Thomas De Quincey's discussion of the human mind in his *Suspiria de Profundis* (1845): "What else than a natural and mighty palimpsest is the human brain? Such a palimpsest is my brain; such a palimpsest, oh reader! is yours. Everlasting layers of ideas, images, feelings, have fallen upon your brain softly as light. Each succession has seemed to bury all that went before. And yet, in reality, not one has been extinguished." With his references to "endless strata [covering] up each other in forgetfulness," De Quincey offered a Romantic vision of the mind, one indebted to nineteenth-century geology and archaeology with their characteristic way of describing fossils and recovered edifices.[29] Perhaps De Quincey remembered *Illustrations of the Huttonian Theory of the Earth* (1802) in which John Playfair wrote that fossil remains constitute a figurative "memory preserved in those archives, where nature has recorded the revolutions of the globe."[30] In responding to the scene before him, Watson fuses geological and archaeological commonplaces with the De Quincean palimpsest of the mind. On that silvery slope, the past has been preserved through the accretion of indistinct characters: one sign is superimposed ineradicably upon another, a smudged trace attesting to a continuum that connects the prehistoric past to the present. All distinctions between the brutal Selden and the civilized baronet, between the cunning Stapleton and Holmes, dissolve. They are united in that barely decipherable smudge upon the rocky slope, asserting that the prehistoric past persists into the present moment – but not, as Dr. Mortimer's articles might argue, through reversion or atavism. Watson's account has implicitly rejected the biological determinism of Cesare Lombroso, for whom the reversion to the savage remains a purely hereditary phenomenon. Rather, in connecting Selden with Sir Henry, and Stapleton with Holmes, Watson suggests that there are figurative depths to the self that are to be associated with a primitive past that has never disappeared: the Carlylean film of consciousness always rests upon the depths of the involuntary and the unconscious.[31]

Such depths have already been suggested by the Grimpen Mire, as Watson transforms it into something other than a representation of Darwinian nature. For it will be out of a "dense, white fog" gathering over the Grimpen Mire that the hound of the Baskervilles is to appear, as Holmes, Watson, and Inspector Lestrade wait outside Merripit House to spring their trap on Stapleton: "The moon shone on it, and it looked like a great shimmering ice-field, with the heads of the distant tors as rocks borne upon its surface" (*Hound*, II, 755). The "fog-wreaths" drift across the moor, "crawling round both corners of [Merripit House] and roll[ing] slowly into one dense bank, on which the upper floor and the roof [float] like a strange ship upon a shadowy sea." What emerges from that "dense white sea, with the moon silvering its upper edge" (II, 756) proves to be overwhelming. Watson recalls: "Never in the delirious dream of a disordered brain could anything more savage, more appalling, more hellish be conceived than that dark form and savage face which broke upon us" (II, 757). The hound figuratively springs from the mind of Stapleton, a poet manqué who in "a flash of genius" has conceived a way to exploit the Baskerville legend and, through the use of phosphorous paint, "to make [his] creature diabolical" (II, 762). Like Wordsworth's "silent sea of hoary mist" gazed upon by "the full-orbed Moon" – the "type/Of a majestic intellect" (*Prelude*, Book XIV, ll. 42, 53, 66–67) – Gladstone's silver cloud of time has been internalized: the Devon landscape, the fog, and the moon all provide a vision of the human mind. The figurative sea of fog becomes associated with Stapleton, a man who is able to negotiate the depths of the Grimpen Mire and to penetrate to the island with the abandoned tin mine at its center until, at last, the Mire's "tenacious grip" (*Hound*, II, 760) seizes him and reclaims him.

Such a vision of consciousness – at once indebted to Coleridge, Wordsworth, Carlyle, and De Quincey – may have proved too elusive for readers of *The Strand* in 1902. However, Doyle was to return in 1910 to familiar landscapes – and themes – in "The Adventure of the Devil's Foot." In this story Sherlock Holmes's "iron constitu- tion" has almost given way as a result of overwork and "occasional indiscretions" (*Complete Sherlock Holmes*, II, 955) – a return, I assume, to the use of cocaine or morphine, associated with Romantic pre- occupations with dreams and the mystery of human consciousness.[32] In the company of Dr. Watson, Holmes retreats to a cottage at Poldhu Bay on Cornwall's Lizard Peninsula: in "a country of rolling moors, . . . there were traces of some vanished race which had passed utterly away, and left as its sole record strange monuments of stone, irregular mounds which contained the burned ashes of the dead, and curious earthworks which hinted at prehistoric strife" ("Devil's Foot," II, 955). Once again traces of modern England seem almost to have disap- peared, as a forgotten time reasserts itself in enduring relics. Holmes even turns to the study of "the ancient Cornish language," and, like others before him (including Charles Lyell), he "conceive[s] the idea that it was akin to the Chaldean, and had been largely derived from the Phœnician traders in tin" (II, 955). Historical philology points always to the past, to the roots of the present in a time before written language.[33]

Cornwall has become yet another fantastic "land of dreams" ("Devil's Foot," II, 955) in which Holmes and Watson investigate the mysterious death of Brenda Tregennis and the inexplicable madness of her two brothers, all three apparently stricken while at a game of cards. It is the death of the surviving brother, Mortimer Tregennis – who will prove to be his sister's murderer – that provides the clue that explains how a young woman has apparently been frightened to death and her two brothers driven to insanity. Holmes finds a brownish powder on the smoke-shield of the lamp in the room in which he and Watson have come upon the body of Mortimer Tregennis, his "limbs . . . convulsed and his fingers contorted as though he had died in a very paroxysm of fear" (II, 963). The powder proves to be the residue of an African drug derived from the devil's-foot root, a drug that "stimulates those brain centres which control the emotion of fear, and . . . either madness or death is the fate" of anyone exposed to it, a fate whose cause "European science would be [powerless] to detect" (II, 969).

Holmes and Watson expose themselves to the fumes of the powder, experimenting with its powers. They have an experience akin to the one on the Devon moor when Stapleton's demonic hound leaps from the cloud of white fog. At the first whiff of the fumes Watson's "brain and . . . imagination [are] beyond all control":

> A thick, black cloud swirled before my eyes, and my mind told me that in this cloud, unseen as yet, but about to spring out upon my appalled senses, lurked all that was vaguely horrible, all that was monstrous and inconceivably wicked in the universe. Vague shapes swirled and swam amid the dark cloud-bank, each a menace and a warning of something coming, the advent of some unspeakable dweller upon the threshold, whose very shadow would blast my soul.
>
> ("Devil's Foot," II, 965)

Through the agency of the drug Holmes and Watson are returned to those lower nervous centers of nineteenth-century neurology, physiology, and evolutionary anthropology that in the Eurocentric sciences of the day were to be studied in the peoples of the East and Africa. The past dwells within such nervous centers and also within Holmes and Watson, just as in *The Hound of the Baskervilles* it exists in Selden and Stapleton, each identified with a primitive era in the past. It waits only to be released and to emerge from those figurative mists of time that so obscure it.

In the midst of the mystery of the "Cornish horror" ("Devil's Foot," II, 955), it is fitting that Holmes diverts himself in "the pursuit of neolithic man" and that, at the conclusion of the case, he returns "to the study of those Chaldean roots which are surely to be traced in the Cornish branch of the great Celtic speech" (II, 961, 970). The roots of the human species, of language, and of human consciousness itself are to be found in the vicinity of the Mediterranean and in Africa, to which Dr. Leon Sterndale returns in a self-imposed exile for avenging the death of Brenda Tregennis by murdering her brother, Mortimer. It is an appropriate penance that the man who has brought the devil's-foot root to England should vow "to bury [him]self in central Africa" (II, 970), yet another land of dreams associated with a prehistoric past that survives, figuratively, into the present in the peoples amongst whom Sterndale will live out his days.[34]

III

Both Sherlock Holmes's preoccupation with the origins of the Celtic language and Dr. Leon Sterndale's self-exile in central Africa may return us to *The Hound of the Baskervilles* and to Dr. Watson's insistent references to the peasants on the Devon moor, those ignorant people who believe in the existence of a phantom hound that defies the laws of nature. In relying upon an evolutionary perspective to render his experience intelligible both to himself and to others, Watson echoes the language and the arguments of anthropologists like E. B. Tylor and James Frazer. In *Primitive Culture* (1871) Tylor prefaced his discussion of the development of the human intellect and human culture with words that reveal the basis of Holmes's study of the Chaldean and the Celtic in "The Devil's Foot": "The study of language has, perhaps, done more than any other in removing from our view of human thought and action the ideas of chance and arbitrary invention, and in substituting for them a theory of development by the co-operation of individual men, through processes ever reasonable and intelligible where the facts are fully known."[35] From a uniformitarian perspective the study of language involves, inevitably, the study of mind. Tylor even espoused a credo akin to the one that informs Holmes's scientific use of the imagination: "Rudimentary as the science of culture still is, the symptoms are becoming very strong that even what seem its most spontaneous and motiveless phenomena will, nevertheless, be shown to come within the range of distinct cause and effect as certainly as the facts of mechanics" (*Primitive Culture*, I, 18).

Tylor set out to look "backward from our own times, [so that] the course of mental history may be traced" (*Primitive Culture*, I, 273). Through the study of "the history and præ-history of man" it becomes possible "to establish a connexion between what uncultured ancient men thought and did, and what cultured modern men think and do" (II, 443). From a Eurocentric – and racist – perspective, Tylor studied existing primitive people as if they were living fossils, exemplary of a previous stage of human development. But he also turned to "the modern European peasant" whose beliefs and customs "have altered little in a long course of centuries": it is possible to "draw a picture where there shall be scarce a hand's breadth difference between an English ploughman and a negro of Central Africa" (I, 7). Through the doctrine of survivals Tylor argued that there are "processes, customs, opinions, and so forth, which have been carried on by force of habit into a new state of society different from that in which they had their original home, and they thus remain as proofs and examples of an older condition of culture out of which a newer has been evolved" (I, 16). The so-called peasants of the Devon moor engage in such customs when they burn the litigious Mr. Frankland in effigy. At that moment there is perhaps "scarce a hand's breadth difference" between them and the negroes of that Central Africa to which Dr. Leon Sterndale returns: they resort to practices, according to E. B. Tylor, whose roots extend into a past of which they are themselves ignorant.[36]

In his dogmatic fashion Tylor turned to suggestive figures of speech as he hoped to eradicate superstition and a misguided belief in the supernatural: "It is quite wonderful, *even if we hardly go below the surface of the subject*, to see how large a share stupidity and unpractical conservatism and dogged superstition have had in preserving for us *traces* of the history of our race" (*Primitive Culture*, I, 156, emphasis added). Tylor's project was to expose and root out such traces of the past, to usher in the age of reason and science so that no one will yield to superstitious belief in the supernatural or engage in practices that suggest primitive error. In the closing pages of *Primitive Culture* he explained his goal: "To impress men's minds with a doctrine of development, will lead them in all honour to their ancestors to continue the progressive work of past ages. . . . It is a harsher, and at times even painful, office . . . to expose the remains of crude old culture which have passed into harmful superstition, and to mark these out for destruction" (II, 453). It is this office that Holmes takes up as he scoffs at Dr. Mortimer for having "quite gone over to the supernaturalists" (*Hound*, II, 681), while Watson relies on prevailing notions of common sense rather than "descend to the level of [the] poor peasants, who are not content with a mere fiend dog but must needs describe him with hell-fire shooting from his mouth and eyes" (II, 727).

Yet when Mr. Frankland speaks in passing of his contempt for the local police, his words reveal how the rationalist program of Tylor subverts itself even in the language it uses to espouse its aims. Frankland has refused to inform the police of the boy who attends one of the men living on the moor in a neolithic stone hut. In his pique he observes that the police have "treated [him] shamefully" by not interfering with the Fernworthy folk who have pillaged him in effigy: "Nothing would induce me to help the police. . . . For all they cared it might have been me, instead of my effigy, which these rascals burned at the stake" (*Hound*, II, 738). Frankland may not understand that for Tylor the ceremony would be the "unconscious record" of primitive beliefs and customs "rooted in the depths of savage life" and persisting "below the surface of the subject" – and of human consciousness (*Primitive Culture*, I, 104, 129, 156). Nor could he be expected to know that in an 1888 talk before the Royal Anthropological Institute, Tylor further developed his figure of speech in discussing matriarchal and patriarchal societies. The figurative language that deals with surfaces and depths led Tylor to observe: "the institutions of man are as distinctly stratified as the earth on which he lives. They succeed each other in series substantially uniform over the globe, independent of what seem the comparatively superficial differences of race and language, but shaped by similar human nature acting through successively changed conditions in savage, barbaric, and civilised life."[37]

Tylor's avowedly evolutionary anthropology encouraged the excavation of the human past and the discovery in the customs of nineteenth-century peasant folk – such as the ritual burning of effigies – the vestiges of the barbaric and even the savage past, with the goal of rooting out such vestiges and eradicating them. The program was to be pursued by James G. Frazer in *The Golden Bough* (1890). Throughout the various editions of a work whose subtitle was to become "The Roots of Religion and Folklore," Frazer continued with a vengeance the work of excavation as he exposed current superstitions and folk practices as the remains of Tylor's "crude old culture," treating religions – Christianity among them – as the vestiges of superstition and intellectual error. But in his discussion of religion, myth, and ritual, Frazer was not to usher in an age of Comtean positivism. Rather – and nowhere more clearly than in his analysis of the significance of effigies in various observances – he hinted at modes of consciousness and subterranean desires that precede and coexist with the Enlightenment rationality that he promoted.[38]

It is ironic that Tylor and Frazer suggested a vision of the mind that may produce the awe and wonder that Tyndall experienced atop the Matterhorn, where he had been "led to the outer rim of speculative science, for beyond the nebulæ scientific thought has never hitherto ventured" (*Fragments*, p. 455). Beyond the nebulae remains the mystery of the origins of consciousness. Neither the anthropology of Tylor and Frazer nor the evolution hypothesis to which they seemed to defer would solve "the ultimate mystery of this universe" (p. 455): science will not explain the nature of human consciousness. The investigation of consciousness can only lead us (once again in Tyndall's words) to "lower our heads, and acknowledge our ignorance, priest and philosopher, one and all": "the problem of the connection of body and soul" remains "insoluble" (p. 421) – particularly, in the world of *The Hound of the Baskervilles*, with Watson's vision of the enigmatic Man on the Tor.

The granite pinnacle of Black Tor and the figure of the man standing upon it return us to *The Golden Bough* and those geological figures of speech to which Frazer turned (and that, ironically, subvert his own

project). Frazer opened his book with the famous discussion of a ceremony from the time of imperial Rome, describing the ritual that
occurred periodically in a wood dedicated to Diana, in the vicinity of
the modern Italian village of Nemi. In that wood, according to the texts
that Frazer had consulted, there presided a priest who had gained his
position by murdering his predecessor; and the priest was himself fated
to be succeeded by the man who would kill him. In such a ritual Frazer
sought clues to "detect the motives which led to its institution."[39]
Through Tylor's doctrine of survivals Frazer set out to find in the institution of the priesthood at Nemi the vestigial remains of even earlier
customs and beliefs, perhaps reaching back into the era of Stapleton's
"Neolithic man – no date," and beyond. In this way Frazer pursued "a
clue to the real meaning" (*Golden Bough*, II, 365) of the mistletoe that
is the golden bough of antiquity. He would expose the origins of those
mistaken beliefs that continued to influence men and women of his
own time who, in burning an effigy on the Devon moor, reenact
perhaps in another form the ritual at Nemi: "No one will probably deny
that such a custom savours of a barbarous age and, surviving into imperial times, stands out in striking isolation from the polished Italian
society of the day, like a primeval rock rising from a smooth-shaven
lawn" (I, 2–3).

The primeval rock recurs in a 1908 lecture by Frazer that reveals, in
an extended figure of speech, his anxieties about the uneducated masses
in Great Britain and on the Continent. He returned to the language of
the *Golden Bough*, speaking of "the smooth surface of cultured society
[that] is sapped and mined by superstition."[40] Alarmed by the "intellectual savagery" of "a mass, if not the majority, of people in every civilized country," Frazer observed: "We appear to be standing on a volcano
which may at any moment break out in smoke and fire to spread ruin
and devastation among the gardens and palaces of ancient culture
wrought so laboriously by the hands of many generations" ("Social
Anthropology," p. 170). Frazer returned to a geological analogy to deal
with the social upheaval that he feared. Yet his "unseen forces" can be
transformed into psychological ones that persist not only within "the
minds of the vulgar," who only nominally conform to "the will of their
betters," but also in the minds of Frazer's "enlightened minority" (pp.
170–71). They persist as well in Doyle's Stapleton and Holmes, each of
whom is possessed of "hidden fires" (see *Hound*, II, 713, 745).

Frazer's "unseen forces" by which "the ground beneath our feet is
... honeycombed" ("Social Anthropology," p. 170) become manifested
in *The Hound of the Baskervilles* in the Black Tor, that "sharp pinnacle of

granite" rising out of the wilderness of the Devon moor. The tor becomes primary, enduring, never to be eradicated, the virtual bedrock upon which the landscape rests. With its igneous origins the tor reveals the presence of subterranean phenomena: it points backward to a geological epoch when the earth may have been in a molten state; it hints of that far distant moment when Mr. Vestiges' "universal Fire Mist" may have preceded matter in its present form. In the words of Tyndall:

> Many who hold [to the nebular hypothesis] would probably assent to the position that, at the present moment, all our philosophy, all our poetry, all our science, and all our art – Plato, Shakspeare [*sic*], Newton, and Raphael – are potential in the fires of the sun. We long to learn something of our origin. If the Evolution hypothesis be correct, even this unsatisfied yearning must have come to us across the ages which separate the unconscious primeval mist from the consciousness of to-day.
>
> (*Fragments*, pp. 453–54)

Tyndall's Romantic musings defy the confident rationalism of Tylor or Frazer, even as they reject Lombroso's biological determinism.

With its muted allusions to *Paradise Lost*, Tyndall's "Scientific Use of the Imagination" has informed Dr. Watson's vision of the Man on the Tor, the figure outlined against the moon, rising above yet allied to the depths of the moor and the Grimpen Mire. There is perhaps no separation between Tyndall's "unconscious primeval mist" and "the consciousness of to-day." Such consciousness coexists with the unconscious phenomena from which it has emerged. Frazer's primeval rock becomes not merely a relic of a former era, at best a survival of a barbarous age; it also becomes the foundation upon which the smooth-shaven lawn of a polished society rests as it thinly covers something primordial and ineradicable, a possibility suggested by Frazer in a telling figure of speech in his 1908 talk: "The surface of society, like that of the sea, is in perpetual motion; its depths, like those of the ocean, remain almost unmoved" ("Social Anthropology," p. 171). Such an insight, Carlylean in its implications, informs Watson's feeling that for someone on the bosom of the moor all traces of modern England have been effaced. As Tyndall suggested, there is no need to fear the "Evolution hypothesis": there remain the mysteries of human motivation that are suggested by the curious parallels between the ritualized murders in the wood near Nemi and the designs of Stapleton upon the life of Sir Henry Baskerville as he seeks to prove himself stronger and craftier than the man he would succeed.

In Watson's depiction of the Man on the Tor, a vision of the mind takes shape – one influenced, I would like to think, not only by Tyndall and, however indirectly, by *Paradise Lost* but also by Tyndall's friend Charles Darwin, someone not unacquainted with Milton's epic poem (a copy of which he carried with him throughout his voyage on the *Beagle*). We can return to Darwin's narrative of the voyage and his description of the Chilean earthquake of 1835: "A bad earthquake at once destroys the oldest associations: the world, the very emblem of all that is solid, has moved beneath our feet like a crust over a fluid; – one second of time has conveyed to the mind a strange idea of insecurity, which hours of reflection would never have created."[41] In this description Darwin turned implicitly to the nebular hypothesis and to theories of the earth's molten core in order to capture a sudden, irreversible revolution in worldview. For Darwin the earth had moved upon its foundations, undermining the orthodoxies that once sustained him. Yet the moment makes itself available to other interpretations, in which a prevailing common sense and scientific reason become, like Natural Theology, a figurative crust riding upon a molten fluid that suggests Romantic depths of the mind.

There may well be traces of Darwin's account of the Chilean earthquake – distant, unnamed, almost undetectable – in "Scientific Use of the Imagination" and *The Hound of the Baskervilles*. Tyndall and Doyle may have responded to Darwin's language, to the implications of the fact that the ground has moved beneath his feet to reveal the insubstantiality of the earth's surface and of a Carlylean film of consciousness that rests upon the fluid depths of the self. But Tyndall had already moved beyond the appropriations of figurative language from Milton, Nichol, Darwin, and others to meditate upon the very origin of the abstractions by which men and women contrive to live. Standing upon the Matterhorn, he observed: "I have no right to intrude upon you, unasked, the unformed notions which are floating like clouds, or gathering to more solid consistency, in the modern speculative scientific mind" (*Fragments*, p. 451). Here the nebular hypothesis provides not only a metaphor for the mind but also a subtle critique of the claims of science to empirical knowledge. For as Tyndall implies, it is out of metaphor itself that scientific theories and principles emerge. Dr. Watson echoes Tyndall as he describes the "figure of a man upon the tor" who stands "with his head bowed, as if he were brooding over that enormous wilderness of peat and granite . . . before him." In the act of brooding Sherlock Holmes conjures up a worldview out of the landscape upon which he muses. In rendering the man on the tor, Watson –

perhaps unwittingly – reveals that over the course of time a diffused nebulosity of figurative language coalesces into abstraction, convincing us that we tread upon Darwin's solid crust of empirical fact, when all the time there remains a domain beneath the "emblem of all that is solid," the fluid domain of metaphor.[42]

Epilogue: A Retrospection

> Darwin, in short, is the extraordinary man who, all by himself, embodied the only three beings proclaimed worthy of respect by Baudelaire – for he pulled down an old order, and came to know a large part of the new world that he created. *Il n'existe que trois êtres respectables: le prêtre, le guerrier, le poète. Savoir, tuer, et créer.* There exist only three beings worthy of our respect: the priest, the warrior, and the poet. Know, kill, and create.
>
> Stephen Jay Gould, *The Structure of Evolutionary Theory* (2002)

The Hound of the Baskervilles (1901–02) closes with the requisite coda of the detective novel, the summing up of the case in a coherent narrative organized chronologically and causally with no apparent omissions – with no enigmas, conundrums, or hieroglyphic puzzles unresolved. At first glance, the effect of such "A Retrospection" seems to consolidate the implicit worldview of the art of detection modeled on the reconstructions of the nineteenth-century historical disciplines. In his summing up Sherlock Holmes invokes empirical data, rejects appeals to the supernatural, and offers a narrative account that forgoes teleological claims of any sort, whether theistic or positivistic.

All of this is suggested when Dr. Watson asks Sherlock Holmes how, "if Stapleton came into the succession, . . . could he explain the fact that he, the heir [to the Baskerville title], had been living unannounced under another name so close to the property? How could he claim it without causing suspicion and inquiry?" Holmes responds: "It is a formidable difficulty, and I fear that you ask too much when you expect me to solve it. The past and the present are within the field of my inquiry, but what a man may do in the future is a hard question to answer."[1] Here, Holmes voices the credo of those practitioners of William Whewell's "palætiological sciences" that had culminated in the *Origin of Species* (1859). In "A Retrospection" Holmes allies himself with Charles Lyell (1797–1875), Charles Darwin (1809–1882), and John Tyndall (1820–1893), if not with E. B. Tylor (1832–1917) and James G. Frazer (1854–1941) whose Comtean self-assurance led to their anticipation of a future freed of those religious superstitions that they dismissed as vestiges of primitive modes of thought.

However, the retrospection with which *The Hound of the Baskervilles* ends only seems to consolidate a new common sense that John Stuart Mill had called for in "The Spirit of the Age" (January–May 1831). An age of transition was to lead to a new, secular worldview, a philosophical naturalism to be promoted by a scientific clerisy and accepted by the laity, by the men and women who were to read Arthur Conan Doyle's Sherlock Holmes stories and novels, if not the writings of Lyell, Darwin, and Thomas Huxley (1825–1895). But, we are not to forget Dr. Mortimer's curious equivocation as he begins to lose confidence in what Holmes calls "the ordinary laws of Nature" (*Hound*, II, 684) and appears to "have quite gone over to the supernaturalists" (II, 681). Mortimer's lapse points to the experience of others who had promoted "the ordinary laws of Nature" – men like Robert Chambers (1802–1871), Alfred Russel Wallace (1823–1913) and, of course, Doyle himself – only to embrace spiritualism in their later years. They had once turned away from the "Supernatural Christianity" that Winwood Reade had repudiated in *The Martyrdom of Man*.[2] They had rejected, in Doyle's words, "the whole Christian faith," but could find no resting-place in "an agnosticism, which never for an instant degenerated into atheism."[3] Wallace observed in a letter of September 1860 that "Darwin has given the world a *new science*, and his name should, in my opinion, stand above that of every philosopher of ancient or modern times."[4] Darwin had promoted a new worldview that, however coherent and sweeping, offered no solace in a universe of chance and necessity. The materialist philosophy of Darwin, Huxley, and Tyndall was not to be borne by many confronting a universe so conceived, in which death is final, the extinguishing forever of the mysterious consciousness that John Tyndall celebrated in "Scientific Use of the Imagination" (1870).[5]

Perhaps such men are to be seen as apostates to the cause of Uniformitarianism. However, there are those in the scientific community today who, with a belief in "the ordinary laws of Nature," point out the inadequacy of the evidence to which Darwin turned or seek modifications of the evolutionary hypothesis of the *Origin of Species*. Henry Gee, the senior editor of *Nature*, deals once again with the imperfections of the geological record, arguing "that Deep Time can never support *narratives of evolution*. . . . What we need is an antidote to the historical approach to the history of life – a kind of 'anti-history' that recognizes the special properties of [a] Deep Time" that, unavailable to direct observation, will not support any narrative that offers a causal story of organic life.[6]

No less committed to the working of natural law everywhere in the universe, the late Stephen Jay Gould sought in his magnum opus, *The Structure of Evolutionary Theory* (2002), to modify the twentieth-century synthesis that revitalized evolutionary thought by joining Mendelian genetics to the Darwinian mechanism of Natural Selection. Gould argued for a change in a prevailing orthodoxy that embraces Darwinian gradualism, seeking a new concensus, within a naturalistic tradition: "But [such a] concensus is premature and we can only see the resulting shape of [a] revised and unified theory through a glass darkly – though in the future, no doubt, face to face."[7]

In his wry allusion to I Corinthians 13, Gould offered his version of Sherlock Holmes's claim that "the past and the present are within the field of [his] inquiry, but what a man [or a culture?] may do in the future is a hard question to answer." This is particularly true of the United States, and increasingly of Great Britain, at this moment when both Creationists and proponents of Intelligent Design offer their differing critiques of Darwinian evolution and seek to challenge its place in the classrooms of public (state-supported) schools. Creation science, as Ronald L. Numbers has explained, rejects the claims of geologists about the antiquity of the earth; appeals to catastrophies as instances of divine intervention; and returns to the doctrine of special creation by disputing paleontological interpretations of the fossil record.[8] While Creationists tend to read Genesis literally, the proponents of Intelligent Design accept the antiquity of the earth; the extinction and transmutation of species; and the uniform operation of natural law, up to a point. In his 1990 manifesto, "Evolution as Dogma: The Establishment of Naturalism," Phillip E. Johnson writes as a theist, promoting a "competing worldvie[w]" to the "philosophical naturalisim" of what he identifies as the "dominant culture."[9] Johnson refashions Creationism in language like that of nineteenth-century Natural Theology:

> the very fact that the universe is on the whole orderly, in a manner comprehensible to our intelligence, is evidence that we and it were fashioned by a common intelligence. What is truly a miracle . . . is

the emergence of a being with consciousness, free will, and a capacity to understand the laws of nature in a universe which in the beginning contained only matter in mindless motion.

("Evolution as Dogma," p. 71)

Phillip E. Johnson and others have set out to challenge the concensus of a "dominant culture" that was from the start open to various critiques, both theistic and naturalistic, and that was never dominant in the way that Johnson argues. In *The Hound of the Baskervilles* Doyle fully grasped how illusory may be the solutions of the fictional detective and how ephemeral the confident claims of those historical disciplines grounded in a philosophical naturalism. As Sherlock Holmes reconstructs the events of the Baskerville case without "referring to [his] notes," he admits that he "cannot guarantee that [he carries] all the facts in [his] mind," even though he asserts, "I do not know that anything essential has been left unexplained" (*Hound*, II, 766, 761, 766). However, if Watson's account has been compromised by omissions and appeals to memory, so is that of Holmes even as he boasts of having "made certain of the hound, and . . . guessed at the criminal before ever we went to the west country" (II, 765). Unfortunately, Stapleton, the nominal criminal, is not available to confirm Holmes's account, his corpse "forever buried," perhaps somewhere "in the heart of the great Grimpen Mire" (II, 760). Stapleton's disappearance constitutes a negative fact to suggest the conditional nature of all narrative reconstructions of a past "for ever forging, day and night, in the vast iron-works of time and circumstance."[10]

Just as problematic is Holmes's explanation of Stapleton's motives, a necessary link in the causal chain that he offers to Watson. Within the context of a class-conscious society based on the rule of primogeniture, he reduces Stapleton's motives to a desire for status and wealth. As the son of Rodger Baskerville, the younger brother of Sir Charles who had gone off to South America, Stapleton would be heir to the Baskerville title and estate upon the death of Sir Henry. But the various names assumed by Stapleton attest both to the weakness of his claim to the baronetcy and to the instability of his identity and the volatility of motives perhaps incomprehensible even to himself. The "flash of genius" that transformed the "terrible creature" – part bloodhound, part mastiff – into something "diabolical" (*Hound*, II, 762, 757, 762) implies a realm of consciousness beyond the confident rationalism of late-Victorian Britain. Stapleton's various stratagems suggest motives that Holmes chooses not to consider. In presenting his wife, Beryl as his sister, Stapleton establishes a complex situation reminiscent of those in Edgar Allan Poe's "The Purloined Letter" (1844) and in Charles Dickens's *Bleak House* (1852–53) and *The Mystery of Edwin Drood* (1870). Stapleton and Sir Henry, in their relationship to Beryl Stapleton, are enmeshed in circumstances not to be explained only by social or economic aspirations. At one point in Watson's account Stapleton comes upon Beryl and Sir Henry in a moment of ambiguous intimacy: "absorbed in their conversation . . . Sir Henry suddenly drew Miss Stapleton to his side. . . . He stooped his head to hers, and she raised one hand as if in protest. Next moment I saw them spring apart and turn hurriedly round . . . [Stapleton] was running wildly towards them. . . . He gesticulated and almost danced with excitement in front of the lovers. What the scene meant I could not imagine" (*Hound*, II, 718–19). Watson's inability to fathom the significance of the moment, especially for Stapleton, and Holmes's silence upon it fail to deal with those other motives that inform Stapleton's complex plotting.

Without a consideration of such motives, Holmes's chain of cause and effect, his web of meaning, remain unsatisfying. Perhaps that explains the elegiac tone pervading Watson's narrative, an acknowledgment that the fictional detective offers no satisfactory resolutions to the mysteries that he confronts, just as there is no end to the debates swirling about evolutionary hypotheses, then and now. As Watson, Sir Henry, and Dr. Mortimer near Baskerville Hall upon their arrival in Devon, "a tinge of melancholy [lies] upon the countryside, which [bears] so clearly the mark of the waning year": "Yellow leaves carpeted the lanes and fluttered down upon us as we passed. . . . we drove through drifts of rotting vegetation – sad gifts . . . for Nature to throw before the carriage of the returning heir of the Baskervilles" (*Hound*, II, 700–1). The year is waning, along with the orthodoxies that once sustained men and women in the nineteenth century. In their stead a Darwinian Nature presents only "sad gifts," signs of unending change in a universe of chance and necessity.[11] Such random change may obliterate the past, even as it prepares for an unpredictable future, both for Phillip E. Johnson's "competing worldviews," and for the human species set precariously atop "the very summit of the organic scale," separated from and connected to those supposedly lesser species that have preceded it, "still bearing in [its] bodily frame the indelible stamp of [its] lowly origin."[12]

The Hound of the Baskervilles offers its own check to the bent of certain narratives that celebrate the triumph of the modern.[13] The *Descent of Man* returns us to the episode of the Man on the Tor, to "the figure of a man" that is "outlined as black as an ebony statue" against the "shining background" of the moon (*Hound* II, 726). As "the very spirit of that terrible place" (II, 726), the man could be seen to body forth the final consolidation of a Darwinian worldview as he broods upon the scene before him. But, in vanishing from sight, the figure becomes suggestive not only of the ephemeral status of the human species in a universe of unending change, but also of a worldview that had only *seemed* to consolidate itself within the consciousness of men and women.

In the somber tone of his account, Dr. Watson has responded to Darwin's *"new science"* and to its unnerving implications. Darwin offered to men and women a vision of the reign of contingency in the realms of nature and the human, even as inexorable natural law acted in both realms. This is a vision without solace as Darwin's observation in his *Autobiography* (completed just before his death) reveals: "With respect to immortality, . . . the consideration of the view now held by most physicists, [is] namely that the sun with all the planets will in time grow too cold for life. . . . it is an intolerable thought that [man] and all other sentient beings are doomed to complete annihilation."[14] In rejecting "the immortality of the human soul" (p. 92) in a universe so conceived, Darwin resigned himself to the implications of the nebular hypothesis and the necessary "death of the sun" and the planetary system that it sustains. Darwin's is a stoicism that few, to this day, can embrace. Our human response in the future to such a prospect remains beyond our capacity to predict, for "the past and the present [may be] within the field of [our] inquiry, but what . . . [we] may do in the future is a hard question to answer."[15]

Notes

Introduction

1. John Stuart Mill, "The Spirit of the Age, I," in *Newspaper Writings by John Stuart Mill, December 1822 – July 1831*, eds Ann P. Robson and John M. Robson, *Collected Works of John Stuart Mill*, ed. John M. Robson, 33 vols (Toronto: University of Toronto Press, 1965–91), XXII, 228. All further references are to this volume and appear in the text.
2. For the classic essay on common sense, see Clifford Geertz, "Common Sense as a Cultural System," in *Local Knowledge: Further Essays in Interpretive Anthropology* (New York: Basic Books, 1983), pp. 73–93. Historians and philosophers of science with a constructivist orientation have begun to use the word "concensus" to discuss the conditional nature of a prevailing scientific paradigm, pointing to the problematic nature of any prevailing agreement amongst members of a scientific community.
3. For a discussion of Romantic historicism, with passing references to Mill, see James Chandler, *England in 1819: The Politics of Literary Culture and the Case of Romantic Historicism* (Chicago: University of Chicago Press, 1998).
4. In "The Spirit of the Age, II," Mill referred to Laplace, if only in passing: "It does not follow that all men are not to inquire and investigate. . . . It is right that they should acquaint themselves with the evidence of the truths which are presented to them, to the utmost extent of each man's intellect, leisure, and inclination. Though a man may never be able to understand Laplace, that is no reason he should not read Euclid" (*Collected Works*, XXII, 242).
5. See Ronald L. Numbers, *The Creationists* (New York: Alfred A. Knopf, 1992); and Robert T. Pennock, ed., *Intelligent Design Creationism and its Critics* (Cambridge, Mass.: MIT Press, 2001). It may be unnecessary to direct readers to recent controversies over the teaching of evolutionary hypotheses in secondary schools in various regions of the United States.
6. Stephen Knight, *Form and Ideology in Crime Fiction* (Bloomington: Indiana University Press, 1980), p. 62.
7. Dennis Porter, *The Pursuit of Crime: Art and Ideology in Detective Fiction* (New Haven: Yale University Press, 1981), p. 1. All further references are to this edition and appear in the text.
8. Ronald R. Thomas, *Detective Fiction and the Rise of Forensic Science*, Cambridge Studies in Nineteenth-Century Literature and Culture, no. 26 (Cambridge, Eng.: Cambridge University Press, 1999), p. 10, emphasis added. All further references are to this edition and appear in the text.
9. Edgar Allan Poe, "The Murders in the Rue Morgue," in *Edgar Allan Poe: Poetry and Tales*, ed. Patrick F. Quinn (New York: Library of America, 1984), pp. 403–4. All further references to this or other Poe stories are to this edition and appear in the text.
10. Winwood Reade, *The Martyrdom of Man* (1872; reprint, Stark, Kans.: De Young Press, 1997), pp. 364, 430.

11. Hayden White, *Metahistory: The Historical Imagination in Nineteenth-Century Europe* (Baltimore: Johns Hopkins University Press, 1973), pp. 1–2, 29. All further references are to this edition and appear in the text.
12. See Kenneth Burke, "The Philosophy of Literary Form," in *The Philosophy of Literary Form: Studies in Symbolic Action*, 3rd edn (Berkeley: University of California Press, 1973), pp. 110–11.
13. See James Chandler, *England in 1819*, p. xvi.
14. Catherine Gallagher and Stephen Greenblatt, "Introduction," in *Practicing New Historicism* (Chicago: University of Chicago Press, 2000), p. 15.
15. Ernst Mayr, *The Growth of Biological Thought: Diversity, Evolution, and Inheritance* (Cambridge, Mass.: Belknap Press, 1982), p. 521. All further references are to this edition and appear in the text. Also, see Stephen Jay Gould, *The Structure of Evolutionary Theory* (Cambridge, Mass.: Belknap Press, 2002): "Darwin knew that evolution would not win respect until methods of historical inference could be established and illustrated. . . . He therefore set out to formulate rules for inference in history. I view the *Origin* as one long illustration of these rules" (p. 99).
16. Charles Darwin, *The Origin of Species by Means of Natural Selection or The Preservation of Favoured Races in the Struggle for Life*, ed. J. W. Burrow (1859; reprint, New York: Penguin Books, 1968), p. 316, emphasis added. All further references are to this edition and appear in the text.
17. Charles Lyell, *Principles of Geology, Being an Attempt to Explain the Former Changes of the Earth's Surface, by Reference to Causes Now in Operation*, 3 vols (1830–33; reprint as *Principles of Geology*, Chicago: University of Chicago Press, 1990–91), III, 1. All further references are to this edition and appear in the text.
18. See Hans Aarsleff, *The Study of Language in England, 1780–1860* (Princeton: Princeton University Press, 1967), for the classic account of Sir William Jones's role in the discipline of philology and of Trench as a popularizer of historical philology.
19. Sir William Jones, *The Works of Sir William Jones. With the Life of the Author, by Lord Teignmouth*, 13 vols (London: John Stockdale and John Walker, 1807), III, 135. All further references are to this edition and appear in the text.
20. See Sir Francis Darwin, introduction to *Evolution by Natural Selection*, by Charles Darwin and Alfred Russel Wallace (Cambridge, Eng.: Cambridge University Press, 1958), pp. 23–38.
21. "Charles Darwin's Sketch of 1842," in *Evolution by Natural Selection*, p. 54, emphasis added. All further references to the "Sketch" or the *Essay* are to this edition and appear in the text.
22. For a more recent discussion of Richard Chenevix Trench, see John Willinsky, "At Trench's Suggestion, 1858–1878," in *Empire of Words: The Reign of the OED* (Princeton: Princeton University Press, 1994), pp. 14–34.
23. There are various important surveys of Natural Theology and of the debates about the age of the earth, the extinction of species, and the geological and zoological past. See Charles Coulston Gillispie, *Genesis and Geology: A Study in the Relations of Scientific Thought, Natural Theology, and Social Opinion in Great Britain, 1790–1850* (Cambridge, Mass.: Harvard University Press, 1951); John C. Greene, *The Death of Adam: Evolution and its Impact on Western Thought* (Ames: Iowa State University Press, 1959); Roy Porter, *The Making of*

Geology: Earth Science in Britain, 1660–1815 (Cambridge, Eng.: Cambridge University Press, 1977); and Martin J. S. Rudwick, *The Meaning of Fossils: Episodes in the History of Palaeontology*, 2nd edn (New York: Science History Publications, 1976).

24. Richard Chenevix Trench, *On the Study of Words: Lectures Addressed (Originally) to the Pupils of the Diocesan Training-School, Winchester*, 9th edn (New York: W. J. Widdleton, 1863), p. 20. All further references are to this edition and appear in the text.

25. Richard Chenevix Trench, *English Past and Present* (New York: Redfield, 1855), pp. 17, 15–16, emphasis added. All further references are to this edition and appear in the text.

26. See Willinsky, *Empire of Words*, for a discussion of how Trench's providential, imperialist perspective was to appear in the *Oxford English Dictionary* in spite of Murray's positivist claims for the project.

27. Richard Chenevix Trench, *On Some Deficiencies in Our English Dictionaries. Being the Substance of Two Papers Read Before the Philological Society, Nov. 5, and Nov. 19, 1857* (London: John W. Parker and Son, 1857), p. 4. All further references are to this edition and appear in the text.

28. In Notebook B (1837–38), one of the notebooks he kept as he moved toward his evolution hypothesis, Darwin drew a figure resembling a bush rather than the Tree of Life of the *Origin*. See *Charles Darwin's Notebooks, 1836–1844: Geology, Transmutation of Species, Metaphysical Enquiries*, ed. Paul H. Barrett, Peter J. Gautrey, Sandra Herbert, David Kohn, and Sydney Smith (Ithaca: Cornell University Press, 1987), pp. 179–80.

29. See Mayr, *Growth of Biological Thought*, pp. 487–88; and Gould, *Structure of Evolutionary Theory*, pp. 125–69. Also, see Fredric Jameson's discussion of nominalism and the postmodern in *Postmodernism, or, The Cultural Logic of Late Capitalism* (Durham, N.C.: Duke University Press, 1991), pp. 181–259.

30. James Chandler in *England in 1819* and Catherine Gallagher and Stephen Greenblatt in *Practicing New Historicism* make similar observations about the fictive nature of the constructs supporting *any* historical discipline. My aim is to suggest how the *Origin of Species* suggested similar conclusions.

31. For a critique of the narratives of the modern, see Stephen Toulmin, *Cosmopolis: The Hidden Agenda of Modernity* (New York: Free Press, 1990).

32. See "Proposal for the Publication of a New English Dictionary, by the Philological Society" (1858); and Rudwick, *Meaning of Fossils*, pp. 251–52.

33. See John Tyndall, "Scientific Use of the Imagination," in *Fragments of Science: A Series of Detached Essays, Addresses and Reviews*, 5th edn (London: Longmans, Green, 1876), pp. 423–58.

34. For discussions of the nebular hypothesis, Nichol, and *Vestiges*, see Simon Schaffer, "The Nebular Hypothesis and the Science of Progress," and James A. Secord, "Behind the Veil: Robert Chambers and *Vestiges*," in *History, Humanity and Evolution: Essays for John C. Greene*, ed. James R. Moore (Cambridge, Eng.: Cambridge University Press, 1989), pp. 131–94.

35. Sir Arthur Conan Doyle, *The Hound of the Baskervilles*, in *The Complete Sherlock Holmes*, 2 vols (Garden City, N.Y.: Doubleday, 1930), II, 687. All further references are to this edition and appear in the text.

36. M. M. Bakhtin, "The Problem of the Text in Linguistics, Philology, and the Human Sciences: An Experiment in Philosophical Analysis," in *Speech Genres*

and Other Late Essays, eds Caryl Emerson and Michael Holquist, trans. Vern W. McGee, University of Texas Press Slavic Series, no. 8 (Austin: University of Texas Press, 1986), p. 124, emphasis added.

37. See George Rosie, *Hugh Miller: Outrage and Order. A Biography and Selected Writings* (Edinburgh: Mainstream Publishing, 1981).

38. Hugh Miller, *The Testimony of the Rocks; or, Geology in its Bearings on the Two Theologies, Natural and Revealed* (Boston: Gould and Lincoln, 1857), p. 311, emphasis added. All further references are to this edition and appear in the text.

39. For a recent discussion of the New Science and the Book of Nature, see Steven Shapin, *The Scientific Revolution* (Chicago: University of Chicago Press, 1996). For a discussion of nineteenth-century Natural Theology, see John Hedley Brooke, "The Fortunes and Functions of Natural Theology," in *Science and Religion: Some Historical Perspectives*, Cambridge History of Science, ed. George Basalla (Cambridge, Eng.: Cambridge University Press, 1991), pp. 192–225.

40. Hugh Miller, *Foot-Prints of the Creator: or, the Asterolepis of Stromness* (London: Johnstone and Hunter, 1849), p. 229.

41. Daniel Defoe, *Robinson Crusoe*, ed. Michael Shinagel, 2nd edn (New York: W. W. Norton, 1994), p. 58. All further references are to this edition and appear in the text.

42. Hugh Miller, "Our Novel Literature," in *Essays: Historical and Biographical [,] Political and Social [,] Literary and Scientific*, 7th edn (London: William P. Nimmo, 1875), pp. 463, 465–66, emphasis added.

43. See Dorothy L. Sayers, "The Omnibus of Crime (1928–29)," in *The Art of the Mystery Story: A Collection of Critical Essays*, ed. Howard Haycraft (New York: Biblo and Tannen, 1976), p. 74; A. E. Murch, *The Development of the Detective Novel*, rev. edn (Port Washington, N.Y.: Kennikat Press, 1968), pp. 25, 69, 177; and Julian Symons, *Bloody Murder: From the Detective Story to the Crime Novel: A History*, rev. edn (New York: Viking, 1985), pp. 27–28, 33.

44. M. Cuvier, *Essay on the Theory of the Earth*, trans. Robert Kerr (Edinburgh: William Blackwood, 1813), pp. 98–99. All further references are to this edition and appear in the text.

45. See James Chandler, "Representing Culture, Romanticizing Contradiction: The Politics of Literary Exemplarity," in *England in 1819*, pp. 155–202.

46. See Paolo Rossi, *The Dark Abyss of Time: The History of the Earth and the History of Nations from Hooke to Vico*, trans. Lydia G. Cochrane (Chicago: University of Chicago Press, 1984), pp. 85–101, for a discussion of Voltaire's resistance to the "idea of a change in the earth" (p. 95).

47. Gideon Algernon Mantell, *The Wonders of Geology; or, A Familiar Exposition of Geological Phenomena; Being the Substance of a Course of Lectures Delivered at Brighton*, 3rd edn, 2 vols (London: Relfe and Fletcher, 1839), I, 20, emphasis added. All further references are to this edition and appear in the text. Henry Gee discusses such issues in *In Search of Deep Time: Beyond the Fossil Record to a New History of Life* (New York: Free Press, 1999).

48. The Romantic origins of the fictional detective have been remarked upon by Ross Macdonald (Kenneth Millar) in "The Writer as Detective Hero," in *Detective Fiction: A Collection of Critical Essays*, ed. Robin W. Winks (Englewood Cliffs, N.J.: Prentice-Hall, 1980): "[Sherlock Holmes's] drugs, his

secrecy and solitude, his moods of depression (which he shared with [Poe's] Dupin) are earmarks of the Romantic rebel then and now. Behind Holmes lurk the figures of nineteenth-century poets, Byron certainly, probably Baudelaire, who translated Poe and pressed Poe's guilty knowledge to new limits" (p. 181). In *Bloodhounds of Heaven: The Detective from Godwin to Doyle* (Cambridge, Mass.: Harvard University Press, 1976), Ian Ousby traces the changes in Doyle's depiction of Holmes as he ceases to be associated with Decadence and is transformed into the gentleman and the specialist (pp. 158–64).

49. William Whewell, *History of the Inductive Sciences, from the Earliest to the Present Times*, 3 vols (London: John W. Parker, 1837), III, 481.

50. Ross Macdonald, "The Writer as Detective Hero," in *Detective Fiction*, p. 186.

51. For recent discussions of the validity of the concept of culture, see Christopher Herbert, *Culture and Anomie: Ethnographic Imagination in the Nineteenth Century* (Chicago: University of Chicago Press, 1991); and Alan Liu, "Local Transcendence: Cultural Criticism, Postmodernism, and the Romanticism of Detail," *Representations*, no. 32 (fall 1990): 75–113.

52. See Brooke, *Science and Religion*: "There was no linear succession of scientific insights, inexorably culminating in Darwin's theory of natural selection" (p. 227). Also, see James A. Secord, "Lifting the Veil," in *Victorian Sensation: The Extraordinary Publication, Reception, and Secret Authorship of "Vestiges of the Natural History of Creation"* (Chicago: University of Chicago Press, 2000), pp. 515–32.

Chapter 1   "The Murders in the Rue Morgue": Edgar Allan Poe's Evolutionary Reverie

1. M. M. Bakhtin, *The Dialogic Imagination: Four Essays*, ed. Michael Holquist, trans. Caryl Emerson and Michael Holquist, University of Texas Press Slavic Series, no. 1 (Austin: University of Texas Press, 1981), p. 4.

2. Michael McKeon, *The Origins of the English Novel, 1600–1740* (Baltimore: Johns Hopkins University Press, 1987), p. 20.

3. I am using Thomas S. Kuhn, *The Structure of Scientific Revolutions*, 2nd edn (Chicago: University of Chicago Press, 1970), to discuss the implications of detective fiction. For other discussions of detective fiction, see John G. Cawelti, *Adventure, Mystery, and Romance: Formula Stories as Art and Popular Culture* (Chicago: University of Chicago Press, 1976); Stephen Knight, *Form and Ideology in Crime Fiction* (Bloomington: Indiana University Press, 1980); Dennis Porter, *The Pursuit of Crime: Art and Ideology in Detective Fiction* (New Haven: Yale University Press, 1981); D. A. Miller, *The Novel and the Police* (Berkeley: University of California Press, 1988); and Ronald R. Thomas, *Detective Fiction and the Rise of Forensic Science*, Cambridge Studies in Nineteenth-Century Literature and Culture, no. 26 (Cambridge, Eng.: Cambridge University Press, 1999).

4. See Charles Coulston Gillispie, *Genesis and Geology: A Study in the Relations of Scientific Thought, Natural Theology, and Social Opinion in Great Britain, 1790–1850* (Cambridge, Mass.: Harvard University Press, 1951).

5. See Neal C. Gillespie, *Charles Darwin and the Problem of Creation* (Chicago: University of Chicago Press, 1979); and George Levine, *Darwin and the Nov-*

elists: Patterns of Science in Victorian Fiction (Cambridge, Mass.: Harvard University Press, 1988). For a discussion of creationism in the United States, see Ronald L. Numbers, *The Creationists* (New York: Alfred A. Knopf, 1992). Also, see Robert T. Pennock, ed., *Intelligent Design Creationism and its Critics: Philosophical, Theological, and Scientific Perspectives* (Cambridge, Mass.: MIT Press, 2001).

6. See Kenneth Burke's "The Philosophy of Literary Form," in *The Philosophy of Literary Form: Studies in Symbolic Action*, 3rd edn (Berkeley: University of California Press, 1973), pp. 110–11.

7. Edgar Allan Poe, "The Murders in the Rue Morgue," in *Edgar Allan Poe: Poetry and Tales*, ed. Patrick F. Quinn (New York: Library of America, 1984), p. 411. All further references to this story and to other Poe works are from this edition and appear in the text.

8. For a discussion of detective fiction, Poe's detective stories, and Poe's knowledge of Laplace, see John T. Irwin, *The Mystery to a Solution: Poe, Borges, and the Analytic Detective Story* (Baltimore: Johns Hopkins University Press, 1994), pp. 322, 338–39, and 352.

9. For discussions of this episode, see Burton R. Pollin, "Poe's 'Murders in the Rue Morgue': The Ingenious Web Unravelled," in *Studies in the American Renaissance, 1977*, ed. Joel Myerson (Boston: Twayne Publishers, 1978), pp. 235–59; and Irwin, *Mystery to a Solution*, pp. 349–56. Pollin suggests that the narrator's train of thought is empty of meaning; Irwin provides a reading dealing with social issues.

10. Charles Darwin, *Journal of Researches into the Geology and Natural History of the Various Countries Visited by H.M.S. Beagle, Under the Command of Captain Fitzroy, R.N. from 1832 to 1836* (London: Henry Colburn, 1839), p. 369.

11. See P[ierre] S[imon] Laplace, *The System of the World*, trans. J. Pond, 2 vols (London: Richard Phillips, 1809), II, 354–75.

12. Quoted in Stephen G. Brush, "The Nebular Hypothesis and the Evolutionary Worldview," *History of Science*, 25 (1987): 251.

13. See Brush, "The Nebular Hypothesis and the Evolutionary Worldview."

14. William Paley, *Natural Theology: or, Evidences of the Existence and Attributes of the Deity, Collected from the Appearances of Nature*, 3rd edn (London: R. Faulder, 1803), p. 414.

15. Thomas Chalmers, *On the Power, Wisdom, and Goodness of God, as Manifested in the Adaptation of External Nature to the Moral and Intellectual Constitution of Man*, A New Edition (Philadelphia: Carey, Lea and Blanchard, 1836), pp. 17–18, emphasis added. All further references are to this edition and appear in the text.

16. See Simon Schaffer, "The Nebular Hypothesis and the Science of Progress," in *History, Humanity and Evolution: Essays for John C. Greene*, ed. James R. Moore (Cambridge, Eng.: Cambridge University Press, 1989), pp. 131–64.

17. For discussions of these issues, see Gillispie, *Genesis and Geology*; and Jack Morell and Arnold Thackray, *Gentlemen of Science: Early Years of the British Association for the Advancement of Science* (Oxford: Clarendon Press, 1981). For a discussion of the response to the nebular hypothesis in the United States, see Ronald L. Numbers, *Creation by Natural Law: Laplace's Nebular Hypothesis in American Thought* (Seattle: University of Washington Press, 1977).

18. See Schaffer, "Nebular Hypothesis and the Science of Progress."

19. J[ohn] P[ringle] Nichol, *Views of the Architecture of the Heavens: In a Series of Letters to a Lady*, 3rd edn (Edinburgh: William Tait, 1839), p. 189. All further references are to this edition and appear in the text.
20. See Brush, "Nebular Hypothesis and the Evolutionary Worldview," and Numbers, *Creation by Natural Law*, for discussions of how Lord Rosse's resolution of the nebula in Orion into already formed stars was later used by proponents of Natural Theology to refute the nebular hypothesis.
21. See *Ovid's Fasti*, trans. Sir James George Frazer, Loeb Classical Library, no. 253 (New York: G. P. Putnam's Sons, 1931), pp. 296–301, v. 493–544.
22. See Pollin, "The Ingenious Web Unravelled," pp. 253–54. Pollin does not deal with Cuvier's explanation of the etymology of the name, Ourang-Outang. For a nineteenth-century discussion of cosmogony and Cuvier, see "Cuvier's Theory of the Globe," review of *A Discourse on the Revolutions of the Surface of the Globe, and the Changes thereby Produced in the Animal Kingdom*, by Baron G. Cuvier, *Southern Review*, 8 (1831–32): 69–88: the essay attacked "the doctrine of atoms, with all its train of atheistical notions," even as it rejected explanations invoking "the immediate agency of the Creator when events can be accounted for by secondary causes"; it concluded by quoting Cuvier's English editor, who refers to the "fertile womb" of nature.
23. Baron Cuvier, *The Animal Kingdom, Arranged According to its Organization, Serving as a Foundation for the Natural History of Animals, and an Introduction to Comparative Anatomy*, 4 vols (London: G. Henderson, 1834–37), I, 47–48.
24. See Hans Aarsleff, *The Study of Language in England, 1780–1860* (Princeton: Princeton University Press, 1967).
25. James Burnett, Lord Monboddo, *Antient Metaphysics: or, The Science of Universals*, 6 vols (1779–99; reprint, New York: Garland Publishing, 1977), IV, 26. All further references are to this edition and appear in the text. For further discussions of the Ourang-Outang by Lord Monboddo, see *Of the Origin and Progress of Language*, 2nd edn, Vol. I (Edinburgh: J. Balfour, 1774).
26. See Michel Foucault, *Madness and Civilization: A History of Insanity in the Age of Reason*, trans. Richard Howard (New York: Pantheon Books, 1965); and Edward W. Said, *Culture and Imperialism* (New York: Alfred A. Knopf, 1993).
27. See Irwin, *Mystery to a Solution*, for his discussion of the mind–body relation in the detective story, in Poe's stories and, specifically, in "The Murders in the Rue Morgue."
28. For the classic psychoanalytic reading of Poe's works, see Marie Bonaparte, *The Life and Works of Edgar Allan Poe: A Psycho-Analytic Interpretation*, trans. John Rodker (London: Imago Publications, 1949). For a discussion of Doubling in "The Murders in the Rue Morgue," see Irwin, *Mystery to a Solution*, and his discussions of the motif in this story and in detective fiction generally.
29. *Charles Darwin's Notebooks, 1836–1844: Geology, Transmutation of Species, Metaphysical Enquiries*, eds Paul H. Barrett, Peter J. Gautrey, Sandra Herbert, David Kohn, and Sydney Smith (Ithaca: Cornell University Press, 1987), pp. 263–64. I have followed the notation system used by the editors.
30. In "The Nebular Hypothesis and the Science of Progress," Simon Schaffer argues that Darwin, Robert Chambers, and John Stuart Mill, as well as Poe, were all persuaded by John Pringle Nichol's version of the nebular hypothesis (see pp. 144–45).

31. Robert Chambers, *"Vestiges of the Natural History of Creation" and Other Evolutionary Writings*, ed. James A. Secord (Chicago: University of Chicago Press, 1994), pp. 26, 360. All further references are to this edition and appear in text. For discussions of *Vestiges*, see Milton Millhauser, *Just Before Darwin: Robert Chambers and "Vestiges"* (Middletown, Conn.: Wesleyan University Press, 1959); and James A. Secord, "Behind the Veil: Robert Chambers and *Vestiges*," in *History, Humanity and Evolution*, pp. 165–94; and Secord, *Victorian Sensation: The Extraordinary Publication, Reception, and Secret Authorship of "Vestiges of the Natural History of Creation"* (Chicago: University of Chicago Press, 2000).

32. See Dwight Thomas and David K. Jackson, *The Poe Log: A Documentary Life of Edgar Allan Poe, 1809–1849* (Boston: G. K. Hall, 1987), pp. 723–24. All further references appear in the text. In "The Nebular Hypothesis and the Science of Progress" Schaffer argues that Poe heard John Pringle Nichol's New York lectures of 1847–48 (p. 145).

33. [Adam Sedgwick], review of *Vestiges of the Natural History of Creation*, [by Robert Chambers], *The Edinburgh Review*, 82 (July 1845): 25–26, 39.

34. See Irwin, *Mystery to a Solution*, on labyrinths in detective fiction. For a discussion of "The Gold-Bug," see Michael J. S. Williams, *A World of Words: Language and Displacement in the Fiction of Edgar Allan Poe* (Durham, N.C.: Duke University Press, 1988), pp. 127–40.

Chapter 2   "The Gold-Bug," Hieroglyphics, and the Historical Imagination

1. For a popular account of the decipherment of the Rosetta Stone, see Maurice Pope, *The Story of Decipherment: From Egyptian Hieroglyphs to Maya Script*, rev. edn (London: Thames and Hudson, 1999), pp. 60–84.

2. Edgar Allan Poe, "The Murders in the Rue Morgue," in *Edgar Allan Poe: Poetry and Tales*, ed. Patrick F. Quinn (New York: Library of America, 1984), p. 397. All further references to this and other Poe tales are to this edition and appear in the text.

3. See J. Hillis Miller, "Line," in *Ariadne's Thread: Story Lines* (New Haven: Yale University Press, 1992), pp. 1–27.

4. For a history of William Kidd, see Robert C. Ritchie, *Captain Kidd and the War against the Pirates* (Cambridge, Mass.: Harvard University Press, 1986).

5. See Mary P. Winsor, "Jan Swammerdam," in vol. 13 of *Dictionary of Scientific Biography*, ed. Charles Coulston Gillispie (New York: Charles Scribner's Sons, 1976), pp. 168–75. For discussions of the emerging Enlightenment concensus, see John Hedley Brooke, *Science and Religion: Some Historical Perspectives*, Cambridge History of Science, ed. George Basalla (Cambridge, Eng.: Cambridge University Press, 1991); David C. Lindberg and Ronald L. Numbers, eds, *God and Nature: Historical Essays on the Encounter between Christianity and Science* (Berkeley: University of California Press, 1986); Steven Shapin and Simon Schaffer, *Leviathan and the Air-Pump: Hobbes, Boyle, and the Experimental Life* (Princeton: Princeton University Press, 1985); Steven Shapin, *The Scientific Revolution* (Chicago: University of Chicago Press, 1996); and Stephen Toulmin, *Cosmopolis: The Hidden Agenda of Modernity* (New York: Free Press, 1990).

6. See William Coleman, *Georges Cuvier, Zoologist: A Study in the History of Evolution Theory* (Cambridge, Mass.: Harvard University Press, 1964). Also see Nicolaas A. Rupke, *The Great Chain of History: William Buckland and the English School of Geology (1814–1849)* (Oxford: Clarendon Press, 1983).

7. William Whewell, *History of the Inductive Sciences, From the Earliest to the Present Times*, 3 vols (London: John W. Parker, 1837), III, 474. All further references are to this edition and appear in the text.

8. M. Cuvier, *Essay on the Theory of the Earth*, trans. Robert Kerr (Edinburgh: William Blackwood, 1813), pp. 1–2. All further references are to this edition and appear in the text.

9. For a discussion of the epigraph to "The Gold-Bug," see *Tales and Sketches, 1843–1849*, vol. 3 of *Collected Works of Edgar Allan Poe*, ed. Thomas Ollive Mabbott (Cambridge, Mass.: Belknap Press, 1978), pp. 844–45.

10. Throughout my discussion of "The Gold-Bug," I am indebted to John T. Irwin's *American Hieroglyphics: The Symbol of the Egyptian Hieroglyphics in the American Renaissance* (New Haven: Yale University Press, 1980); and to his *The Mystery to a Solution: Poe, Borges, and the Analytic Detective Story* (Baltimore: Johns Hopkins University Press, 1994).

11. Review of *Essay on the Hieroglyphic System of M. Champollion, Jr. and on the Advantages which it Offers to Sacred Criticism*, by J. G. H. Greppo, trans. Isaac Stuart, *The North American Review*, 32 (1831): 96, 119. For an account of the decipherment of the Rosetta Stone, see Erik Iversen, *The Myth of Egypt and its Hieroglyphs in European Tradition* (Copenhagen: Gec Gad, 1961).

12. See J. G. H. Greppo, *Essay on the Hieroglyphic System of M. Champollion, Jun. and on the Advantages Which it Offers to Sacred Criticism*, trans. Isaac Stuart (Boston: Perkins and Marvin, 1830), pp. 35–52. All further references are to this edition and appear in the text. The discussion of "the scarabee" occurs on p. 42.

13. For an account of the study of language in the nineteenth century, see Hans Aarsleff, *The Study of Language in England, 1780–1860* (Princeton: Princeton University Press, 1967). Also, see Walter J. Ong, *Orality and Literacy: The Technologizing of the Word* (New York: Methuen, 1982).

14. See Ritchie, *Captain Kidd*, pp. 228–38. Ritchie also deals with and dismisses legends of buried pirate treasure.

15. See Ian Hodder, *Reading the Past: Current Approaches to Interpretation in Archaeology* (Cambridge, Eng.: Cambridge University Press, 1986). For the relevance of "The Gold-Bug" to the new intellectual history, see Dominick LaCapra, *Rethinking Intellectual History: Texts, Contexts, Language* (Ithaca: Cornell University Press, 1983).

16. For discussions of these issues, see Ellison A. Smyth, Jr., "Poe's Gold-Bug from the Standpoint of an Entomologist," *The Sewanee Review*, 18 (1910): 67–72; and J. K. Van Dover and John F. Jebb, "Planting the Genre on Sullivan's Island," in *Isn't Justice Always Unfair? The Detective in Southern Literature* (Bowling Green, Ohio: Bowling Green State University Popular Press, 1996), pp. 28–46. There was an eighteenth-century account of pirates, published in 1724, that Poe may have known: see Captain Charles Johnson, *A General History of the Robberies and Murders of the Most Notorious Pirates*, ed. Arthur L. Hayward (London: Routledge and Kegan Paul, 1926). Some have speculated that Captain Johnson was a pseudonym for Daniel

Defoe, suggesting connections between *Robinson Crusoe* (1719) and "The Gold-Bug." See Mabbott, *Tales and Sketches*, III, 801, note.

17. Charles Lyell, *Principles of Geology, Being an Attempt to Explain the Former Changes of the Earth's Surface, by Reference to Causes Now in Operation*, 3 vols (1830–33; reprint as *Principles of Geology*, Chicago: University of Chicago Press, 1990–91), I, 76–77. All further references are to this edition and appear in the text.

18. In the introduction to C. Lemmonnier, *A Synopsis of Natural History: Embracing the Natural History of Animals, with Human and General Physiology, Botany, Vegetable Physiology and Geology*, trans. Thomas Wyatt (Philadelphia: Thomas Wardle, 1839), the translator wrote, "to Students in Geology, who wish to extend their inquiries, we would respectfully recommend 'Lyell's Elements of Geology,' for a first book, and his larger work, entitled, 'Lyell's Principles of Geology'" (p. iv). In *The Poe Log: A Documentary Life of Edgar Allan Poe, 1809–1849* (Boston: G. K. Hall, 1987), Dwight Thomas and David K. Jackson observe that Thomas Wyatt "engage[d] Poe to assist in preparing *The Conchologist's First Book* . . . Poe [wrote] 'the Preface and Introduction,' as well as translating 'from Cuvier, the accounts of the animals.'" In the same year (1838) "Poe assist[ed] Wyatt in preparing the latter's *Synopsis of Natural History*" (p. 259).

19. For a recent discussion of cryptography in Poe's detective stories, see Shawn James Rosenheim, *The Cryptographic Imagination: Secret Writing from Edgar Poe to the Internet* (Baltimore: Johns Hopkins University Press, 1997), pp. 19–86.

20. For an account of Austen Henry Layard's life, see Gordon Waterfield, *Layard of Nineveh* (London: John Murray, 1963). For an account of Heinrich Schliemann's life, see David A. Traill, *Schliemann of Troy: Treasure and Deceit* (New York: St. Martin's Press, 1995).

21. For a psychoanalytic reading of Poe's stories, see Marie Bonaparte, *The Life and Works of Edgar Allan Poe: A Psycho-Analytic Interpretation*, trans. John Rodker (London: Imago, 1949). For observations that might lead to a feminist analysis, see Luce Irigaray, "This Sex Which is Not One," in *This Sex Which is Not One*, trans. Catherine Porter (Ithaca: Cornell University Press, 1985), pp. 23–33. Also, see Rosenheim, *Cryptographic Imagination*, pp. 60–64.

22. *North American Review*, 32 (1831): 97, 102.

23. See Hans Aarsleff, *Study of Language*; and Irwin, *American Hieroglyphics*, pp. 3–40.

24. See "Egypt" in vol. 4 of *Supplement to the Fourth, Fifth, and Sixth Editions of the Encyclopædia Britannica* (Edinburgh: Archibald Constable, 1824), pp. 55–56. Young's authorship of "Egypt" is discussed by Alexander Wood in his *Thomas Young, Natural Philosopher: 1773–1829* (Cambridge, Eng.: Cambridge University Press, 1954), p. 262. Wood notes that Young also contributed the article on "Languages" in volume five of the *Supplement*.

25. There is no evidence that Poe knew Thomas Young's *An Account of Some Recent Discoveries in Hieroglyphical Literature, and Egyptian Antiquities* (London: John Murray, 1823). Yet, in following the controversy over priority in the decipherment of the Rosetta Stone, Poe might have been led to it. In his preface Young wrote of the allure of "secret treasure" (p. x) and of "the train of occurrences that [had] accidentally led [him] to engage in [such] pursuits" (p. xiv). At one point he described an episode of 1821 and his surprise at

receiving an inscribed papyrus: "a most extraordinary chance had brought into my possession a document which was not very likely, in the first place, ever to have existed, still less to have been preserved uninjured, for my information, through a period of near two thousand years: but that this very extraordinary translation should have been brought safely to Europe, to England, and to me, at the very moment when it was most of all desirable to me to possess it . . . would, in other times, have been considered as affording ample evidence of my having become an Egyptian sorcerer" (p. 58).

26. For a relevant reading of "The Gold-Bug," see Michael J. S. Williams, "Conclusion: Allegories of Reading," in *A World of Words: Language and Displacement in the Fiction of Edgar Allan Poe* (Durham, N.C.: Duke University Press, 1988), pp. 122–52.

27. "The Gold-Bug," as others have noticed, can be seen as a response to and a commentary on Daniel Defoe's *Robinson Crusoe* (1719) with its Calvinist version of what was to become the central position of Natural Theology with its emphasis on the Argument from Design and the revelations of the New Testament.

28. Jan Swammerdam, *The Book of Nature; or, The History of Insects: Reduced to Distinct Classes, Confirmed by Particular Instances, Displayed in the Anatomical Analysis of Many Species*, trans. Thomas Flloyd, revised by John Hill (London: C. G. Seyffert, 1758), pt. 1, 1; pt. 2, 153.

29. Galileo Galilei, *The Assayer*, trans. Stillman Drake, in *The Controversy on the Comets of 1618*, eds Stillman Drake and C. D. O'Malley (Philadelphia: University of Pennsylvania Press, 1960), pp. 183–84. In *Cryptographic Imagination*, Rosenheim writes of "the detective's ability to read the world as a text . . . as a form of magic" (p. 67).

30. Francis Bacon, *The Advancement of Learning*, in *Francis Bacon*, ed. Brian Vickers, Oxford Authors (Oxford: Oxford University Press, 1996), pp. 125–26.

31. Sir Thomas Browne, "Hydriotaphia: Urne-Burial or, a Brief Discourse of the Sepulchrall Urnes Lately Found in Norfolk," in *The Works of Sir Thomas Browne*, ed. Geoffrey Keynes, 4 vols (Chicago: University of Chicago Press, 1964), I, 142–43. All further references to this and other essays by Browne are to this edition and appear in the text. Throughout, my discussion has been influenced by John T. Irwin's discussions of "Urne-Burial" and "The Garden of Cyrus" in his *Mystery to a Solution*.

32. See William B. Ashworth, Jr., "Catholicism and Early Modern Science," in *God and Nature*: "An emblematic worldview, which sees nature as a vast collection of signs and metaphors, was a staple feature of Renaissance thought, but in the seventeenth century Bacon, Descartes, Galileo, and their followers rejected the notion that everything in nature carries a hidden meaning. Nature instead was to be taken at face value and investigated on its own terms" (pp. 156–57).

33. See James R. Moore, "Geologists and Interpreters of Genesis in the Nineteenth Century," in *God and Nature*: "The Baconian compromise, like all political compromises, could be maintained only so long as the parties concerned fulfilled its terms . . . So long as naturalists proved their biblical orthodoxy by furnishing evidence of God's wisdom, goodness, and power; so long as exegetes accepted from naturalists the 'true sense' of the natural

historical portions of the Scriptures; and so long as naturalists and exegetes alike remained content with the social relations that sustained and were sanctioned by their endeavors – to that extent the compromise prevailed" (p. 335).

34. Friedrich Nietzsche, *Beyond Good and Evil: Prelude to a Philosophy of the Future*, trans. Walter Kaufmann (New York: Random House, 1966), pp. 21, 27–28.

35. John Locke, *An Essay Concerning Human Understanding*, ed. Alexander Campbell Fraser, 2 vols (1894; reprint, New York: Dover Publications, 1959), I, 121. For a discussion of how the "white paper" of the mind becomes transformed into the blank page of the universe, see Arthur Danto, "Perspectivism," in *Nietzsche as Philosopher* (New York: Macmillan, 1965), pp. 68–99. For a more recent discussion, see Steven D. Hales and Rex Welshon, *Nietzsche's Perspectivism* (Urbana: University of Illinois Press, 2000).

36. See Daniel Hoffman, "Disentanglements," in *Poe Poe Poe Poe Poe Poe Poe* (1972; reprint, New York: Vintage Books, 1985), pp. 103–33.

Chapter 3 *Bleak House*, the Nebular Hypothesis, and a Crisis in Narrative

1. Charles Dickens, *Bleak House*, Oxford Illustrated Dickens (Oxford: Oxford University Press, 1987), p. 15. All further references are to this edition and appear in the text.

2. For representative critics who discuss the present-tense narrative in *Bleak House*, see Harland S. Nelson, "*Bleak House*," in *Charles Dickens*, Twayne's English Authors Series, no. 314 (Boston: Twayne Publishers, 1981), pp. 145–89; Norman Page, "*Bleak House*": *A Novel of Connections*, Twayne's Masterwork Studies, no. 42 (Boston: Twayne Publishers, 1990); and Graham Storey, *Charles Dickens: "Bleak House,"* Landmarks of World Literature (Cambridge, Eng.: Cambridge University Press, 1987).

3. See Jacques Monod, *Chance and Necessity: An Essay on the Natural Philosophy of Modern Biology*, trans. Austryn Wainhouse (New York: Alfred A. Knopf, 1971).

4. J[ohn] P[ringle] Nichol, *Views of the Architecture of the Heavens. In a Series of Letters to a Lady*, 3rd edn (Edinburgh: William Tait, 1839), pp. 142–43. All further references are to this edition and appear in the text.

5. It was Richard Owen who coined the term "dinosaur" in 1841. See Nicolaas A. Rupke, *Richard Owen: Victorian Naturalist* (New Haven: Yale University Press, 1994). For accounts of the careers of Laplace and Buckland, see Charles Coulston Gillispie, *Pierre-Simon Laplace, 1749–1827: A Life in Exact Science* (Princeton: Princeton University Press, 1997); and Nicolaas A. Rupke, *The Great Chain of History: William Buckland and the English School of Geology (1814–1849)* (Oxford: Clarendon Press, 1983).

6. Constance A. Lubbock, ed., *The Herschel Chronicle: The Life-Story of William Herschel and his Sister Caroline Herschel* (Cambridge, Eng.: Cambridge University Press, 1933), p. 310, emphasis added. Also, see Charles Coulston Gillispie, *Pierre-Simon Laplace*, pp. 166–75; and Roger Hahn, "Laplace and the Mechanistic Universe," in *God and Nature: Historical Essays on the Encounter*

between Christianity and Science, eds David C. Lindberg and Ronald L. Numbers (Berkeley: University of California Press, 1986), pp. 256–76.

7. Dickens owned the fifth edition of Nichol's *Architecture of the Heavens* (1845) and the first edition of *Thoughts on Some Important Points Relating to the System of the World* (Edinburgh: William Tait, 1846). See J. H. Stonehouse, ed., *Catalogue of the Library of Charles Dickens* and *Catalogue of the Library of W. M. Thackeray* (London: Piccadilly Fountain Press, 1935), p. 84. For discussions of the nebular hypothesis and John Pringle Nichol, see Milton Millhauser, *Just Before Darwin: Robert Chambers and "Vestiges"* (Middletown, Conn.: Wesleyan University Press, 1959); Simon Schaffer, "The Nebular Hypothesis and the Science of Progress," in *History, Humanity and Evolution: Essays for John C. Greene*, ed. James R. Moore (Cambridge, Eng.: Cambridge University Press, 1989), pp. 131–64; James A. Secord, "Behind the Veil: Robert Chambers and Vestiges," in *History, Humanity and Evolution*, pp. 165–94, and his encyclopedic, *Victorian Sensation: The Extraordinary Publication, Reception, and Secret Authorship of "Vestiges of the Natural History of Creation"* (Chicago: University of Chicago Press, 2000).

8. Robert Chambers, *"Vestiges of the Natural History of Creation" and Other Evolutionary Writings*, ed. James A. Secord (Chicago: University of Chicago Press, 1994), p. 30. All further references are to this edition and appear in the text.

9. See Millhauser, *Just Before Darwin*; Secord, "Behind the Veil," in *History, Humanity and Evolution*, pp. 165–94, and his *Victorian Sensation*.

10. See Edgar Johnson, *Charles Dickens: His Tragedy and Triumph*, 2 vols (New York: Simon and Shuster, 1952), II, 702–18; and Fred Kaplan, *Dickens: A Biography* (New York: William Morrow, 1988), p. 265.

11. Charles Dickens, "The Poetry of Science," review of *The Poetry of Science, or Studies of the Physical Phenomena of Nature*, by Robert Hunt, in *Miscellaneous Papers, Plays and Poems*, vol. 35 of *The Works of Charles Dickens*, ed. B. W. Matz (London: Chapman and Hall, 1908), p. 61. See K. J. Fielding and Shu-Fang Lai, "Dickens, Science, and *The Poetry of Science*," *Dickensian*, 93 (spring 1997): 5–10.

12. Robert Hunt, *The Poetry of Science, or Studies of the Physical Phenomena of Nature* (London: Reeve, Benham, and Reeve, 1848), p. 17. All further references are to this edition and appear in the text.

13. [Adam Sedgwick], review of *Vestiges of the Natural History of Creation*, [by Robert Chambers], *Edinburgh Review*, 82 (July 1845): 3. All further references appear in the text.

14. For discussions of the responses to *Vestiges*, see Millhauser, *Just Before Darwin*; and Secord, *Victorian Sensation*.

15. William Whewell, *Indications of the Creator. Extracts, Bearing upon Theology, from the History and the Philosophy of the Inductive Sciences* (London: John W. Parker, 1845), p. 12. All further references are to this edition and appear in the text.

16. See Galileo Galilei, *The Assayer*, trans. Stillman Drake, in *The Controversy on the Comets of 1618*, eds Stillman Drake and C. D. O'Malley (Philadelphia: University of Pennsylvania Press, 1960), pp. 183–84. Also, see Steven Shapin, *The Scientific Revolution* (Chicago: University of Chicago Press, 1996).

17. See Ernst Mayr, "The Multiple Meanings of Teleological," in *Toward a New Philosophy of Biology: Observations of an Evolutionist* (Cambridge, Mass.: Harvard University Press, 1988), pp. 38–66.

18. For discussions of a new awareness of time, see Paolo Rossi, *The Dark Abyss of Time: The History of the Earth and the History of Nations from Hooke to Vico*, trans. Lydia G. Cochrane (Chicago: University of Chicago Press, 1984); and Martin J. S. Rudwick, *Scenes from Deep Time: Early Pictorial Representations of the Prehistoric World* (Chicago: University of Chicago Press, 1992).

19. For a discussion of *Bleak House* as a "document about the interpretation of documents," see J. Hillis Miller, "Interpretation in Dickens' *Bleak House*," in *Victorian Subjects* (Durham, N.C.: Duke University Press, 1991), pp. 179–99.

20. Charles Lyell, *Principles of Geology, Being an Attempt to Explain the Former Changes of the Earth's Surface, by Reference to Causes Now in Operation*, 3 vols (1830–33; reprint as *Principles of Geology*, Chicago: University of Chicago Press, 1990–91), III, 1–2.

21. See Martin J. S. Rudwick, *The Great Devonian Controversy: The Shaping of Scientific Knowledge among Gentlemanly Specialists* (Chicago: University of Chicago Press, 1985); and James A. Secord, *Controversy in Victorian Geology: The Cambrian-Silurian Dispute* (Princeton: Princeton University Press, 1986).

22. At this point it should be clear that my reading of *Bleak House* will diverge from that of George Levine's "Dickens and Darwin," in *Darwin and the Novelists: Patterns of Science in Victorian Fiction* (Cambridge, Mass.: Harvard University Press, 1988), pp. 119–52. George Levine has offered one context in which to consider the novel; I shall provide a different one that will lead in a different direction.

23. Adam Sedgwick, preface to *A Discourse on the Studies of the University of Cambridge*, 5th edn (London: John W. Parker, 1850), pp. cxli, xix. All further references to the preface, the body, and the appendices of the *Discourse* are to this edition and appear in the text.

24. See J. Hillis Miller, "Line," in *Ariadne's Thread: Story Lines* (New Haven: Yale University Press, 1992), pp. 1–27.

25. The parallels between this situation in *Bleak House* and that in Edgar Allan Poe's "The Purloined Letter" (1844) involving Minister D— and two royal personages are clear. Dickens met Poe in March, 1842, during his first visit to the United States. Later, Poe wrote to Dickens, asking him for help in finding an English publisher for his works. See Kenneth Silverman, *Edgar A. Poe: Mournful and Never-Ending Remembrance* (New York: HarperCollins, 1991), pp. 198–200; and vol. 4, *The Letters of Charles Dickens: 1844–1846*, eds Kathleen Tillotson and Nina Burgess, Pilgrim Edition (Oxford: Clarendon Press, 1977), p. 523.

26. Hugh Miller, *Foot-Prints of the Creator: or, The Asterolepis of Stromness* (London: Johnstone and Hunter, 1849), pp. 280, 279. There is no evidence that Dickens knew *Foot-Prints of the Creator*, or Miller's earlier, widely read, *The Old Red Sandstone; or New Walks in an Old Field* (Edinburgh: John Johnstone, 1841). Dickens did receive a copy of *The Testimony of the Rocks; or, Geology in its Bearings on the Two Theologies, Natural and Revealed* (Edinburgh: Thomas Constable, 1857), from the author's wife; the book was published posthumously after Miller's suicide in 1856. For Dickens's gracious letter to Mrs.

Miller, see vol. 8, *The Letters of Charles Dickens: 1856–1858*, eds Graham Storey and Kathleen Tillotson, Pilgrim Edition (Oxford: Clarendon Press, 1995), pp. 315–16.

27. For discussions of metonymy and the concept of cause and effect, see David Hume, "Of the idea of necessary connexion," in *A Treatise of Human Nature*, ed. L. A. Selby-Bigge, 3 vols in 1 (1888; reprint, Oxford: Clarendon Press, 1964), pp. 155–72; and J. Hillis Miller, "The Fiction of Realism: *Sketches by Boz, Oliver Twist*, and Cruikshank's Illustrations," in *Victorian Subjects*, pp. 119–77.

28. Richard Chenevix Trench, *On the Study of Words: Lectures Addressed (Originally) to the Pupils of the Diocesan Training-School, Winchester*, 9th edn (New York: W. J. Widdleton, 1863), pp. 12–13, 93.

29. Sir Arthur Conan Doyle, *A Study in Scarlet*, in *The Complete Sherlock Holmes*, 2 vols (Garden City, N.Y.: Doubleday, 1930), I, 23.

30. At this point in my discussion of *Bleak House*, I offer an interpretation that differs with D. A. Miller's interpretation of the novel: see "Discipline in Different Voices: Bureaucracy, Police, Family, and *Bleak House*," in his *The Novel and the Police* (Berkeley: University of California Press, 1988), pp. 58–106. For a more recent Foucauldian reading of the novel, see Ronald R. Thomas, "Photographic Memories in *Bleak House*," in *Detective Fiction and the Rise of Forensic Science*, Cambridge Studies in Nineteenth-Century Literature and Culture, no. 26 (Cambridge, Eng.: Cambridge University Press, 1999), pp. 131–49.

31. For various readings of Esther Summerson's experiences and of the significance of her illness, see Lawrence Frank, "'Through a Glass Darkly,'" in *Charles Dickens and the Romantic Self* (Lincoln: University of Nebraska Press, 1984), pp. 97–123; Jasmine Yong Hall, "What's Troubling about Esther? Narrating, Policing, and Resisting Arrest in *Bleak House*," *Dickens Studies Annual: Essays on Victorian Fiction*, 22 (1993): 171–94; Robert Newsom, *Dickens on the Romantic Side of Familiar Things: "Bleak House" and the Novel Tradition* (New York: Columbia University Press, 1977); Michael Ragussis, "The Ghostly Signs of *Bleak House*," *Nineteenth-Century Fiction*, 34 (1979): 253–80; Judith Wilt, "Confusion and Consciousness in Dickens's Esther," *Nineteenth-Century Fiction*, 32 (1977): 285–309; and Alex Zwerdling, "Esther Summerson Rehabilitated," in *Charles Dickens: New Perspectives*, ed. Wendell Stacy Johnson (Englewood Cliffs, N.J.: Prentice-Hall, 1982), pp. 94–113.

32. Edgar Allan Poe, "The Gold-Bug," in *Edgar Allan Poe: Poetry and Tales*, ed. Patrick F. Quinn (New York: Library of America, 1984), pp. 585, 581.

33. For discussions of the Higher Criticism, see John Hedley Brooke, *Science and Religion: Some Historical Perspectives*, Cambridge History of Science, ed. George Basalla (Cambridge, Eng.: Cambridge University Press, 1991), pp. 263–74; Adrian Desmond, *Huxley: From Devil's Disciple to Evolution's High Priest* (Reading, Mass.: Addison-Wesley, 1997), pp. 278–98, 315–16; and Basil Willey, "George Eliot: Hennell, Strauss and Feuerbach," in *Nineteenth Century Studies: Coleridge to Matthew Arnold* (New York: Columbia University Press, 1949), pp. 204–36.

34. See Richard T. Gaughan, "'Their Places are a Blank': The Two Narrators in *Bleak House*," *Dickens Studies Annual: Essays on Victorian Fiction*, 21 (1992): 79–96, for a Bakhtinian reading of the novel.

35. For a history of the nineteenth-century belief in progress, see Peter J. Bowler, *Fossils and Progress: Paleontology and the Idea of Progressive Evolution in the Nineteenth Century* (New York: Science History Publications, 1976).

36. See Monod, *Chance and Necessity:* he writes of "'absolute coincidences,' those, that is to say, which result from the intersection of two totally independent chains of events. Suppose that Dr. Brown sets out on an emergency call to a new patient. In the meantime Jones the contractor's man has started making emergency repairs on the roof of a nearby building. As Dr. Brown walks past the building, Jones inadvertently lets go of his hammer, whose (deterministic) trajectory *happens* to intercept that of the physician, who dies of a fractured skull. We say he was a victim of chance. . . . Chance is obviously the essential thing here, inherent in the complete independence of two causal chains of events whose convergence produces the accident" (p. 114, emphasis added). In *The Structure of Evolutionary Theory* (Cambridge, Mass.: Belknap Press, 2002), the late Stephen Jay Gould also invokes Jacques Monod's "chance" and "necessity" in discussing "Darwinism" (p. 144).

37. See Slavoj Žižek, *Looking Awry: An Introduction to Jacques Lacan through Popular Culture* (Cambridge, Mass.: MIT Press, 1991), pp. 48–66, for a Lacanian discussion of how detective fiction seeks to subvert the conventions of the realistic novel. At one point Žižek observes: "Teleology is always a retroactive illusion" (p. 78).

38. Throughout, my discussion of *Bleak House* has been informed by the concept of the paradigm shift. See Neal C. Gillespie, *Charles Darwin and the Problem of Creation* (Chicago: University of Chicago Press, 1979), especially "Positivism and its Consequences" (pp. 1–18); Thomas S. Kuhn, *The Structure of Scientific Revolutions*, 2nd edn (Chicago: University of Chicago Press, 1970); and Frank Palmeri, "History of Narrative Genres after Foucault," *Configurations: A Journal of Literature, Science, and Technology*, 7, no. 2 (1999): 267–77.

Chapter 4   News from the Dead: Archaeology, Detection, and *The Mystery of Edwin Drood*

1. Charles Dickens, *Bleak House*, Oxford Illustrated Dickens (Oxford: Oxford University Press, 1987), p. 877. All further references are to this edition and appear in the text.

2. See Robert M. Young, *Darwin's Metaphor: Nature's Place in Victorian Culture* (Cambridge, Eng.: Cambridge University Press, 1985); and Leonard G. Wilson, "Charles Lyell," in vol. 8 of *Dictionary of Scientific Biography*, ed. Charles Coulston Gillispie (New York: Charles Scribner's Sons, 1973), pp. 563–76.

3. For the account book of *All the Year Round*, and, where available, the names of authors of unsigned articles, see Ella Ann Oppenlander, *Dickens' "All the Year Round": Descriptive Index and Contributor List* (Troy, N.Y.: Whiston Publishing, 1984). For a discussion of the history and publication of *The Mystery of Edwin Drood*, see Margaret Cardwell, introduction to *The Mystery of Edwin Drood*, by Charles Dickens, Clarendon Dickens (Oxford: Clarendon Press, 1972), pp. xiii–l.

4. "Natural Selection," *All the Year Round*, 7 July 1860, 295. All further references appear in the text. Writing to Lyell in June, 1860, Darwin observed of

"Species," the first *All the Year Round* review article: "There is notice of me in penultimate no' of 'All the Year Round', but not worth consulting; chiefly a well-done hash of my own words." Darwin to Charles Lyell, 14 June 1860, vol. 8, *The Correspondence of Charles Darwin: 1860*, eds Frederick Burkhardt, Duncan M. Porter, Janet Browne, and Marsha Richmond (Cambridge, Eng.: Cambridge University Press, 1993), pp. 253–54.

5. "Species," *All the Year Round*, 2 June 1860, 176. All further references appear in the text.

6. For the passage paraphrased, see Charles Darwin, *The Origin of Species by Natural Selection or the Preservation of Favoured Species in the Struggle for Life*, ed. J. W. Burrow (1859; reprint, New York: Penguin Books, 1968), p. 456. All further references are to this edition and appear in the text.

7. "How Old Are We?", *All the Year Round*, 7 March 1863, 32. All further references appear in the text.

8. Dickens owned editions both of the *Origin of Species* and the *Antiquity of Man*. See J. H. Stonehouse, ed., *Catalogue of the Library of Charles Dickens* and *Catalogue of the Library of W. M. Thackeray* (London: Piccadilly Fountain Press, 1935), pp. 26, 75. See George Levine, "Dickens and Darwin," in *Darwin and the Novelists: Patterns of Science in Victorian Fiction* (Cambridge, Mass.: Harvard University Press, 1988), pp. 119–52, for a discussion of the reviews of the *Origin* in *All the Year Round*.

9. See Albert D. Hutter, "Dismemberment and Articulation in *Our Mutual Friend*," *Dickens Studies Annual: Essays on Victorian Fiction*, 11 (1983): 136–37: "as we move from *Bleak House* to *The Mystery of Edwin Drood*, the detective function becomes yet more complex because Dickens' view of writing and of perception itself becomes more sophisticated. The novelist is now less omniscient. . . . Dickens' novels of the 1860s, like those of Wilkie Collins, are particularly concerned with questions of epistemology: . . . the explication of a mystery becomes less important than the *process* of perception and solution."

10. Charles Dickens, *The Mystery of Edwin Drood*, ed. Margaret Cardwell, Clarendon Dickens (Oxford: Clarendon Press, 1972), p. 11. All further references are to this edition and appear in the text.

11. For a discussion of the controversies surrounding the unresolved mysteries in the novel, see Cardwell, introduction to *The Mystery of Edwin Drood*, pp. xiii–l.

12. My reading of *Edwin Drood* is indebted throughout to Philippa Levine, *The Amateur and the Professional: Antiquarians, Historians and Archaeologists in Victorian England, 1838–1886* (Cambridge, Eng.: Cambridge University Press, 1986); and to A. Bowdoin Van Riper, *Men among the Mammoths: Victorian Science and the Discovery of Human Prehistory* (Chicago: University of Chicago Press, 1993). Also, see John C. Greene, *The Death of Adam: Evolution and its Impact on Western Thought* (Ames: Iowa State University Press, 1959); and Paolo Rossi, *The Dark Abyss of Time: The History of the Earth and the History of Nations from Hooke to Vico*, trans. Lydia G. Cochrane (Chicago: University of Chicago Press, 1984).

13. Richard Chenevix Trench, *On the Study of Words: Lectures Addressed (Originally) to the Pupils of the Diocesan Training-School, Winchester*, 9th edn (New York: W. J. Widdleton, 1863), pp. 94–95. All further references are to this edition and appear in the text.

14. For discussions of Trench, see Hans Aarsleff, *The Study of Language in England, 1780–1860* (Princeton: Princeton University Press, 1967), pp. 230–47; and John Willinsky, "At Trench's Suggestion, 1858–1878," in *Empire of Words: The Reign of the OED* (Princeton: Princeton University Press, 1994), pp. 14–34.
15. Thomas Wright, *The Celt, the Roman, and the Saxon: A History of the Early Inhabitants of Britain, Down to the Conversion of the Anglo-Saxons to Christianity*, 2nd edn (London: Arthur Hall, Virtue, 1861), p. v. All further references are to this edition and appear in the text.
16. In her *The Amateur and the Professional*, Philippa Levine quotes Richard M. Dorson's claim in *The British Folklorists: A History* (Chicago: University of Chicago Press, 1968) that Wright "perfectly [typifies] the early Victorian antiquary-scholar" (p. 14). Although there is no evidence that Dickens owned *The Celt, the Roman, and the Saxon*, he did have in his library copies of three other works by Wright. See J. H. Stonehouse, ed., *Catalogue*, p. 120.
17. For a discussion of the town of Rochester and the books to which Dickens might have turned for its history, see Wendy S. Jacobson, *The Companion to "The Mystery of Edwin Drood"* (London: Allen and Unwin, 1986), pp. 49–50.
18. For discussions of these issues, see Alain Schnapp, "The Invention of Archaeology," in *The Discovery of the Past*, trans. Ian Kinnes and Gillian Varndell (New York: Harry N. Abrams, 1997), pp. 275–315; and Van Riper, *Men among the Mammoths*, pp. 117–43, 184–221.
19. For discussions of the idea of progress, see Peter J. Bowler, *Fossils and Progress: Paleontology and the Idea of Progressive Evolution in the Nineteenth Century* (New York: Science History Publications, 1976); and Levine, *The Amateur and the Professional*, pp. 70–100.
20. See Schnapp, *Discovery of the Past*, pp. 286, 314.
21. For a discussion of Staple Inn and the inscription, see Jacobson, *Companion*, pp. 108–10.
22. For discussions of imperialism in general and of British imperialism in the nineteenth century, see John Barrell, *The Infection of Thomas De Quincey: A Psychopathology of Imperialism* (New Haven: Yale University Press, 1991); Patrick Brantlinger, *Rule of Darkness: British Literature and Imperialism* (Ithaca: Cornell University Press, 1988); Ania Loomba, *Colonialism/Postcolonialism* (New York: Routledge, 1998); Edward W. Said, *Culture and Imperialism* (New York: Alfred A. Knopf, 1993), and his *Orientalism* (New York: Pantheon Books, 1978); and Sara Suleri, *The Rhetoric of English India* (Chicago: University of Chicago Press, 1992).
23. See G[iovanni Battista] Belzoni, *Narrative of the Operations and Recent Discoveries within the Pyramids, Temples, Tombs, and Excavations in Egypt and Nubia; and of a Journey to the Coast of the Red Sea, in Search of the Ancient Berenice; and Another to the Oasis of Jupiter Ammon* (London: John Murray, 1820). For discussions of Belzoni's life, see Stanley Mayes, *The Great Belzoni* (London: Putnam, 1959); and [W. H. Wills and Mrs. Hoare], "The Story of Giovanni Belzoni," *Household Words*, 1 March 1851, 548–52.
24. "Latest News from the Dead," *All the Year Round*, 11 July 1863, 473. All further references appear in the text.
25. See Maurice Pope's popular account, *The Story of Decipherment: From Egyptian Hieroglyphs to Maya Script*, rev. edn (London: Thames and Hudson, 1999).

26. Edward Robinson, introductory note to *Nineveh and its Remains: With an Account of a Visit to the Chaldæan Christians of Kurdistan, and the Yezidis, or Devil-Worshippers; and an Inquiry into the Manners and Arts of the Ancient Assyrians*, by Austen Henry Layard, 2 vols (New York: George P. Putnam, 1849), I, ii–iii.

27. Austen Henry Layard, *A Popular Account of Discoveries at Nineveh* (New York: Harper and Brothers, 1854), p. 294. All further references are to this edition and appear in the text. Dickens owned several of Layard's books: see Stonehouse, *Catalogue*, p. 71.

28. For an account of Layard's life, see Gordon Waterfield, *Layard of Nineveh* (London: John Murray, 1963). For discussions of the friendship between Dickens and Layard, see Michael Cotsell, "Politics and Peeling Fresoes: Layard of Nineveh and *Little Dorrit*," *Dickens Studies Annual: Essays on Victorian Fiction*, 15 (1986): 181–200; Fred Kaplan, *Dickens: A Biography* (New York: William Morrow, 1988), pp. 296, 330–31; and Nancy Aycock Metz, "Little Dorrit's London: Babylon Revisited," *Victorian Studies*, 33 (spring 1990): 465–86.

29. Charles Dickens, *Pictures from Italy*, in *American Notes and Pictures from Italy*, Oxford Illustrated Dickens (Oxford: Oxford University Press, 1987), p. 364. All further references are to this edition and appear in the text.

30. Quoted in Glyn Daniel and Colin Renfrew, *The Idea of Prehistory*, 2nd edn (Edinburgh: Edinburgh University Press, 1988), p. 46.

31. For discussions of the establishment of human prehistory, see Glyn Daniel, *A Hundred and Fifty Years of Archaeology* (Cambridge, Mass.: Harvard University Press, 1976); Daniel and Renfrew, *Idea of Prehistory*; Donald K. Grayson, *The Establishment of Human Antiquity* (New York: Academic Press, 1983); and Van Riper, *Men among the Mammoths*.

32. Charles Lyell, *The Geological Evidences of the Antiquity of Man*, 3rd edn (London: John Murray, 1863), p. 68. All further references are to this edition and appear in the text. Dickens owned the third edition; see Stonehouse, *Catalogue*, p. 75.

33. William Whewell, *History of the Inductive Sciences, from the Earliest to the Present Times*, 3 vols (London: John W. Parker, 1837), III, 481. All further references are to this edition and appear in the text.

34. For discussions of geology in nineteenth-century Britain, see Stephen Jay Gould, *Time's Arrow, Time's Cycle: Myth and Metaphor in the Discovery of Geological Time* (Cambridge, Mass.: Harvard University Press, 1987); Rachel Laudan, *From Mineralology to Geology: The Foundations of a Science, 1650–1830* (Chicago: University of Chicago Press, 1987); Roy Porter, *The Making of Geology: Earth Science in Britain, 1660–1815* (Cambridge, Eng.: Cambridge University Press, 1977); Nicolaas A. Rupke, *The Great Chain of History: William Buckland and the English School of Geology (1814–1849)* (Oxford: Clarendon Press, 1983); and Leonard G. Wilson, *Charles Lyell: The Years to 1841: The Revolution in Geology* (New Haven: Yale University Press, 1972).

35. Charles Lyell, *Principles of Geology, Being an Attempt to Explain the Former Changes of the Earth's Surface, by Reference to Causes Now in Operation*, 3 vols (1830–33; reprint as *Principles of Geology*, Chicago: University of Chicago Press, 1990–91), I, 448. All further references are to this edition and appear in the text.

36. For a discussion of the argument over the status of fossils throughout several centuries, see Martin J. S. Rudwick, *The Meaning of Fossils: Episodes in the History of Palaeontology*, 2nd edn (New York: Science History Publications, 1976).
37. My interpretation of Lyell's discussion of the Temple of Jupiter Serapis and *Edwin Drood* has throughout been influenced by recent discussions of archaeology: see, especially, Ian Hodder, *Reading the Past: Current Approaches to Interpretation in Archaeology* (Cambridge, Eng.: Cambridge University Press, 1986).
38. See J. Hillis Miller, "Line," in *Ariadne's Thread: Story Lines* (New Haven: Yale University Press, 1992), pp. 1–27.
39. For speculations on the setting and the time of the events depicted in *Edwin Drood*, see Jacobson, *Companion*, pp. 49–50, 83, and 149.
40. See Barrell, *Infection of Thomas De Quincey*; Brantlinger, *Rule of Darkness*; and Suleri, *Rhetoric of English India*. For a recent popular history of British India, see Lawrence James, *Raj: The Making and Unmaking of British India* (New York: St. Martin's Press, 1997).
41. See Brantlinger, *Rule of Darkness*; Jacobson, *Companion*, p. 137; and James, *Raj*, pp. 233–98.
42. For representative psychological readings of *Edwin Drood*, see Lawrence Frank, *Charles Dickens and the Romantic Self* (Lincoln: University of Nebraska Press, 1984), pp. 187–237; Beth F. Herst, *The Dickens Hero: Selfhood and Alienation in the Dickens World* (New York: St. Martin's Press, 1990); Eve Kosofsky Sedgwick, *Between Men: English Literature and Male Homosocial Desire* (New York: Columbia University Press, 1985), pp. 161–200; and Ronald R. Thomas, *Dreams of Authority: Freud and the Fictions of the Unconscious* (Ithaca: Cornell University Press, 1990), pp. 219–37.
43. See D. A. Miller, *The Novel and the Police* (Berkeley: University of California Press, 1988), for a Foucauldian reading of nineteenth-century detective fiction, especially of *Bleak House* and Wilkie Collins's *The Moonstone* (1868). Also, see Ronald R. Thomas, *Detective Fiction and the Rise of Forensic Science*, Cambridge Studies in Nineteenth-Century Literature and Culture, no. 26 (Cambridge, Eng.: Cambridge University Press, 1999). Miller and Thomas offer readings of nineteenth-century detective fiction that functioned both to police consciousness and to impose the normative values of a society.
44. For discussions of these issues, see Neal C. Gillespie, *Charles Darwin and the Problem of Creation* (Chicago: University of Chicago Press, 1979), pp. 1–40; Rudwick, *Meaning of Fossils*, pp. 164–217; and Van Riper, *Men among the Mammoths*, pp. 117–83.
45. For discussions of Victorian anthropology and its various schools, see George W. Stocking, Jr., *Victorian Anthropology* (New York: Free Press, 1987); and his more recent *After Tylor: British Social Anthropology, 1888–1951* (Madison: University of Wisconsin Press, 1995).
46. Edward B. Tylor, *Primitive Culture: Researches into the Development of Mythology, Philosophy, Religion, Language, Art, and Custom*, 7th edn, 2 vols in 1 (New York: Brentano's, 1924), I, 1. All further references are to this edition and appear in the text.
47. See Kaplan, *Dickens*, p. 554. Also, see Edgar Johnson, *Charles Dickens: His Tragedy and Triumph*, 2 vols (New York: Simon and Schuster, 1952), II, 1142–58.

48. I am responding to David Lowenthal, *The Past is a Foreign Country* (Cambridge, Eng.: Cambridge University Press, 1985), p. xvi, and to the title of his book that alludes to L. P. Hartley's *The Go-Between* (London: Hamish Hamilton, 1953).

Chapter 5   Sherlock Holmes and "The Book of Life"

1. Ernst Mayr, "Darwin, Intellectual Revolutionary," in *Toward a New Philosophy of Biology: Observations of an Evolutionist* (Cambridge, Mass.: Harvard University Press, 1988), p. 182. Also, see Robert M. Young's comments on the triumph of Uniformitarianism in Darwin's *Origin of Species* in his *Darwin's Metaphor: Nature's Place in Victorian Culture* (Cambridge, Eng.: Cambridge University Press, 1985).
2. In *Victorian Sensation: The Extraordinary Publication, Reception, and Secret Authorship of "Vestiges of the Natural History of Creation"* (Chicago: University of Chicago Press, 2000), James A. Secord observes: "More than any other book of the modern era, the *Origin* has been endowed by successive generations of readers with the classic's timeless, transcendent power. The *Origin* is among the most pervasive remnants of the Victorian world . . . , yet it simultaneously forces much of that world into oblivion," obscuring the fact that it was part of a larger cultural movement (pp. 515–16).
3. Charles Darwin, *Journal of Researches into the Geology and Natural History of the Various Countries Visited by H. M. S. Beagle, Under the Command of Captain Fitzroy, R.N. from 1832 to 1836* (London: Henry Colburn, 1839), p. 369.
4. Sir Arthur Conan Doyle, *Memories and Adventures* (Boston: Little, Brown, 1924), p. 26. All further references are to this edition and appear in the text.
5. Sir Arthur Conan Doyle, *The Sign of Four*, in *The Complete Sherlock Holmes*, 2 vols (Garden City, N.Y.: Doubleday, 1930), I, 137. All further references to the novel and other Holmes stories or novels appear in the text.
6. Winwood Reade, *The Martyrdom of Man* (1872; reprint, Stark, Kans.: De Young Press, 1997), p. 377. All further references are to this edition and appear in the text. Significantly, Reade here echoed *Vestiges of the Natural History of Creation*.
7. In *Bloodhounds of Heaven: The Detective in English Fiction from Godwin to Doyle* (Cambridge, Mass.: Harvard University Press, 1976), Ian Ousby refers to *The Martyrdom of Man* and comments briefly on its significance for Doyle (p. 155).
8. On the generic status of *Vestiges of the Natural History of Creation*, see Milton Millhauser, *Just Before Darwin: Robert Chambers and "Vestiges"* (Middletown, Conn.: Wesleyan University Press, 1959), pp. 58–85; and Secord, *Victorian Sensation*, pp. 41–76.
9. Adam Sedgwick, *A Discourse on the Studies of the University of Cambridge*, 5th edn (London: John W. Parker, 1850), pp. xvi–xvii.
10. Charles Dickens, *Bleak House*, Oxford Illustrated Dickens (Oxford: Oxford University Press, 1987), p. 1. All further references are to this edition and appear in the text.
11. Here, Reade would seem to echo Hegel: see Georg Wilhelm Friedrich Hegel, "The Oriental World," in *The Philosophy of History*, trans. J. Sibree, rev. edn (1899; reprint, New York: Dover Publications, 1956). Relevant discussions of British racism in the nineteenth century are to be found in Patrick

Brantlinger, *Rule of Darkness: British Literature and Imperialism, 1830–1914* (Ithaca: Cornell University Press, 1988); Cynthia Eagle Russett, *Sexual Science: The Victorian Construction of Womanhood* (Cambridge, Mass.: Harvard University Press, 1989); and George W. Stocking, Jr., *Victorian Anthropology* (New York: Free Press, 1987).

12. Edward B. Tylor, *Primitive Culture: Researches into the Development of Mythology, Philosophy, Religion, Language, Art, and Custom*, 7th edn, 2 vols in 1 (New York: Brentano's, 1924), II, 453.

13. Ludwig Feuerbach, *The Essence of Christianity*, trans. George Eliot [Marian Evans] (1854; reprint, New York: Harper and Row, 1957), p. 14. For a classic discussion of George Eliot and the Higher Criticism, see Basil Willey, "George Eliot: Hennell, Strauss and Feuerbach," in *Nineteenth Century Studies: Coleridge to Matthew Arnold* (New York: Columbia University Press, 1949), pp. 204–36. More recent discussions of the Higher Criticism in mid-Victorian England may be found in passing in John Hedley Brooke, *Science and Religion: Some Historical Perspectives*, Cambridge History of Science, ed. George Basalla (Cambridge, Eng.: Cambridge University Press, 1991); Adrian Desmond, *Huxley: From Devil's Disciple to Evolution's High Priest* (Reading, Mass.: Addison-Wesley, 1997); and Adrian Desmond and James Moore, *Darwin* (New York: Warner Books, 1991).

14. Edgar Allan Poe, "Eureka: A Prose Poem," in *Edgar Allan Poe: Poetry and Tales*, ed. Patrick F. Quinn (New York: Library of America, 1984), p. 1357.

15. John Tyndall, "Scientific Use of the Imagination," in *Fragments of Science: A Series of Detached Essays, Addresses and Reviews*, 5th edn (London: Longmans, Green, 1876), p. 455.

16. Ian Ousby discusses the "Book of Life" in *Bloodhounds of Heaven* without connecting it to *The Martyrdom of Man* (p. 154).

17. William Whewell, *History of the Inductive Sciences, from the Earliest to the Present Times*, 3 vols (London: John W. Parker, 1837), III, 481. All further references are to this edition and appear in the text.

18. William Paley, *Natural Theology: or, Evidences of the Existence and Attributes of the Deity, Collected from the Appearances of Nature*, 3rd edn (London: R. Faulder, 1803), pp. 1–2. All further references are to this edition and appear in the text.

19. See Brooke, "The Fortunes and Functions of Natural Theology," in *Science and Religion*, pp. 192–225; Jacques Roger, "The Mechanistic Conception of Life," in *God and Nature: Historical Essays on the Encounter between Christianity and Science*, eds David C. Lindberg and Ronald L. Numbers (Berkeley: University of California Press, 1986), pp. 277–95; and Stephen Toulmin, *Cosmopolis: The Hidden Agenda of Modernity* (New York: Free Press, 1990), especially pp. 107–17.

20. For a discussion of such issues, see Mayr, "The Multiple Meanings of Teleological," in *Toward a New Philosophy of Biology*, pp. 38–66.

21. Charles Darwin, *The Various Contrivances by which Orchids are Fertilized by Insects*, 2nd edn, vol. 17 of *The Works of Charles Darwin*, eds Paul H. Barrett and R. B. Freeman (1877; reprint, New York: New York University Press, 1988), p. 1. All further references are to this edition and appear in the text. I am indebted to Neal C. Gillespie's *Charles Darwin and the Problem of Creation* (Chicago: University of Chicago Press, 1979), for directing me to this text.

22. See Charles Darwin, *The Origin of Species by Means of Natural Selection or The Preservation of Favoured Races in the Struggle for Life*, ed. J. W. Burrow (1859; reprint, New York: Penguin Books, 1968), pp. 139–42.

23. Other studies have dealt in passing with Darwinian themes in the Sherlock Holmes stories and novels. See Jacqueline A. Jaffe, *Arthur Conan Doyle*, Twayne's English Authors Series, no. 451 (Boston: Twayne Publishers, 1987); Rosemary Jann, *The Adventures of Sherlock Holmes: Detecting Social Order*, Twayne's Masterwork Series, no. 152 (New York: Twayne Publishers, 1995); Ian Ousby, *Bloodhounds of Heaven*; and Ronald R. Thomas, *Detective Fiction and the Rise of Forensic Science*, Cambridge Studies in Nineteenth-Century Literature and Culture, no. 26 (Cambridge, Eng.: Cambridge University Press, 1999).

24. George Combe, *The Constitution of Man Considered in Relation to External Objects*, 6th edn (Edinburgh: John Anderson, Jun., 1836), p. xi. All further references are to this edition and appear in the text.

25. "Cerebral Physiology," *The Zoist: A Journal of Cerebral Physiology and Mesmerism, and their Application to Human Welfare*, 1 (1843–44): 16–17.

26. Robert Chambers, *"Vestiges of the Natural History of Creation" and Other Evolutionary Writings*, ed. James A. Secord (Chicago: University of Chicago Press, 1994), pp. 335–36. For discussions of the tradition in which George Combe, John Elliotson, and Mr. Vestiges participated, see Adam Crabtree, *From Mesmer to Freud: Magnetic Sleep and the Roots of Psychological Healing* (New Haven: Yale University Press, 1993); and Fred Kaplan, *Dickens and Mesmerism: The Hidden Springs of Fiction* (Princeton: Princeton University Press, 1975).

27. For various discussions of a naturalistic approach to the study of brain and mind, see Edwin Clarke and L. S. Jacyna, *Nineteenth-Century Origins of Neuroscientific Concepts* (Berkeley: University of California Press, 1987); Adam Crabtree, *From Mesmer to Freud*; Anne Harrington, *Medicine, Mind, and the Double Brain: A Study in Nineteenth-Century Thought* (Princeton: Princeton University Press, 1987); L. S. Hearnshaw, *A Short History of British Psychology: 1840–1940* (London: Methuen, 1964); and Robert M. Young, *Mind, Brain and Adaptation in the Nineteenth Century: Cerebral Localization and its Biological Context from Gall to Ferrier* (Oxford: Clarendon Press, 1970).

28. Charles Darwin, *The Expression of the Emotions in Man and Animals* (1872; reprint, Chicago: University of Chicago Press, 1965), p. 12, emphasis added. All further references are to this edition and appear in the text.

29. For a discussion of the *Expression of the Emotions*, see Paul Ekman, introduction to *The Expression of the Emotions in Man and Animals*, 3rd edn, by Charles Darwin (Oxford: Oxford University Press, 1998), pp. xxi–xxxvi. Throughout the *Expression of the Emotions*, Darwin refers to Winwood Reade in footnotes.

30. For discussions of the tendency to equate so-called savages with women and children in an emerging evolutionary anthropology, see Russett, *Sexual Science*; and Stocking, *Victorian Anthropology*.

31. [Thomas Carlyle], "Characteristics" (review of *An Essay on the Origin and Prospects of Man*, by Thomas Hope, and *Philosophische Vorlesungen*, by Friedrich von Schlegel), *Edinburgh Review*, 54 (1831): 358.

32. William B. Carpenter, *Principles of Human Physiology, with their Chief Applications to Psychology, Pathology, Therapeutics, Hygiène, and Forensic Medicine*,

4th edn (Philadelphia: Blanchard and Lea, 1855), p. 589. Darwin's annotated copy of the fourth edition is in the Darwin Collection of the Cambridge University Library: see vol. 5, *The Correspondence of Charles Darwin: 1851–1855*, eds Frederick Burkhardt and Sydney Smith (Cambridge, Eng.: Cambridge University Press, 1989), p. 340, n. 8.

33. See Lucille B. Ritvo, *Darwin's Influence on Freud: A Tale of Two Sciences* (New Haven: Yale University Press, 1990). Also, see Henri F. Ellenberger, *The Discovery of the Unconscious: The History and Evolution of Dynamic Psychiatry* (New York: Basic Books, 1970); and Frank J. Sulloway, *Freud, Biologist of the Mind: Beyond the Psychoanalytic Legend* (New York: Basic Books, 1979).

34. Sigmund Freud, "Fragment of an Analysis of a Case of Hysteria," in vol. 7 of *The Standard Edition of the Complete Psychological Works of Sigmund Freud*, ed. and trans. James Strachey (London: Hogarth Press, 1953), pp. 77–78. In *Detective Fiction and the Rise of Forensic Science*, Ronald R. Thomas quotes the same passage to suggest an emphasis on the physiological rather than the psychological: see "The Lie Detector and the Thinking Machine," pp. 21–39. In *Freud, Race, and Gender* (Princeton: Princeton University Press, 1993), Sander L. Gilman touches upon Freud's "*resistance* to the language of biological determinism" (p. 7, emphasis added).

35. See Desmond and Moore, *Darwin*, pp. 375–87.

36. For a survey of attitudes toward "madness" – and epilepsy – in nineteenth-century Britain, see Andrew Scull, *The Most Solitary of Afflictions: Madness and Society in Britain, 1700–1900* (New Haven: Yale University Press, 1993).

37. *Charles Darwin's Notebooks, 1836–1844: Geology, Transmutation of Species, Metaphysical Enquiries*, eds Paul H. Barrett, Peter J. Gautrey, Sandra Herbert, David Kohn, and Sydney Smith (Ithaca: Cornell University Press, 1987), p. 263.

Chapter 6 Reading the Gravel Page: Lyell, Darwin, and Doyle

1. Sir Arthur Conan Doyle, "The Final Problem," in *The Complete Sherlock Holmes*, 2 vols (Garden City, N.Y.: Doubleday, 1930), I, 480. All further references to other Holmes stories or novels are to this edition and appear in the text.

2. See Richard Lancelyn Green and John Michael Gibson, *A Bibliography of A. Conan Doyle*, Soho Bibliographies, no. 23 (Oxford: Clarendon Press, 1983), pp. 76–77. Also, see John Dickson Carr, *The Life of Sir Arthur Conan Doyle* (New York: Harper and Brothers, 1949).

3. See W. W. Robson, introduction to *The Hound of the Baskervilles: Another Adventure of Sherlock Holmes*, by Arthur Conan Doyle, ed. W. W. Robson, Oxford Sherlock Holmes (Oxford: Oxford University Press, 1993), pp. xi–xxix.

4. For an account of Lyell and Darwin and their concern with "Uniformitarianism" or "Actualism," see Robert M. Young, *Darwin's Metaphor: Nature's Place in Victorian Culture* (Cambridge, Eng.: Cambridge University Press, 1985).

5. Richard Kirwan, *Geological Essays* (London: D. Bremner, 1799), pp. iii–iv.

6. M. Cuvier, *Essay on the Theory of the Earth*, trans. Robert Kerr (Edinburgh: William Blackwood, 1813), pp. 1–2.

7. Charles Lyell, *Principles of Geology, Being an Attempt to Explain the Former Changes of the Earth's Surface, by Reference to Causes Now in Operation*, 3 vols (1830–33; reprint as *Principles of Geology*, Chicago: University of Chicago Press, 1990–91), I, 73. All further references are to this edition and appear in the text.

8. Mrs. Lyell, ed., *Life, Letters and Journals of Sir Charles Lyell, Bart.*, 2 vols (London: John Murray, 1881), I, 251.

9. Among the numerous works on narrative in general and detective fiction specifically that influence my reading of *The Hound of the Baskervilles*, I would like to acknowledge my debt to Peter Brooks, *Reading for the Plot: Design and Intention in Narrative* (New York: Alfred A. Knopf, 1984); Umberto Eco and Thomas A. Sebeok, eds, *The Sign of Three: Dupin, Holmes, Peirce* (Bloomington: Indiana University Press, 1983); Steven Marcus, "Freud and Dora: Story, History, Case History," in his *Representations: Essays on Literature and Society* (New York: Random House, 1975), pp. 247–310; and Tzvetan Todorov, *The Poetics of Prose*, trans. Richard Howard (Ithaca: Cornell University Press, 1977): see especially Todorov's "The Typology of Detective Fiction," pp. 42–52.

10. The discussion that follows has been influenced by William C. Dowling, *Jameson, Althusser, Marx: An Introduction to "The Political Unconscious"* (Ithaca: Cornell University Press, 1984); Wolfgang Iser, *The Implied Reader: Patterns of Communication in Prose Fiction from Bunyan to Beckett* (Baltimore: Johns Hopkins University Press, 1974); and Louis O. Mink, "Narrative Form as a Cognitive Instrument," in *The Writing of History: Literary Form and Historical Understanding*, eds Robert H. Canary and Henry Kozicki (Madison: University of Wisconsin Press, 1978), pp. 129–49.

11. For a discussion of the lingering influence of the Lockean model of the mind on nineteenth-century British thought, see Robert M. Young, *Mind, Brain and Adaptation in the Nineteenth Century: Cerebral Localization and its Biological Context from Gall to Ferrier* (Oxford: Clarendon Press, 1970). Also, see Michael S. Kearns, *Metaphors of Mind in Fiction and Psychology* (Lexington: University Press of Kentucky, 1987).

12. Charles Darwin, *The Origin of Species by Means of Natural Selection or The Preservation of Favoured Races in the Struggle for Life*, ed. J. W. Burrow (1859; reprint, Penguin Books, 1968), p. 440, emphasis added. All further references are to this edition and appear in the text.

13. My discussion has been influenced by Martin J. S. Rudwick, *The Meaning of Fossils: Episodes in the History of Palaeontology*, 2nd edn (New York: Science History Publications, 1976); and by Michael Ruse, *The Darwinian Revolution: Science Red in Tooth and Claw* (Chicago: University of Chicago Press, 1979). In "The Adventure of the Empty House," the first story in *The Return of Sherlock Holmes* (1903–04), Holmes explicitly employs the family tree to explain why Colonel Sebastian Moran "began to go wrong": "There are some trees, Watson, which grow to a certain height, and then suddenly develop some unsightly eccentricity. You will see it often in humans. I have a theory that the individual represents in his development the whole procession of his ancestors, and that such a sudden turn to good or evil stands for some strong influence which came into the line of his pedigree. The person

becomes, as it were, the epitome of the *history* of his own family" (*Complete Sherlock Holmes*, II, 494, emphasis added).

14. See John T. Irwin, *American Hieroglyphics: The Symbol of the Egyptian Hieroglyphics in the American Renaissance* (New Haven: Yale University Press, 1980); and Erik Iversen, *The Myth of Egypt and its Hieroglyphs in European Tradition* (Copenhagen: Gec Gad, 1961).

15. For accounts of this episode, see Sidney Spokes, *Gideon Algernon Mantell, LL.D., F.R.C.S., F.R.S., Surgeon and Geologist* (London: John Bale, Sons and Danielsson, 1927), pp. 29–30, 84–85; and *The Journal of Gideon Mantell, Surgeon and Geologist, Covering the Years, 1818–1852*, ed. E. Cecil Curwen (London: Oxford University Press, 1940), pp. 59–62. For a more recent account of Mantell's career, see Dennis R. Dean, *Gideon Mantell and the Discovery of Dinosaurs* (Cambridge, Eng.: Cambridge University Press, 1999).

16. Gideon Algernon Mantell, *The Wonders of Geology; or, A Familiar Exposition of Geological Phenomena; Being the Substance of a Course of Lectures Delivered at Brighton*, 3rd edn, 2 vols (London: Relfe and Fletcher, 1839), I, 127–28.

17. I have concentrated on Gideon Mantell, rather than on Sir Richard Owen, because there seem to be no explicit references to Owen in the Holmes stories to the best of my knowledge. In *The Lost World* (1912) Professor Challenger alludes to Mantell by mentioning the Sussex physician who had discovered and named the fossil dinosaur, the Iguanodon. Doyle apparently shared with Mantell an enthusiasm for Cuvier rather than Owen. In "The Five Orange Pips," in *The Adventures of Sherlock Holmes*, Holmes echoes observations made in "The Book of Life": "The ideal reasoner . . . would, when he had once been shown a single fact in all its bearings, deduce from it not only all the chain of events which led up to it but also all the results which would follow from it. As Cuvier could correctly describe a whole animal by the contemplation of a single bone, so the observer who has thoroughly understood one link in a series of incidents should be able to accurately state all the other ones, both before and after" (*Complete Sherlock Holmes*, I, 224–25).

18. For discussions of Lyell and the *Principles of Geology*, see Stephen Jay Gould, *Time's Arrow, Time's Cycle: Myth and Metaphor in the Discovery of Geological Time* (Cambridge, Mass.: Harvard University Press, 1987); and Nicolaas A. Rupke, *The Great Chain of History: William Buckland and the English School of Geology (1814–1849)* (Oxford: Clarendon Press, 1983). For discussions of a nineteenth-century geological controversy that touches on issues of epistemology and narrative, see Martin J. S. Rudwick, *The Great Devonian Controversy: The Shaping of Scientific Knowledge among Gentlemanly Specialists* (Chicago: University of Chicago Press, 1985); and James A. Secord, *Controversy in Victorian Geology: The Cambrian–Silurian Dispute* (Princeton: Princeton University Press, 1986).

19. Christopher Clausen's "Sherlock Holmes, Order, and the Late-Victorian Mind," in *The Moral Imagination: Essays on Literature and Ethics* (Iowa City: University of Iowa Press, 1986), pp. 51–85, and Geoffrey H. Hartman's "Literature High and Low: The Case of the Mystery Story," in *The Poetics of Murder: Detective Fiction and Literary Theory*, eds Glenn W. Most and William W. Stowe (New York: Harcourt Brace Jovanovich, 1983), pp. 210–29, explore the unsatisfactory nature of the ending to *The Hound of the Baskervilles* in particular and to detective stories in general.

20. Thomas H. Huxley, "Palæontology and the Doctrine of Evolution," in *Discourses: Biological & Geological*, vol. 8 of *Collected Essays* (1894; reprint, London: Macmillan, 1908), p. 342. All further references to the essay appear in the text. For a discussion of Huxley and detective fiction, see Ian Ousby, *Bloodhounds of Heaven: The Detective in English Fiction from Godwin to Doyle* (Cambridge, Mass.: Harvard University Press, 1976), pp. 153–55.

21. Rudwick, *Meaning of Fossils*, p. 252. In *Huxley: From Devil's Disciple to Evolution's High Priest* (Reading, Mass.: Addison-Wesley, 1997), Adrian Desmond provides a different version of the episode (pp. 471–85). Also, see Ernst Mayr, *The Growth of Biological Thought: Diversity, Evolution, and Inheritance* (Cambridge, Mass.: Belknap Press, 1982), pp. 71, 520–23.

22. In *Detective Fiction and the Rise of Forensic Science*, Cambridge Studies in Nineteenth-Century Literature and Culture, no. 26 (Cambridge, Eng.: Cambridge University Press, 1999), Ronald R. Thomas explores such issues, particularly in his discussions of Raymond Chandler and Dashiell Hammett, but without an emphasis on epistemology.

23. See Jerome Bruner, *The Culture of Education* (Cambridge, Mass.: Harvard University Press, 1996), pp. 130–49.

24. Thomas S. Kuhn, *The Structure of Scientific Revolutions*, 2nd edn (Chicago: University of Chicago Press, 1970), pp. 65, 67, 77.

25. See Jan Golinski, *Making Natural Knowledge: Constructivism and the History of Science*, Cambridge History of Science, eds George Basalla and Owen Hannaway (Chicago: University of Chicago Press, 1998).

26. See Dowling, *Jameson, Althusser, Marx*, p. 95. Also, see Bruner, *Culture of Education*: "Narrativized realities . . . are too ubiquitous, their construction too habitual or automatic to be accessible to easy inspection. We live in a sea of stories, and like the fish who (according to the proverb) will be the last to discover water, we have our own difficulties grasping what it is like to swim in stories" (p. 147).

27. Edgar Allan Poe, "The Gold-Bug," in *Edgar Allan Poe: Poetry and Tales*, ed. Patrick F. Quinn (New York: Library of America, 1984), p. 585. All further references to Poe stories are to this edition and appear in the text.

28. For a provocative discussion of "The Narrative of Arthur Gordon Pym," see Irwin, *American Hieroglyphics*, pp. 43–235.

29. See Harold Bloom, "The Internalization of Quest-Romance," in *Romanticism and Consciousness: Essays in Criticism*, ed. Harold Bloom (New York: W. W. Norton, 1970), pp. 3–24; and Ross Macdonald, "The Writer as Detective Hero," in *Detective Fiction: A Collection of Critical Essays*, ed. Robin W. Winks (Englewood Cliffs, N.J.: Prentice-Hall, 1980), pp. 179–87.

30. Charles Darwin, *Journal of Researches into the Geology and Natural History of the Various Countries Visited by H.M.S. Beagle, Under the Command of Captain Fitzroy, R.N. from 1832 to 1836* (London: Henry Colburn, 1839), p. 227. All further references are to this edition and appear in the text.

31. For accounts of Darwin's experiences on H.M.S. *Beagle*, see Janet Browne, *Voyaging*, vol. 1 of *Charles Darwin: A Biography* (New York: Alfred A. Knopf, 1995); and Adrian Desmond and James Moore, *Darwin* (New York: Warner Books, 1991). For a discussion of the arbitrary nature of the international dateline, see Dava Sobel, *Longitude: The True Story of a Lone Genius Who Solved the Greatest Scientific Problem of His Time* (New York: Walker, 1995).

32. See John McPhee who has dealt with similar issues in his "The Gravel Page," *The New Yorker*, 29 January 1996, 44–69.

Chapter 7 *The Hound of the Baskervilles*, the Man on the Tor, and a Metaphor for the Mind

1. Sir Arthur Conan Doyle, *Memories and Adventures* (Boston: Little, Brown, 1924), p. 26. All further references appear in the text.
2. M. M. Bakhtin, "The Problem of the Text in Linguistics, Philology, and the Human Sciences: An Experiment in Philosophical Analysis," in *Speech Genres and Other Late Essays*, eds Caryl Emerson and Michael Holquist, trans. Vern W. McGee, University of Texas Press Slavic Series, no. 8 (Austin: University of Texas Press, 1986), p. 124, emphasis added.
3. In the chapter I shall consider John Tyndall as a Romantic materialist. In his recent biography of Thomas Henry Huxley, Adrian Desmond refers to Tyndall's "poetic materialism": see *Huxley: From Devil's Disciple to Evolution's High Priest* (Reading, Mass.: Addison-Wesley, 1997), p. 366: his "poetic materialism was enough to drive . . . [St. George] Mivart to damn Tyndall's 'creed.' . . . But there was a magnificent determinism to it."
4. For discussions of the various issues raised by those promoting biological determinism, see Stephen Jay Gould, *The Mismeasure of Man*, rev. edn (New York: W. W. Norton, 1996); and for an authoritative survey of nineteenth-century anthropology, see George W. Stocking, Jr., *Victorian Anthropology* (New York: Free Press, 1987).
5. Sir Arthur Conan Doyle, *The Hound of the Baskervilles*, in *The Complete Sherlock Holmes*, 2 vols (Garden City, N.Y.: Doubleday, 1930), II, 671. All further references to Holmes stories or novels are to this edition and appear in the text.
6. For recent discussions of such issues in relation to the Sherlock Holmes stories and novels, see Rosemary Jann, *The Adventures of Sherlock Holmes: Detecting Social Order*, Twayne's Masterwork Series, no. 152 (New York: Twayne Publishers, 1995); and Ronald R. Thomas, *Detective Fiction and the Rise of Forensic Science*, Cambridge Studies in Nineteenth-Century Literature and Culture, no. 26 (Cambridge, Eng.: Cambridge University Press, 1999).
7. For discussions of Havelock Ellis's life and career and of his importance as a popularizer of nineteenth-century science, including discussions of the criminal and sexuality, see Phyllis Grosskurth, *Havelock Ellis: A Biography* (New York: Alfred A. Knopf, 1980); and Cynthia Eagle Russett, *Sexual Science: The Victorian Construction of Womanhood* (Cambridge, Mass.: Harvard University Press, 1989).
8. Havelock Ellis, *The Criminal* (1890; reprint, New York: AMS Press, 1972), pp. 102, 106. All further references are to this edition and appear in the text.
9. For an account of nineteenth-century British classical evolutionism and anthropology, see Stocking, *Victorian Anthropology*; and Stocking, *After Tylor: British Social Anthropology, 1888–1951* (Madison: University of Wisconsin Press, 1995).
10. Cesare Lombroso, *Crime: Its Causes and Remedies*, trans. Henry P. Horton, Patterson Smith Reprint Series in Criminology, Law Enforcement, and

Social Problems, no. 14 (1911; reprint, Montclair, N.J.: Patterson Smith, 1968), pp. 368–69, 373.

11. For discussions of the discipline of prehistoric archaeology in the 1860s, and the decades to follow, the coining of the term *neolithic* by John Lubbock, and other relevant facts, see Glyn Daniel and Colin Renfrew, *The Idea of Prehistory*, 2nd edn (Edinburgh: Edinburgh University Press, 1988); Donald K. Grayson, *The Establishment of Human Antiquity* (New York: Academic Press, 1983); and A. Bowdoin Van Riper, *Men Among the Mammoths: Victorian Science and the Discovery of Human Prehistory* (Chicago: University of Chicago Press, 1993).

12. For discussions of Darwin and nineteenth-century British literature, see Gillian Beer, *Darwin's Plots: Evolutionary Narrative in Darwin, George Eliot and Nineteenth-Century Fiction* (London: Routledge and Kegan Paul, 1983); and George Levine, *Darwin and the Novelists: Patterns of Science in Victorian Fiction* (Cambridge, Mass.: Harvard University Press, 1988).

13. Charles Darwin, *The Descent of Man, and Selection in Relation to Sex*, 2 vols in 1 (1871; reprint, Princeton: Princeton University Press, 1981), II, 405. All further references are to this edition and appear in the text.

14. Thomas Henry Huxley, *Evidence as to Man's Place in Nature* (London: Williams and Norgate, 1863), p. 112. For a discussion of Huxley, see James G. Paradis, *T. H. Huxley: Man's Place in Nature* (Lincoln: University of Nebraska Press, 1978). For a recent life of Huxley, see Desmond, *Huxley*.

15. See John Tyndall, "Scientific Use of the Imagination," in his *Fragments of Science: A Series of Detached Essays, Addresses and Reviews*, 5th edn (London: Longmans, Green, 1876), pp. 423–58. All further references to Tyndall's essays are to this edition and appear in the text.

16. For a biography of Tyndall, see A. S. Eve and C. H. Creasey, *Life and Work of John Tyndall* (London: Macmillan, 1945). For a discussion of the X Club, see Adrian Desmond and James Moore, *Darwin* (New York: Warner Books, 1991), pp. 525–28. Also, see Desmond, *Huxley*, pp. 327–30.

17. Robert Chambers, *"Vestiges of the Natural History of Creation" and Other Evolutionary Writings*, ed. James A. Secord (Chicago: University of Chicago Press, 1994), p. 30. All further references are to this edition and appear in the text. For further discussions of *Vestiges*, see Secord's introduction; also, see Secord, "Behind the Veil: Robert Chambers and *Vestiges*," in *History, Humanity and Evolution: Essays for John C. Greene*, ed. James R. Moore (Cambridge, Eng.: Cambridge University Press, 1989), pp. 165–94. Secord's *Victorian Sensation: The Extraordinary Publication, Reception, and Secret Authorship of "Vestiges of the Natural History of Creation"* (Chicago: University of Chicago Press, 2000) has superseded all previous discussions of *Vestiges*.

18. See Simon Schaffer, "The Nebular Hypothesis and the Science of Progress," in *History, Humanity and Evolution*, pp. 154–55. For an earlier discussion of *Vestiges*, see Milton Millhauser, *Just Before Darwin: Robert Chambers and "Vestiges"* (Middletown, Conn.: Wesleyan University Press, 1959).

19. J[ohn] P[ringle] Nichol, *Views of the Architecture of the Heavens. In a Series of Letters to a Lady*, 3rd edn (Edinburgh: William Tait, 1839), p. 187. All further references are to this edition and appear in the text.

20. For a recent discussion of Milton and materialism, see John Rogers, *The Matter of Revolution: Science, Poetry, and Politics in the Age of Milton* (Ithaca:

Cornell University Press, 1996). For earlier discussions see Walter Clyde Curry, *Milton's Ontology, Cosmogony and Physics* (Lexington: University of Kentucky Press, 1957); and Denis Saurat, *Milton: Man and Thinker* (New York: Dial Press, 1925).

21. John Milton, *Paradise Lost*, in *Complete Poems and Major Prose*, ed. Merritt Y. Hughes (New York: Odyssey Press, 1957), pp. 351–52; Book VII, ll. 220; 225–27; 232–37.

22. "Character of Mr. Wordsworth's New Poem, The Excursion," in *The Complete Works of William Hazlitt in Twenty-One Volumes: Centenary Edition*, ed. P. P. Howe, 21 vols (London: J. M. Dent and Sons, 1930–34), XIX, 10, emphasis added.

23. Percy Bysshe Shelley, "Mont Blanc," in *Shelley: Poetical Works*, ed. Thomas Hutchinson (London: Oxford University Press, 1968), p. 532, ll. 1–6.

24. William Wordsworth, *The Prelude, or Growth of a Poet's Mind*, ed. Ernest de Selincourt, rev. Helen Derbishire, 2nd edn (Oxford: Clarendon Press, 1959), p. 481, Book XIV, ll. 40–42.

25. For a discussion of the nebular hypothesis and Darwin, see Schaffer, "The Nebular Hypothesis and the Science of Progress." Also, see Nora Barlow, ed., *The Autobiography of Charles Darwin: 1809–1882* (London: Collins, 1958), p. 92: "With respect to immortality, nothing shows me how strong and almost instinctive a belief it is, as the consideration of the view now held by most physicists, namely that the sun with all the planets will in time grow too cold for life. . . . Believing as I do that man in the distant future will be a far more perfect creature than he now is, it is an intolerable thought that he and all other sentient things are doomed to complete annihilation after such long-continued slow progress. To those who fully admit the immortality of the human soul, the destruction of our world will not appear so dreadful."

26. [Thomas Carlyle], "Characteristics" (review of *An Essay on the Origin and Prospects of Man*, by Thomas Hope, and *Philosophische Vorlesungen*, by Friedrich von Schlegel), *Edinburgh Review*, 54 (1831): 358, 353.

27. Quoted in Daniel and Renfrew, *Idea of Prehistory*, p. 46.

28. Quoted in Glyn Daniel, *A Hundred and Fifty Years of Archaeology* (Cambridge, Mass.: Harvard University Press, 1976), p. 63.

29. Thomas De Quincey, *Suspiria de Profundis: Being a Sequel to "The Confessions of an English Opium-Eater,"* in *The Collected Writings of Thomas De Quincey*, ed. David Masson, 14 vols (London: A. and C. Black, 1896–97), XIII, 346, 348.

30. John Playfair, *Illustrations of the Huttonian Theory of the Earth* (Edinburgh: William Creech, 1802), p. 8.

31. For a discussion of detective fiction and Victorian preoccupations with memory and mind, see Gillian Beer, "Origins and Oblivion in Victorian Narrative," in *Sex, Politics, and Science in the Nineteenth-Century Novel*, ed. Ruth Bernard Yeazell, Selected Papers from the English Institute, 1983–84 (Baltimore: Johns Hopkins University Press, 1986), pp. 63–87. At this point in my reading of *The Hound of the Baskervilles*, I offer an interpretation different from Ronald R. Thomas's claim in *Detective Fiction and the Rise of Forensic Science* that nineteenth-century detective fiction rejected Romantic versions of human consciousness.

32. For discussions of opium and Romanticism, see Virginia Berridge and Griffith Edwards, *Opium and the People: Opiate Use in Nineteenth-Century*

England (New York: St. Martin's Press, 1981); and Alethea Hayter, *Opium and the Romantic Imagination* (Berkeley: University of California Press, 1968).

33. See Hans Aarsleff, *The Study of Language in England, 1780–1860* (Princeton: Princeton University Press, 1967). In a letter dated 15 May 1865 Charles Lyell wrote to William Pengelly, whose excavations of a cave near Brixham Hill, Devon, helped to establish the antiquity of man: "How old do you imagine the Cornish language to have been? Professor Nilsson . . . believes that the Phœnicians had a tin trade with the Cassiterides . . . twelve hundred years B.C. and that their trade lasted a thousand years." See *A Memoir of William Pengelly, of Torquay, F.R.S. Geologist, With a Selection from His Correspondence*, ed. Hester Pengelly (London: John Murray, 1897), p. 165.

34. The issue of ethnocentrism, racism, and nineteenth-century science, especially evolutionary anthropology, is discussed in various places; see Russett, *Sexual Science*; Stocking, *Victorian Anthropology*; and Sara Suleri, *The Rhetoric of English India* (Chicago: University of Chicago Press, 1992). Dr. Leon Sterndale may well be based on Winwood Reade and his *Savage Africa* (1863).

35. Edward B. Tylor, *Primitive Culture: Researches into the Development of Mythology, Philosophy, Religion, Language, Art, and Custom*, 7th edn, 2 vols in 1 (New York: Brentano's, 1924), I, 18. All further references are to this edition and appear in the text.

36. For recent critiques of the concept of culture that Tylor promoted, see Christopher Herbert, *Culture and Anomie: Ethnographic Imagination in the Nineteenth Century* (Chicago: University of Chicago Press, 1991); and Alan Liu, "Local Transcendence: Cultural Criticism, Postmodernism, and the Romanticism of Detail," *Representations*, no. 32 (fall 1990): 75–113.

37. Edward B. Tylor, "On a Method of Investigating the Development of Institutions, Applied to Laws of Marriage and Descent," *Journal of the Anthropological Institute of Great Britain and Ireland*, 18 (1888): 269; quoted in Stocking, *After Tylor*, p. 8.

38. For discussions of the intellectual traditions informing *The Golden Bough*, see Robert Ackerman, *J.G. Frazer: His Life and Work* (Cambridge, Eng.: Cambridge University Press, 1987); and Ackerman, *The Myth and Ritual School: J.G. Frazer and the Cambridge Ritualists*, Theorists of Myth, no. 2 (New York: Garland, 1991); Marc Manganaro, *Myth, Rhetoric, and the Voice of Authority: A Critique of Frazer, Eliot, Frye, & Campbell* (New Haven: Yale University Press, 1992); Stocking, *Victorian Anthropology*, pp. 144–237; and Stocking, *After Tylor*.

39. James G. Frazer, *The Golden Bough: The Roots of Folklore and Religion*, 2 vols in 1 (1890; reprint, New York: Avenel Books, 1981), I, 3. All further references are to this edition and appear in the text.

40. J[ames] G. Frazer, "The Scope of Social Anthropology," in *Psyche's Task: A Discourse Concerning the Influence of Superstition on the Growth of Institutions*, 2nd edn (1913; reprint, London: Dawsons of Pall Mall, 1968), p. 170. All further references are to this edition and appear in the text. I am indebted to George W. Stocking, Jr., for directing me to this lecture in his *After Tylor*.

41. Charles Darwin, *Journal of Researches into the Geology and Natural History of the Various Countries Visited by H.M.S. Beagle, Under the Command of Captain Fitzroy, R.N. from 1832 to 1836* (London: Henry Colburn, 1839), p. 369. The story of Darwin's pocket edition of *Paradise Lost* has become legendary. In

Darwin, Desmond and Moore state that on the voyage of the *Beagle* Darwin "carried a pocket edition [of *Paradise Lost*] everywhere, inspired by its vision of a prehistoric world torn by titanic struggle" (p. 124).

42. I am here responding to Donald P. Spence, *The Freudian Metaphor: Toward Paradigm Change in Psychoanalysis* (New York: W. W. Norton, 1987). For the larger significance of metaphor for our understanding of ourselves and our universe, see George Lakoff and Mark Johnson, *Metaphors We Live By* (Chicago: University of Chicago Press, 1980); and George Lakoff and Mark Turner, *More than Cool Reason: A Field Guide to Poetic Metaphor* (Chicago: University of Chicago Press, 1989). This vision of metaphor as the basis of human understanding is more fully connected to Western philosophy by George Lakoff and Mark Johnson in their *Philosophy in the Flesh: The Embodied Mind and its Challenge to Western Thought* (New York: Basic Books, 1999).

Epilogue

1. Sir Arthur Conan Doyle, *The Hound of the Baskervilles*, in *The Complete Sherlock Holmes*, 2 vols (Garden City, N.Y.: Doubleday, 1930), II, 766. All further references are to this edition and appear in the text.
2. Winwood Reade, *The Martyrdom of Man* (1872; reprint, Stark, Kans.: De Young Press, 1997), p. 430.
3. Sir Arthur Conan Doyle, *Memories and Adventures* (Boston: Little, Brown, 1924), pp. 26, 27.
4. Alfred Russel Wallace, *My Life: A Record of Events and Opinions*, 2 vols (London: Chapman and Hall, 1905), I, 372–73. All further references are to this edition and appear in the text.
5. In February 1867, Robert Chambers wrote to Wallace, "I have for many years *known* that [the phenomena] of spiritualism are real, as distinguished from impostures; and it is not of yesterday that I concluded they were calculated to explain much that has been doubtful in the past, and when fully accepted, revolutionize the whole frame of human opinion on many important matters" (*My Life*, II, 285). John Tyndall was to remain skeptical to the end, writing to Wallace in the 1870s, "Your sincerity and desire for the pure truth are perfectly manifest. If I know myself, I am in the same vein. . . . Supposing I join you [at a séance], will you undertake to make the effects evident to my senses? . . . Will you, in short, permit me to act towards your phenomena as I act, and successfully act, in other departments of nature?" (*My Life*, II, 278). For accounts of the various encounters with spiritualism engaged in by Chambers, Wallace, and Doyle, see Milton Millhauser, "The Shadow," in *Just Before Darwin: Robert Chambers and "Vestiges"* (Middletown, Conn.: Wesleyan University Press, 1959), pp. 165–90; Peter Raby, *Alfred Russel Wallace: A Life* (Princeton: Princeton University Press, 2001); and Daniel Stashower, *Teller of Tales: The Life of Arthur Conan Doyle* (New York: Henry Holt, 1999).
6. Henry Gee, *In Search of Deep Time: Beyond the Fossil Record to a New History of Life* (New York: Free Press, 1999), pp. 4–5, emphasis added.
7. Stephen Jay Gould, *The Structure of Evolutionary Theory* (Cambridge, Mass.: Belknap Press, 2002), p. 167.

8. See Ronald L. Numbers, *The Creationists* (New York: Alfred A. Knopf, 1992).

9. Phillip E. Johnson, "Evolution as Dogma: The Establishment of Naturalism," in *Intelligent Design Creationism and its Critics: Philosophical, Theological, and Scientific Perspectives*, ed. Robert T. Pennock (Cambridge, Mass.: MIT Press, 2001), pp. 68, 66. All further references are to this edition and appear in the text.

10. Charles Dickens, *The Mystery of Edwin Drood*, ed. Margaret Cardwell, Clarendon Dickens (Oxford: Clarendon Press, 1972), p. 118.

11. See Gould, *Structure of Evolutionary Theory*: "variation [in individual organisms] must be *unrelated to the direction of evolutionary change*; . . . This fundamental postulate gives Darwinism its 'two step' character, the 'chance' and 'necessity' of [Jacques] Monod's famous formulation" (p. 144).

12. Charles Darwin, *The Descent of Man, and Selection in Relation to Sex*, 2 vols in 1 (1871; reprint, Princeton: Princeton University Press, 1981), II, 405.

13. For critiques of the modern, see Michel Foucault, *The Order of Things: An Archaeology of the Human Sciences* (New York: Pantheon Books, 1970); Jean-François Lyotard, *The Postmodern Condition: A Report on Knowledge*, trans. Geoff Bennington and Brian Massumi, Theory and History of Literature, no. 10 (Minneapolis: University of Minnesota Press, 1984); and Stephen Toulmin, *Cosmopolis: The Hidden Agenda of Modernity* (New York: Free Press, 1990).

14. Nora Barlow, ed., *The Autobiography of Charles Darwin: 1809–1882* (London: Collins, 1958), p. 92.

15. For a Darwinian investigation of the history of human societies, see Jared Diamond, *Guns, Germs, and Steel: The Fates of Human Societies* (New York: W. W. Norton, 1997). At one point Diamond observes, "Thus, the difficulties historians face in establishing cause-and-effect relations in the history of human societies are broadly similar to the difficulties facing astronomers, climatologists, ecologists, evolutionary biologists, geologists, and paleontologists" (p. 424). For a recent discussion of the historical imagination in a similar vein, see John Lewis Gaddis, *The Landscape of History: How Historians Map the Past* (Oxford: Oxford University Press, 2002).

Index

Compiled by Sue Carlton